Dear Reader,

For the holidays, Arabesque is pleased to offer four wonderful and inspiring stories in *A Season of Miracles.* From bestselling romance authors Rochelle Alers, Adrianne Byrd, Kayla Perrin, and Janice Sims, the miracle of love and faith that is part of the magic of the holiday season is revealed in so many ways. In *A Season of Miracles,* love comes in many ways: out of tragedy, in reconnecting with family, through fate and through prayer, and sometimes through miracles.

In "Shepherd Moon" by Rochelle Alers, a tragic Christmas Eve accident that happened long ago brings together two people who have all but given up on love. But can they find a way to forgive and forget the past? And will they ever find love in this holiest of seasons?

For some, the holidays can bring unhappy memories. In "Wishing on a Starr" by Adrianne Byrd, a woman finds the courage to face her past, and in so doing learns the meaning of love and family.

Sometimes fate brings lovers together, as in Kayla Perrin's inspiring romantic story "Blind Faith." When a woman's car careens off the highway, she finds herself desperately praying for help. But she soon learns that love can sometimes be the best lifesaver.

When it seems that everything that can go wrong does go wrong, it is sometimes hard to feel thankful. In "A Christmas Serenade" by Janice Sims, a woman finds that out of misfortune can come opportunity, romance, and even love.

In these four stories we hope you find inspiration and romance, and continue to believe in the miracle of love.

Happy holidays,

Evette Porter
Editor

A SEASON OF MIRACLES

ROCHELLE ALERS, ADRIANNE BYRD, KAYLA PERRIN AND JANICE SIMS

ARABESQUE®

East Baton Rouge Parish Library
Baton Rouge, Louisiana

A SEASON OF MIRACLES

An Arabesque title published by Kimani Press 2006

Copyright © 2005 by BET Publications, LLC

ISBN-13: 978-1-58314-813-6
ISBN-10:   1-58314-813-2

The publisher acknowledges the copyright holders
of the individual works as follows:

SHEPHERD MOON
Copyright © 2005 by Rochelle Alers

WISHING ON A STARR
Copyright © 2005 by Adrianne Byrd

BLIND FAITH
Copyright © 2005 by Kayla Perrin

A CHRISTMAS SERENADE
Copyright © 2005 by Janice Sims

www.kimanipress.com

Printed in U.S.A.

CONTENTS

SHEPHERD
MOON

ROCHELLE ALERS

Suppose one of you has a hundred sheep and loses one of them—what does he do? He leaves the other ninety-nine sheep in the pasture and goes looking for the one that got lost until he finds it.

—Luke 15:4
—Good News Bible—Today's English Version

CHAPTER 1

Rhianna Campbell slowed the rental car as she entered the town limits for Shepherd, New York, population 642. A smile, the first one in hours, curved the corners of her mouth. Shepherd was undergoing a population boom. When she'd moved away ten years before, the official census was 598.

The tiny hamlet nestled in the picturesque Hudson Valley was frozen in time. There were no malls or multiplex movie theaters. How, she mused, was a town able to survive without at least one Wal-Mart or fast-food restaurant?

During one of their biannual reunions, her parents told her that a fast-food chain executive had tried to bribe several town officials to get their approval to erect a fast-food burger outlet in Shepherd, but the lifelong residents went to the county's district attorney with the scheme. The general consensus was that as long as Campy's remained open for business, another eating establishment had as much chance of opening in Shepherd as a snowball in hell.

Grief had sent Rhianna fleeing from her hometown, and now a family emergency had brought her back. Turning off the county road, she continued along an unlit winding stretch of roadway until the two-story brick building that housed the Hudson Valley Communities Hospital came into view. She maneuvered into a space in the visitors lot and shifted into park. It took a full minute before she was able to shut off the engine and get out of the car.

Vivid memories of speeding to the hospital after receiving a call at her parents' restaurant that Errol Sutherland and his parents had been transported to the hospital after their car skidded off an icy road, crashing into a tree and exploding on impact, came flooding back.

Rhianna knew the moment she walked into the hospital and met Emery Sutherland's pain-filled gaze that he'd lost his parents and identical twin brother. She had lost her high school sweetheart, fiancé, and a part of herself on that cold and snowy Christmas Eve.

Turning up the collar of her lightweight jacket, Rhianna quickened her pace as she walked toward the entrance. She was chilled to the bone. Living in southern California had thinned her blood.

Bright lights, antiseptic smells, and the soft squishing sound of rubber soles on highly polished tiles greeted her as she made her way to the information desk. A clerk gave her a pass, her father's room number, and a stern warning that visiting hours would end in fifteen minutes.

Rhianna stepped into an elevator and took it to the second floor. Less than a minute later she walked into her father's room. Anna Campbell rose from a chair beside her husband's bed.

"You came."

Rhianna nodded as she closed the distance between her and her mother. Wrapping her arms around the older woman's waist, she kissed her cheek. "Mom, you know I had to come."

Anna eased back, smiling up at her only child. She and Reid reunited with their daughter twice a year, but each time she saw Rhianna, she had changed. Now she'd cut her shoulder-length curly hair into a pixie style that flattered her delicate features and made her look a lot younger than thirty-three.

Her daughter's looks were striking: tall, slender, high cheekbones, slightly slanting dark brown eyes, short buttonlike nose, and a lush mouth that made most people— men in particular—give her a second look. The California sun had darkened her taupe-brown skin.

Rhianna glanced over at Reid Campbell, his chest rising and falling in a slow, measured rhythm. The beeping sounds from the machines monitoring his vitals and his ragged breathing through the tube in his mouth reverberated throughout the small private room.

She released Anna and walked over to the bed. Abrasions on his forehead, his right cheek, and chin marred his handsome face, while his right arm was immobilized over his chest by a sling.

"Daddy, what did you do to yourself?" she whispered, as she leaned down and kissed his thinning gray hair.

Reverberated

"He can't hear you. He's in a drug-induced coma."

Rhianna knees weakened. "Coma?"

"He hit his head when he fell, and there's some swelling in his brain. His doctor wants him sedated until it goes down."

"But you told me he hurt his arm. You said nothing about a head injury."

Anna ignored her daughter's strident tone. "If I'd told you the seriousness of your father's injuries you'd have been a basket case before your jet landed."

Running a hand over her short hair, Rhianna nodded. "You're probably right."

"I know I'm right." Anna's voice was soft, conciliatory. "He's going to make it, sweetheart."

Turning away from the figure in the hospital bed, she blinked back tears. "How long is he going to be like this…hooked up to these tubes and machines?"

Exhaling a long breath, Anna shook her head. "I don't know."

Anna had called Rhianna at her Los Angles home, leaving a message on her voice mail that her father had fallen and was admitted to the hospital. Rhianna returned from her early morning jog, picked up the message, called her boss to tell him that she had a family emergency, then went into superwoman mode. An hour after listening to her mother's voice, she found herself in a taxi en route to LAX. She used the time to call her boss back to inform him that she was taking an extended family leave. She managed to get a stand-by reservation, and then spent the next four hours in the airport before she boarded a nonstop Los Angeles–New York connection.

ignored strident tone

"Your father forgets that he's a cook whenever he tries to play Mr. Fix-It-Yourself," Anna continued with a frown.

Rhianna stared at her mother. Petite, silver-haired, fifty-eight-year-old Anna had given up a career as a kindergarten teacher to marry Reid and help him run Campy's.

"What was he doing this time?"

The dimples in Anna's cheeks deepened as she compressed her lips. "He fell off a ladder."

"What was he doing…" The announcement that visiting hours had ended halted Rhianna's query. "Tell me about it on the way out."

Rhianna held Anna's hand as they walked from Campy's parking lot to the restaurant's rear entrance. The original clapboard siding she remembered had been replaced with white vinyl siding and the windows in the three-story farmhouse with a wraparound porch now sported dark red shutters. The restaurant took up the first floor; her family occupied the second and third. Soft golden light filtered through the curtains in the bedrooms on the second floor.

She was still reeling from the disclosure that Reid had attempted to single-handedly renovate the restaurant to include a party room where Shepherd's retirees could gather for their breakfast specials, card games, and club meetings.

Her father had always liked tinkering around the house and the restaurant, hammering or tightening a screw here and there. But he'd never attempted to build anything. The year he'd put together a dollhouse for her eighth birthday was the exception.

[handwritten: ↗ much ; Illumination]

Anna unlocked the door, pushed a button on a wall panel, and light illuminated the storeroom. A smile softened Rhianna's face as she was surrounded by the familiar structure that had been home for two thirds of her life. The distinctive aroma of apple pie lingered in the air. Anna was renowned for baking the best apple pie in the Hudson Valley.

She walked into the dining room and stopped. Nothing had changed. Campy's was reminiscent of a 1950s soda shop with a counter and stools, bright red leather booths and a large colorful jukebox with compact discs instead of vinyl 45s, which were popular when her parents were teenagers. A slight frown appeared between her eyes. It was the first week in December, yet nothing in the restaurant hinted at the holiday season.

"Where are the decorations?"

Anna removed her red knit cap and fluffed up her silver curls. "We stopped putting them up years ago."

"How long ago?"

Anna stared at the black and white tiled floor. "Once you left Shepherd, Christmas never felt the same for me and your father."

Rhianna closed her eyes for several seconds. "You know why I couldn't stay."

"I understood why you wanted to go away for a while, but I didn't think you'd never come back."

She did not want to argue with her mother, they'd done enough of that before she moved to the West Coast. "I'm back now, Mom."

"For how long, Rhianna?"

She heard the pain in Anna's voice and recognized the pain in her eyes. "For as long as it will take for Daddy to fully recover." She hugged her mother. "Why don't you go upstairs and try to get some sleep."

"What are you going to do?"

She stared at the colorful clock over the jukebox. "I'm going to hang out here until I'm ready for bed. My circadian rhythm is out of whack because of the three-hour time difference."

Anna's gaze met and fused with Rhianna's. "I've missed you so much," she said in a hushed tone.

She flashed a wry smile. "Please go to bed, Mom, before you have me bawling my eyes out."

Anna nodded. "I'm going, but I want you to consider one thing."

"What's that, Mom?"

"Emery Sutherland returned to Shepherd to bury his parents and brother and he stayed."

"He stayed to raise his brothers and sisters."

"True. But he sacrificed what could've become a rewarding career as a vet to take over his father's business."

Rhianna felt as if her composure was under attack. Her mother was at it again. No one could lay a guilt trip on better than Anna McCray-Campbell. She called her parents every Sunday night, and at least once a month Anna hinted that she wanted her to move back to Shepherd. Her response was always the same: *I like California and my job as a hotel banquet manager.*

"Good night, Mother."

Anna turned her head rather than let Rhianna see her

expression. She'd hit a nerve. Whenever her daughter called her *Mother* she knew she had shaken her resolve.

"Good night, baby girl."

Rhianna sat in her favorite booth, staring into nothingness. It was where she'd sat with Errol Sutherland planning their wedding and a future that promised forever—a future that ended in a ball of fire.

Hours later her lids grew heavy and fatigue swept over her like a heavy blanket. She got up, walked out of the dining room, opened a door, then climbed the staircase that led to her bedroom. Her eyes were drooping as she showered, pulled a flannel nightgown over her head, and slipped under several handmade quilts. She fell into a deep, dreamless sleep within minutes of her head touching the pillow.

Rhianna woke up feeling disoriented Friday morning, her body still on Pacific Time. She lay, staring up at the ceiling until she realized she was in her old bedroom. Everything that had happened over the past twenty-four hours, coupled with the image of her motionless father in the hospital bed, his breathing regulated by a machine, swept over her and the tears fell, streaking her face, streaming into her hair and soaking the pillow. She cried until spent, then left her bed and walked on trembling legs to the adjoining bathroom to complete her morning routine.

She descended the staircase and opened the door leading to the restaurant's storeroom. The smell of coffee, bacon, and eggs wafted toward her nostrils, and reminded her that the only thing she'd eaten in the past twenty-four hours was an airline bag lunch. The babble of voices, rattle of utensils, and waitresses calling out orders reminded her that she was truly home.

She hadn't taken more than half a dozen steps into the dining room when she saw him. Sitting in a booth reading a newspaper was the mirror image of the man with whom she'd fallen in love. Her heart slammed against her ribs as she stared at Emery Sutherland's bowed head.

His close-cropped hair was liberally sprinkled with flecks of gray. He was only thirty-six, yet he was graying prematurely. Even though she couldn't see all of his face, she was able to recall his large penetrating dark-brown eyes, strong chin, and chiseled cheekbones. Emery had removed his jacket and a pair of broad shoulders and massive biceps were outlined under a waffle-knit crewneck pullover.

Emery was the reason she'd fled Shepherd, because every time she saw him she was reminded of his identical twin, reminded that the man she loved enough to offer her innocence to was lost to her forever. Turning quickly, she retreated to the kitchen.

Emery Sutherland's head came up, his eyes narrowing in concentration. There was something about the tall woman in a pair of fitted jeans that was vaguely familiar.

His attention was averted as he watched the wall-mounted flat panel television; he read the crawl along the bottom of the screen. A winter storm watch was in effect for counties ranging from Westchester to Onondaga. He'd planned to fly to up to Ithaca later that afternoon to confer with a former professor at Cornell University's New York College of Veterinary Medicine. But with the threat of snow and sleet he would have to cancel the meeting.

Removing a cell phone from his jacket pocket, Emery scrolled through the directory and punched in his mentor's number. The geneticist answered the call after the second ring. It took less than sixty seconds to reschedule their meeting for the following week—weather permitting.

He'd committed to participate in a research study concentrating on sheep breeding, and communications with the octogenarian would've been easier if Dr. Maddox had not eschewed computers.

Emery entered all of his data into a computer, but was forced to travel to Ithaca to discuss his findings with the brilliant geneticist. The man's eccentricity did not bother Emery because it had been years since he'd been involved with veterinary medicine.

Propping an elbow on the table, he closed his eyes and tried recalling where he'd seen the strange woman before.

CHAPTER 2

Rhianna found Anna in the kitchen dicing onions. Gary Tobin, Campy's long-time short-order cook, dropped one of the eggs that had been cradled in his enormous hand when he recognized her.

"Joey! Come clean up this mess." His deep voice reverberated throughout the kitchen when he shouted for the young college student who doubled as a dishwasher/busboy. Reaching for another egg, Gary glared at Rhianna. "I guess it took your father cracking his melon to get you to come back home."

She smiled at the irascible middle-aged man who never seemed to age. His round sable-brown face reminded her of statues of Buddha.

"Hello, Mr. Gary. How have you been?"

Gary rolled his eyes at her as he cracked two eggs and dropped them onto the heated skillet. "I should ask how have you been. You're nothing but a bag of bones. What are you eating in La-La Land? Seaweed and tofu?"

Rhianna patted his thick shoulder. "No. But, I can honestly say that I've missed your cooking."

He waved his spatula. "Sit down and I'll fix something that'll stick to your ribs."

Rhianna picked up an apron, and tied it around her waist. She washed her hands and selected a knife from a stack on a shelf. Sitting down beside Anna, she reached for an onion.

"How often does Emery come here to eat?"

Anna lifted an eyebrow as she continued dicing. She'd noticed Rhianna's swollen lids. It was apparent she'd been crying.

"Four or five times a week. Why?"

"I just saw him. I thought I was looking at a ghost."

"Errol's ghost?"

"Yes."

Anna's hands stilled. Shifting on her stool, she stared at her daughter's strained expression. "Are you all right?" Rhianna nodded. "Why were you crying?"

Biting down on her lower lip, Rhianna averted her head. "The extent of Daddy's injuries hit me hard this morning."

"He's going to be all right, sweetheart."

"He's in a coma, Mom."

"A *drug-induced* coma," Anna insisted softly.

"I wish I had your confidence," she countered, turning back to stare at her mother.

A slight smile softened Anna's full mouth. "It's called

faith. I've always believed in miracles, and I believe your father will walk out of that hospital on his own two feet before Christmas."

Angling an arm around Anna's neck, Rhianna kissed her soft, scented cheek. "I pray you're right."

And she would pray for her father's recovery. That was something she hadn't been able to do for Errol. The medical examiner's report indicated Errol and his parents died instantly, their charred bodies burned so badly that a funeral service was conducted with closed caskets.

Anna saw the blank look in Rhianna's eyes. "Is Emery the reason you left Shepherd? Because he reminded you of his twin?"

She wanted to lie and say no, but there was never a time when she hadn't been truthful with her parents. "Yes."

"Just because they looked alike was not a reason for you to run away."

"I didn't run away," she said defensively.

"I'm not going to mince words," Anna countered. Her tone had become chilly. "You never would've left Shepherd if you'd been in love with Errol."

"I *was* in love with Errol," she argued softly, and not caring whether she sounded defensive. "I'm still in love with him."

Anna shook her head. "No, sweetheart. You thought you were in love."

Rhianna wavered, trying to comprehend what she was hearing. "How can you say that when you helped me plan my wedding?"

"I'm a mother. And mothers want to see their children happy."

"I know what love feels like, Mother."

"If you truly were in love, then seeing Errol's identical twin would've never affected you."

"You make it sound as if I was infatuated with his looks."

Anna gave her a long, penetrating stare. "Weren't you?"

Rhianna's jaw dropped. "Of course not." Her mother's expression spoke volumes. She didn't believe her.

There was no doubt she'd been taken with Errol's good looks, as were most of the girls at their high school. It wasn't his looks as much as it was his happy-go-lucky attitude that drew her to him. He was three years her senior, and she could not believe it when he'd taken an interest in her; she'd done nothing to elicit his attention. One date became two, then halfway through her sophomore year she and Errol were acknowledged as a couple.

Errol graduated from high school and elected not to go to college. He went to work for his father in their general contracting business. The night of her senior prom he proposed marriage and she accepted. Her parents weren't pleased when she showed them the ring Errol had given her, but reluctantly gave them their blessing.

"You're never going to be able to move forward with your life if you don't reconcile your past." Anna's soft voice broke into her musings.

"I've moved on, Mom."

"Have you really?"

"Yes, I have."

"Rhianna, do you still like your eggs scrambled?" Gary asked loudly.

"Yes."

Wiping her hands on a damp towel, she slipped off the stool to see what Gary had prepared for her. Talking about Errol with her mother had unsettled her as much as seeing Emery again. Did Anna really believe she was so shallow that she would marry a man because of his looks?

Anna was wrong about Rhianna reconciling her past. Returning to Shepherd had proven that. Even though she continued to mourn the loss of her first lover, she had dated occasionally. She'd given one man her passion without offering him her love; falling in love a second time was not an option.

Rhianna accepted a plate from Gary filled with grits, scrambled eggs, strips of ham, and a fluffy biscuit, and walked into the dining room. The booth Emery had occupied was empty. The table had been cleaned and a place setting with an overturned coffee mug awaited the next diner. She walked over and sat down to the subtle sensual scent of a man's cologne.

They may have looked alike, but that's where the resemblance ended. Anna's words came rushing back. She was right—Errol never wore cologne or aftershave. He claimed soap and water were enough.

A waitress came over with a pot of freshly brewed coffee and filled the mug. Rhianna did not recognize the woman. In fact, she did not recognize any of the dining room staff. Next year, Campy's would celebrate its thirtieth year of offering the residents of Shepherd some of the best home-cooked food in the region.

She did not want to think of the restaurant's future once her parents retired.

* * *

The morning and afternoon sped by for Rhianna as she observed the space her father had attempted to renovate. He planned to expand the enclosed back porch to accommodate at least twenty additional diners.

She returned her rental and rode back to the hospital with Anna for afternoon visiting hours. She met with the neurologist, listening as he outlined in laymen's terms his course of treatment for her father. CAT scans indicated a slight swelling, which the doctor predicted would subside quickly.

Reid's disability impacted directly on Anna and Gary, and Rhianna volunteered to assume her mother's job of supervising the staff and assisting in food preparation for lunch and dinner.

She and Anna left the hospital, holding hands. "I'm going to drop you back home, then I have to shop for a coat," Rhianna said, holding the passenger-side door open for Anna.

"Were you serious about staying?" Anna asked, after Rhianna had taken her seat behind the wheel.

"Yes."

Rhianna started up the sedan, but did not shift into gear. Turning slightly, she stared into Anna's clear brown eyes. She and her mother looked nothing alike. Both had curly hair, but Anna's was softer, silkier.

"What about your position with the hotel?"

"I'm entitled to sixty days of family leave, but if it exceeds that, then I'll request a transfer to a northeast location."

Anna smiled. "I don't want to put any pressure on you,

but you have to know that your father and I want you living closer to us. We aren't getting any younger. "

"Lighten up with the guilt, Mom." She smiled at Anna. "I'll think about it. Okay?"

"Don't think too long," Anna mumbled under her breath, as Rhianna backed out of the space.

"I'm going to stop at the nursery to pick up some plants and lights to decorate the restaurant," she said, deftly changing the subject. "I'm looking forward to celebrating Christmas where I don't have to see palm trees and Styrofoam snowmen."

Anna reached over and switched on the radio to a station that featured holiday music. The perfectly pitched voice of Whitney Houston singing, "Do You Hear What I Hear," came through the speakers.

The two women sang along with the familiar songs until they arrived at Campy's. Anna got out and Rhianna reversed direction, heading for her favorite boutique in an upscale shopping center.

Emery heard the smoky feminine voice and went completely still. His head came up and he stared at the woman standing only twenty feet away.

Now that he'd heard the voice he knew the mystery woman's identity. Rhianna Campbell may have changed her looks, but not her contralto voice. Her short hairdo, stylish tan cashmere swing coat, and imported loafers screamed big city elegance.

He wasn't sure whether it was coincidence or serendipity that he and Rhianna were at Jansen's Nursery at the same time. He'd ordered a plant to be sent to her father at the hospital; she had placed an order for poinsettias and wreaths to be delivered to Campy's.

Emery had waited a long time to confront Rhianna, and now that she'd returned to Shepherd he realized his ten-year wait was over.

CHAPTER 3

After three days in Shepherd Rhianna felt restless—an emotion she hadn't experienced in a long time. The first time it happened was after she'd relocated to Los Angeles. It took more than a year to become acclimated to one season and make new friends.

Adjusting to her position as a banquet manager was easier and rewarding. Each affair, whether business or personal, ended satisfactorily because she believed customer approval was paramount to hotel profits.

She alternated visiting hours with Anna, going in the evenings, whereas her mother sat at her husband's bedside during the afternoon, talking quietly to him, even though he wasn't able to hear her. Rhianna had suggested hiring a private duty nurse once he was discharged, but Anna's vehement opposition to having another woman take care of her husband made it moot.

Once the townsfolk heard she had returned to Shepherd, Campy's business tripled. The curious wanted to see how she looked after a ten-year absence, and many welcomed her back home with bright smiles and hugs.

She'd closed Campy's, but hadn't yet gone upstairs, content in sitting in the near-dark dining room and listening to one of her favorites songs on the jukebox. A tapping sound caught her attention. Sitting up straighter, she listened intently. Someone was rapping on the door.

Pushing out of the booth, she walked over to the door and peered through a pane of glass. Porch lanterns and tiny white bulbs strung around leafless branches provided enough light for her to see the face of the man that had sent her fleeing from Shepherd as if the hounds of hell were pursuing her. Why, she wondered, had Emery Sutherland come to Campy's after closing time?

A wave of moisture swept over her body. She'd told herself that she was ready to face him, but was she? "What do you want?" she shouted at the door.

"I need to talk to you."

She swallowed. Why was it she remembered his face and not his voice? It was a lower register than Errol's, a mellow, seductive baritone.

"We're closed, Emery. Please come back tomorrow."

There was a pause before he said, "Please, open the door, Rhia."

Her pulse quickened. He was the only one she knew that always shortened her name. She stared at the door as if it would solve her dilemma. Should she ignore Emery and go upstairs, or open the door?

But she knew the answer before the question had formed in her mind. She *had* to open the door and once and for all put *all* of the ghosts from her past to rest.

"Wait a minute."

She made her way across the dining room and into a smaller room where her father had set up his office. Switching on a light, she pressed several buttons on a panel, deactivating the security system.

By the time she returned to open the door for Emery she was in complete control of her emotions. If she had changed in ten years, so had he.

A short sheepskin-lined jacket failed to mask the power in his upper body. At six-two, he had bulked up considerably, although his face was leaner, high cheekbones even more pronounced. What hadn't changed was the attractive cleft in his strong chin.

"Please come in."

Emery walked into the restaurant. His expressionless face gave no indication of what he was feeling at that moment—a long simmering rage that refused to die out.

His gaze moved over Rhianna as he noted the obvious changes in her appearance. Despite his deep-rooted anger he admitted to himself that he liked her with short hair. What he didn't like was seeing her so thin. She was tall, therefore the loss of weight made her look almost emaciated.

Rhianna motioned to a booth. "Would you like to sit down?"

Emery shook his head. "No. What I have to say won't take that long."

Crossing her arms under her breasts, she nodded. "Spit it out."

Assuming a similar pose, Emery angled his head. "I want to thank you for screwing up my little sister's head."

Her back stiffened. "What!" The word exploded from her mouth.

He walked forward a step, bringing them less than a foot apart. "Don't tell me you don't remember promising Debbie that you'd always be there for her. That's a helluva thing to tell an eight-year-old who'd just lost her brother and parents. You stayed in Shepherd long enough to garner everyone's sympathy as Errol's grieving fianceé before you took off for sunny California, leaving me with a little girl who cried herself to sleep every night because she wanted everything to be the way it was before her play sister deserted her.

"I hated you, Rhia, for giving my sister hope when there was none. She was so messed up that she was forced to go into counseling after she began running away to see if she could find you. It took four long years before she was able to acknowledge that you were never coming back to Shepherd."

Rhianna stared, tongue-tied, unable to form a comeback to counter Emery's virulent attack. Her heart pounded in her chest and in her ears, the roaring sound making it impossible to hear what he was saying. She stared at his mouth as if she was trying to read lips, and, through the roaring din, managed to breathe out two words.

"Get *out!*" Emery looked at her for several seconds, then turned on his heels and walked out of Campy's, leaving her staring at the space where he had been.

She stood in the same spot, not moving, until she felt her calves cramping, then forced herself to put one foot in front of the other as she made her way over to the door and locked it. Moving like a robot, Rhianna reset the alarm, extinguished the lights, and walked slowly up the staircase to her third floor bedroom; she entered the room, closed the door softly, and headed for the cushioned window seat in an alcove. She sat down, pulling her knees to her chest, and tried to make sense of Emery's verbal assault. She had promised his sisters, especially Deborah, that she would always be their big sister, but that was before the tragic accident that decreased the Sutherland household from eight to five in the blink of an eye.

And in the weeks following the funeral she could not and did not remember what she'd done or said. What she did remember were her mother's tears when she announced that she was leaving Shepherd and moving to California.

Rhianna stared at the tiny white bulbs entwined in the trees planted around the house. She'd held the ladder while the busboy strung hundreds of feet of lights that shimmered like tiny sparkling diamonds. Christmas had always been her favorite time of the year, with the exchange of gifts, parties, pageants, songs, cards, and prayers for peace and good will toward men. That was before that tragic Christmas Eve.

She hadn't celebrated Christmas for ten years, but since returning to Shepherd she'd promised herself that she would try to recapture the normalcy missing in her life since she had—as her mother charged—run away.

A wry smile twisted her mouth. It was apparent peace and good will were not a part of Emery Sutherland's life. He'd harbored hate and resentment toward her for almost a decade, attacking her without warning and not giving her the opportunity to explain herself. He could believe whatever he wanted to believe, but the next time she and Emery crossed paths she knew she would be more than prepared for him.

Rhianna slept fitfully, and when she slipped out of bed hours before dawn, she felt as if she hadn't slept at all. The virulent words Emery had hurled at her had tormented her throughout the night.

She walked on bare feet to the bathroom to shower. There was no need to stay in bed when all she could do was twist and turn restlessly. She showered, patted her skin dry, then moisturized her body with a thick perfumed cream. The cold weather had attacked her sensitive skin with a vengeance.

Dressed in a pair of chocolate wale cords, a white wool turtleneck sweater, and brown low-heeled boots, she slipped her arms into an Old Navy blue pea coat before reaching for the keys to her father's truck. Moving over to the desk where she'd sat years before doing homework and typing papers, she scribbled a note on a pad: *Went for a drive. Be back soon. R.*

She folded the piece of paper in half as she walked the length of the hallway and descended the staircase. Stopping at her mother's bedroom, she slipped the note under the door.

As she passed the living room the clock on the fireplace mantel chimed the half hour. It was four-thirty, much too early to drop in on someone unannounced, but she didn't much care. If Emery could come to Campy's after closing hours and insult her to her face in her family-owned place of business, then she had no qualms about returning the gesture.

She left through the rear of the house. The frozen earth made crunching and crackling sounds under her booted feet as she walked toward the two-car garage. The readout on the large digital thermometer mounted on the side of the house registered eighteen degrees. The prediction of a major snowstorm was downgraded to snow showers that had left the Hudson Valley covered with several inches of white powder and turned the countryside into a Currier & Ives winter wonderland postcard.

She drove slowly, her gaze never straying from the icy roadway in front of the glare of her headlights. She didn't realize how tense she'd been until she pulled into the driveway leading to Emery's house. The structure was similar to many in the region: two or three stories, wraparound or enclosed porch, set on enough acreage that children could play with wild abandon. It was dark, but still she could make out changes to the large farmhouse. Shutters had been added to the many windows.

Rhianna cut off the engine, pushed opened the door, and, before she could alight from the truck, saw a pair of glowing eyes staring up at her. Not much had changed. The Sutherlands had always kept dogs as pets.

"Hey there, boy," she whispered. The dog moved closer and she recognized it as a border collie. She headed for the front porch, the dog lopping along at her heels.

Rhianna mounted the stairs, stared at the solid door painted a dark forest green, then rang the bell. The sound echoed melodiously throughout the interior.

Without warning, the door opened and her mouth went suddenly dry as she stared numbly at the wide bare chest of the tall man looming over her. A pair of jeans rode low on his slim hips. It was apparent he'd thrown them on at the last moment because he hadn't bothered to snap the waistband.

He frowned, his eyes level under drawn brows. "What are you doing here?"

"I need to talk to you," she said, repeating the very words he'd spoken hours before.

Emery scratched his stubbly jaw. "There's nothing to talk about."

Rhianna refused to relent. "I beg to differ with you. Either you let me in, or you can step outside. It's your call."

His frown deepened. "If you don't leave my property I'm going to call the sheriff and have you arrested for trespassing."

A swift shadow of anger swept over her face. "No, you won't, Emery. You're going to listen to what it is I have to say. You owe me that much."

"I owe you nothing," he spat at her.

"You're not the only one hurting," she said, as if he hadn't spoken. "I loved your brother. I loved everything about him, and when he died I wanted to die, too." Her eyes filled with tears. "The day after you buried Errol and your parents I locked myself in my bedroom with my father's gun, trying to get up enough nerve to shoot myself." Her shoulders shook as tears overflowed and rolled down her face. "I sat up all night with the gun in my lap, laughing and crying. I laughed at all of the silly things Errol and I used to do together, then I cried because I was too much of a coward to take my own life."

Sniffling, she wiped angrily at her tears with the back of her hand. "I couldn't stay, Emery. Not whenever I saw you I saw Errol. If I didn't go away I would've lost my mind, because the pain was too much to bear." Pulling back her shoulders, she lifted her chin in a gesture that indicated defiance. "I'm sorry I bothered you."

Turning quickly, she ran down the porch steps to where she'd parked the truck. Her hands were shaking uncontrollably as she tried turning the key. The engine caught and with a squeal of rubber hitting the concrete, she sped away from Emery and the shocked expression freezing his features.

Emery did not move, unmindful of the cold air nipping at his exposed skin. Guilt slapped at him, leaving invisible welts as he recalled Rhianna's impassioned admission. What if she had taken her own life? He did not want to imagine how the act would've impacted her parents.

At the age of twenty-six his dream of becoming a veterinarian was deferred when he found himself surrogate father to two younger brothers and sisters. He dropped out of veterinary school, took control of his father's general contracting business, and divided what free time he had to checking homework, refereeing squabbles between sixteen-year-old Kirk, Paul, fourteen, thirteen-year-old Brielle, and eight-year-old Deborah. He attended back-to-school night conferences with their respective teachers, as well as concerts and intramural games.

A fellow student whom he had hoped to marry had ended their relationship because she wasn't prepared to take on a ready-made family.

Emery had sacrificed a career he'd wanted all of his life, marriage, and children of his own for his grieving siblings. And, not once had he ever regretted it. The day he escorted Debbie to her dorm room at Penn State made everything worthwhile. His troubled little sister had turned her life around, made the high school honor roll two years in a row, and was accepted into the college of her choice.

No, he thought, he hadn't done too badly. He was now Uncle Emery to three nieces and two nephews. Brielle had called to inform him that everyone was invited to her house in Scranton, Pennsylvania, for Christmas. It had taken years, but the Sutherlands had accepted the loss of their loved ones and had begun celebrating the holiday again.

Stepping back into the house, Emery slammed the door so hard the windows rattled. After he'd gone to Campy's to unload on Rhianna, he'd returned home feeling like a bully. He'd blindsided her, spewed his venom, then walked away like a coward.

He closed his eyes, but he could not shut out the sight of Rhianna's tears. He would more willingly face a rabid dog than see a woman cry.

Emery opened his eyes and expelled a lungful of air. How could he send Reid Campbell a plant and card wishing him a speedy recovery, after all Reid had done for the

Sutherlands, then turn around and insult the man's daughter? He may have been getting older, but certainly not wiser. He couldn't retract what he'd said to Rhianna, but he would try to make amends—to her and to Reid.

The sound of a kettle's whistle shattered the silence in the house—a six-bedroom house that was much too big for one person. He'd thought about selling it when he sold Sutherland and Sons General Contracting, but once he committed to breeding sheep for a research project, he'd changed his mind. It was a three-year study, which meant he would be forced to remain in Shepherd until he was almost forty. Then he would decide what he wanted to do with the rest of his life.

CHAPTER 4

Rhianna returned to Campy's experiencing both relief and shame. She'd disclosed to Emery why she could not continue to live in Shepherd, but she had also told him something she'd never revealed to another living soul. The inability to cope with grief and loss had sucked her into a morass where she hadn't wanted go on living. But she had survived and moved on with her life, while accepting the reality that Errol was never coming back.

She hung up her jacket in the office and made her way to the kitchen. By the time Gary arrived she'd brewed several pots of coffee, diced ingredients for omelets, emptied the dishwasher, and set out place settings on the tables in the booths.

"Very nice," he crooned, staring at the plastic bowl filled with diced ham, onion and green and red peppers. "Your daddy taught you well," he said, smiling.

She returned his smile. "Thank you."

Washing his hands in a stainless steel sink, he gave Rhianna a sidelong glance. "Are you still thinking about running a bed-and-breakfast?"

There had been a time when all she'd talked about was turning Campy's into a B&B. That was before she'd earned a degree in business with a concentration in hotel and restaurant management. Instead of serving three meals a day, she'd planned to offer the patrons a sumptuous brunch and gourmet dinners.

"I haven't thought about that in a long time," she admitted. The telephone rang, and she picked up the receiver on the wall phone. "Good morning. Campy's."

"Rhianna, this…this is Nicole."

"What's wrong, Nicole?" She hadn't recognized the waitress's voice.

"My throat is on fire. I hope I don't have strep."

"Have you been to the doctor?"

"I'm going to the walk-in clinic as soon as it opens."

"Let me know if you're going to need more time off."

"I will. But I hate to leave you stranded."

"Don't worry about it, Nicole. Just feel better."

She ended the call, reaching for an apron. "Nicole won't be in today," she told Gary. "She has a sore throat."

He squinted at the board with the personnel work schedules. "You can call Penny and have her come in."

Rhianna shook her head, tying the apron around her waist. "Penny hasn't had a day off in more than a week. I'll fill in for Nicole."

Gary lifted a gray eyebrow. "Are you sure you remember how to wait tables?"

She gave him a saucy smile. "Watch me."

The last time she attempted to wait tables was the year she turned fourteen. Then, when she'd tried balancing several plates on her arm as she'd seen other more experienced waitresses do, it spelled disaster. Food and broken dinnerware littered the floor. Undaunted, she'd apologized and returned to the kitchen to duplicate the order.

Picking up a pad and pencil now, she walked into the dining room. The early morning regulars were already seated in booths and at the counter. Those who commuted to New York City usually came on the weekends, but those who were either retired or worked locally breakfasted at Campy's several times each week.

She hesitated, but didn't stop when she spied Emery sitting in the booth he'd occupied before. He'd shaved, and he wore a crewneck sweater over his jeans, yet she could not forget the image of his stubbly jaw, defined pectorals, and abs that lingered around the fringes of her mind. Although crying and shaken she still had been aware of how he looked standing barefoot in the doorway with the soft glow of light throwing his body in relief.

Their gazes met and fused as she approached his table. Pencil poised, she smiled. "May I take your order?"

His dark eyes widened as he noticed for the first time why his brother had been so taken with Rhianna Campbell. She was enchanting. Not classically beautiful, but delicate, ardently feminine. She wore no makeup, not even lipstick, yet something about her radiated a sensuality he hadn't noticed in any other woman he'd met.

Her lashes swept down across her cheekbones, and he

was lost, lost and hypnotized by a woman who, if she'd married his brother would've been a part of his family, someone he would've regarded as a sister; however, his thoughts were anything but brotherly.

"I'll have the usual."

Rhianna lifted an eyebrow. "And that is?"

Relaxing, Emery rested an arm over the back of the seat. "Oatmeal with low-fat milk, a large orange juice, one slice of wheat toast with strawberry preserves and black coffee."

She scrawled his order on the pad, using symbols only she could decipher. "Decaf or regular?" There came a noticeable pause and she glanced at Emery, believing he hadn't heard her, but he was staring at her as if she were a stranger.

Suddenly it hit her. Errol and Emery may have been identical twins, but there were subtle differences. Emery's face was leaner, more angular, his jaw stronger, and his eyes were not as dark as Errol's had been.

"What did you say?" he asked, as if coming out of a trance.

"I asked whether you wanted regular of decaf coffee."

"Regular."

She nodded. "I'll be right back with your coffee."

Rhianna knew she had to get away from Emery before she embarrassed herself. She'd found herself drawn to her late-fiancé's brother not because of their marked resemblance, but because he emanated a virility that stoked a sensual fire that had been banked for far too long.

She gave Gary Emery's order, and, as she returned to take the orders of the diners sitting at the counter debating Sunday's football scores, Anna appeared. She looked awful.

"Have you been you sleeping?" she asked Anna in a harsh whisper. There were dark circles under her eyes that made them appear sunken in their sockets.

Anna sighed audibly. "Not really. I don't like sleeping alone." A sad smile trembled over her lips. "The only time your father and I haven't shared a bed was when I went to the hospital to have you. Sometimes he makes me so mad that I want to spit tacks, but after being married to the same man for almost forty years I find myself more in love with him with each passing day."

Wrapping her arms around her mother's shoulders Rhianna kissed her forehead. "I want you to go back to bed. Gary and I have everything under control."

"Who's going to make dinner?"

"What are the Monday night specials?"

"Roast chicken and meatloaf."

"I'll handle it," she said, smiling.

"Are you sure, sweetheart?"

"Of course I'm sure. It's been a long time, but I still know my way around a kitchen. Now, please go upstairs and try to get some sleep." Her father, a professional chef, had taught her to cook before she celebrated her twelfth birthday.

Anna nodded. "Wake me up in time to go to the hospital."

"We'll go together." She would go see her father early because she wanted to be back in time to help Gary prepare the dishes for the dinner menu.

She kissed her mother again unaware of a pair of dark eyes watching the tender interchange. The sound of a ringing bell propelled her into action as Rhianna walked into the kitchen to pick up her orders.

Rhianna entered Campy's with her step lighter than it had been since her return to Shepherd. Her father's neurologist reported that he planned to bring Reid out of the coma over the next twenty-four hours. But Reid would remain in the hospital for at least another week undergoing tests to make certain he hadn't sustained any permanent brain damage.

Her shoulder bag bulged with the number of cards that had accompanied the plants and flowers crowding every flat surface in Reid's hospital room. Whenever she got a free moment she planned to send out thank you cards to those wishing her father a speedy recovery.

The first thing she noticed, as the storm door closed behind her, was a large vase filled with a bouquet of white baby roses and blue and green hydrangeas sitting on the counter. A satin ribbon in a soft seafoam green circled the mouth of the crystal vase. The flowers had been delivered to the restaurant instead of to the hospital.

Linda, the waitress who worked the three-to-nine shift, gave her a wide grin. "Somebody must really like you, Rhianna."

She stopped in midstride. "What?"

Linda, a single mother with three children, had gone to school with Rhianna. The attractive blond married her high school sweetheart a month after graduating, had three children in rapid succession, then left her husband because he preferred sleeping to working.

"The flowers are for you."

Rhianna walked to the counter and removed the envelope stapled to the clear blue cellophane protecting the delicate blooms. She took out a card, her heart stopping, then starting up again as she read the bold script: *SORRY— Please call me—Emery.* He'd written his phone number below his name.

He'd apologized with one word, a request, and his name and number scrawled on a tiny square of vellum. Emery hadn't changed that much. He was known as the quiet twin, whereas Errol talked enough for both of them.

She slipped the card into the envelope and tucked it into her bag with the others. Emery had sent her flowers as a peace offering, and she would accept his apology. Both of them had said things they could never retract, things about the past that would remain in the past.

"Aren't you going to tell me who sent them?" Linda asked, her hazel eyes filled with amusement and curiosity.

Rhianna gave her a saucy smile. "Nope."

Linda rolled her eyes. "Damn. You're not even back a week and already some guy is chasing you."

"What makes you so certain they're from a guy?"

"The colors. A woman would've selected either pink, red, or even yellow roses."

She regarded the pale, cool colors. "You're probably right."

"So, are they from a man?"

"I'm not telling," Rhianna teased. She picked up the vase and carried it into the office.

She wouldn't tell Linda who had sent her the flowers because she probably would misinterpret Emery's intent. He only wanted to apologize, not court her.

And she would call him—after she closed Campy's.

Emery took off his boots, leaving them on a mat in the mudroom. He'd spent the past three hours checking the two-dozen ewes in the barn he'd built before committing to the research study. All but two ewes had come into heat. He'd mated them with a lone young ram and Emery hoped the ewes would lamb in either late April or early May.

He stripped off his jeans, sweater and underwear, leaving them in a large wicker basket next to a front-loading, stackable washer-dryer. The telephone rang as he walked out of the mudroom to the half-bath off the kitchen. He picked up the receiver on a wall phone before the third ring.

"Hello."

"Emery?"

A slow smile spread across his face when he heard the contralto voice. "Yes, Rhia."

"You wanted me to call you."

"Yes, I did." His smile faded. "I wanted to apologize—"

"You did that with the flowers," she countered, interrupting him. There came a pregnant pause. "Thank you. They're beautiful."

He smiled again. "I'm glad you like them. I want to apologize," he repeated, "and I want to talk to you about something."

There came another pause. "What about?"

"It's something I don't want to discuss on the phone."

He glanced at the clock over the sink. It was nine forty-five. "Are you still in the restaurant?"

"Yes. Why?"

"Wait there for me. I'll be over in half an hour."

"If it's all right with you, I'd rather come to your place."

Rhianna's suggestion that they meet at his house left Emery momentarily speechless. He tried coming up with reasons why she didn't want him to come to Campy's, but drew a blank.

"Okay."

"I'll be over in about forty minutes," she said.

"I'll be here waiting for you."

"Goodbye, Emery."

"Later, Rhia."

Emery hung up and walked into the bathroom. He hadn't expected Rhianna to accept his apology, but was glad she had, because it would make it easier for him to propose something he believed would absolve him of his guilt and help her father.

Rhianna pulled into the driveway and parked behind Emery's pickup truck. Motion sensors brightened the area like daylight. She got out and walked the short distance to the expansive wraparound porch. A large live pine wreath festooned with tiny fragrant pinecones and a red velvet bow was attached to the front door. She rang the bell and within seconds it opened.

"Please come in," Emery said, greeting her with a friendly smile.

Warmth, the scent of Emery's cologne, and burning

wood wrapped around her, beckoning and welcoming her into his home.

Wiping her booted feet on the thick straw doormat, she returned his smile, her gaze moving quickly over him. The last time she'd come she'd caught him off guard and in a state of half-dress. Tonight he wore a faded sweatshirt with his jeans. A pair of thick white cotton socks covered his feet.

"How's your dad coming along?" Emery asked.

"The doctor's prognosis is very encouraging. Hopefully, he'll be out of the hospital some time next week." Rhianna did not tell Emery about her father's head injury.

She stepped into the entryway and went completely still. Recessed lights, highly polished parquet flooring, and a massive fieldstone fireplace in the living room caught her immediate attention.

"You've made some changes."

Emery nodded. "I've made a lot of changes. Let me take your coat, then I'll give you a tour."

She shrugged out of the coat, handing it to him. He hung it on a brass coatrack. Leaning against a wall, she bent over to remove her boots, but was thwarted when Emery hunkered down and caught her ankle, forcing her to rest a hand on his shoulder to maintain her balance.

Rhianna swallowed a moan as she registered heat and solid muscle under her fingertips. What was there about Emery Sutherland that made her knees shake like gelatin and her pulse beat a little too quickly?

Despite their uncanny resemblance to each other, Errol and Emery's personalities were complete opposites. Errol had been outgoing, exhibiting an *I-don't-give-a-damn* attitude, whereas Emery was serious, brooding, and studious. Girls literally threw themselves at Emery, who'd always politely declined their advances. He was focused on one thing: becoming a veterinarian. He graduated from high school and enrolled in college, whereas Errol went to work for his father.

She did not have time to recover from the jolt of awareness snaking through her body when she recoiled again. Emery had caught her hand, holding it firmly within his larger grasp, the calluses on his palms indicating he was no stranger to manual labor.

"We'll start with the upstairs and work our way down." Nodding, she followed him up a curving staircase with delicately carved newel posts.

"How's your family?" she asked. She had to say something, anything to take her mind off the strength of the large hand cradling hers.

"They're all doing well for themselves. Kirk is married and lives in D.C. with his wife and two sons. He's now an assistant curator for the Smithsonian. Paul is a teacher and became a father for the first time this summer. His wife gave birth to twin girls."

Rhianna smiled. "Were they identical?"

Emery nodded, smiling. "Yes. They're beautiful."

"Spoken like a proud uncle."

His smile widened. "You've got that right."

"What about Brielle?"

"She's also married with a daughter and lives in Scranton, Pennsylvania. She's an interior decorator. After I renovated the house she offered to decorate it. It's a little fancy for my tastes, but I'm getting used to it."

Rhianna followed Emery up another flight of stairs to the attic. "How is Debbie?" She held her breath as she waited for Emery's response. He'd harbored a ten-year grudge against her because of Deborah.

"She's great. She entered Penn State this fall and hopes to become a lawyer."

"That's wonderful news."

"It is," he agreed. "Once I dropped her off at college I was no longer a surrogate father, but an older brother and uncle."

She gave him a sidelong glance. "What are you going to do now?"

He stopped on the top stair, staring down at her. "I plan to do all of the things I've put on hold for the past ten years."

Rhianna wanted to ask him if his plans included marriage and fatherhood. Linda had given her an update on most of the kids they'd gone to school with, and the chatty woman was more than willing to reveal that Emery Sutherland was one of Shepherd's most eligible bachelors.

All conversation ended when Rhianna stepped into a space the width and length of the thirty-five-hundred square-foot house. Tilting her head, she stared up at Palladian windows and skylights bringing the outdoors inside.

"This is where I spend most of my time," Emery said close to her ear.

She shivered noticeably, as much from his moist breath

feathering over her ear as from his closeness. "You did all of this?" Her voice was filled with awe.

A king-size platform bed was positioned under an eave, while a desk, drop leaf table, computer worktable, and bookcases lined an entire wall. A large-screen television resting on its own stand, a home theater, and stereo system were set up to the right of the wood-burning fireplace. It was a place to sleep, relax, and commune with the spectacular Hudson River Valley landscape.

"Yes. It took me nearly a year to put in a new floor, walls, windows, fireplace, and the bathroom."

Rhianna eased her hand from Emery's loose grip and walked over to a floor-to-ceiling window. From where she stood she could see for miles. Spotlights shimmered off the frozen surface of a large pond.

"Do the kids still skate on the pond?"

Emery closed the distance between him and Rhianna, his gaze caressing the soft curves of her body outlined in charcoal-gray wool. The twin set matched a pair of tailored slacks. There was something about Rhianna that was so alluring that he found it hard to keep his thoughts straight.

"Yes, they do."

"I miss ice skating."

"Do you want to go?"

"Go where?" she asked, not turning around.

"Skating?"

Rhianna closed her eyes, recalling how she'd waited every winter for the town officials to declare the pond safe enough for skating. She'd learned to ice skate before she entered the first grade, and it had quickly become her favorite winter sport.

"When?"

Emery smiled. "Whenever you want. Do you want to go now?"

Rhianna turned, her shoulder brushing Emery's chest. Her expression mirrored disbelief. "You're joking, aren't you?"

His gaze lowered, as did his voice when he said, "I never joke, Rhia."

She looked at him as if he'd lost his mind. He'd sent her flowers and a note asking that she call him because he'd wanted to discuss something with her. If he'd wanted her to go out with him, then he just should've asked.

"I can't...not tonight."

Emery lifted an curving eyebrow. "When?"

"Tomorrow," she said quickly.

A hint of a smile touched his mobile mouth. "Good."

"Is it really *that* good, Emery?" Rhianna asked. "Couldn't you have asked another woman to go skating with you?"

"I could've, but I asked you."

"Why?"

His expression changed, sobering. "It's been a long time since I've been on skates, and even longer since we've skated together."

Rhianna berated herself for thinking Emery wanted to date her. What he wanted was to relive a time when their lives were predictable and carefree. Once she'd begun dating Errol she and the Sutherlands skated together every weekend.

"What time tomorrow?"

"I'll come by Campy's after closing." Reaching out, he

cupped her elbow, directed her over to a tapestry-covered love seat in front of the fireplace, sat and pulled her down beside him. "I asked you to come here tonight because I want to talk to you about Campy's."

Rhianna stared at him staring back at her. His eyes were serious as was his expression, and she wondered what Emery wanted with her parents' restaurant, a business establishment into which they'd poured their life's blood and savings.

CHAPTER 5

Emery stared at the smoldering embers in the fireplace instead of at the woman next to him. What he proposed to tell Rhianna had nothing to do with what he was feeling or was beginning to feel for her.

"Tell your father that I'm going to finish his construction project."

Rhianna wanted to tell Emery that she wasn't able to tell Reid anything. Not until he was conscious. "Why?"

Stretching out his long legs, Emery crossed his sock-covered feet at the ankles. "Reid came to me once he decided to renovate the back porch, asking my advice about specs and materials he'd need to accommodate an additional twenty customers. I'd offered to help him, but he turned me down. I know he wanted to complete it before Christmas, but with a broken arm we know that will never happen."

Rhianna sat up straighter. "Why are you offering to do this?"

Turning his head, Emery met her steady gaze. "Because it's the least I can do for your mother and father. After my folks died they fed my family until I hired a housekeeper. My mother always did the cooking, so we were all totally helpless in the kitchen. Reid and Anna had become my angels because I was overwhelmed with running my dad's contracting business, making certain everyone got to school on time and that they did their homework."

She shook her head. "I didn't know."

"You couldn't know, because you'd left."

Rhianna dropped her gaze. "I left when I should've stayed."

Emery covered her hand with one of his. "You did what you had to do to save yourself."

"I left, but I had to come back."

He gave her fingers a gentle squeeze before releasing them. "Are you back to stay?"

She paused. There was only the sound of their breathing and an occasional hiss of falling embers behind the decorative fireplace screen. He'd asked her the same question her mother had posed to her. And the answer was the same for both.

"No. I'll stay here until my father is able to return to work."

Rhianna wasn't certain whether she'd ever be able to live in Shepherd again; and if she returned to the East Coast she wanted to move closer to New York City.

"Christmas is less than three weeks away. Do you think you'll be able to have everything done by that time?"

Emery lifted a shoulder. "I don't know. I'll take a look at it tomorrow morning."

"When are you going to find the time?"

"What do you mean?"

"Don't you have your own construction projects?"

Emery lifted his eyebrows and smiled at her. "I sold the business four months ago."

Her eyes widened. Sutherland and Sons General Contracting had been in business as long as Campy's.

"But why, Emery?"

He held up his hands, fingers outstretched. "I grew up believing I'd use these hands as a veterinary surgeon, but that never happened because I had to run electrical wires, replace roofs, or install plumbing. I hated my father for making me work with him during school vacations when all I wanted was to hang out with friends. But in the end it all came in handy, because instead of waiting for a handout from social services I was able to support my family."

Rhianna curbed the urge to touch him. "Was it hard, Emery?"

He gave her a sad smile. "It was in the beginning. My brothers and sisters acted out, the men who were used to taking orders from my dad challenged me, and I'm ashamed to admit that I lost my temper and fired all of them. Two days later I hired them back. I suppose it worked because it was the last time they challenged me."

Reaching over she placed her hand on his forearm. "I'm sorry I wasn't here to help you with Debbie."

Emery stared at the small hand resting on his arm.

"Maybe we all had to go through what we went through to get to where we are now."

She blinked once. "You're probably right."

He covered her hand with his. "I know I'm right, Rhia, because you never would've come back if not for a family emergency." The look in his eyes dared her to refute him. Much to his surprise she smiled and nodded.

"I'll tell my mother that you'll finish the expansion. I need you to give me an estimate for the materials and your labor."

His hands curled into tights fists, causing the muscles to bunch up in his arms. He flung off her hand. "I'm not offering to help your father because I expect to be paid."

"My father would never accept a handout."

Emery sprang to his feet and glared at Rhianna. "It's not a handout, Rhia. It's apparent you've been away so long that you forgot people in small towns help one another in a crisis. It's best that you don't come back to Shepherd to live because you'd never fit in."

Rhianna stood up, her eyes narrowing as fury held a chokehold on her throat, not permitting her to speak. "I'm leaving before I forget my manners and insult you in your home," she said, once she regained her voice.

She turned and headed across the expansive space; strong fingers curled around her upper arm, stopping her retreat. Rhianna lost her balance. A small gasp escaped her as Emery held her upright.

Closing her eyes, she quickly forgot her anger as she melted against his stronger body. Why did she find herself fighting with him whenever they were alone? Was it because he was alive and Errol was dead, because she was attracted to him, or because she was still angry with Errol because he'd driven too fast and on occasion had drunk too much and he had been responsible for the accident that killed him and his parents?

"Please don't leave, Rhia."

"I'm sorry, Emery."

They'd spoken in unison.

Emery turned her around to face him. Her eyes glistened with unshed tears. "Please forgive me for opening my mouth before I engaged my brain."

Rhianna successfully blinked back tears. "It's all right, Emery. I'm sorry if I insulted you when I offered to pay you."

A slow sensual smile parted his lips. "Apology accepted. I want this to be the last time we argue about minutiae."

Peering up at him through her lashes, she smiled. "You've got yourself a deal. You did promise to give me a tour of the house."

Reaching for her hand, Emery cradled it in the crook of his elbow. "As I said before, I hang out here most of the time when I'm not checking on the sheep."

"Sheep?" He nodded. "You're a shepherd?"

Emery threw back his head and laughed, the rumbling sound coming up from his chest. "No. I'm a sheep breeder."

Her expression mirrored disbelief. "You're raising sheep in Shepherd, New York."

"What goes around comes around. After all that's how Shepherd got its name." There had been a time when the lush valley was dotted with countless sheep, goat, and dairy farms.

"What are you breeding them for?"

"Their wool. The ones I'm working with have much finer fleece than most North American breeds. It's similar to the soft under hair of the Kashmir goat."

"Are you saying their wool would be comparable to cashmere?"

"That's what we're hoping to achieve. And if successful, then we won't have to rely on India, Iran, and Mongolia for their wool."

Rhianna studied his face for a long moment. "So, instead of becoming a vet you've become a farmer."

He angled his head. "Farmer, breeder—it's all the same."

"Do you find it rewarding?"

"I *make* it rewarding."

Rhianna replayed his answer over and over in her head as she followed Emery in and out rooms that were renovated with recessed lighting, new floors, and windows. Baseboards and molding were scraped, sanded, and covered with varnish to bring out their natural wood grain.

Brielle had chosen furnishings in keeping with an early twentieth-century farmhouse. Side tables, armoires, lamps, chandeliers, sofas, and chairs were simple and elegant. The imported hand-knotted wool rugs covering the living and dining room floors were exquisite. Emery left her in the living room as he retreated to the rear of the house.

She stood in the living room in front of the fireplace. The mantel was crowded with family photographs. She studied a picture of Debbie at her high school graduation.

Surrounded by her brothers, sister, and in-laws, she'd stared into the camera lens, smiled, and flashed a victory sign. Rhianna's gaze shifted to the photos of newborns and toddlers. Another generation of Sutherlands confirmed they were still prolific.

Emery walked into the living room and saw Rhianna staring at his family's photographs, wondering if she was looking for one of Errol. Once he'd begun the refurnishing of the house—room by room—the eight-year project had signaled a healing for him. He'd gathered all of the photographs with his brother and parents and sent them to Brielle. She kept the ones she wanted and distributed the others to Kirk, Paul, and Deborah. He didn't need a photograph of Errol to remember what he looked like. All he had to do was look in a mirror.

"I'll follow you home."

She turned at the sound of the deep voice. Emery had put on a barn jacket over his sweatshirt. "That's okay. I'll get home all right."

He closed the distance between them and held out his hand. "Let's go."

Rhianna wrinkled her nose at him. "I've haven't been away so long that I don't know how to find my way home."

Emery grasped her fingers and dropped a kiss on her knuckles. "Now, that's debatable." He led her to the entryway where she retrieved her boots and coat.

They walked the short distance to their vehicles. Rhianna maneuvered out of the driveway, Emery following a short distance behind her in his truck. Minutes later, she pulled into the driveway alongside Campy's.

Emery got out of his truck, but left the engine running. He walked Rhianna to a side door. "I'll be over about six."

She smiled up at him. "Thank you for everything."

He reached down and cradled her face between his palms. "There's no reason to thank me." Lowering his head, he brushed a light kiss over her mouth. "Good night."

Rhianna was certain he could hear her heart pumping wildly in her chest. It was only a mere brushing of lips, but her mouth was on fire.

Her eyelids fluttered wildly. "Good night, Emery." Her voice had dropped an octave from the rising desire she was helpless to control.

"Now, go inside before you catch a chill."

There was an icy edge to his command, but Emery could not control the shiver of awareness arcing through his body. Kissing Rhianna had melted the frozen passion surrounding his heart—a passion he'd withheld from every woman since Tonya gave him back his ring.

Rhianna unlocked the door, then closed it behind her; she listened for the sound of Emery's truck. She waited as the seconds ticked off. A frown formed between her eyes when she encountered silence.

She opened the door and went completely still. Emery hadn't moved. The light over the door threw long and short shadows over his lean face. A rush of wanting settled in her middle and she sagged against the doorframe. Her instinctive response to him was swift and overwhelming.

"Go home, Emery," she pleaded in a soft whisper.

He took a step, bringing him inches from her. "I can't," he countered. He couldn't until he discovered what it was

about Rhianna Campbell that rekindled feelings he
thought long dead.

The pit of Rhianna's stomach churned in anxiety. "What
do I have to do to make you leave?"

Emery came closer without moving. He dipped his head
until their breaths mingled. "Kiss me."

Standing on tiptoe, she touched her lips to his, giving
herself freely to the passion of his kiss.

Emery moved his mouth over Rhianna's, devouring its
softness and sweetness. He'd asked Rhianna to kiss him
when he wanted more—much more. He wanted her in his
bed—naked, flesh-to-flesh, and heart to heart and man to
woman. Why her and not some other woman? Why the
woman who was to have become his sister-in-law?

He forgot all of the whys as his mouth moved to the column of her neck and breathed a kiss there. "Thank you,
Rhia. I can go home now."

Rhianna stood motionlessly, watching Emery as he
walked back to his vehicle and drove away. She ran her
tongue over her bottom lip, tasting him again. Bringing
her fingertips to her mouth she blew a kiss to the cold,
silent night.

"Good night, Emery."

Stepping back, she closed and locked the door. His taste
and touch lingered with her as she prepared for bed. She
slipped under a mound of blankets and switched off the
bedside lamp. The last thing she remembered before
sleep claimed her was that the more time she spent with
Emery the more she recognized distinct differences between the twin brothers.

CHAPTER 6

Emery woke before dawn, and instead of getting out of bed he lingered, staring up at the skylight. He didn't know what possessed him to ask Rhianna to kiss him because he usually did not act or react on impulse. But there was something about her that kept him a little off balance, made him a little less confident than he presented.

Running a hand over his face, he let out a deep breath. He did not want to acknowledge the obvious—he was lusting after his dead twin brother's fiancée.

Mixed feelings swirled through him as his mind reeled in confusion. He'd always interacted with Rhianna as he had with his sisters, but their roles changed after Errol's death. He'd comforted her along with his siblings, and whenever she clung to him she elicited in him an overwhelming urge to take care of her.

Days before Rhianna left Shepherd, Tonya made her feelings known. The woman he'd hoped to marry admitted that she hadn't been prepared to become a stepmother or compete with his dead brother's fiancée for his attention. He'd stood there unable to form a reply even after she left his ring on a table and walked out of his life. He'd believed Tonya's jealousy was totally unfounded until now—now that he'd seen Rhianna again and now that he'd kissed her. Perhaps Tonya recognized something he hadn't wanted to acknowledge at that time—his feelings for Rhianna went beyond their role of brother and sister-in-law.

Throwing back the blanket, he swung his legs over the side of the bed. He had to get up and check on the sheep before going to Campy's. Every morning he fed and watered the flock, then turned them out into a fenced-in pasture before he returned to clean the barn. He relied on the three border collies to protect the sheep from coyotes and other stray dogs.

Emery entered Campy's carrying a toolbox. His gaze swept around the small café-restaurant. He nodded to the early morning regulars as he made his way to the rear of the building. Shrugging out of his jacket, he placed it on a makeshift worktable Reid had constructed when he placed a piece of plywood over two sawhorses.

"What are you doing in here?"

He glanced over his shoulder to find Anna Campbell in the doorway, hands resting on her hips.

He smiled at her. "Didn't Rhia tell you?"

A slight frown creased her smooth forehead. "Tell me what?"

"I'm going to finish the expansion."

Her frown deepened. "When did you decide this?"

"Rhia and I discussed it last night."

She shook her head. "You don't have to do this, Emery."

"Yes, I do," he countered softly. "It's the least I can do to repay you and Reid for what you've done for my family."

"We did what anyone else would've done considering the circumstances."

"You're wrong, Anna. What you and Reid did went beyond love thy neighbor."

"I appreciate your help, but I don't want to take you away from your own work."

Emery gave her a reassuring smile. "That's not a problem. I'll come by and work after closing hours. That way the noise won't disturb your customers."

Clasping her hands together, Anna's features became more animated. It looked as if Reid was going to get his wish. Her husband had become so obsessed about expanding the restaurant that after a while she refused to discuss it with him. She thought when he'd contacted Emery for his advice he would let the younger man do the work. Much to her surprise, Reid decided to embark on his do-it-yourself project, which resulted in him injuring himself.

Rhia and I discussed it last night. It was apparent her daughter felt comfortable and confident enough with Emery to meet with him. Her mouth curved into an unconscious smile. Emery was the reason Rhianna had fled her hometown, and perhaps she would enlist him to help her daughter change her mind and come back to live in Shepherd.

"How can I thank you, Emery?"

"You did that ten years ago," he said with a significant lifting of his eyebrows. "After I finish what your husband started, then we'll be even."

"Okay," Anna said with a wide smile. "Would you like anything special for breakfast?"

"No. Just my usual."

"I'll let you get back to your work."

Emery removed a retractable tape measure, pencil, and pad from the box. He made notations on the pad as he measured walls and floor space. Climbing on the ladder propped against a wall, he measured the ceiling. Three-quarters of an hour later he'd filled several pages with diagrams with accompanying measurements for windows, electrical outlets, load-bearing walls, a solid floor construction, and a ventilation system. The task was daunting for someone with his experience, and Emery could not understand what would make Reid attempt to tackle it by himself.

He left his toolbox in a corner and made his way to a bathroom to wash his hands. His mind was working overtime as he calculated how long it would take him to finish the space before Christmas. He planned to put up the walls, lay the floor, and install the windows first, then tackle the electrical installation and ventilation. He always left the painting for last.

Emery walked out of the bathroom and into the restaurant, hoping to see Rhianna, but was disappointed when Nicole came over to his booth carrying a carafe of coffee. She turned over a mug and filled it with the steaming brew.

"The usual, Emery?"

"Yes, Nicole."

He did not know why she asked him the same thing every morning. It was only on a rare occasion that he ordered the country breakfast: grits, eggs, bacon, ham or sausage, and biscuits.

He retrieved his cell phone, scrolled through the directory and punched in the number for the company where he'd bought all of his materials for Sutherland and Sons General Contracting. He called in his order with a request that everything should be delivered to Campy's.

His breakfast arrived and he ate slower than usual, hoping Rhianna would show up. She still hadn't put in an appearance when he paid his check, and he called himself every kind of fool for coming on to her.

She'd admitted that seeing him reminded her of Errol, and he had taken advantage of her vulnerability when he asked her to kiss him. He clamped his teeth tightly, welcoming the pain radiating in his lower jaw.

He'd made a fool of himself, and he swore a silent oath that it would not happen again.

Rhianna overslept for the first time in a long time. The sun was high in the sky as she scrambled from her bed, wondering why her mother had not come to wake her up.

She showered and dressed quickly, then raced down to the restaurant. Breakfast was over, and Nicole sat at the counter reading the newspaper. The television was muted with closed captions, while the soulful wail of a flugelhorn came through the jukebox speakers. She found her mother in the office, sitting at a desk writing checks.

"Good morning, Mom."

Anna peered at Rhianna over a pair of half-glasses. "It's more like good afternoon."

She sat down on a worn chair next to an antique desk Anna had picked up at a tag sale.

"Why did let me sleep so late?"

"When you didn't get up, I figured you needed your sleep. What time did you go to bed?" Anna asked, as she scrawled her signature on a check.

"It had to be after midnight. I went to see Emery last night." Anna's head came up and stayed as she told her about Emery's offer to finish the renovations, but not about kissing him or the promise to go skating with him later that night.

Her mother gave her a long, penetrating stare. "Are you certain you're going to be all right with Emery hanging out here?"

"Very certain," she said with a quiet confidence.

"So, whatever it was about him that made you leave has been resolved?"

"Yes."

Lacing her fingers together in a prayerful gesture, Anna flashed a grateful smile. "It does my heart good to hear that. Now, I pray for your father's speedy recovery."

"Aren't they supposed to stop sedating him today?"

Anna nodded. "His doctor asked that we don't come to the hospital until he's fully conscious."

Vertical lines appeared between Rhianna's eyes. "When will that be?"

"Probably some time tomorrow afternoon. Meanwhile I need you to come to the bank with me. I want to add your signature to the business account. Once your father's home I'm going to be spending most of my time with him."

Rhianna picked up a flyer announcing an annual fundraising dinner-dance to benefit homeless and infirmed children. "Who left these?"

"The president of the Chamber of Commerce asked me to put them out for our customers."

"Are you going, Mom?" The event was next week.

"No, sweetheart. Not without your father. But, you should go and represent Campy's." She opened one of the desk drawers, took out an envelope and handed it to Rhianna. "I paid for the invitations and sent in our donation."

"I didn't bring anything to wear."

Anna smiled. "After we finish our bank business we can go to that little boutique in Yorktown Heights you like so much. They still carry the most darling little outfits for evening wear."

Rhianna found it impossible not to return her mother's enchanting dimpled smile. She'd lost count of the number of times she and Anna shared what they'd called their mother–daughter away days. Once each month they'd get up early and spend the entire day together, dining out, sightseeing, and shopping. The shopping was what Rhianna loved most.

"I need a cup of coffee. Then I'll be ready to leave."

"I only have a few more checks to write. I meant to tell you that everybody says they love the Christmas decorations."

Nodding, Rhianna stood up and walked out of the office. She'd placed electric candles in each of the many windows; positioned red poinsettia plants on a stepladder in the shape of a pine tree next to the jukebox, and hung a massive wreath on the front door. She liked the tiny white lights entwined in the leafless trees most.

She went behind the counter and filled a mug with coffee, then sat down beside Nicole and picked up a section of the newspaper. She was on her second cup when Anna told her she was ready to leave.

Rhianna locked the door behind the cleaning man. Seconds later the telephone rang. She contemplated whether to answer the call or let the answering machine pick it up. The restaurant had closed more than an hour before. At the last moment she picked up the receiver.

"Campy's."

"Are we still on for tonight?"

Her heart beat a double-time rhythm as she recognized the sensual baritone voice. "Yes." The word came out in a breathless sigh.

"How soon can you be ready?"

"I just have to get my skates."

"I'll be here."

"Where are you, Emery?"

A soft chuckle came through the earpiece. "I'm standing on the porch. I was waiting for Mr. Archer to leave."

It was her turn to laugh softly. "There are laws against stalking."

"There's a difference between stalking and waiting for my date."

Rhianna froze, her fingers tightening around the receiver. "I'll be right out." She pressed a button and ended the call. *My date.* What she'd wanted to tell Emery was that she wasn't his date, but an old friend who'd agreed to go ice-skating with him.

She'd returned to Shepherd to help her family with their restaurant, not become involved with a man.

Rhianna left through a side door and came around to the porch. Emery leaned against a massive column holding up the second floor, his arms crossed over a heavy knit sweater. He straightened slowly with her approach.

"Hello."

Emery stared at Rhianna. He didn't think he would ever get used to the throaty timbre of her sensual voice, and didn't want to. She was dressed for skating—knitted cap, bulky sweater under a short jacket, and wool slacks.

"Hey." He came off the porch, his gaze fusing with hers. "Are you ready?"

Rhianna nodded, but wanted to ask Emery what he meant by ready. Ready for what he considered a date, ready for him, ready to open herself up enough to fall in love again? He took her skates from her loose grip, reached for her hand and led her to his pickup.

"It feels like snow," she said softly as he opened the passenger-side door.

Emery hoisted her up onto the seat with a minimum of effort. "It's too cold."

"There's a haze around the moon."

A knowing smile parted his mouth. "So, the girl still has a little country in her."

"I'm not that citified," she retorted, rolling her eyes at him.

"Yeah, right," he drawled. "I bet you'll fall down within five minutes of lacing up your skates."

"Bite your tongue, Emery Sutherland."

Chuckling under his breath, Emery closed the door and came around the vehicle. He got in behind the wheel, grinning broadly. Rhianna had no idea how much she'd changed—in looks and demeanor. She'd left Shepherd a shy girl, and returned a very sexy woman.

Rhianna sat on a bench beside Emery, lacing up her skates, as a biting wind stabbed her exposed skin like sharp needles. They had the pond to themselves. If it had been the weekend there was no doubt it would've been crowded with skaters of every age from sunrise and far beyond sunset. She completed the task and slipped her stiff fingers into a pair of fur-lined gloves.

Emery stood up, cupped her elbow, easing her gently to her feet. Leaning against his length, she managed to keep her balance until they reached the frozen pond. Then, without warning, her feet went out from under her, and she would've fallen if not for the strong hand on her forearm.

"Careful."

Rhianna wrapped her arms around Emery's waist, pressing her face to his shoulder. "Don't move yet. I need to get my balance."

Emery nodded. Rhianna needed to get her balance while everything about her kept him off balance. Emotions he'd never experienced with any other woman, including Tonya, surfaced.

He wanted Rhianna, the wanting surpassing the desire to take her to bed to slack his sexual frustration. He could do that with other women, what he'd shared with every woman he'd slept with over the past ten years. He hadn't realized it, until now, that they were only temporary, a poor substitute to the woman in his arms.

Why Rhianna Campbell? He didn't know, and didn't want to know, because he'd spent years denying his feelings for a girl who'd fallen in love with his brother. He spent years telling himself that Errol was blessed to have found someone with whom to live, laugh, and love. But after Errol lost control of his new car, killing himself and their parents, he'd called his twin king of fools.

Emery felt a shudder shake Rhianna. Lowering his head, he pressed his mouth to her forehead. "What's the matter, darling?" The endearment had slipped out unbidden.

Another shiver swept over Rhianna's body, the cold replaced by a swath of heat. Easing back, she stared up at Emery. The bright overhead lights flattered the elegant ridge of cheekbones that gave his face the appearance of a high fashion male model. Large, deep-set, dark eyes regarded her intently.

"I'm freezing," she said in a half-truth. She was cold *and* hot at the same time because of frigid below-freezing temperatures and the man holding her to his heart.

He lowered his head until their mouths were inches apart. "I know a way to heat us up."

Her gloved fingers tightened on his sweater. "We can't, Emery," she whispered, even though there was no one around to hear them.

Emery's lids lowered. "Yes, we can, Rhia." She shook her head. His hold on her upper arms tightened as he pulled her closer. "I am not my brother." He had enunciated each word.

This time she nodded. Emery wasn't Errol, and she wasn't the same person who'd left Shepherd ten years before. She'd dated men for all of the wrong reasons, and she'd slept with one for a multitude of reasons: she was lonely, tired of sleeping alone, and she wanted to see whether she could finally exorcise her deceased lover's ghost, and she had failed miserably—until now.

"I know you're not Errol. I realized that the moment you kissed me last night." A sense of strength came to her as her defenses began to subside.

One of Emery's hands moved up and cradled the back of her head. "I'm not Errol, nor do I want to replace him in your heart, but I don't want to hurt you. "

She closed her eyes for several seconds. "You can't, Emery, because I will never permit my heart to overrule my head again."

"Where do we go with this?"

She lifted her eyebrows. "I don't know."

"Neither do I, but I promise to be truthful with you. I've always liked you."

Her gaze widened in astonishment, but Emery plunged on recklessly. "I suppose I wanted you a long time ago, but you were dating my brother and I wouldn't allow myself to entertain anything licentious."

Rhianna stood there, amazed, shaken and unable to believe what she was hearing. Emery Sutherland—the quiet twin, the straight-A student, the consummate all-around athlete, and valedictorian had had a crush on her.

"Why didn't you say something?"

"I did."

"To whom?"

"Errol."

"He knew that you liked me?"

Emery inclined his head. "But, why did he come onto me if he knew you were interested in me?"

His expression changed, and Rhianna recognized the cold dignity that was the Emery she remembered. "Sibling rivalry."

"But…but he was your twin."

"He was my brother, Rhia. Just like Cain and Abel were brothers."

She never knew, never suspected there had been enmity between the two. If Emery was telling her the truth, then did that mean he was the good twin and Errol the bad one?

"I don't believe you," she said in a quiet voice.

"You don't have to," Emery countered. "I'd never lie about Errol." Smiling, his mood changed like quicksilver. Grasping her hands he pulled her further out onto the ice. "Let's skate before it gets too late."

Once Rhianna gained her balance and footing, she found herself gliding over the icy surface as she had as a child. As she executed dips and turns the conversation she'd had with her mother came rushing back in vivid clarity: *You never would've left Shepherd if you'd been in love with Errol.* Had Anna seen what she hadn't been able to see? That it was Emery she loved, not Errol.

She laid her head on his shoulder as he led her over the frozen surface as if they were on a dance floor. She'd always preferred skating with Emery because he didn't twirl her around and around until she found she wasn't able to stand upright. And whenever she fell Errol laughed hysterically until she demanded he help her up.

They skated to music without words or sound, and Rhianna could not rid her mind of the fact that she may have convinced herself that she was actually in love with Errol, when in reality it was Emery she really loved and wanted.

Emery used every inch of the pond as he told her that he'd ordered the supplies needed to complete the renovations in the rear of the restaurant, and he would start work tomorrow after Campy's closed.

They skated and talked about everything—but themselves. A light snow had begun falling when they took off their skates and walked back to the pickup.

He drove to Campy's, leaving her at the side door; this time he did not have to ask her to kiss him. Wrapping her arms around his neck, Rhianna pulled his head down and kissed him with a hunger that longed to be assuaged. The kiss ended, both breathing heavily.

Rhianna was the first one to move. "Good night, Emery."

He winked at her. "Good night, Rhia."

They turned at the same time, she opening and closing the door behind her as Emery made his way to his truck. She climbed the staircase to her third-floor bedroom, walked over to a window, and stared out at the snow blanketing the countryside. It was so quiet that she felt as if the world was holding its breath while it contemplated its next move, and she was no different.

Emery had admitted he liked her, but she had yet to admit the same.

And, she did like him.

A lot.

And the liking had nothing to do with his resemblance to her deceased fiancé.

CHAPTER 7

Rhianna sat at Reid Campbell's bedside, cradling his uninjured hand, always mindful of the IV taped to its back. It had taken twenty-four hours for her father to become alert enough to recognize familiar faces.

Reid stared at his daughter, his gaze softening. He couldn't speak above a whisper. The tube used to facilitate breathing made swallowing painful.

"You're back." His voice was low and raspy.

She smiled. "Yes, Daddy, I'm back."

Reid closed his eyes as his chest rose and fell in an even rhythm. "Good."

That was the last word he uttered as Rhianna sat with him for more than an hour, bringing him up-to-date on what had happened in her life since their last telephone conversation.

"Emery is going to finish the renovations on the back

porch. He's hoping to have everything finished before Christmas. Mom told me that you wanted to host an open house, but what I don't understand is why you did not want to wait until next year for Campy's thirtieth anniversary."

Smiling, she continued her monologue. "I know Mom tried to talk you out of tackling it by yourself. But I know once you set your mind to do something, no one or nothing can get you to change it."

"Don't…"

Rhianna went completely still. She'd thought Reid was asleep. "Don't what, Daddy?"

She waited for him to speak again, until visiting hours ended, then left, wondering what her father was protesting.

Rhianna totaled the daily receipts, prepared a deposit ticket, and put them in the wall safe. She'd had to count the cash twice. The whirring sound of a saw made it hard for her to concentrate.

Things were almost back to normal. Her father had been released from the hospital with a recommendation from his doctor that he limit his daily activities. Anna spent all of her time helping Reid adjust to his temporary disability, while Rhianna stepped into her mother's role of running Campy's.

She quickly realized that managing the mom-and-pop restaurant was more daunting than she first thought. She was responsible for opening and closing, ordering foodstuffs, scheduling work shifts, payroll, accounts receivable and payables, and food preparation.

Emery usually arrived before closing time, waited until she locked the door behind the last customer, then began working. He'd erected a large sheet of heavy-gauge plastic over the work area to keep dust and debris from seeping back into the restaurant area.

Leaning back on her chair, Rhianna ran her fingers through her short hair. She still hadn't done any of her own Christmas shopping, and didn't know when she would get the time to do it. Her gaze shifted, lingering on the computer. A knowing smile softened her mouth. She would shop online.

"What are you smiling about?"

Swiveling in her chair, she saw Emery standing in the doorway. Her jaw dropped, but she recovered quickly. A damp white T-shirt, a pair of low-rise jeans, work boots, and the white bandana on his head screamed virility.

"I just solved my Christmas shopping dilemma. I've decided to shop online."

Emery pulled off the bandana, pushing it into a back pocket of his jeans. "Smart move," he said, walking into the office. He'd shopped for his nieces and nephews months before.

His gaze lingered on Rhianna's face, noting the changes. Her cheeks had filled out and the shadows under her eyes had disappeared. She radiated a delicate sensuality he found mesmerizing.

"I'm through for the night. The walls are up."

Pushing back the chair, she stood up. "Can I see what you've done?"

"Not until I lay the floor."

Rhianna came around the desk, sitting on a corner, her gaze meeting and fusing with Emery's. "Have I thanked you for what you're doing for my folks?"

He angled his head. "I don't think so."

She stared up at him through her lashes. "Thank you, Emery."

Taking two long strides, he closed the distance between them, wrapped his arms around her waist and eased her to her feet. "You're welcome," he crooned softly. "I don't believe I've thanked you."

Her eyebrows lifted. "For what?"

"For coming home," Emery crooned, as his head came down. His mouth brushed hers, the sensation soft and velvety as the brush of a butterfly's wings.

Rhianna opened her mouth to tell him that she'd come back, but not to stay, giving him the advantage he needed when his tongue slipped between her parted lips.

She gasped, sinking into his strength. His kiss sang through her veins and heated her blood. His mouth demanded a response and she answered, curving her arms under his shoulders and pressing her breasts to his hard chest as shivers of wanting and delight held her in a grip from which she did not want to escape.

I want him, I want him, I want him so much, sang the silent refrain in her heart and in her head. She drank in the sweetness of his kiss, the power in his body, and the virility that made her a prisoner of her own lust. Even when she'd believed she was in love with Errol she never felt the aching desire she felt for Emery.

Emery eased the hem of Rhianna's shirt from the waistband of her jeans, his fingers caressing the silky flesh on her back. He undid the clasp on her bra, freeing her breasts. Cupping the small, firm mounds of flesh, squeezing them gently, he groaned when they swelled against his palms.

He rotated his hips and permitted her to feel the hardness he was helpless to control. He wanted Rhianna, couldn't remember when he didn't want her. He'd loved her for more than half his life; loved her when he'd pledged his future to another.

"Come home with me tonight, darling," he whispered against her moist, parted lips.

Rhianna rested her forehead on his shoulder. "I can't, Emery."

"I'll make certain you get up in time to open the restaurant. If you want, you can meet my research subjects."

Her heart pounded in her chest as she struggled to regain control of the runaway passion surging through her body. There was no way she would her permit her desire for the man holding her to his heart to cloud her judgment. She'd told Emery that she would never permit her heart to overrule her head again.

They were adults, not having to answer to anyone, and if she was going to share Emery's bed, then she owed it to him to establish ground rules for what would follow.

"Not tonight," she continued. Her voice was low and hauntingly sensual.

Emery didn't realize he'd been holding his breath until the band constricting his chest made breathing difficult. He winked at her. "No rush, no pressure."

Rhianna closed her eyes, exhaling softly, and when she opened them her steady gaze was filled with confidence. "And no strings, Emery."

The three words would've aroused old fears and uncertainties in Emery, but now he was older, more secure. He'd lost Rhianna once because he hadn't made his feelings known to her. It would not happen again.

He gave her a long, penetrating look. "Okay. No strings."

Rhianna's smile was dazzling. Somehow she hadn't expected Emery to go along with her mandate, but he had. Perhaps, like her, he wasn't looking for someone with whom he could settle down, that he didn't want Miss Right, but Miss Right Now.

She'd stopped looking for Mr. Right after losing Errol. Every man she met she compared with him. Some were intelligent, but lacked the requisite social etiquette. Others had money and social status, yet watching moss grow had elicited more excitement. And there was one who truly was an Adonis, but dumb as dirt.

However, Emery was the exception and not an option. She could not and would not lose her heart to another Sutherland man. She would enjoy whatever he offered, and once her father recovered from his injuries, she planned to return to Los Angeles and the life she'd made for herself.

Emery watched a myriad of expressions cross Rhianna's delicate features and wondered what it was she was thinking about. Suddenly it hit him. What if she had a boyfriend—someone waiting for her in California? Was that the reason she was willing to go into a liaison without a commitment? Men did it every day, so why not a woman?

"I won't be by Saturday night."

Emery mentioning Saturday night reminded Rhianna that she'd committed to attending Shepherd's Chamber of Commerce dinner-dance.

"That's okay, because I won't be here either. I'm going to the Chamber's fundraiser."

"So am I. Are you going with your mother?"

She hesitated. Her parents had paid for tickets for two. "No. I'm going alone."

"You don't have to go alone."

"Why?"

"You can go with me."

Rhianna rested her palms on his solid pectorals. "What happened to your date?"

He smiled at her. "Don't have one."

"Why not?"

"I couldn't find anyone I wanted to go with me."

She affected an attractive moue, bringing his gaze to linger on her lush mouth. "So, I'm your last choice?"

His eyes crinkled in a smile. "You're my *only* choice."

She sobered quickly. "What if I hadn't come back, Emery? Who would you've taken?"

His expression stilled and grew serious. "No one. It wouldn't be the first time I've attended a local function alone. I've made it a practice not to date any woman who lives in Shepherd. The town is too small. Folks too nosy and it would be uncomfortable if we decide to stop seeing each other."

"How is that different from you and I?"

Emery ran his forefinger down the length of her nose. "You don't live in Shepherd."

"You're right, Emery." He'd just reminded her that she was a visitor, nothing more than a tourist in her hometown. "I'll come and meet your sheep Saturday night."

"Before or after the dinner-dance?"

"Before. If it's all right with you I'll get dressed at your place."

"It's more than all right. Good night, darling." He kissed her again, then turned and walked out of the office.

Rhianna waited a full minute, then whispered, "Good night Emery."

Emery rapped lightly on the door, listening for movement on the other side.

"Come in."

He recognized the female voice, but it wasn't the one he'd expected to hear. He pushed open the door and walked in. Anna sat behind the desk, a phone cradled between her chin and shoulder; she motioned for him to sit.

Anna wrote down the telephone number, her gaze shifting from the pad in front of her to the man sitting several feet away. It had been a long time since she'd seen Emery unshaven, but there was something about the stubble on his jaw that made him appear more rugged than usual.

She'd gone to high school with his mother, who'd been prom queen and the prettiest girl at Shepherd High; she'd passed her striking good looks on to her twin sons.

Anna ended the call and smiled at Emery. "Hello. I take it you were looking for Rhianna?"

He nodded. "Yes. I told her that I'd pick her up around five."

"She's upstairs with Reid. I'm certain she'll be down momentarily. By the way, I want to thank you for escorting my daughter to the Chamber dance tonight."

Emery draped one leg over the opposite knee and stared at the scuffed toes on his boots. "I'm honored that she agreed to go with me. Having her as my date will be quite a change from taking my sisters."

"How are your sisters?"

He smiled. "They're quite well, thank you."

He'd continued the tradition begun by his father of supporting the local Chamber of Commerce. He paid dues and attended the annual fundraising dinner-dance whenever he escorted his sisters to the event.

However, Emery didn't want to talk about his sisters. He was anxious to spend as much time with Rhianna as he could before he had to bring her home later that night.

"I won't keep Rhia out too late," he said in a quiet voice.

Anna sat up straighter and laced her fingers together. "I'm not as concerned with you bringing her home as making sure she's safe."

Emery's head rose up and he met Anna's steady stare. "You know?"

A mysterious smile deepened the dimples in the older woman's cheeks. "I've known for years, Emery."

Uncrossing his legs, he placed both feet on the carpeted floor. "Why didn't you say something?"

"It wasn't my place to tell my daughter how you felt about..." Anna's words trailed off when Rhianna walked into the small room.

"Tell me what?"

Emery stood up, his gaze taking in everything about Rhianna in one sweeping look. Her short hair was styled in tiny ringlets that framed her narrow face.

"That it's impolite to keep your young man waiting," Anna lied smoothly.

"Emery's not my young man," Rhianna said, reaching for Emery's hand and lacing her fingers through his. "We're friends."

What she didn't tell her mother was that Emery was a friend who'd kissed her with a passion that made her knees weak, a friend who'd touched her body and made her hot as a pat of butter on a heated surface. A friend who made her want to strip naked and lie in his strong embrace and experience why she'd been born female.

Emery couldn't pull his gaze away from Rhianna. Even without makeup she looked incredible. He squeezed her fingers. "Well, friend, are you ready to meet my flock?"

"I have to get my bags."

"Where are they?"

Rhianna met Emery's curious gaze. "I left them at the side door."

There was no way she was going to walk through the restaurant area with Emery carrying an overnight and garment bag. Before they darkened the door, the gossip would be all over town that Reid Campbell's girl was spending the night with Emery Sutherland. The fact that they would attend the fundraiser together was enough to start tongues wagging.

He nodded and said, "I'll meet you around there."

"Thank you," she said so softly he had strained his ears to hear what she'd said. Shifting, she smiled at her mother. "I'll see you tomorrow."

Anna lifted an eyebrow as she regarded her daughter. "Have fun. Don't bother about getting up early. I'll open up."

"But I usually open up," Rhianna countered.

A mysterious smile lifted the corners of Anna's mouth. "Please don't argue with your mother, sweetheart." She waved a hand. "Now go and have a wonderful time."

Rhianna's smile matched Anna's. "I will."

She left the office and made her way down a narrow hallway that led to the opposite end of the structure where the Campbells maintained their living quarters.

She opened the door and seconds after she'd stepped in the small space she found herself in Emery's arms, his mouth coming down on hers, stealing the breath from her lungs.

Rising on tiptoe, she deepened the kiss that flamed like smoldering heat from joined metals. Her hands cradled his face, the emerging whiskers biting into the tender skin on her palms. She inhaled the smell of soap mingling with his body's natural scent.

"I've missed you," he murmured against her moist, parted lips.

Rhianna anchored a hand against his chest, pushing him back. "You're crazy. We just saw each other last night." He'd finished laying the floor around eleven.

Tightening his hold on her waist, Emery pulled her close again. "That was almost eighteen hours ago."

He kissed her again, the tip of his tongue tantalizing the recesses of her mouth and eliciting a strong thrumming between her thighs. The delicious sensations went on and on until she went weak in his embrace, collapsing against the wall of his chest like a soft breeze ruffling a delicate leaf.

Emery knew he had to stop or he would either take Rhianna where they stood or embarrass himself by spilling his passions like an inexperienced adolescent during his first sexual encounter. Reluctantly, he released her.

He picked up an overnight bag and matching garment bag off a straight-back chair and took them to where he'd parked his truck, leaving Rhianna to close and lock the door behind her. He waited by the passenger-side door, helped her in, then sat down beside her. An uneasy silence filled the vehicle as he drove away from Campy's. There was so much he wanted to say, but he would wait—wait until later that night.

CHAPTER 8

Rhianna stood several feet away from Emery inside a tightly woven fence, watching as he checked the foot of the lone ram. Three border collies stood guard outside the fence. The area where the sheep were turned out to pasture covered almost half an acre.

The first thing Rhianna noticed about the sheep was their fleece. It wasn't tightly curled as she'd seen in other breeds; it was longer and crinkly like goat hair.

"Do they stay out here overnight?"

Emery straightened from his kneeling position. "No. All but two ewes have come into estrous and have mated with Bully Boy."

"When do you expect them to lamb?"

"Late April or early May."

"Why so late?"

"Once I decided to participate in the study I only had

enough time to build the barn, but not enough to install a heating system. If I'd bred the ewes in August, then they would've lambed in January."

"Aren't you afraid of stray dogs or a coyote attacking them?"

Emery opened the gate and whistled sharply between his teeth. On cue three dogs raced in and herded the sheep out of the fenced-in area and over a rise to the small barn where they would spend the night.

"Not at all. The two males would've attacked you if you hadn't been with me, while Lady is a bit more gentle. She'll probably be the one to protect the lambs."

"Lady and I have met."

Cupping her elbow, Emery led her back to the truck. "When?"

"The first night I came to see you."

Raising his eyebrows, he stared at her delicate profile. "Oh, that was the night you came and cussed me out."

She stopped and faced him. "I didn't curse you, Emery Sutherland."

"It sounded like cussing to me."

Rhianna rested her hands on her hips. "If I'd really *cussed* you out, then you never would've spoken to me again. Because when I cuss someone they stay cussed."

Bending slightly, Emery swung her up in his arms and spun her around and around. "If that's the case, then I hope never to get on the wrong side of you."

Rhianna wrapped her arms around his neck to keep her balance. "Put me down, Emery."

He stopped spinning. "Why?'

"Because I'm too big to carry."

"Too big or too heavy?"

She punched him softly on the shoulder. "You got jokes about my weight."

"No. When you first came back here I thought you were a little skinny for my taste. I like my woman to have some meat on her bones."

Rhianna froze as she stared at him. She could barely make out his features in the stream of light coming from the pickup's headlights.

"Who said I was your woman?"

"I didn't."

"Neither did I."

He kissed the end of her nose. "Would you like to be my woman, Rhia?"

Her whole being seemed to be filled with waiting, a waiting that had eluded her for ten long, lonely years. Every time Emery looked at her she saw a longing in his gaze that echoed her own. Each time he kissed or touched her she wanted to surrender all of the love she'd locked away from every man to him. Could she, for the short time she would spend in Shepherd, open her heart to love again?

"I don't know, Emery."

"What don't you know, darling? Is it because Errol was my brother?" he asked, not waiting for her reply. Rhianna closed her eyes and nodded. Lowering his head, Emery kissed her cold lips. "Will you promise me one thing?"

She opened her eyes. "What?"

"Let me prove to you that I'm not my brother."

There was another time when Emery told her that he

wasn't his brother, and his kisses had proven that. Aside from their physical resemblance there was nothing about Emery that reminded her of Errol. The two were as different as night was from day.

Resting her head on his shoulder, she whispered a silent prayer for strength. "Okay."

Rhianna followed Emery into a bedroom that once belonged to his parents. When he had taken her on a tour of the large farmhouse she'd been taken aback with the four-poster king-size bed in a room with all-white furnishings: duvet, curtains, carpet, love seat with a chenille throw, and padded bench at the foot of the bed. Cream-colored wallpaper dotted with tiny yellow and pale green flowers provided a cheerful backdrop to the otherwise pristine space.

Emery placed her garment bag on a hook inside a closet door and left the overnight case on the floor next to the bench. "I'll be downstairs whenever you're ready." The cocktail hour was scheduled for seven, a sit-down dinner at eight, and dancing at ten.

Rhianna winked at him. "I'll see you later."

She removed her makeup and toiletries from the bag, walked into the adjoining bathroom, and was transported back to another era. The claw foot bathtub and pedestal sink were exquisite, made of pale blue with darker blue veins running through the porcelain. The soft blue and white furnishings in the bathroom were the perfect complement for the pristine near-white bedroom.

She turned on the silver plated faucets in the tub and added a cupful of perfumed body wash under the running water. The sensual bouquet of Bulgarian rose, calla lily and Mandarin combined with white musk and woods wafted in the air.

Stripping off her clothes, Rhianna settled down in the warm water, sighing softly as she closed her eyes. Earlier that morning she'd gone to a day spa where she'd had her hair washed, conditioned, and trimmed; an esthetician had given her a facial; a nail technician, a manicure and pedicure; and a masseuse, a full body massage. She left the spa feeling better than she had in weeks. Not wanting to keep Emery waiting, she picked up the bath sponge.

Emery stood at the foot of the staircase, temporarily paralyzed, his heart beating in double-time as he watched Rhianna descend. When he did move it was to anchor an arm over the banister to maintain his balance.

His gaze, fixed on her slender feet in a pair of black peau de soie high heel pumps, moved slowly up to her shapely legs in sheer black hose and up further to the outline of her slender body. The pencil skirt ended at her knees, the fitted peplum jacket flared at her tiny waist. But it was what she wore under the jacket that garnered his rapt attention. A soft swell of dark brown flesh rose and fell over the décolletage of a black bustier covered with sequins and bugle beads. A matching fringed shawl was tossed casually over one shoulder. A certain part of Emery's body refused to listen to the dictates of his brain, and he knew he had to get her out of the house before he wouldn't be able to leave.

He walked up the staircase to meet her, extending his hand while forcing a smile. He couldn't stop the gasp that escaped his parted lips when he saw her face. Makeup had dramatically brought out the glossy sheen in her slanting dark brown eyes, and a hint of raspberry on her high cheekbones matched the shimmering shade on her lush mouth. Magnificent Tahitian pearls were suspended from a cascade of bezel-set diamond drop earrings in her pierced lobes. She applied a gel to her hair and spiked the curls at the crown. Rhianna Campbell radiated a dark sensual beauty that literally took his breath away.

"You look beautiful." He was unable to conceal his awe in the compliment.

Slowly, a secret smile softened Rhianna's mouth. She hadn't been able to decide whether to buy the black tuxedo suit or another slinky black dress, so she'd decided to purchase both. She thought of the stir the backless dress would probably cause among the townsfolk and had chosen to wear the suit.

She stared up at Emery through her lashes, unaware of the seductiveness of the gesture. "Thank you."

Her admiring gaze swept over him quickly. His close-cropped hair, smooth jaw, and a tailored navy suit, stark white shirt, platinum-gray silk tie, and imported slip-ons competed with his face for attention. Reaching up, she pressed her thumb to the slight indentation in his chin, and then leaned forward, her lips replacing her fingers.

"You look good enough to eat." It wasn't until the words were out that she realized how ribald they sounded.

Emery's thick, black eyebrows lifted slightly. "Not if I don't eat you first."

Rhianna was growing more uncomfortable the longer

they lingered in his house. "Let's go before we miss the cocktail hour."

Wrapping an arm around her waist, Emery led her off the stairs, across the living room and out of the house. Lady rose from where she lay on a mat in the corner of the porch. "I'll see you later, girl."

Rhianna glanced at the large border collie. "Why doesn't she hang out with the other dogs?"

"She's more of a house dog. Buster and Olaf were bred to herd sheep."

Shifting her tiny purse, she slipped the shawl off her shoulder and wrapped the silk-lined cashmere throw around her body. The night air was dry, the temperature hovering at freezing. Emery led her to a dark, low-slung, two-seater sports car. He'd left the engine running.

He opened the door for her, waiting until she was seated and belted-in, then closed it. He sat down behind the wheel, shifted into gear, and, with a powerful burst of speed, the car shot forward.

Rhianna's fingers curled into tight fists when she re-membered sitting beside Errol whenever he exceeded the speed limit. She stole a glance at the speedometer. Emery was just under the speed limit, so why did it feel as if he was driving too fast?

Resting her back against the leather seat, she closed her eyes and tried to think of everything else but the man sitting less than a foot away from her. Why, she thought, couldn't she have fallen in love with any man but the brother of her first lover? Her eyes flew open as her pulse raced uncontrol-lably and she wondered where that thought had come from.

Was she in love with Emery? Had she always been in love with him? Had she accepted Errol because he'd become a substitute for someone who'd always acted as if she did not exist, the man who'd always treated her like a younger sister?

She sat staring through the windshield replaying all of the encounters she'd shared with Emery as realization washed over her like the numbing effect of an ice-cold shower. Whenever she came to the Sutherland house for dinner Emery usually found an excuse not to join them. It had taken him more than six months to congratulate her on her engagement to his brother, and two weeks later he announced that he planned to marry a fellow student.

He'd loved her and she'd loved him, but the difference was she hadn't known it at the time. But now she was given a second chance with Emery. What she didn't know was where it would lead. She planned to remain in Shepherd only until she exhausted her family leave. If Emery promised more, then she would stay. If not, then she would go back to Los Angeles and the life she'd made for herself.

Emery maneuvered into a long driveway leading to the Vandervoot Mansion. The manor house, erected on a hill that overlooked the Hudson River, once belonged to a family who traced their roots back to a Dutch sea merchant who'd settled in the valley before it was ceded to English rule. The present-day Vandervoots, who did not want to maintain the eighteen-room mansion, sold the property to a group of businessmen, who turned it into a country club with a nearby nineteen-hole golf course. Various businesses, social organizations, and couples rented the grand ballrooms for weddings and fundraisers.

A red-jacketed valet opened the door for her as Emery came around the car to take her arm. Pulling her close to his side, he pressed his mouth to her ear. "You know there's going to be talk?"

She nodded. There was no doubt her attending the event would generate a lot of gossip about her dating her late fiancé's brother. "I don't care, Emery."

The fingers at her waist tightened. "Good."

Lights from half a dozen chandeliers lit up the first floor ballroom as if it were the middle of the day. Rhianna recognized people with whom she'd gone to school, their parents, and their grandparents. A quiet hush fell over those milling around the entrance as she walked in with Emery's arm around her waist.

Tilting her chin, she glanced up at him smiling down at her. There was no way those standing close to them could miss the silent, passionate exchange. When she removed her shawl and handed it to Emery to leave in the coatroom several audible gasps were heard above the babble coming from the ballroom. The bustier had worked it magic, enhancing her B-cup to a full C.

Slipping the coat check ticket into the breast pocket of his jacket, Emery took Rhianna's hand, brought it to his mouth and kissed her smooth knuckles.

She smiled, saying, "Let's mingle, darling."

Rhianna spent most of the cocktail hour sipping champagne, nibbling hors d'oeuvres, and talking to people she hadn't seen in a decade.

Emery found himself a part of a group of men debating

the merits of modernizing downtown Shepherd. Some wanted to keep the look of an early twentieth-century main street, whereas others wanted to update the storefronts to compete with a few of the nearby malls.

"What do you think, Sutherland?" asked one of the officers.

Emery saw several pairs of eyes staring at him. They wanted to discuss revitalizing downtown Shepherd when he wanted to be with Rhianna. As it was they didn't spend as much time together as he'd wanted.

"I like Main Street the way it is. It harkens back to a time of innocence that's missing nowadays. But if you want to compete with the malls, then I suggest you enclose it. Replace the streetlights with gaslight-types. The walls of the mall can be stained glass and the ceiling made with solar heating panels that will offset exorbitant heating and cooling costs. If any new businesses decide they want in, then their storefronts must conform to the existing architecture."

A tall man with a florid face and snow-white hair reached over and pumped Emery's right hand. "Hot damn, Sutherland! I think you're on to something. How would you like to join the planning board?"

"I'll let you know," he said, not wanting to commit to another project. He had enough with his breeding experiment. "Gentlemen, I don't want to appear rude, but I need to get back to Miss Campbell."

He made his way over to Rhianna. "Meet me at the bar," he whispered softly, as he headed in the direction of the nearest portable bar.

Emery ordered a Rusty Nail. By the time Rhianna joined

him he'd downed half the drink and eaten several puffed pastries. A knowing smile crinkled the skin around his eyes. Not only was she sexy, but she also had a sexy walk. He wasn't disappointed when she wrapped her arm around his waist inside his suit jacket.

Leaning forward, she affected a sensual smile. "What do you say we blow this place and go where it's not so crowded?"

His eyebrows shot up. "Are you sure?"

Rhianna kissed his smooth jaw. The scent of his after-shave was hypnotic. "Very sure."

"Where?"

Her eyes widened, prisms of light reflecting in their dark velvet depths. "Your place."

Emery placed the tumbler on the bar before reaching for her hand. "Let's go."

They stopped long enough to retrieve her shawl and wait for his car to be brought around. Within an hour of leaving to drive to the Vandervoot Mansion, Emery and Rhianna retraced their steps as they climbed the staircase leading to the top floor of his house.

Rhianna stood in the middle of Emery's bedroom and stared up at the skylights. Light from a half moon was the only illumination, bathing the space with an eerie glow.

Emery removed his jacket, draping it over the back of a club chair before he walked over and turned on the stereo. The hauntingly beautiful voice of Sarah Brightman flowed from concealed speakers. He came back to Rhianna, offering his hand.

"May I have this dance?"

Smiling, she raised her arms and arced them under his shoulders as he wrapped his arms around her waist. They moved together, breathed together, as they'd done the night they skated under the shadowy moon, losing track of time; however, tonight there were no shadows across their hearts.

Without warning, Emery caught Rhianna under her knees and lifted her effortlessly, carrying her across the room to the bed. Pulling back a pale gray comforter, he placed her gently on the crisp, cool sheets, then joined her, his gaze meeting and fusing with hers. Slowly, methodically, he undressed her: shoes, jacket, bustier, garter belt, stockings, and finally the black lace triangle that teased more than concealed. Her breasts were silvered in the flattering light, rising and falling above her narrow ribcage.

He undressed himself, then sat back staring at the woman whom he loved and waited more than half his life for, and now that he had her in his bed there was no need to rush—not when he had all night to drown in the pleasure of her fragrant silky body.

His large hand took her face and held it gently. "Look at me, darling." Her lids fluttered before she complied. "I love you." And he did love her. He'd loved her for so long that he couldn't remember when he hadn't. "Tonight it can only be you and I," he whispered, "because I will not make love to you if I have to share you with someone in your past."

Rhianna knew to whom he was referring. A part of her would always love Errol. But he was her past and Emery was her present. "You can't expect me to exorcise him completely from my heart."

Emery kissed the end of her nose. "I'd never ask you to, Rhia. Errol was my brother *and* my twin. I'll love and miss him until the day I die. He came between us when he was alive. But I don't want it to happen again now that he's gone."

She trailed her fingers down the side of his face. "He won't," she whispered, "because this time I won't let him."

Emery's hand grazed her hip and a delicious shiver of wanting raced through her. He licked the corners of her mouth as she tried capturing his darting tongue. His tongue was everywhere—her hair, eyes, mouth, and the base of her throat. She arched her back off the mattress when his mouth covered her breasts, his teeth tightening on her nipples until they hardened and swelled to bursting. She felt drugged by his scent, the power in his hard body and the strong pulsing against her mound.

His hand had trailed up between her thighs, his touch leaving her core wet and throbbing. "Emery," she sobbed, the harsh uneven rhythm of her breathing signaled she was going over the edge.

Emery felt the bite of Rhianna's fingernails on his shoulders. He shifted her body, reached over and removed a condom from the drawer of a bedside table. He opened the foil packet and slipped the latex sheath over his aroused flesh.

His knees parted hers as he positioned his hardness at the entrance to her femininity. "Do this with me, baby."

Rhianna opened her legs wider, gasping softly as she felt her flesh stretching until it closed around Emery's sex. They lay joined, not moving and taking pleasure in their oneness. Tears welled up behind her eyelids as a feeling of indescribable joy filled her heart. She loved Emery. She'd always loved him, but had been too flighty to realize it.

She'd left Shepherd because of Emery, not Errol. She'd been too afraid to show the emotions she had transferred to his brother because she feared he would reject her as he'd done all of the other girls who'd flirted shamelessly with him.

Emery pressed his mouth to the column of Rhianna's scented neck. "You feel so good," he crooned in a deep, quiet voice.

Her hands curled into tight fists on his back. "Don't talk."

He nuzzled her ear. "What do you want me to do?"

"Love me. Just love me, Emery."

He smiled. "That, my darling, is the easiest thing anyone has ever asked me to do."

And he did love her, moving in and out of her hot, wet body in long, powerful thrusts before slowing and rolling his hips until both were mindless with ecstasy that threatened to tear apart their very souls.

Rhianna welcomed Emery into her body, into her heart, and into her life. He did more than just satisfy a physical need. He'd touched a part of her that no man had ever come near. She could feel the heat of his body course down the length of hers, and she couldn't control the screams of delight rushing from the back of her throat.

"Baby…oh baby…baby," Emery chanted over and over as eruptions of erotic ecstasy hurtled him beyond the point of no return. Lowering his head, he growled out the last of his passion into the pillow cradling Rhianna's head.

He floated back to earth and reality; an overwhelming feeling made him want to weep with joy. There had been a time when he'd prayed for things to be as they'd been before that tragic Christmas Eve—before he lost his parents and brother—before Rhianna left Shepherd. But she'd come back when his family couldn't. For that he whispered a reverent prayer of gratitude.

Rhianna sighed audibly as the tremors inside her heated thighs and groin faded. Wrapping her arms around Emery's head, she smiled. "It was wonderful."

He chuckled softly. "You were wonderful."

"You're so right, Emery."

"What about?"

"You are *not* your brother."

Emery had no comeback as he rolled off her body and lay on his back. There was no doubt Rhianna had made a comparison as to his and Errol's lovemaking. He'd never competed with his twin—in or out of bed.

"I believe it would be best if we didn't mention Errol's name in bed."

Rising on an elbow, Rhianna stared at Emery. His expression was a mask of stone. "He's gone, Emery, and you're here."

Emery knew she was right, and he wondered how long would he have to compete with a dead man for a woman they both loved. He cupped the back of her head and brushed a light kiss over her parted lips.

"How would you like to go into the city with me next weekend?"

Settling back on the pillow, Rhianna rested her head on his shoulder. "What do you have planned?"

"Have you seen *Phantom of the Opera*?"

"No."

"You would like to see it?"

"Yes."

"We'll make a day of it. I'll get the tickets for a Saturday matinee. Afterwards we can have dinner at Tavern on the Green before going to Rockefeller Center to see the tree. If I can convince you to spend the night with me we can go skating at either Rockefeller Center or at the Wollman Rink before we come back."

Her fingertips traced the ridges of his pectorals and the muscles defining his abs. "When did you come up with this well thought-out plan?"

Emery caught her hand, stopping it before it moved lower. "I just thought of it. I think it's pretty clever. Don't you?"

Moving with the agility of a cat, she straddled him. "I think you have a swelled head."

His flesh stirred under the softness of her buttocks. "That's not the only thing swelling right now."

Rhianna sprang off him, her face burning in shame. She had no idea sitting on Emery would arouse him so quickly. "No…I mean yes, I'd love to go into the city with you."

Throwing back his head, Emery laughed until Rhianna covered his mouth with her hand. They rolled from one side of the large bed to the other, their impromptu wrestling ending with Emery slipping on another condom and entering her in a raw act of possession that shattered them into tiny fragments of unspoken passion.

CHAPTER 9

Rhianna walked into Campy's Sunday afternoon and stopped short. Her father sat at the counter with a pad and pencil, attempting to write with his left hand. The early morning crowd was gone, and only two diners lingered in booths reading newspapers.

She closed the distance between her and Reid, looping an arm around his neck and kissing his cheek. "The cast is coming off in three weeks, Dad."

He turned and smiled at her. Reid Campbell was as handsome at fifty-nine as he'd been at nineteen. Tall and slender, the chef had gained ten pounds since graduating from high school, and he had lost some hair on the crown of his head, but his open and friendly disposition had remained the same.

"I wanted to see if I could sign my name using my left hand."

Rhianna sat down next to Reid. "There's no need for you to sign your name because I can sign checks if Mom isn't around."

Reid's smile faded as his dark slanting eyes narrowed. "For how long, baby girl?"

"How long what?"

"Are you going to stay around?"

"Dad, I'm home."

"For how long?" Reid repeated.

"Daddy don't—"

"Dammit! Don't daddy me, Rhianna!"

She noticed the customers were staring at them. "Daddy, please. There's no need to tell everyone our business," she chided softly.

Reid gave his daughter a long, penetrating stare. "I thought maybe with you taking up with Emery you'd change your mind and come back home."

Her eyes widened like silver dollars. "Who told you that?"

"You did, baby girl." Reid's voice had softened considerably. "The word is that you and Emery left the fundraiser before the cocktail hour ended. And when you didn't come home last night I figured you'd spent the night with him."

Rhianna struggled to control her rising temper. "I'm a grown woman. I didn't think I had to answer to anyone as to my whereabouts."

"You don't have to tell me you're grown, but let me remind you where you are. This is a small town and folks tend to gossip."

"What about you, Daddy? How do you feel about me and Emery?"

Reid's expression softened, attractive lines fanning out around his eyes. "I think he's one of the finest young men Shepherd has ever produced."

"You didn't answer my question."

"I'm not going to answer it. Whatever it is you feel for him you will have to figure out on your own."

Rhianna stomped her foot as she had when she was a child. Her father could be the most exasperatingly stubborn man on the face of the earth. "Where's my mother?"

Reid lifted his dark eyebrows. "My *wife* happens to be in the kitchen."

Turning on her heels, she stalked out of the restaurant's dining room and into the kitchen, running into Anna. "I'm sorry, Mom."

Anna held on to her arm. "Slow down. What's the matter?"

"Your husband knows exactly what buttons to push to make me lose it."

"My husband or your father?"

"Both!"

Anna pulled her over to a tall stool. "Sit down and talk to me."

Rhianna told her mother everything. About leaving the fundraiser, spending the night with Emery, how she cooked breakfast for him, and Reid's comments about town gossip and her staying in Shepherd.

Anna hugged and kissed her daughter's forehead. "I'm glad you found someone you like being with. But, I have to agree with your father about the gossip. I want you to remember that not only are people talking about you, but also Emery. Even after you leave and go back to Los

Angeles, he still has to live here. And since he ended his engagement with that girl he met in veterinary school, no one has ever seen him with another woman. That means he's managed to keep his private life very private."

Rhianna nodded. Emery had admitted to her that he'd never date a woman who lived in Shepherd because he hadn't wanted to invite gossip. But he was dating a woman who was living in Shepherd—even if it was for a short time.

"Why me, Mom? Why has he elected to advertise our…" Her words trailed off. What were they having—an affair, relationship or a liaison?

"I'm surprised you have to ask that question. He loves you, Rhianna. And he wants everyone to know that he loves you."

She met her mother's gaze, holding it. "He's admitted to loving me."

"Do you love him?"

"I think I do."

"Think?"

Rhianna worried her lower lip between her teeth, knowing she couldn't deny the evidence any longer. She had fallen in love with Emery Sutherland as a shy teenager and only accepted Errol because he was as close as she would ever get to the boy who'd captured her heart and never let it go.

"I know I love him. I've always loved him."

Anna smiled that all-knowing smile parents affected. "What are you going to do about it?"

"I'm going to wait for him to make the first move."

"I hope you don't wait too long," Anna mumbled to herself.

"What did you say?"

"Nothing. Grab an apron and help me put up a few pies."

Rhianna knew no amount of coaxing could get Anna to open up once she decided a subject was moot. She washed her hands and reached for an apron. "What if I make a few sweet potato pies?"

Anna smiled and folded her hands on her hips. "I believe that would make a lot of folks happy." Rhianna had earned the reputation of making the best sweet potato pies in the Hudson River Valley.

She rolled out four graham cracker and pecan crusts, filling them with whipped sweet potatoes blended with the traditional ingredients, as well as ground nutmeg, lemon zest, and ginger. She baked the pies for thirty minutes before adding a praline topping. Then they went back into the oven for an additional twenty minutes.

She baked, sautéed, and stir-fried, while Emery hammered, drilled, and tightened nuts, bolts, and installed windows. She didn't get to see him until hours after the restaurant's closing.

Emery shook Rhianna gently. She sat in a booth, her head resting on folded arms. "Wake up, baby."

Her head came up, and she stared at him as if he were a stranger. "What?"

"I'm leaving. You need to set the alarm."

Massaging her eyes with her fingertips, she moaned softly. "I must have fallen asleep."

Cupping her elbow, Emery pulled her to her feet. "I'll see you in a couple of days."

Rochelle Alers

All remnants of sleep vanished. "Where are you going?"

"I'm flying up to Ithaca early tomorrow morning to meet with the breeding study committee. I also have to arrange for the exchange of two ewes that haven't come into heat."

"Maybe they're rams, not ewes."

Smiling, he cradled her face. "I'm certain they're ewes."

"Have you thought of going back to veterinary school?"

"Yes, but I'll have to wait until I complete the breeding study." Lowering his head, he kissed the pulse at the hollow of her throat. "I have to go."

Her arms circled his neck. "I'm going to miss you."

Emery moved his mouth over hers, devouring its softness. "Me, too."

He was there, then he was gone, leaving Rhianna staring at the space where he'd been. She told him that she'd miss him when she wanted to tell him that she loved him.

She knew it was only a matter of time before she would be forced to tell Emery what lay in her heart.

Emery sat forward on the leather seat and closed the partition between him and the limo driver. "Now, let's see what you're hiding under this coat," he whispered to Rhianna.

"No." She clutched the fur-lined silk raincoat tighter. "You'll just have to wait until we get to the theater."

"No," he repeated. "Then I'm not going to be responsible for body slamming some pervert for ogling my woman."

A slight frown appeared between her eyes, eyes accentuated with smoky gray and muted gold shadows. "When did you become a badass?"

Emery traced the delicate curve of her jaw with his finger. "The day I used brawn instead of brains to earn a living."

Within a year of running Sutherland and Sons Contracting he doubled the small company's projects. He satisfied all business loans, invested a portion of the profits—something his father refused to do—and, when each of his siblings graduated high school, saved enough money to cover their college expenses.

She blinked once. "You wouldn't."

"Wouldn't do what?"

"Fight."

He angled his head, struggling to keep straight face. "Hell yeah. I don't think you want to see me throw down."

Rhianna stared at Emery, trying to decide whether he was serious or joking. At six-two and weighing about two-twenty, she had no doubt that he would be able to handle himself in a physical altercation. Releasing the front of her coat, she shifted, shrugging off the coat and baring her back.

Emery's eyes bulged from their sockets. "Oh…" He swallowed the expletive poised on the tip of his tongue. An expanse of smooth dark brown skin, from the nape of her neck to the small of her back, was laid bare for anyone's gaze.

Biting back a smile, Rhianna pulled the coat up and over her shoulders. She hadn't been able to resist the garment when she went shopping with her mother. The black crepe de chine sheath dress had a squared neckline with capped sleeves and a hemline that ended midway at her calves. A front slit displayed a generous amount of leg with each step.

She peered at him over one shoulder. "Do you like it?"

Placing a hand on her stocking-covered knee, Emery leered at her. "Very much." His hand moved up between her legs. "If your intent was to seduce me, then you succeeded." Without warning, he cupped the back of her knees, turning her around to face him.

She let out a small yelp when he anchored her feet on his shoulders and lowered his head. "No, please no," she gasped, as he raised her hips at the same time he lowered his head. She couldn't believe he was going to make love to her in the back seat of a moving limousine.

The very air inside the car seemed electrified, and her whole being seemed filled with waiting for Emery to finish what she'd begun. There was no doubt the dress was made for seduction, but she'd found herself the victim of her own scheme.

Emery cradled Rhianna's hips in his hands and pressed a kiss on the lace thong. Her legs were trembling. He inhaled her perfume and the sweet musky essence of her femininity. He kissed her again, committing her fragrance to memory.

He released her hips, pulling down the hem of her dress, and raised his head. Her eyes wide, glittered with a passion that sucked him in and would not let him go.

She wanted him!

She wanted to make love to him as much as he wanted her.

He moved to the opposite end of the wide seat and stared out the window. Rhianna Campbell was dangerous— as dangerous and potent as a narcotic. And now that he'd sampled her addictive properties he knew he could not let her go. He would do any and everything short of deliberately getting her pregnant to force her to stay in Shepherd.

* * *

Rhianna stood in the elevator, holding hands with Emery as he sung the words to "Music of the Night," in her ear. Within minutes of the first note she knew it wasn't the first time Emery had seen the musical.

The costumes, set decorations, and the music held sway over her from the first note until the final curtain. She barely had time to recover from the magnificence of the performance when they were back in the limo for the ride to Central Park and Tavern on the Green.

She shared a bottle of wine with Emery and ordered broiled salmon and pale asparagus spears in a setting with mirrored walls and sparkling chandeliers that set the stage for a magical retreat from reality for several hours.

She'd found herself scowling at other women whose gazes lingered too long on her date whenever they passed their table. It wasn't her dress that had attracted attention, but her lover's body and face.

"How many times have you seen *Phantom of the Opera*? she asked as the elevator opened at the top floor.

Emery reached into the pocket of his topcoat and removed the magnetic key. "I saw it for the first time in London in 1986. Then a couple of times after it came to Broadway."

Rhianna recalled Errol's outrage when Emery spent a month in Europe while he remained in the States to work on several construction projects with his father, who reminded him that he was a full-time employee. Errol sulked and grumbled until Emery returned.

Emery slipped the key into the slot, waited for the green light, and pushed open the door. A wall of glass provided an unobstructed view of the Hudson River and New Jersey. The limousine driver had delivered their luggage to the hotel while they were at the theater.

"Come in, darling."

Rhianna moved into the entryway like a zombie. Vases of fresh flowers and dozens of tea lights crowded every flat surface. Emery closed the door and led her across the living room, beyond a utility kitchen, and into a bedroom with a large four-poster bed draped in yards and yards of white organza. The flickering candles in wrought-iron candelabras threw long and short shadows on the walls of the sitting room. A smile trembled over her lips.

"It's perfect, Emery."

He closed the distance between them and pulled her close to his chest. "That's because you're perfect."

Wrapping her arms around his neck, she buried her face against his warm throat. "Thank you, my love."

Emery reached up and cradled her face. "Am I, Rhia?"

"What, Emery?"

"Your love?"

Rising on tiptoe, she pressed her lips to his, caressing his mouth more than kissing it. "Yes," she sighed, parting her lips to his probing tongue. Her tongue mated with his as she gave herself up to his marauding mouth.

He was her love, her beginning, end, and everything in between. She loved his gentleness, generosity, thoughtfulness, and sexual magnetism that made her want to lie with him for an eternity.

The telephone rang and Emery went to answer it as she slipped out of her coat and shoes. Sitting on an armchair, she unhooked her nylons and rolled them down her legs unaware that Emery watched her every move. She stood up and walked into a bathroom spa. A sunken tub, twin showers, a steam room and stalks of bamboo, and candles lining a dressing table beckoned one to come and stay awhile.

Rhianna returned to the bedroom to retrieve her toiletries, smiling at Emery as he unbuttoned his shirt. "I'm going to relax in the tub for a while."

He wiggled his eyebrows. "Would you like company?"

Her face grew warm. She'd never shared a bath or a shower with a man. "I'd love company."

Rhianna shifted on her side and pressed her face against Emery's smooth chest. "You smell like me," she whispered in the stillness of the room.

He dropped a kiss on her damp hair. "You smell good, feel good, and taste even better."

She giggled like a little girl. "You're so good for a woman's ego."

"Not any woman, baby. Just you."

A comfortable silence followed as Rhianna listened to the beating of her own heart. "I love you, Emery." His muscles tensed, then relaxed. "I left Shepherd because I was too much of a coward to face the truth."

"Which was?"

"I was secretly in love with you."

Emery gritted his teeth in frustration. Her declaration of love should've had him jumping for joy, but he instead felt disappointment. "I love you and you love me, and meanwhile we've lost ten years." Ten years in which she could've become his wife and the mother of his children.

Tears filled her eyes and streaked her cheeks. She'd gone into voluntary exile for nothing. Relocating to Los Angeles had grieved her parents and Debbie Sutherland because of her fear and cowardice.

"I'm so sorry." The apology was ripped from the depths of her soul.

Emery felt the moisture on his shoulder and his heart turned over. "No, baby. Please, don't cry." The floodgates opened as he attempted to comfort Rhianna. She sobbed silently. Pushing himself up to a sitting position, he pulled her over his lap, rocking her gently as if she were a child.

He opened his mouth to ask her marry him, and closed it when he recalled her pronouncement of "no strings," which reminded him that although they slept together she hadn't indicated she wanted to take their relationship to another level.

"I'm sorry," she repeated. Her husky voice seemed to echo in the expansive space.

Emery combed his fingers through her short hair. "There's no need to apologize, sweetheart. It's just that I'm not good with a woman's tears."

She laughed softly. "So, Mr. Badass is not so bad after all."

He flipped her on her back; she let out an audible gasp of surprise. She barely had time to catch her breath when his mouth covered hers before charting and mapping every inch of her body. He kissed her throat, ears, and the column of her neck, her armpits, ribs, and belly. Then he drank deeply—between her thighs—as she writhed, moaned, and pleaded for him to stop. He did, pausing only to protect her from an unplanned pregnancy.

Her pleas became moans of satisfaction when he entered her wet, hot flesh and began a dance of desire that made them forget there was a world outside the penthouse suite.

Rhianna sobbed again, not in sorrow, but in pleasure. Her breasts swelled, legs trembled, and blood scalded her flesh as she gave herself up to the ecstasy wrought from her. She'd confessed to loving him and now her body communicated in its own way.

Wrapping her legs around Emery's waist, she arched her hips, welcoming his powerful thrusts. Together they found the tempo that bound their bodies and hearts together— for an eternity.

CHAPTER 10

E mery sat on a wooden bench trying and failing to concentrate on the daily observations he always entered into the laptop balanced on his knees. The cold wind coming through cracks in the unheated barn chilled his fingers, while the sensual memories of the weekend in New York City heated his blood. He adjusted the screen to counter the glare from an overhead lighting fixture. Staring at the blinking cursor, he began typing:

Saturday, December 24:
Time: 0400.
Weather conditions: Clear 0–9C.
    All trimmed, tagged, and mated ewes appear to be in good health.
    #12 and #17 have come into estrus. Will delay return and isolate for breeding.

Plan to clip wool on Bully Boy from neck to belly in the region of penis, and mark with paste on breast and forelegs for mating with #12 and #17. If mating fails, researcher/breeder requests delivery of vigorous, well-grown, early-maturing ram lamb A.S.A.P.

All will be turned out to pasture for exercise. Winter pasture is good.

He saved what he'd typed into the computer. Problems with the flock, if there were to be any, would manifest before and after lambing, whereas Emery's quandary with regard to a slip of a woman who'd become entwined in his life was the cause of his many sleepless nights. The only time he was able to sleep undisturbed was when they shared a bed.

How had he become so used to having Rhianna in his life in a manner of weeks when it had taken months and on a rare occasion a year before he'd opened himself up to other women?

Rhianna was able to complete his sentences and laughed hysterically at his corny jokes. They respected each other's space—he by not pressuring her to see him when she had to help out at Campy's, and she when he had to spend hours examining and observing the sheep.

He'd done and said everything he could to let her know how much he loved her, but "will you marry me?" He'd lost Rhianna once because he hadn't made his feelings known, and he didn't want to lose her again if he proposed marriage and she rejected him. His loss then would be more profound; it would be a final pronouncement that they would not share a love and future that promised forever.

He stared at the date: *December 24*, Christmas Eve and the tenth anniversary of his brother and parents' death. The telephone call and the events that followed the fatal accident were as vivid today as they had been a decade before. Even though his grief had eased, Emery didn't believe he would ever accept the loss.

He and Errol were inseparable as children, but once they entered adolescence their relationship changed when they became competitors. Whether it was for their parents' attention, other girls, or grades, the gauntlet had been thrown down and a cold war had begun.

Emery had graduated at the top of his class, whereas Errol came in at twenty-three in a class of eighty-six. Errol set a school passing record as a football quarterback for Shepherd High, and he had broken a sixteen-year record as a point guard for the basketball team. The only arena where there was no competition was with the opposite sex.

Errol hadn't given Rhianna Campbell a passing thought or glance until Emery mentioned that he liked her. Within days the rumors were circulating at the high school that Errol Sutherland and Rhianna Campbell were a couple. Emery watched his brother romance the woman who unknowingly had captured his heart with her beauty, brains, and outgoing personality. Once Reid and Anna Campbell officially announced their daughter's engagement to Errol Peter Sutherland, Emery knew it was time to move on and stop pining for what would never be. But now Errol was gone and Rhianna had come back to Shepherd, and in a season of miracles he'd been given a second chance at love.

For the first time in a long time Emery looked forward to Christmas. His plans included driving to Scranton and reuniting with his family for the holiday. A slow smile crinkled his eyes. He spoke to Debbie at least twice a month since she enrolled in Penn State, and he looked forward to seeing if she was as mature as she sounded on the phone.

Rhianna wiped the back of her hand over her forehead, leaving streaks of flour in her eyebrows. She'd spent the last two days baking pies, and making cutout cookies and decorating them in festive holiday colors. Her parents had decided to host a Christmas Eve open house to kick off a yearlong celebration, which would culminate with Campy's thirtieth anniversary.

Reid's decision to close on Mondays had gotten a thumb's up from Anna, who'd complained that operating seven days a week had become too stressful. She longed to indulge in a full day of beauty at her favorite spa, or take a train ride into Manhattan to visit a museum or to take in the sights.

The subject of her musings walked into the kitchen. "These are ready, Mom."

Anna clasped her hands, smiled and nodded her approval. "They look too pretty to eat." The sugar, chocolate, and gingerbread cookies were a big hit with the young children who'd come into the restaurant with their parents and older siblings.

Rhianna washed her hands in one of the three stainless steel sinks. "Please tell Joey to load the SUV with the trays for the hospital and nursing home."

Nearly two-dozen trays of cookies and petit fours were covered in colorful plastic wrap and tied with either red or green ribbon. A card reading, COMPLIMENTS OF CAMPY'S, was stapled to each one. There was a tray for the members of the local sheriff's office, bank employees, and volunteer fire department.

Anna glanced at the wall clock. It was only ten o'clock. "You're leaving now?"

Rhianna smiled at her mother over her shoulder. "Yes. I want to get back here before the big crush."

Campy's Christmas Eve Open House had begun at six that morning and would end twelve hours later. Long-time customers and those who came in once in a while would be offered an all-you-can eat buffet breakfast, lunch, and dinner—gratis. It was Reid and Anna Campbell's way of saying thank you to those who made Campy's a landmark eating establishment in the historic Hudson River Valley.

"I think you'd better go upstairs and wash your face, Miss Betty Crocker," Anna teased. "You've got flour all over your face."

Rhianna dried her hands, then took off the net covering her hair. "I plan to shower and change anyway. I must smell like confectionary sugar and ginger."

Anna kissed her daughter's cheek. "Thank you, sweetheart."

"For what?"

The older woman's expression changed, becoming wistful. "For being here. For helping out, and for being the best daughter a mother could ever ask for."

Tears welled in Rhianna's eyes, shimmering like precious jewels, but did not fall. "Stop it, Momma." Emotion had lowered her voice an octave.

Blinking back her own tears, Anna sniffled. "Let me go and get Joey so he can bring everything out to the truck."

Rhianna took off her apron, and left the kitchen through a back door. She'd deliberately pushed herself to exhaustion so that she would not be reminded that she was spending Christmas Eve in Shepherd, New York.

She'd come home to help her family and had fallen in love with a man whom she'd always loved, a man who looked like one to whom she'd given her innocence. She would always love Errol because what she'd had with him was merely a dress rehearsal for what she hoped to share with Emery.

Emery entered Campy's and encountered a cacophony of sounds and mouthwatering smells. The jukebox blared an upbeat contemporary holiday song. The counter and booths were crowded with people ranging from fretful infants to octogenarians, who laughed loudly as they called out to one another.

Linda, the waitress who usually worked the late shift, winked at him. "All of the food is in the back, handsome."

Emery hadn't come to eat, but to see Rhianna before he left for Pennsylvania. His gaze searched the crowd. She wasn't there. He walked to the rear of the expanded restaurant. Gary and Nicole stood behind a long table filled with chafing dishes serving those waiting on line.

He'd finished renovating the back porch two days before. He'd laid a black and white vinyl floor, painted the walls a soft antique white, and installed recess lights along with several rows of track lights and heating and cooling vents. The French doors running the length of the porch made it appear larger than it actually was and provided breathtaking views of the Hudson River.

He waved to Gary and walked back into the restaurant's main dining room. He met Linda again. "Have you seen Rhianna?"

The waitress shook her head. "Not this morning. I do know she was up late last night working in the kitchen. Do you want me to find out where she is?"

"No," Emery said quickly. "I'll see her later. Thanks, Linda."

"No problem, Emery. Merry Christmas."

He smiled at her. "Merry Christmas to you and your family."

She returned his smile with a bright one of her own. "Thank you. The same to yours."

As Emery turned to retrace his steps, the cell phone on his waist rang. He glanced at the display, a slight frown creasing his smooth brow as he plucked the tiny phone off his belt. Quickening his pace, he pushed open the door and stepped onto the front porch. The noise inside Campy's had escalated.

"Hello, Dr. Maddox."

"Hello back to you and merry Christmas, son." The elderly veterinarian had a strong, deep, rumbling voice that belied his age.

Emery smiled as he walked to the parking lot where he'd left his sports car. "Same to you."

"I spent all morning debating whether to call you, but in the end I decided to give you your Christmas present a little early."

Emery stopped. "What are you talking about?" His voice had dropped to a whisper.

"Now, you know I still have what the young folks call *juice* over at the college, and I was able to convince several of my ex-colleagues to waive your residency requirement because you were the only one who agreed to participate in the breeding study. And I don't have to tell you that the trustees didn't want to turn down that much grant money put up by the sheep breeders association. You'll get an official notification after the new semester begins, but I want to be the first to call you Doctor Sutherland. Congratulations."

Emery, momentarily speechless in his surprise, closed his eyes and whispered a silent prayer of gratitude. He'd left veterinary school with only six months left to complete his residency. It had taken ten years, but come the new year he would become Emery Patrick Sutherland, Doctor of Veterinary Medicine. He'd done it! He'd fulfilled his life-long dream of becoming a veterinarian thanks to his former professor and mentor, Dr. Alan Maddox.

"Thank you, Doctor Maddox," he said reverently.

"There's no need to thank me, Doctor Sutherland. You've more than earned your degree. Remember I told you after your first week in my class that you were one of the brightest students I'd encountered in all of my years of teaching. Now, you have a merry Christmas and a new year filled with all good things."

Emery's smile was dazzling. "Thank you. I wish the same for you and your family. I was going to wait until after the holidays to call and let you know that there's no need to pick up twelve and seventeen. Both have come into heat."

"Maybe the girls are late bloomers."

"No doubt they are. Look for me to come up around the middle of next month."

"You don't have to fly up anymore."

"Why?"

"My grandson has moved off campus and is now living with me and his grandmother. The boy is a whiz with computers. You can send me your findings and statistics electronically and he'll retrieve it for me. We can get together after the spring lambing to toss back a few."

Emery grimaced, shaking his head even though the brilliant geneticist couldn't see him. The last time he'd gone out with Alan Maddox to toss back a few he woke up the next day with the hangover from hell.

"That's a bet," Emery said reluctantly. "Merry Christmas, Doctor Maddox."

"Same to you, Emery."

"Have a good one," he said, using Alan's usual parting remark.

"You have a good one, too."

Emery ended the call and slipped the phone back on his waistband. He'd been reluctant to participate in the breeding study because of his contracting business. It had taken more than six months of telephone calls from Alan Maddox to convince him to head the study. Once he committed, he began a plan of action to sell his father's business. A long-time employee approached him and made him an offer he would've been a fool to refuse. He sold everything, including the name. What he refused to sell were his tools and the pickup truck.

He lingered in the parking lot, hoping to catch a glimpse of Rhianna, while taking furtive glances at his watch. He had to leave now, or he'd never be able to avoid the heavy holiday traffic.

He turned the key in the ignition and drove out of the parking lot. It wasn't until he left the environs of Shepherd that he stopped glancing up at his rearview mirror with the hope he would see Rhianna's vehicle.

CHAPTER 11

Emery, sprawled on a leather love seat with his long legs hanging over an arm, stared at the flickering flames behind the decorative fireplace screen.

His youngest sister, Deborah, sat in front of the fire with her legs folded in a yoga position. Not only did she sound different, but she also looked very different. Her room-mate had braided her hair in an intricate design that resembled a delicate spider web. He, Errol, and Deborah resembled their late mother, whereas Kirk, Brielle, and Paul looked more like their father.

"You're different, Emery."

He smiled. "So are you, Debbie."

Uncrossing her legs, she spun around on her bottom to face him. "You know what I mean."

He lifted a questioning eyebrow. "No, I don't."

She crossed her legs again. "I know Christmas has always

been difficult for you. It's never been easy for any of us. But this is the first time I can remember you laughing and acting silly."

"Ten years is a long time to mourn, baby girl."

"Don't baby girl me, Emery Sutherland. And in case you haven't noticed, I'm not a baby anymore. What's up with you?"

Emery sat up and planted his sock-covered feet firmly on the thick carpet. "Who *is* he?"

Deborah rolled her eyes, while sucking her teeth loudly. "Don't change the subject, Emery."

"I hope you're practicing safe sex."

"Who's practicing safe sex?" asked a beautifully modulated female voice.

Emery pointed at Deborah, who sat with her mouth gaping. "I hope she is."

Brielle folded her lithe body into an armchair and ran her fingers through her dreadlocked shoulder-length hair. "Debbie and I already had *that* conversation."

Debbie stuck her tongue out at her brother. "And for your information I'm not ready to sleep with anyone."

"Good for you. Just make certain he's worth it."

Deborah narrowed her eyes at Emery. "Now, to get back to the topic at hand. What's going on in your life since you have the house to yourself?"

Emery wondered how much he should tell his sisters. And Deborah was right. This Christmas Eve gathering was vastly different from the others when a pall always hung over the festivities. He decided to be truthful and told

Brielle and Deborah everything. Why Rhianna had come back to Shepherd and that they were seeing each other.

Brielle twisted her face. "That's nasty, Emery. How can she mess around with brothers?"

"It's not nasty, Ellie" Deborah said in defense of Rhianna.

"And why not?" Brielle countered.

Deborah gave her sister a long, penetrating look. "Because it was Emery Rhianna liked all along."

Emery sat forward. "How did you know that?"

Deborah held his questioning stare. "I use to watch her with Errol. It was like she forced herself to be funny or silly because he liked to fool around so much. But whenever she was around you she was like a different person. And she used to stare at you when she thought you weren't looking. It wasn't until I finally got my head together that I knew she had chosen the wrong brother."

"You saw all that?" Brielle asked her sister.

"Yeah, I did."

"But you were so young."

"I have eyes don't I?" Deborah retorted.

Sighing, Emery slumped back against the love seat. "You saw what I couldn't see—at least not until now.

"What are you going to do about it, big brother," Brielle teased with a sly smile.

He lifted an eyebrow. "What do you mean?"

"When are you going to give me a sister-in-law I can get along with? You know I can't stand Kirk and Paul's wives. Both of them are nothing but heifers. I'm certain if Jack had a sister I probably wouldn't get along with her either."

"That's because you think you're a diva," Emery said, deadpan.

Brielle tilted her chin and waved a hand, the pompous gesture eliciting laughs from Deborah and Emery.

"Think? Now both of you know I'm the bomb diggity."

"I'll admit that you've got some talent," Emery conceded.

Brielle rolled her head on her neck and snapped her fingers. "I'm talent personified. Now, to get back to the topic at hand," she said, repeating what Deborah said minutes before. It had been their mother's favorite saying whenever their father attempted to evade her queries. "Are you going to ask her to marry you, or wait another ten years? By that time you'll be too old to think about making babies."

"How old is Jack? Forty or forty-one?" His sister had married a man seventeen years her senior.

"Ease up off my husband," Brielle warned. "He gave me a beautiful daughter."

"That he did," Emery said, pushing to his feet. "Good night, ladies."

"You better ask her to marry you," Deborah said to his broad back.

"Good night, Debbie," he drawled as he made his way out of the family room and up the winding staircase to the second floor bedroom where he always slept whenever he visited Brielle and her family.

She'd met her husband when she was commissioned to decorate the tax attorney's office, and after a three-month whirlwind courtship she married the confirmed bachelor in a private ceremony with only family members in attendance. A year later she and Jack became the parents of a little girl, whom they named Maxine in memory of her maternal grandmother.

The large house was quiet. The children were permitted to open one gift—they would open the rest after breakfast on Christmas Day. Emery had done all of his shopping early and had everything shipped directly to Brielle's house.

He knew he had to make a decision before he returned to Shepherd the next day. He had to know whether Rhianna would become a part of his future. If not, then he would have to exorcise her from his mind *and* his heart.

Rhianna stared numbly at the earrings nestled on a bed of white velvet. Her mother had given her the magnificent diamond and Tahitian pearl earrings she'd worn to the Chamber of Commerce's fundraiser.

Her gaze lifted. "Why are you giving me these?" Her father had given them to Anna for their twenty-fifth wedding anniversary. The twelve-millimeter pearls and flawless diamonds had cost Reid a small fortune.

"You've always admired them," Anna said softly.

"But they were a gift from Daddy."

"I've only worn them twice. They're too heavy for my lobes." Moving off her bed, Anna reached into the drawer of a bedside table and withdrew a small velvet box. "He just gave me these for Christmas."

Rhianna sat down next to her mother and took the box from her hand. "My word!" she gasped. Reid had given Anna a pair of pear-shaped blond diamond studs. The yellow stones were the perfect compliment for the yellow-orange undertones in her smooth face.

"They're beautiful, Mom. Wear them in good health."

"I don't know why your father buys me these baubles."

"They're called bling nowadays," Rhianna said with a wide grin.

Anna waved a hand. "Bling, baubles, or whatever," she drawled. "When do I get a chance to dress up?"

"You will, Mom."

"When?"

Reaching into a back pocket of her jeans, Rhianna handed her mother a small envelope. She'd given her parents gifts cards, a Waterford vase, and bottles of their favorite fragrances. She hadn't realized she was holding her breath until tightness in her chest made breathing difficult. She bit down on her lower lip when Anna read the handwritten note. Anna dropped the note card, extended her arms, and Rhianna went into her embrace.

"I...don't...don't believe it," Anna said, her voice breaking with raw emotion.

Rhianna had spent a restless night reexamining her conscience, and when Christmas Eve slipped into Christmas Day she reached a decision she knew would change her life—forever.

Working in Campy's kitchen wasn't work, but fun. She enjoyed interacting with people with whom she'd grown up and gone to school. She'd come to know the regulars who preferred hanging out at Campy's to the senior center.

She'd come to appreciate how hard her parents worked to make their business a success.

She'd also come to value her mother's sage advice and her father's understanding.

She'd fled Shepherd because she couldn't face one man, and ten years later her love for that man was critical after she decided she wanted to spend the rest of her life in Shepherd.

"Believe it, because I'm staying. Of course I have to go back to L.A. to hand in my resignation and clean out my apartment, but I'll be back."

"You're going to resign?"

Rhianna nodded. "Yes."

"Why, Rhianna?"

"Now, why are you asking the child why, Anna?" Reid asked from the doorway.

Anna stared at her husband. "Because…" Her words trailed off when she saw his expression.

Rhianna kissed her mother's scented cheek. "I'm going out to drop off a few gifts." She slipped off the bed and winked at Reid. "I'll see you later," she said as she left the room.

Waiting until he heard fading footsteps, Reid walked into the bedroom, closing the door behind him. He stood at the foot of the antique brass bed, shaking his head from side to side.

"Baby," he drawled softly. "You just had to ask."

Anna sat up straighter. "What are you talking about?"

"She said she's staying. Shouldn't that be enough?"

Going to her knees, Anna crawled the length of the bed, her gaze narrowing. "What are you hiding from me, Reid Campbell?"

Reid smiled at the woman whom he loved more with every sunrise. "Can you keep a secret?"

Eyes wide, Anna stared at him in disbelief. "I've never been one to spread gossip."

Leaning over, Reid whispered in his wife's ear. She covered her mouth with a hand, fell back to the mattress, kicking her legs like a child. Her husband joined her on the bed and they laughed until tears streaked their faces.

Raising his injured arm above his head, Reid turned on his side and smiled at Anna. His gaze moved slowly over her face. "When was the last time I told you that I loved you?"

Anna traced the outline of his mouth with a forefinger. "I think it was last night. No...it had to be this morning." She pressed her mouth to his. "I love you, Reid Campbell."

"I love you more, Anna Campbell."

"Love you even more," she countered.

They continued the game that had sustained their marriage when Reid was drafted and sent to Vietnam, during the lean years after he'd opened Campy's, and through the tragedies of two miscarriages before they celebrated the birth of the baby girl who would become their only child.

* * *

Rhianna maneuvered into the driveway leading to Emery's house and parked behind his pickup. She'd expected him to attend the open house, but when he hadn't she managed to hide her disappointment, laughing when she felt like crying.

Sheer exhaustion became her best friend. She'd crawled into bed before midnight Christmas Eve and did not wake up again until two the following afternoon. She knew Christmas would always be a difficult season for the Sutherlands because it was a reminder of the loss of their loved ones. She'd lost Errol, but miraculously had rediscovered love with his brother.

She cut off the engine and reached for the decorative shopping bag on the passenger seat. As soon as she stepped out of the vehicle she saw the large dog.

Rhianna scratched her behind her ears. "Hey, Lady."

The dog barked loudly, but did not follow her as she climbed the steps leading to the porch, illuminated by lamps and light filtering through the sheers covering the windows on the first floor.

She rang the bell and waited, then rang it again as Lady continued to bark frantically. When Emery did not answer the door, she left the shopping bag on a cushioned rocker and walked off the porch. Lady raced back and forth barking and whining.

She stared at the agitated canine. "What's the matter, girl?"

Lady ran a few yards, stopped and then came back to her. It was obvious the dog wanted Rhianna to follow her. Her heart lurched before pounding a runaway rhythm. A feeling of dread swept over her. Had something happened to Emery?

"Take me to Emery, Lady," she shouted, following the dog as she loped away from the house. Daylight had faded and nighttime temperatures had dropped dramatically. A full moon in star-littered sky silvered the countryside and provided enough light for Rhianna to see where she was going. Lady was heading for the pastures where the sheep grazed.

Torturous thoughts gripped her, and she refused to think of anything happening to Emery.

"No," she whispered, breathing heavily. "Please. Not again," she gasped, trying to catch her breath as she quickened her pace.

She said every prayer she'd been taught as a child as she scrambled up a rise and came to a complete stop. Standing in the valley was a lone sheep; its plaintive bleating echoed in the silent night.

Moving slowly, Rhianna approached the ewe, debating how she was going to get her back to the barn. There was no way she could possibly lift the animal as she'd seen Emery execute in one smooth motion.

Going to her knees, she wrapped her arm around Lady's neck. "Get her back to the barn, girl." The dog whined deep in its throat, but did not move. It was apparent it only followed Emery's commands.

The mournful bleating sent shivers up and down Rhianna's back as she moved closer. She knew nothing about sheep except that they frightened easily and were easy prey for coyotes. Reaching out tentatively, her hand touched the untagged ear. The ewe backed up, bleating louder.

"You're going to have to help me, sweetie," she crooned, hoping not to startle the animal. A sharp whistle rent the air and Lady sprang into action and chased the ewe across the pasture.

Rhianna turned slowly, her eyes widening in shock as she saw Emery standing several feet away, arms crossed over his chest. His straight white teeth gleamed brightly in the moonlight.

"You have to learn to whistle if you're going to hang out with my sheep."

Her lower lip trembled as she smiled through a shimmer of tears. The man she loved more than she'd ever expected to love stood before her, tall, powerful, and safe.

"How did you know where to find me?"

"When I saw your truck in the driveway I knew you couldn't have gone too far on foot."

She nodded. "I followed Lady."

Emery stared at Rhianna, his eyes making love to her face. Two days—that's all it took for him to acknowledge that he would love this woman until he drew his last breath.

Lowering his arms, he closed the distance between them, taking her hands and pulling her close to his body. "Merry Christmas, darling."

A tender smile softened her mouth as Rhianna said, "Thank you. Merry Christmas to you, too."

Emery dropped her hands and wrapped his arms around her waist. "I don't want you to leave Shepherd. I want you here with me." He knew his request was selfish, but he was beyond being polite or correct.

Rhianna buried her face against his warm throat. "What are you prepared to do to make me change my mind?" He didn't know she'd planned to stay.

Easing back, he stared at her staring back at him. "All I can offer you is a lifetime of love. Will that be enough?"

A dazzling smile parted her lips. "It's not bad for a start."

He lifted his eyebrows. "You want more?"

"Yes. I want to dissolve our agreement of no strings."

A slight frown appeared between his eyes. "Are you talking about a commitment?"

Rhianna nodded. "Yes."

"To me a commitment is forever. Are you ready for that?"

"What comes under the heading of forever?"

"Marriage, children, PTA meetings, summer camp, anniversaries, graduations, and, on occasion, mind-blowing sex. Are you ready for all of that?"

Curving her arms under his shoulders, Rhianna rested her head on his chest. The scent of his cologne clung to the fibers of his sweater. "How many children are you talking about?"

"Enough to fill up every bedroom in the house with noise and mayhem."

She smiled. There were six bedrooms in Emery's house, excluding his attic retreat. "That's a lot of babies."

"No, darling. That's a lot of mind-blowing baby-making

sex." Emery went down on one knee, staring up at her. "Rhianna Campbell, will you marry me?"

Rhianna stared at Emery as if he'd lost his mind. She hadn't expected him to be *that* traditional. She never would've imagined in her wildest dreams that he would propose marriage in an open field under a Shepherd moon. Emery had just offered her what she'd wanted from the first time she realized her heart beat a little too quickly when their gazes met. He'd said the four magic words every woman hoped to hear from the man she loved. He was offering her a chance to let go of her past and plan for a future filled with love and passion.

"Yes," she whispered. The tears came before she could stop them.

Emery sprang up, cradling her to his chest. "Don't cry, baby. Please don't cry."

"I...I can't...help it," she said, hiccupping.

Lowering his head, Emery covered her mouth with his, cutting off her soft sobs. He showered kisses around her lips and along her jaw. "Thank you, darling. Thank you," he whispered over and over.

Rhianna snuggled closer to his hard, hot body. "When do you want to get married?"

"Next week."

"You're kidding?"

He shook his head slowly. "No, I'm not. I've been in love with you for more than half my life, and I've exhausted all of my patience."

"What about my parents?"

"What about them, Rhia?"

"I'm certain my mother is going to want a ceremony and a little something afterwards."

"Reid and Anna know what to do."

The heavy lashes that shadowed her cheeks flew up. "My parents know?"

"Yes, baby. I told your father that I was in love with you, and that I planned to ask you to marry me."

"What did he say?"

" 'Go for it!' "

She had to smile. "That sounds like my father. I'd like to wait a little longer."

"How long?"

"A couple of months. I'm going to call my boss and let him know that I'm resigning. Don't forget that I have to go back to Los Angeles to close up my apartment."

A muscle twitched in Emery's jaw. He'd admitted to Rhianna that he was very short on patience. "How's February?"

She nodded. "I'd love a Valentine's Day wedding."

"Then Valentine's it is." He reached for her hand. "Let's get back to the house. I want to give you your Christmas present."

"What did you get me?"

Emery patted the hand tucked into the bend of his elbow. "You'll see."

Resting her head against his shoulder, Rhianna smiled up at Emery. "I left your gift on the porch."

"What did you get me?" he asked, repeating her query.

"You'll see soon enough."

As they walked back to the large house that had been filled with happiness and sorrow, and would soon be filled with joy again Emery told Rhianna about his telephone conversation with Alan Maddox.

She leapt into his arms, kissing him passionately. "I can't believe it. You're finally going to be Doctor Sutherland."

"It's going to take some getting used to, but it's been a long time coming. After the lambing we'll take a belated honeymoon. All of the sheep will be transported back to the college for further study. Late August or early September I'll get another flock and start the breeding process all over again."

Rhianna stared at her fiancé's distinctive profile in the shadowy glow of the full moon. "What do you plan to do once the study is over?"

"One of the conditions of the grant is that I'm expected to chair a series of lectures for a minimum of one year. After that I'll apply to several area veterinary hospitals."

They made their way up the steps to the porch, stopping only to retrieve the shopping bag from the rocker. There was only the sound of their footsteps as they climbed the staircase leading to the top floor.

Rhianna felt flutters in the pit of her stomach as Emery undressed her and carried her to the large bed. The last time they'd shared the bed it had been as man and woman, but this time it would be as fiancé and fiancée. Their words pledging a future together as binding as the vows they would exchange in another few weeks.

Even their lovemaking was different. It was passionate but tempered with tenderness and a love that promised forever.

It was later—after their passions had peaked and their breathing had resumed a normal rate that Rhianna and Emery exchanged Christmas gifts.

He cradled an exquisite bowl of Steuben glass etched with a scene of a shepherd tending his sheep under the light of a large star on his fingertips. Rhianna had also given him compacts discs of all of Andrew Lloyd Webber's musical productions.

He put down the bowl and stacked the discs on a nearby table before learning over and kissing her. "You are incredible."

"So are you."

Moonlight shimmered on the diamonds resting between her breasts. He'd wanted to buy her a ring, but settled on a necklace with three hearts representing yesterday, today and tomorrow. The larger heart made of white gold cradled two smaller ones in rose and yellow gold.

Pulling her into his arms, Emery buried his face in her short hair. "Do you think you'll be able to spare a weekend to go shopping for rings?"

"Do you think we're going to need an entire weekend to select rings?"

"We will if we go into Manhattan to celebrate."

Rhianna giggled. "How will we go in?"

"By limo, of course."

"You are so naughty, Doctor Sutherland."

"I'll show you naughty," he crooned as he swept her off the bed and carried her into the bathroom. They shared a shower, exchanging a passion that ended with them sitting on the floor of the stall, limbs entwined, hearts beating in unison as they truly had become one.

This Christmas would become the first of many more for Rhianna and Emery where the real reason for the season was *LOVE*.

EPILOGUE

Reid and Anna Campbell
Request the pleasure of your company
At the marriage of their daughter
RHIANNA SHILOH
To EMERY PATRICK SUTHERLAND
Brother of BRIELLE SUTHERLAND-HARRIS and
PAUL, KIRK, and DEBORAH SUTHERLAND
Saturday, the Fourteenth of February 2006
Four o'clock in the afternoon
At the First Baptist Church
Brandywine Lane, Shepherd, New York

Reception afterward at
Six o'clock in the evening at
The Vandervoot Mansion
222 Grove Court
Shepherd, New York

WISHING ON A STARR

ADRIANNE BYRD

PROLOGUE

Christmas Eve, Talboton, GA 1990

"I told you, you ain't had no business marryin' that boy," Ma Belle ranted as she paced across the dingy blue-gray carpet in her small shotgun house. "Now he done run off and got himself killed in that damn war."

Seventeen-year old, Gia Hunter sobbed into the cupped palms of her hands. Her short life had been riddled with pain and loss—and it showed no signs of ever ending.

"Now you might as well cut out all that hollerin'. Cryin' never fixed nothin'," Ma Belle continued. "You need to figure out what you gonna to do about that baby. I'm too old to be having another nappy-headed chile runnin' around here. Your sister, Glenda, has plenty—and let's not talk about all those babies that hard-headed brother of yours, Byron, got."

"I c-can take care of my own baby," Gia spat out in between sobs and finally pushed herself out of the rickety dining room chair. "I don't need nobody's help."

"Now where have I heard that before?" Ma Belle settled her hands against her thick hips, while her heated face twisted with a fusion of anger and disappointment. "Oh, yeah. I believe it was Glenda with her first child or maybe it was the sixth."

A waterfall of tears poured down Gia's determined face. Why she thought she could come to her grandmother for support in her time of need she'd never know. She snatched her husband's army dog tags from the table and headed for the door. Her strides were slow, her gait wide.

"Lawd have mercy. Look at you. You're ruining my carpet."

Gia stopped and feverishly wiped away her tears so she could glance down. She still couldn't see anything, but she could feel the moisture running down her legs. "My water broke."

"You don't say." Ma Belle's face flushed burgundy as she turned and hollered toward the back of the house. "Byron, go and pull the car around. It's time to take your sister to the hospital."

Gia's eyes widened as a painful contraction nearly buckled her knees. "But it's too early. I-I'm not due until—" She eased toward the kitchen table.

"No, no. You're not going to ruin my good chairs." Ma Belle strolled over to her and draped a firm arm around her shoulders and redirected her toward the door.

Gia heard Byron's dry calloused feet shuffle across the kitchen floor before she saw his tall, thin frame.

"What's all the yellin' about?" he asked groggily, turning toward the refrigerator.

There wasn't much in the old, olive green icebox, but it didn't stop him from peering inside it twenty times a day.

"Boy, I told you to get the car. Gia is about to have this baby."

"Now?" Byron asked, scratching his large, matted, and lopsided Afro.

"Yes, now," Ma Belle barked.

Another contraction hit Gia and she dropped her husband's dog tags and leaned the majority of her weight against her grandmother. Luckily, Ma Belle was built like the rock of Gibraltar, and she voiced no complaint.

However, her brother was another story. He grumbled and mumbled under his breath while he dressed, and then started the car to drive them toward the Baptist hospital on the edge of town. Ma Belle and Glenda squeezed into the car and everyone fussed about there being another hungry mouth to feed.

Gia tuned them out and focused on the tiny life inside of her. She was about to become a mother...a single mother—just like most of the women in her large and dysfunctional family. She closed her eyes while fresh tears leaked from them.

Jermaine Hunter, her high school sweetheart and husband of one year, smiled back at her. She loved and missed him, but she was also angry with him for leaving her. He was supposed to take her away from all of this. Instead she was stuck in a dead-end town with a tenth-grade education, and no hope of escaping her family's curse of poverty.

She cried out as another tidal wave of pain slammed into her small frame. She could feel something happening between her legs.

"All that hollerin' ain't necessary," Ma Belle preached, but there was an undeniable note of concern laced in her voice.

"I feel the baby's head," Gia panted with worry.

"Oh, hell," Byron grumbled and sped up.

Thanks to the lack of wheel suspension on the thirty-year-old car, she felt every rock and dip in the road. A cramp crept along her spine and Gia swore she was just seconds away from crawling out of her skin.

Glenda reached over and took her hand, and Gia squeezed it with all of her might.

The ten-minute drive felt more like an eternity. And sure enough, the baby's head had already crowned by the time the emergency room nurses took over.

Everything seemed like it was going in slow motion and the pain consumed her. There was no time to administer the epidural. And the tension rose at the announcement of the baby being entangled in the umbilical cord. Gia was instructed to stop pushing, but she wasn't aware that she had been doing so.

The pain lasted so long she had become numb to it. Once she did, Gia fretted over everyone's pensive expressions and deep frowns. Was something wrong?

When the voice in the back of her head reminded her that she was a month early, Gia feared the worst.

"Here we go," the doctor said, glancing up to meet Gia's gaze. "I want you to give me a big push now. Do you think you can do that?"

She nodded even though she was filled with doubt. She couldn't feel the lower part of her body, so how could she muster the strength to push?

"That's it," the doctor encouraged, to Gia's surprise. Seconds later, the room filled with a baby's strangled cry.

"It's a girl," the doctor announced.

"Time—twelve-ten," a nurse announced. "We have ourselves a Christmas baby."

Joy and relief erased her pain instantly. But she was stunned to see a nurse, after cleaning, and wrapping her baby, rush from the room.

"Wait," she called out.

A nurse moved to her side and placed a reassuring hand against her shoulder. "Don't worry. We're going to take good care of her. She's a tiny little thing, but I'm sure she's a fighter." She winked.

More tears spilled down Gia's face. She wanted to see her baby girl. She wanted to see if she could spot some of Jermaine's beautiful features.

However, Ma Belle stepped in, and Gia never got the chance to see her beautiful baby girl.

CHAPTER 1

New York, today

On the first official shopping day of the Christmas season, Daniel Davis couldn't believe he'd agreed to let his daughter, Starr, and her best friend, Neve, drag him to Fifth Avenue to ogle the department store Christmas windows. Moreover, he was stunned by the number of people who crowded around in the freezing cold to do the same thing. Thirty minutes into the trip he grudgingly admitted he was quite impressed with the spectacular displays. "Is there a prize or something involved?" he asked.

Starr playfully rolled her eyes in a way that was adorable even though the gesture usually meant her father was the biggest goofball she'd ever known.

"No, Mr. Davis. Not unless you count drawing in the

most Christmas shoppers. That in itself would be a prize worth fighting for," Neve said, staring dreamily up at him.

Daniel smiled. "I believe you're right."

The teenager beamed a wired smile, while her dimpled cheeks darkened.

Starr elbowed Neve out of her trance and hissed, "Cut it out."

"What?"

Daniel just shook his head at the life-long friends. However, after another hour of bobbing and weaving between shoppers and tourists, he was beginning to feel like an old man.

"Dad, can we go in here to shop for a little while?" Starr asked with anxious eyes.

Daniel glanced up at the name of the store. "Saks Fifth Avenue?" He gave her a dubious look. "I don't think your allowance is going to quite cut it in there."

"Daaad." Starr glanced around, looking as if she hoped no one heard him. "It doesn't cost anything to just look around."

Or to use his credit cards, he wanted to add. Though he sensed a trap, Daniel could feel himself succumbing to her tried-and-true, lost puppy-dog expression. "All right."

The teenagers squealed and turned toward the door.

"Just for a little while," Daniel shouted above the crowd, but he was uncertain if they heard him. By the time he made it inside the door, the girls were gone. He glanced at his watch. "Great. Now I'm going to be here all day."

A petite, Asian salesclerk approached him, wearing a wide smile. "Can I help you with anything, sir?"

"Unfortunately, no." He removed his gloves.

"Ah," she said, brightening. "You must be shopping with your wife. Usually, I can tell, but I didn't see you holding a purse."

Daniel's smile downgraded considerably as his fingers rubbed against his gold wedding band. "Actually…I'm a widower."

"Oh," the woman's smile collapsed on cue as she moved closer. "I'm so sorry. Did she pass recently?"

"It feels that way, but it's been awhile." The flow of traffic increased and Daniel quickly stepped out of the way.

The salesclerk moved with him. "And awhile is…?"

He blinked. "Four years."

Her smiled returned. "My, that has been awhile."

"Yes, it has." This part was always a little tricky for Daniel. Did the glint in the woman's eyes mean she was interested, or were there just too many Christmas lights reflecting off of them? He hoped the latter, because he was guessing that he had a minimum of twenty years on the woman.

To say Daniel was a little rusty at the dating game would be putting it mildly. Starr had even gone so far as to tease him that she never understood how he ever got married in the first place.

"So does this mean you're here with a girlfriend? I'd imagine someone like you has a long line of willing women and an equally long line of broken hearts?"

Daniel laughed awkwardly. "Uh, no. It's nothing like that. I'm just here with my daughter." He moved to check out a table of silk scarves.

Once again, the salesclerk moved with him. "So how old is your daughter?"

"How *old* are you?" Starr's high, tense voice sliced through the conversation.

Turning with a frown, Daniel found his daughter and her best friend glaring up at the salesclerk.

"Oh, this must be your beautiful daughter. I can definitely see the resemblance."

"I'm adopted," Starr said with a no nonsense attitude and obvious disdain. "How old did you say you were?"

"Starr! That's no way to talk to your elders," he reprimanded.

"Er, you know." The woman took a tentative step backward. "I need to be getting back to the other customers. If there's anything I can help you with just let me know." She turned and quickly disappeared among the shoppers.

Daniel glanced back at his daughter in time to see her and Neve high-five each other. "I can't believe you just did that."

"She was too young for you," Starr said simply. "I leave you alone for two minutes and you're rocking the cradle with some nine-year old."

"She's hardly nine."

"Might as well be. Jeez, dad. If I'd known you were that desperate I would've set you up with Neve."

Neve smiled and then looked confused as to whether she had just been insulted or not.

"I'm not taking dating tips from my fourteen-year old."

"I'll be fifteen on Christmas Day," she announced proudly.

"Keep putting your nose where it doesn't belong and I doubt you'll make it that far."

The lost puppy-dog look came back and Daniel resisted being wound around Starr's finger. "I mean it, Starr. I'll not have you talk to grown-ups that way. Know your place."

"Fine." She huffed.

"Excuse me?"

"I mean, yes, sir," she amended.

"That's better." He leaned over and planted a kiss against her forehead.

"You know, I keep telling you that Ms. Roberts, my advance calculus teacher, would be the perfect match for you."

Neve scowled. "I wouldn't say *perfect*."

"Hey, I thought you two wanted to come in here to do some shopping?" He glanced at his watch. "If you're already done then we can head out."

"Actually," Starr peered sheepishly up at him. "I was wondering if I could get an advance on my allowance? I saw this really cute gift I'd like to get you for Christmas."

"You want me to give you money so you can buy me a gift?" he asked to make sure he understood.

"Daaad!"

"I was just checking." He reached inside his jacket and removed his wallet. "How expensive is this gift I'm buying myself?"

Starr's eyes sparkled at the sight of hundred dollar bills and she quickly reached for them. "Thanks, dad," she said, after successfully relieving him of two of the bills. "This should be plenty."

Daniel snatched one of them back. "Don't worry. It's definitely coming out of future allowances."

She frowned, but he held firm.

"Oh, all right." She turned toward her friend. "C'mon. Let's go find him something *cheap*."

He smiled, unfazed. "That's my girl. I'll do the same thing for you."

Starr rolled her eyes.

"Meet you two back here in *one* hour," he called after them.

She nodded.

Daniel continued smiling as he watched her stroll off. "That's my girl."

"Something must be seriously wrong with you. How can you not like Christmas?" Bernadette Frye tugged her friend down Fifth Avenue. "It's the best time of year."

Gia Hunter rolled her eyes and was more than annoyed that she'd allowed her colleague to drag her out in the freezing cold to stare at window displays. "If you're talking about celebrating the birth of Jesus, fine. But if you're talking about gross commercialization, drunken Santas, and off-pitch carolers, then no, it's not my thing."

"Oh, Lord. Don't tell me your middle name is Scrooge or something."

"Why is it when someone doesn't like Christmas they have to be called a Scrooge? Just because I refuse to plunge into debt to buy every single person I know a gift doesn't make me a bad person."

"I'm not saying that," Bernie opted for a softer tone. "I just want you to see that the holidays can be fun. It's the time to surround yourself with family and friends."

Gia clenched her jaw in an effort to suppress her response. Bernie was just trying to be helpful.

"Why is it that you never talk about your family?" Bernie asked.

Gia's irritation returned like a whip. "There's nothing to talk about."

"I know that tone."

"Good. Then you know to drop the subject."

Bernie held up her hands. "As you wish."

As usual, after snapping at her dear friend, Gia felt like a complete ass. Yet, she had sworn years ago that if she ever left Talbotton she would never look back. So far, she'd kept that promise.

"Ooh, we have to go in here," Bernie said, heading toward the door of Saks.

Gia sighed as she followed and glanced at her watch. "Great. Now I'm going to be here all day."

"I'm looking for the perfect gift for Vinny."

"In Saks?" she questioned, thinking of Bernie's mechanic husband whose obsession outside of his wife was any sport with a ball. "This doesn't strike me as his type of store."

"You'd be surprised," Bernie chuckled. "Just help me look around."

Did she have a choice? Bored, Gia strolled behind her friend, trying to muster a smile whenever her friend showed her something "cute" or "precious." After a half hour of this, she was certain that she was quite literally sleepwalking.

"I think my bladder is about to burst," Bernie whispered. "Come with me to the little girls' room."

Gia's face pinched at the thought of how long that line would be.

"Fine. Then wait right here for me. I'll be back in a minute."

"Fat chance."

"You really are no fun when it comes to shopping," Bernie said.

"You can't say I didn't warn you."

"Amen to that."

Gia laughed and then turned toward a brick wall—or rather a man's chest that felt like a brick wall. When she glanced up into deep, brown eyes, her knees buckled. Acqua Di Gio clung lightly to his skin and seduced her instantly.

"Hello," the man's honeyed voice poured over her. His low cropped hair and neatly trimmed mustache was peppered with a few gray strands. Everything about him spelled *sexy*.

She opened her mouth, but wasn't quite sure she'd said anything.

When he smiled, her heart fluttered wildly in her chest. It had been years since she had experienced that. She smiled back, but her gaze floated downward to the woman's blouse he carried in his hands.

"Ah. It's for my daughter," he said, following her gaze. "She and her best friend sort of dragged me down here this morning," he said with a nervous flutter in his voice. "We're supposed to be just looking at windows."

"I was dragged down here under the same ruse," Gia

laughed, but then caught sight of the gold band around his finger.

"Widower," he answered the unasked question, and then added. "If you were wondering."

Her smile ballooned. "I was."

CHAPTER 2

Daniel's chest tightened painfully when the beautiful woman before him smiled. Her warm toffee complexion held just a hint of cinnamon around her cheeks while her feline shaped eyes were perfect for her dark magnetic orbs. A pang of guilt sideswiped him momentarily and he lowered his gaze to fidget with his gold band.

"Is something wrong?"

He covered his sudden unease with a smile and met her steady gaze.

She seemed to recognize something in his expression because her smile softened. "How long have you been a widower?"

"Four years."

She reached for the chain around her neck and, to his surprise, flashed a set of army dog tags and simple gold band. "Fifteen."

Daniel's brows furrowed.

"I married young," she answered the unspoken question shortly before sadness ghosted her eyes.

"Sooo." He decided to break their melancholy mood. "Do you come here often?" he asked, dusting off his pickup lines.

The woman's full lips widened as she shook her head.

He winced. "That was pretty bad, huh?"

"Yeah, I'm afraid so," she laughed.

"Sorry, but it's been awhile."

"I figured as much."

When she laughed again, he sobered at its light, haunting, and lyrical sound. After a few seconds, he realized he was staring. "I'm Daniel," he said, jutting out his hand.

"Gia. Pleased to meet you."

Her hand slid lightly into his and he marveled at its softness. She smelled like a bouquet of spring flowers, which was interesting at the end of the fall season. He stared again, unable to help himself. "I know this is going to sound corny, but have we met before?"

"Boy. You really are bad at this."

"No, no." He laughed. "It's just that— Well, you look familiar."

"I'm certain we've never met."

"Oh?"

"I have a good memory when it comes to handsome men," she said boldly with a twinkle in her eyes.

He smiled. "I'm supposed to do the complimenting. That much I remember."

"Don't worry. You can make it up at dinner."

"Dinner? Oh, dinner. Yes, I would like...wait a minute. I'm supposed to be doing the asking, too," he said cheekily.

"So ask me," she smiled.

Daniel liked her sass. It was a great combination with her ethereal beauty. "Well, Gia, I was wondering if I could interest you in having dinner with me tonight? I happen to know this great restaurant in the Village."

"Can't."

He blinked as his smile evaporated. "Pardon?"

"I can't. I already have plans for tonight," she said sadly, and then brightened. "But I'm free tomorrow night."

His smile ballooned while relief deflated his shoulders. "Tomorrow will be great."

Neve tapped Starr on the shoulder and then quickly pointed across the store. "Ho, alert."

Starr turned away from the shelves of men's sweaters to squint through her glasses. "At least this one looks a little older," she said, still inspecting the woman. "Actually, she's very pretty."

"Yeah, but she could be a gold-digger," Neve warned. "Manhattan is crawling with them. She looks like she's chewed and spit out a few men in her time."

"Will you quit it?" Starr rolled her eyes. "Don't you think it's a little gross for you to have a crush on my dad?"

"I don't have a crush...I'm just...concerned." Neve shrugged. "I've been just as involved as you in trying to find him a new wife. You know, if he and my mother hooked up, then we could be sisters."

Starr nodded, but continued to watch her father. "I thought about that, too, but…" She turned and smiled politely at her best friend. "No offense, but your mother does come off a little desperate at times. She baked him *three* cakes for his birthday."

"What's wrong with that? She likes to bake."

It was on the tip of her tongue to also point out that her mom showed up every Sunday with freshly baked rolls or popped by every Wednesday with chicken Marsala, but Starr decided against it. Instead, her attention returned to her father and the way he practically lit up in front of this beautiful woman. Starr hadn't seen him do that in a long time—four years to be exact.

"Then what about your backup plan?" Neve inquired. "Have you contacted the adoption agency yet?"

Starr sighed. "Not yet. I'm still a little nervous about whether it's a good idea or not. I don't know anything about my real mother. She could be married, dead, or in prison."

Neve glanced back. "They are looking awfully cozy."

"C'mon," Starr coaxed. "Let's see if we can get a little closer."

"I think I can find the place," Daniel said, accepting a business card with Gia's home address written on the back and then flipping it over. "Ah, an interior designer?" He glanced at her. "You probably won't believe this, but I'm in the market for a designer."

"What a coincidence," she said, with a tinge of disbelief. "If you prefer to have a business lunch instead—"

"No, no," he hastily corrected. "Dinner…" he glanced

over her shoulder to catch sight of Starr and Neve ease into view "...will be great. Okay, then. I'll see you tomorrow." He stepped back. "Say eight o'clock?" He took another giant step.

Gia frowned. "Uh, sure. Eight is good."

"Great." He bumped into someone and turned to apologize.

"I'm back," Bernie sang, approaching behind her.

Her thick New York accent penetrated Gia's thoughts and she quickly turned around. "That was fast."

"Turns out the lines weren't so bad. Did you find anything?" Bernie quickly scanned the shelves.

"I found something all right." Gia's gaze traveled back to where she'd last seen Daniel. "But nothing that would remotely interest Vinny," she added when Bernie turned her inquiring eyes on her.

"Tell you what," Bernie sighed. "Why don't we split up? We can zip through here faster that way."

"I don't know what to buy Vinny," Gia whined. "Why don't I look for something for your daughter Tonya. That should be easier."

"Good idea. Meet you back in this very spot in one hour."

That long? Gia smiled. "Deal." She waited until her friend dashed off before she made another futile search for Daniel.

He was gone.

A bubble of hope popped, but Gia's smile lingered. With a head and nose for business, flirting had never been Gia's strong suit, but she was positively stunned by her performance today—stunned and proud.

For years, Gia suffered through countless lectures from her employees that she needed to find a life outside of her work. And for years, she'd lied saying her work was all she needed to be happy. She didn't hate men or think she was better off without them. It's just that she'd been so driven to succeed for so long, she feared she no longer knew how to relate to the opposite sex on an intimate level. Well, long-term anyway.

As loony as that sounded, it was the truth.

Yeah, sure, she dated from time to time, but so far, she hadn't found anyone she could stand to be around more than three dates. But something told her that wouldn't be the case with Daniel—Daniel what?

She stopped strolling the aisles to realize that she'd given him her number, but he'd disappeared before giving her his information. And what was up with him disappearing like that?

Daniel left Saks with Starr and Neve flanked on opposite sides. So far, he'd managed to successfully dodge their needling questions, but if he knew his daughter, and he did, he was certain he wouldn't be able to keep it up for long.

"Admit it, Dad. You liked her," Starr pressed. "I saw how you were looking at her."

"I'm pleading the Fifth."

"You're not on trial," she informed him with an exasperated breath.

"You could've fooled me," he chuckled.

They strolled down the walkway, heading to Rockefeller Center. Memories of Hilary surfaced in the back of his mind while a familiar ache resonated around his heart. At the sight of the Prometheus statue, Daniel drew a deep breath. Twenty-five years ago, he met Hilary at that very fountain.

"Are we coming back here when they light the Christmas tree on Tuesday?" Starr asked out of the blue.

"We have to," Neve insisted. "We have to make a wish."

Daniel frowned. "A wish?"

Simultaneously, the girls rolled their eyes—therefore transforming him into a double dummy, he supposed.

"Everyone is entitled to one wish upon the star. But you have to make it on the first night in order for it to come true," Starr said simply. "Everybody knows that."

"Yeah, yeah. I think I might of heard about that somewhere," he lied and took a moment to do his own series of eye rolling.

"Make fun of it all you want, Daddy, but its true. Mom told me."

His stride slowed. "She did?"

"When I was little." Starr shrugged. "She said she'd only done it twice, but each time, it worked."

Daniel was surprised he'd never heard this story. "What did she wish for?"

"You and me, silly."

The way Starr smiled melted Daniel's heart and he wrapped an arm around her shoulders. "I'm about to be mushy in public," he warned, shortly before he brushed a kiss against her cheek.

Instead of protesting, Starr allowed it, and kissed him back.

"So are you going to call her, Mr. Davis?" Neve asked timidly. "The lady in the store."

He drew a deep breath and watched how Starr's eyes had zeroed back onto him. "I'm going to do more than that," he announced proudly and produced Gia's business card. "I'm taking her to dinner."

Shock colored Starr's expression shortly before her eyes glowed with excitement. "You're kidding me. Let me see it."

She reached for the card, but Daniel quickly jerked it out of reach. At the same time, a sudden gust of wind slipped it out of his fingers. Stunned, Daniel turned a bit too quickly and slipped on a patch of invisible ice.

"Hey, buddy. Watch it."

His fall was everything but graceful. Daniel's arms flailed wide and by the time he landed with an awkward thud, Starr and Neve tumbled on top of him, knocking what little wind he had left out of him. True to form, not a single New Yorker stopped or inquired if they were okay, but Starr and Neve suddenly caught a case of the giggles.

"So glad that I amuse you girls," he groaned. "Do you mind getting off me now, so I can stop looking like a idiot?"

Still laughing, they lumbered slowly to their feet and then did a lousy job trying to help him up.

Bones aching, muscles throbbing, Daniel dusted the snow from his clothes and glanced around. "Please tell me you saw where the card went."

The trio's gazes searched around the snow-covered ground and in between the feet of the bustling crowd. However, after fifteen minutes, they gave up.

"Maybe she's still in the store," Starr said, hopefully.

Daniel glanced at his watch and sighed. "I seriously doubt that. Not to mention the low probability of finding her in that crowd. What was the name of that interior decorating business?" he asked himself and tried to will an image of the card in his mind, but it wasn't working.

Neve patted him on the shoulder. "It looks like you have a wish to make, too, Mr. Davis."

"Yeah, but by Tuesday it'll be too late."

CHAPTER 3

"**D**on't you dare call that gal," Ma Belle spat from her sickbed. "She hasn't come to see me in all these years, so she doesn't need to come and see me now." Her jaw set in a stubborn line, but she was unable to prevent her bottom lip from quivering.

Glenda said nothing as she tucked the blanket tighter around her grandmother.

"You might as well fix your face 'cause I'm not gonna change my mind."

"I didn't say anything," Glenda said, turning and lifting the dinner tray from the nightstand. Everyone knew there was no point in arguing with Ma Belle. She rarely, if ever, changed her mind about anything.

However, Glenda was hardly fooled by the matriarch's blustering. Ma Belle's heart broke the minute Gia escaped Talboton—and it never healed.

The majority of the family thought Gia's dreams of finding a better life in a big city like New York wouldn't last more than a couple of weeks. Some even suggested that she should set her sights on Atlanta—where she would at least be no more than a couple of hours from home and the fall on her face wouldn't be as painful.

But Glenda knew her sister would make it because despite what everybody else believed, Gia had already hit rock bottom.

"Momma, we're out of Coco Puffs."

Glenda glanced at her sixteen-year-old daughter, Jenny, and at her bulging pregnant belly, and felt an overwhelming weariness in her bones.

"Momma, did you hear me?"

"Yes, chile. Just put it on the grocery list and I'll get some more in the morning. Why in the world you want to eat cereal for dinner anyway?" Glenda headed for the kitchen sink to get started on the dishes.

"'Cause that's what I have a craving for," Jenny laughed. "Don't tell me that I have to explain cravings to a woman who's had ten kids."

Glenda bit her lip and warded off the sting of tears. Jenny didn't mean anything by the casual comment, but that didn't stop it from smacking her with the truth of her life.

Gia fled from Talboton to avoid turning into Glenda: an endless baby factory and a woman who fell for every lie every man had ever told her. Glenda pressed a hand to her mouth, but failed to stop a ragged sob.

"Momma, are you okay?" Jenny closed the refrigerator door and waddled next to her.

"I'm fine," she answered, but the tears that followed said otherwise.

"Did I say something wrong?" The concern in Jenny's voice heightened as she slid her arm around her mother's waist. "I'm sorry if I did."

"No, chile. I think I just need to go lie down for a few minutes. Be a dear and finish the dishes for me." Glenda avoided making eye contact and slid out of her daughter's arms to shuffle to her own bedroom in the back of the house. Once she had entered and closed the door behind her, she glanced around the room she had lived in her entire life and drew a deep breath. "Gia, whatever you do, don't you ever come back here."

Miraculously, Gia survived a full day of shopping. Of course the ten-hour venture resulted in only two Christmas gifts, but that was another gripe for another day.

After closing and locking her front door, Gia tossed her keys onto the first end table she passed in the living room and pretended not to notice the flashing light on the answering machine.

"It's my day off," she mumbled under her breath. The first one she'd had in almost four months, three weeks, and two days.

Not that she was counting.

Gia wandered into the kitchen and grabbed a Diet Pepsi from the fridge before meandering to her bedroom where she placed her cell phone on its charger. Like most of the day, her thoughts returned to the wickedly handsome man she'd met at Saks. Her lips curled upward at the memory of his dimpled cheeks and Crest-white smile, but they kept turning south whenever she'd replayed the image of the way the man had taken off.

She sighed as her gaze landed on her little black dress across her bed, still plastic-wrapped from the dry cleaners. The only thing about heading to a private birthday dinner was the meal itself. She was starving.

On cue, Gia's stomach released a mighty growl as if seconding the thought. "Just hang in there," she mumbled under her breath and glanced at her watch. "Two hours until chow time." Popping the top to her soda, she made a beeline toward the adjoining bathroom and turned on the shower to full blast.

She took her time peeling off her clothes and pinning up her hair, but instead of stepping into the shower, Gia froze at the sight of her blurred reflection. Her heart skipped a beat when she caught a glimpse of a younger version of herself with a protruding belly.

Gia drew a shaky breath and inched a trembling hand along her stomach—her flat stomach. Sorrow, her old and faithful friend, swept across her body and squeezed her heart until tears leaked from her eyes.

Blink, her brain screamed. If she blinked, the image would go away and the pain would ease in her chest. But there was that part of her that was still fixated on the young girl's belly and it was just a matter of time before a million "what ifs" crammed into her head.

The phone rang, jarring her daydream and forcing her to blink. She quickly tempered her flash of annoyance with a deep breath before she closed the bathroom door.

Let the answering machine pick it up. If she didn't hurry, she was going to be late. Of course, what she really wanted to do was stay home and rent a movie.

That was how she spent every December—going in hibernation mode and avoiding people. Sighing, she glanced back at the mirror. It was completely steamed over, but she paid it no mind as she pulled open the medicine cabinet.

Gia hesitated for a moment, and then grabbed the vial of Prozac. Only one pill slid around in the bottle. If she was going to survive the holidays, she was definitely going to need to get a refill. Up until a few months ago, Gia was hesitant to seek help for her low energy, irritability, and bouts of prolonged depression. For years she had hated doctors, nurses, and especially hospitals; however, Bernie and Maryann had practically dragged her to a doctor after she had refused to climb out of bed after two weeks of sobbing uncontrollably.

Depression, the doctor had diagnosed proudly. Gia was hardly impressed. Hell, she *knew* she was depressed. She was just in denial on how bad it had gotten. In a way it still didn't make sense. She had accomplished everything she had set out to do and still…

Gia shook her head to change the direction of her thoughts. She plopped the pill into her hand and grabbed her soda again. However, when she went to pop the medicine into her mouth, the damn pill slipped through her fingers and hit the sink. She scrambled to catch it before it rolled down to the drain—but no such luck.

"Damn," she hissed and immediately felt a wave of

panic. For an insane moment, she jabbed her finger down the narrow pipe, but then realized what she was doing and gave up in disgust.

"I have to cancel," she mumbled, fairly conscious of the fact that she might be overreacting; but damn if she could help it. She drew a few deep breaths and then reevaluated the situation. She could surely survive a weekend without her magic pills, she reasoned. It wasn't like she was addicted or anything.

She laughed and finally stepped into the shower.

An hour later, she had showered, applied her makeup, and performed a miracle on her hair before shimmying into her dress.

The fact that she was another year older and the dress still fit her perfectly was reason enough to smile.

"I can do this," she stated with a forced confidence, grabbed her full-length Berber swing coat, and headed out the door.

Starr watched her father intently as they waited to be seated for dinner. "Daddy, I'm sorry you lost that lady's business card," Starr apologized yet again with her bottom lip turned downward in a genuine frown.

Daniel looped his arm around his daughter's shoulders and gave them a gentle squeeze. "Don't worry about it. It's not your fault."

She nodded, but she didn't believe it. No way, after searching high and low for the perfect woman, was Starr going to just give up looking for the woman. Starr wanted to see her father light up again.

"Besides," her father added. "It's not like I have time to be pursuing a relationship right now, anyway."

Starr rolled her eyes. That had been his patented answer since she'd started playing matchmaker. She was guessing that it was some kind of defense mechanism—an annoying one.

"With the practice and taking care of you—"

"Don't." Starr's gaze challenged him. "Don't use me as an excuse, Dad. I'm fine. Of course I don't know for how long if you don't stop babying me all the time." The moment the words were out of her mouth, she regretted them.

Hurt flashed in his eyes as he glanced down at her and allowed his arm to fall from her shoulders.

"Davis party of three," the hostess announced above the steady hum of the crowd.

Daniel, Starr, and Neve worked their way up to the hostess stand where they then followed an attractive woman to their designated table.

Starr continued to feel worse when her father went out of his way to avoid her gaze again. She glanced over at Neve who, in turn, just shrugged and offered no help. "Dad, I didn't mean—"

"Honey, forget about it." He smiled tightly, but still avoided meeting her gaze. "You're just saying how you feel."

Before Starr could respond, the waitress appeared and went over the evening specials. While waiting patiently, Starr reviewed in her mind another way to get her point across. As usual, everything always came out the wrong way.

"I'll give you a few minutes to review the menu," their waitress said and strolled off.

"Dad—"

"If you girls will excuse me. I'm going to run to the men's room." After flashing another plastic smile, he was up and out of his chair before Starr could finish her sentence.

"One of these days, I'm going to stop putting my foot in my mouth," she mumbled.

"Don't be so hard on yourself," Neve said, lowering her menu. "You were just giving him a dose of tough love. And we both know that stuff is supposed to be good for us, but it's really adults who have the hardest time with it."

"You have a point there." Starr crossed her arms and sat back in her chair. "I just wish we hadn't lost that darn card."

"Well, I think it was a sign. I personally didn't like the looks of that lady."

"What was wrong—? You know, never mind." She waved her hand. "I'm starting to think you're not as gung-ho about finding a match for my father as you used to be."

"That's not true. I just really think we should be considering my mother. I mean, don't you want to be sisters?"

She didn't know how she did it, but Starr had marched right into another sticky situation where only tact and saccharine charm could get her out of it. Yet, once again, she never got out what she wanted to say. Instead her gaze drifted to the figure that had just waltzed to the hostess stand. "You're a strong believer in fate, right?"

"Y-yeah," Neve answered slowly.

"Then look who just walked in the door."

Neve turned around in her seat, and then stared open-mouthed at the beautiful woman from Saks Fifth Avenue. "I don't believe it."

Starr smiled. "Looks like Dad doesn't have to make that wish after all."

CHAPTER 4

Daniel washed and dried his hands and then stopped to stare at his reflection in the mirror. As usual, he saw a man who was just barely holding on. The one thing that got him through each day was the idea that his little girl needed him.

That was a lie.

He lowered his gaze and chuckled. Suddenly it was clear as a bell that all this matchmaking Starr and Neve have been doing was for one purpose only: to get him off his daughter's back. If he let go, what would become of the man in the mirror?

"I need some help here, Hilary," he mumbled under his breath. Of course, he'd made that request at least once a day—which was down from the ten times a day four years ago, damn if it wasn't still true. If only Hilary, God, or even

Santa Claus could toss him a vowel, he could figure out a clue as to how to get on with his life.

The door burst open and two gentlemen entered the facilities and consequently ended Daniel's private reflection. He tossed the men a brief smile as he headed out the door. The steady hum of customer chatter and clinking dishes instantly gave him a headache, but he was determined to end the day with the girls on a good note and forced a smile that hardly seemed to fit his face.

When he made his way back over to his table, he was stunned to find it vacant. "Where—"

He turned and made a complete three-sixty, unable to catch a glimpse of the missing teenagers anywhere. His heart instantly shifted into panic mode, but he was still able to keep his wits about him—meaning, he didn't immediately launch into screaming their names at the top of his lungs. Maybe they had just gone to the little girls' room.

He relaxed and settled into his chair. He really needed to do something about his ability to always imagine the worse scenario.

"Are you ready to order, sir?" his smiling waitress asked as she returned to the table.

"Uh, no, ma'am." He smiled and glanced around again. "It seems my daughter and her friend have disappeared for a moment. Maybe you should give us a few more minutes?"

The waitress nodded and strolled off to the next table.

Daniel drew a breath and glanced around again. His gaze skittered to laughing families and eye-gazing couples. This was one of the things he loved about the holidays: people changed. Conversations were no longer filled with stock trades or corporate griping. This time of year people talked about their children's school or church play, organized charity events for the less fortunate, or discussed what would be the perfect gift for the grandparents.

It was like magic—just like Hilary had proclaimed.

The thought brought a smile into Daniel's face. Hilary had been right about so many things he mused, reaching for his iced water.

"Would you marry again if something ever happened to me?" Hilary's voice floated over to him.

Daniel glanced up and was instantly caught up in a memory.

Hilary, beautiful as ever, held his steady gaze. "Come on. Answer the question."

"It's never going to happen," Daniel answered coolly, but felt a small smile tug at his lips. "If anything, I'll die first. I eat badly, I hardly exercise, and I get very little sleep."

"Good point." Hilary nodded with a growing smile. "You'll go first."

Daniel chuckled. "Well, don't look so smug about it. You are going to miss me, right?"

"Immensely," she answered lightning fast and pulled off a look of sincerity that melted his heart.

He reached over and covered her hand, but she gently flipped it over and caressed his palm. He loved it when she did that. The way her fingers would tickle the sensitive area gave him the same wild fluttering in his stomach as her deep sensual kisses. After a moment of watching her, he wondered about her question.

"What about you?" he finally asked. "Would you marry again?"

Her gaze lowered to his hand and then she lifted it to brush a kiss against his knuckles. "If on the rare chance I was able to meet someone as wonderful as you, which is probably unlikely, I'd like to think I would have your blessing to move on."

Another man kissing and making love to his wife didn't exactly bode well with Daniel. He eased his hand out of her grip and leaned back in his chair. "How long are we talking about?"

"What?"

"How long after I'm dead are we talking about. Fifty years, twenty-five years, or two weeks?"

Hilary rocked her head back with a burst of laughter. A few nearby diners glanced in their direction and Daniel apologized for his wife interrupting their meals by flashing them a brief smile.

"You know on second thought, I don't want to know the answer to that question."

"Oh, c'mon, Daniel. I think we should really discuss this. I know I would want you to marry again."

Daniel's brows rose in surprise. "You would?"

Hilary nodded. "I've been thinking about this for a while—"

"Oh, you have?"

"Yeah." She suddenly became somber again. "The question just popped in my head the other night when I was putting Starr to bed. Actually, a lot of questions popped in my head."

He captured her hand again and gave it a gentle squeeze. "Like what?"

"Like—what would I do if one day her birth mother showed up at our door wanting her back?"

"Honey—"

"It could happen. You remember the movie last week with Halle Berry. What would we do in that situation? Before I knew it, I

had a whole list of what ifs and among the top ones—if I passed away, would you marry again?"

She was being serious, he knew, so he forced himself to push past his initial discomfort with the topic.

"Would I marry again?" he repeated, and then drew a deep breath. The idea that there was another woman as wonderful as the woman sitting across from him sounded as far-fetched as discovering life on another planet.

Before Hilary, Daniel remembered clearly how alone he was in a city of more than seven million people. Since she'd walked into his life, there were smiles and laughter every day, and since the adoption of their beautiful little girl, life just kept getting better.

"I don't think so," he finally answered honestly. "I can't imagine my life without you."

Her smile returned. "That is so sweet. But—"

"No," he insisted. "And the point is moot anyway."

Hilary nodded and for a few seconds the subject seemed to be closed. He was wrong.

"I would want you to marry again," she said. "I wouldn't want you to mourn me the rest of your life."

He looked at her incredulously.

"I want you to be happy…always." Her lips quivered at the corners. "That's what we're supposed to want for each other, right?"

Daniel hesitated at the trick question.

She squeezed his hand again. "Right?"

Finally he forced his lips to curl. "Right."

At long last, Daniel closed his eyes and vanquished the memory, but he continued to mumble, "Right."

Watching the stunning woman in red as she walked toward the back of the restaurant, Starr followed her like a moth to a flame. What was it about the woman that enamored her? "Wow," she finally whispered. "I wouldn't mind looking like that when I grow up."

"She's all right," Neve mumbled. "Are you still going to talk to her?"

"Yeah, just give me a minute to think of what to say," Starr answered. In truth she was nervous and didn't understand why—being shy was not one of her characteristics.

"Well, I don't think you should," Neve huffed and crossed her arms. "I mean, look at her. To be wearing something like that she has to have a date or something."

Starr frowned. She hadn't thought of that, but all she had to recall was the way her dad had practically glowed around the woman for her to push the tiny obstacle of a date aside. "I'm going to go talk to her," she announced with newfound courage.

Neve clamped a hand on her friend's shoulder.

When Starr glanced back, she didn't know what to make of her friend's troubled expression. "Look," she started with a patient tone. "It's obvious that my dad likes this lady. You saw how disappointed he looked when he lost her business card."

Neve's gaze skittered downward.

"We've been looking for months for someone to put that kind of smile on his face." She sighed when she noticed the muscles along her friend's jaw pulse. "Besides, we don't have to have my father marry your mom for us to be sisters. We're already family. It's the things that are in our hearts that makes us a family. My mom taught me that."

Neve gave her a sheepish smile and then reached

down into her pants pocket and removed the rumpled business card.

Starr blinked and then reached for it. "You found it?"

"You want a wife for your dad and I wanted a husband for my mom. Maybe I wanted it too badly." Neve's eyes glossed with shimmering tears.

Starr embraced her friend. "We'll find someone—for both of them. And no matter what, we'll always be sisters. Agreed?"

Neve nodded against her shoulder. "Agreed."

The *sisters* slowly eased out of their embrace while still holding on to their smiles. Yet, when they turned back toward the small dock of pay phones, the woman was gone.

"Where did she go?" Neve asked.

Starr glanced around wondering if the woman had passed them while they were talking, but she didn't see her anywhere. "Well." She held up the business card. "At least we still have this."

"Are you going to tell your dad what I did?" Neve asked in alarm.

"No."

"He's going to want to know how we got the card."

Starr nodded and bit her lower lip while she thought for a moment. "I have an idea."

CHAPTER 5

After initially going to the wrong restaurant for Freddy's birthday party, Gia caught up with her good friends, and then had too much to eat and way too much to drink. When she finally managed to pry her eyes open Saturday morning—well, Saturday afternoon—she felt as if she'd been run down by a Mack truck. This was why she wasn't a party person—the consequences far outweighed the benefits.

The telephone blared from the nightstand, but the thing sounded as though it was somehow implanted in her ear. Pressing a pillow against her head, she tried to ignore it; but her teeth rattled and her brain threatened to explode.

Gia groaned and rolled to the edge of the bed and swung out her hand to seize the torturous object. Before she could tuck the phone under her ear, she fell unceremoniously onto the floor, banged her head on the edge of the nightstand, and roared out a succession of curses that would make a veteran sailor blush.

After waiting for the pain to pass, she scrambled across the floor and retrieved the phone. "Hello."

"Uh, yeah. May I speak to Gia Hunter?"

The caller's rich voice dripped like warm honey into Gia's ear and her pain and anger completely evaporated. She had no problem matching the voice to the handsome man she'd met at Saks. "T-this is Gia."

"Did I catch you at a bad time?" he asked with trepidation lacing his voice.

"Yes, uh, I mean, no." She winced. Less than a minute into the conversation and she already sounded like a dunce. "I just woke up…and fell out of bed."

Daniel chuckled. "That explains the cursing."

She laughed.

"Sorry for waking you up. I can call you back later, if you'd like?"

"No. Uh, I mean, that won't be necessary." Gia rolled her eyes at her air-headed behavior. "I'm up now."

He laughed with her, but then an awkward silence vibrated over the line.

Should she say something?

"I have to tell you, I was afraid I would never see you again," Daniel jumpstarted the conversation.

"Oh?" She climbed off the floor.

"Yeah, I lost your business card somewhere near Rockefeller Center, but then this morning I found it bubble-gummed to the bottom of my shoe. You can't imagine my relief."

"Well I'm glad you found it…especially since you left without giving me your number."

"Oh," he managed to sound contrite. "I owe you an explanation for that."

"I am curious…but you don't *owe* me an explanation." Gia rubbed the side of her pounding head and strolled toward her bathroom.

"Then to appease your curiosity, I was trying to get away before my beautiful daughter, who has the best of intentions, by the way, showed up and scared you off."

"Should I be worried?" She switched on a light and winced at her horrible reflection. She looked worse than she felt.

"No, no. Once you get to know her, you hardly notice how she winds you around her finger."

Her smile widened. "She sounds adorable. How old is she?" she asked, opening the medicine cabinet and reaching for the Advil.

"She'll be fifteen on Christmas Day."

Gia froze with her hand clamped around the headache medicine. Her mind instantly filled with images of the delivery room and a nurse rushing off with her newborn child.

"Don't worry. We're going to take good care of her…"

"Of course, I think she's fourteen going on forty." He sighed. "But she's the absolute apple of my eye." Daniel chuckled.

Jolting out of the memory, Gia snatched the Advil out of the cabinet and popped the top.

"What about you?" he asked. "Do you have any kids?"

Gia closed her eyes, but not in time to prevent a lone

tear from streaking down her face as she croaked out the lie she'd told for nearly fifteen years, "No."

"Ma Belle is dying," Glenda announced. She lifted her gaze from her fidgeting fingers to meet Byron's hard stare through the jail's Plexiglas. She watched as her brother's hand tightened around the phone before he finally drew in a deep breath.

"How long?" he asked.

"Doctor said it would be a miracle if she lives until Christmas."

Byron's face lost none of its intensity. She knew he was wondering—hoping that his release date of December twenty-third wouldn't be too late to say his final goodbyes.

"I can't imagine…"

Glenda nodded. He wasn't about to say anything that she hadn't said to herself a thousand times since she was given the news. Ma Belle, though most believed her to be a little rough around the edges, was truly a remarkable woman with the best of intentions. She was a woman with a limited amount of everything: education, money, and resources. Everyone in the family loved her, except maybe…

"Have you talked to Gia?" Byron asked.

Glenda's gaze dropped.

"You have to call her," Byron said.

Glenda closed her eyes. "What's the point? There's nothing she can do."

"Ma Belle would like to see her again."

"That ain't what she's been telling me." Glenda looked up again.

"What Ma Belle says ain't always what she means. We both know that. I might not be the sharpest tool in the toolbox, but even I know Ma Belle's heart been broken ever since Gia left Talboton."

"I seem to recall Gia's heart broken way before she left this stinking town." Glenda grew hot under the collar.

"More reasons for those two to bury the hatchet."

Glenda shook her head. "You just don't understand."

"What's not to understand? Ma Belle encouraged Gia to give up her child for adoption. Gia signed the papers, regretted it, and blamed Ma Belle for forcing her hand. See? Simple."

"Jail has done wonders for—"

"Let's get one thing straight. I ain't proud of being in here. And once I get out I ain't ever coming back. But being locked up makes a man see things differently—you view *time* differently. *You* might not want Gia to come back, but if she's ever going to heal—she has to."

"Okay, young ladies. Are you two ready?" Daniel asked, breezing into the living room and fastening his cuff links.

Starr and Neve glanced up from the current issue of *Seventeen* magazine and frowned at his attire.

"You're not wearing that are you?" Starr asked.

"What?" he asked, and then glanced down at his outfit. "You don't like it?"

Starr's gaze skittered over to her best friend and then ricocheted back to her father. "Well…you look like you're going to one of those boring medical conventions. Don't you have something more…casual in your closet?"

Embarrassment flashed across her father's face as he glanced down again. "This is one of my best suits."

"Exactly my point, Dad. This is a date not a business dinner."

"And lets not forget it's the holidays," Neve added. "You should be casual and fun at the same time."

Starr agreed. "Oh, what about that sweater I bought you for your birthday? That would look nice."

"Yeah. It warms your eyes." Neve nodded.

Starr and her father frowned at the teenager.

Neve shrugged. "What? It's hard not to notice."

Sighing, Starr shook her head and rolled her eyes. "Anyway, I think you should change," she told her father. "If she's an interior designer, she probably has a good sense of fashion, too. You don't want to scare her into thinking you're stuck in the dark ages or something."

A palpable silence stretched between the girls and the lone adult in the room. After a few awkward seconds, Daniel turned and marched back to his bedroom.

Starr smiled, but then turned toward her best friend. "It warms his eyes?"

"Well, it does." Neve shrank deeper into the plush sofa.

A few minutes later, Daniel returned to the living room and sashayed around like a male model sporting his only Sean John outfit. "No autographs. No autographs," he said, pretending the girls were a part of his rock star fan club.

Starr and Neve giggled at his theatrics, and then thrust their thumbs high into the air.

"Now, that I've passed inspection, let's go before I'm late. Starr, did you already pack an overnight bag?"

"Yes, Dad," she moaned, easing out of her chair. She hoped they didn't have to run through their usual checklist of items she might have forgotten. She was only spending the night next door at Neve's. If she had forgotten something, she would just walk back to the house.

"Did you pack your toothbrush?"

"Daaad."

Daniel held up his hands. "All right." He smiled, grabbed her bag by the door, and waited patiently while the girls slid on their coats.

"A few pointers, Dad. When you first show up, make sure you compliment her. But don't just say 'hey, nice shoes' or something crazy like that."

"Make sure you thank her for the date," Neve added.

"Yeah." Starr bobbed her head. "Good manners are still in style."

"That's good to hear," Daniel said sarcastically.

"Dad. We're trying to help you. We all know you're a little rusty."

He looked as if he was about to reprimand her, but then dropped his shoulders and asked, "Is there anything else?"

"Kissing," Starr answered quickly.

"Wait." Daniel held up his hands. "I'm not taking kissing advice from my fourteen…"

Starr stared at him sternly.

"*Almost* fifteen-year old daughter," he amended. "I have to draw the line somewhere."

"When was the last time you kissed the opposite sex?" Starr questioned, cocking her head. "And me and Grandma don't count."

"What do *you* know about kissing?" he asked, and then immediately realized he didn't really want an answer.

Starr stared at him and waited.

"Never mind," her father said, rubbing his temples. "What's the tip?"

"I'm glad you asked." She smiled. "Instead of waiting for the end of the date for that big awkward moment, you should warm her up throughout the date with small kisses."

Daniel frowned.

"You know, when you pick her up, you hand her flowers—you *are* taking her flowers, right?"

"Flowers." He nodded. "That's a good idea."

"Oh, boy. You're worse off than I thought."

"No, I just…forgot." His forehead wrinkled. "What am I doing?" he mumbled. "I'm going to make a fool of myself."

"No you're not. Just thank your lucky Starr that you have her to help you come off smelling like a rose."

Her father's lips sloped unevenly as he tugged one of her pigtails. "Thank you, lucky Starr."

"What do you mean you have a date?" Bernie questioned over the phone. "Since when?"

"Since yesterday—or really this morning," Gia answered as she flitted in and out of her walk-in closet. After a lifetime of having a great metabolism, she grudgingly admitted that if she wanted to remain a size six, she would have to start a medieval practice called *exercise.*

For right now, however, she had a devil of a time trying to find something that flattered her widening hips and rounding bottom. In the end, she settled on a tried and true staple in every woman's closet: the little black dress. It wasn't too dressy or too casual—perfect.

"Why didn't you tell me?" Bernie whined. "Is he ugly or something?"

"Hardly." Gia squeezed her foot into her favorite pumps and twirled a final time in front of a full-length mirror in the bedroom. "I'm nervous," she admitted, and then belatedly remembered that she still had the phone tucked beneath her ear.

"Ooh. He must be really good looking," Bernie commented. "What does he do for a living?"

The doorbell rang and a million butterflies burst from their cocoons inside of her stomach.

"I have to go. He's here." Gia flattened a hand over her heart at the instant memory of Daniel. "Wish me luck."

"Good luck—and I want details tomorrow."

Gia smiled and disconnected the call. At the doorbell's second chime, she smoothed the front of her dress, and then went to answer the door.

When she finally pulled it open, she was stunned to discover that her memory had a faulty wire. The man standing before her was even more devastatingly handsome than she remembered. "Hello."

"Hello," he greeted in a seductive baritone.

His instant smile was infectious and she found herself standing there with a grin that stretched from ear to ear.

"I, uh, brought these for you." Daniel presented a bunch of white carnations and chrysanthemums.

She sucked in a surprised breath and gushed at the beautiful arrangement.

"I hope you like them," he said, and then nervously leaned in and brushed a kiss against her cheek.

Pleasantly surprised, Gia fluttered a hand to her cheek and blushed. "What was that for?"

"I hope it was okay," he said. "I was advised that it was best to get the kiss out of the way."

Gia forced a frown. "But now we don't have anything to look forward to."

"Of course we do."

Her brows rose in curiosity.

"The second kiss."

Gia was smitten by Daniel's boyish charm. "I better put these in some water. Would you like to come in?"

"I thought you'd never ask."

She turned and strolled toward the kitchen. "These are beautiful."

"I'm glad you like them."

"I love them." Gia inhaled the fragrant scent.

"I love the dress," Daniel praised. "You look beautiful."

Gia's smile grew to a ridiculous size while her knees tingled. That definitely had to be a good sign. She had a feeling she was in for a wonderful night and if she played her cards right, she just might end up with Daniel wrapped and placed under her Christmas tree this year. She glanced over her shoulder to sneak another peek at her possible present. "Oh, Santa, baby."

CHAPTER 6

Daniel opened the door to his car and gently ushered Gia into the passenger seat of his silver Cadillac Escalade.

"Thank you." She smiled.

His heartbeat quickened as his lips widened. "You're more than welcome." He closed the door and drew in a breath; however, the gulp of cold air did little to soothe his nervousness. As he walked to the driver's side, his mind scrolled through a list of conversation starters. Once he was settled into his seat, he promptly forgot them all.

"Sooo," Gia sighed. "Where are we going?"

Daniel glanced at her and was instantly entranced by her beautiful eyes and was so enraptured by her growing smile that he forgot how to speak.

"Dinner, movie—do you know?" Gia asked with furrowed brows.

"Huh? Oh, uh—yeah." He glanced away with his face burning from embarrassment. "How does Aureole sound to you?"

"Sounds wonderful. I've never been there, but I've heard great things about the restaurant."

"Then prepare to be in for a treat." He slid his key into the ignition and Nat King Cole's unmistakable voice filtered through the speakers singing "The Christmas Song."

"The holidays come faster every year," Gia marveled.

Unable to ignore the sad tone in her voice, Daniel glanced at her. "You don't like the holidays?"

Sighing, she glanced out the side of her window and seemed reluctant to answer the question.

"Well, not everyone does," he continued as he pulled out into traffic. "I know a part of me is saddened by the commercialization of the season." He glanced over at her in time to see he'd captured her attention again. "But I have to admit that it's my favorite time of the year."

Again she drew a breath, and held on to her smile. "I know what you want me to say, but to be honest—this time of year is usually hard for me. However, this year I'm determined to turn over a new leaf...if I can."

Daniel wanted to inquire further when the voice of reason intervened and told him not push or pry. It was obvious she was holding back and because they were still strangers, he needed to respect her privacy. Yet, his curiosity was still piqued.

"Well. What is it that you do, Mr. Davis?"

"I'm a pediatrician."

"Oh." Her voice lowered. "It's Dr. Davis then?"

"Yes, but you can call me Daniel." He chuckled, but when he looked at her, there was no amusement in her expression. That's odd. Most of the time when he told women he was a doctor, they seemed quite pleased. "Is something wrong?"

"No, no." She tried to cover with a smile, yet it was painfully obvious that something was indeed wrong. In her apartment everything seemed to have been going well. Now it all seemed to have spun on its ear.

Gia returned her attention to the scenery outside of her window.

Ten minutes into the drive, all Daniel could picture in his head was a plane nose-diving from the air. He hadn't crashed and burned this badly since junior high school.

"So are you a native New Yorker?" she asked.

"No." He grabbed hold of the lifeline and held on tight. "Actually, I was born in Tennessee."

"A fellow southerner?" Her voice rose in surprise.

Daniel nodded while cautiously shifting lanes. "Just for a brief time. My family moved when I was two. My father was in the army and we pretty much just bounced from state to state. I even lived in Germany for a couple of years."

When he glanced at her again he was pleased to see a smile had finally returned to her face. "What about you? Where are you from?"

"Georgia."

"Atlanta?"

"Nah," she chuckled softly. "I'm from a tiny place called Talboton—a place where it's easy to get lost and where very few people escape."

"So I take it you're one of the lucky ones?" he joked.

"Luck had very little to do with it." She drew a deep breath. "New York is perfect for me. It's a melting pot of cultures and the pace is as fast and strong as a human heartbeat. I love it."

Daniel caught the way her eyes sparkled as she talked and glanced around. The air between them was charged with her electricity and passion. It was suddenly clear why a small southern town couldn't hold the fiery beauty for long.

Minutes later, they arrived at their destination. The knots in Daniel's stomach remained tight as he stepped out of the car and handed his keys over to the valet. Before entering the building, he offered Gia his arm.

Her winning smile melted another inch of his heart. This time he noticed it held a certain familiarity and he was taken aback by it.

Both handed their coats over at the coat check. At the hostess stand, they were greeted with smiles before being shown to their table.

"This place is beautiful," Gia cooed as she glanced around. "Have you been here before?"

"A few times." He held out her chair.

When she lowered into her seat, he gently slid her closer to the table and whispered in her ear. "The food here is exquisite."

She sucked in her breath. "Then I can't wait."

Before Daniel moved away, he caught the soft floral scent of her hair and the tangy sweet fragrance of her perfume.

"Good evening." Their waitress appeared and immediately rattled off the specials of the day.

Daniel didn't hear a word the woman said. He simply couldn't pull his gaze away from the beauty sitting across from him.

"I'll give you a few minutes to decide," the waitress ended, and then drifted away.

"You're going to have to stop that," Gia said slyly, grinning at him.

"Stop what?"

"Staring at me like that."

A rush of embarrassment scorched his face as he finally succeeded in glancing away. "Sorry."

"No need to apologize," she said warmly. "It's actually kind of sweet...but it's also making me nervous," she confessed.

He was surprised by the information, especially since she seemed so calm, cool, and collected. "In that case, I'll try not to stare."

"Thanks."

"But no promises," he added with a smile.

Gia blushed and made another sad attempt to squash the fluttering in her stomach. Her long bouts of silence weren't caused by indifference or melancholy. She honestly couldn't seem to control her emotions. His lingering gazes had the same effect as a lover's caress and his voice...

She permitted herself a soft sigh. She could easily cuddle up and listen to him talk all night. Her reaction to him was confusing, wonderful, and scary—all at the same time.

When the waitress returned, both confessed that they had yet to take a peek inside the menu and requested a few more minutes to make their decision. Even that turned out to be a game of stolen glances.

The man had no right to look so good, she mused, nor did he have the right to be so perfect. She couldn't remember a man opening car doors, or holding out chairs for her. Not to mention that he also adored his daughter, loved the holidays, and was a physician. And even though she didn't care for doctors, she could easily see herself caring for this one.

Daniel wasn't the kind of man a woman just dated casually. She knew without a doubt, he was the kind you kept—a "death 'til you part" kind. The million-dollar question was whether she was ready for a relationship—truly ready.

A part of her screamed, *yes*. Then there was that part that ebbed at her soul and recycled a question in her mind: What if you get hurt again?

The waitress' third appearance jarred her out of her reverie and she arbitrarily selected an appetizer and an entree.

"Hmm. Those are very good choices," the waitress said, accepting the menu. "And what about you, sir?"

"I'll have what the lady is having," he replied with a smirk and handed over his menu.

When they were left alone, the couple's gazes met once again. How in the world was she going to eat if she couldn't tame those damn butterflies?

"You're going to have to forgive me," Daniel said after the silence. "I'm a little out of practice."

"Don't worry," she assured him. "You're doing fine."

His widening smile stirred her butterflies and she finally gave up in trying to control them. Their conversation remained light and on safe topics until they were halfway through their main course.

"Does dating ever stop feeling like you're cheating on your dead spouse?" Daniel asked out of the blue.

Gia's heart squeezed as she stared into his intense gaze. "It hasn't for me."

Daniel nodded, but then settled back in his chair. "Do you mind telling me about him?"

She clenched her jaw against the threat of tears. It had been so long since she'd talked about her husband. When Jermaine first passed away, everyone had been so busy telling her how she needed to move on, or how to bury the past, that she was reduced to just speaking his name in the confinements of her dark and lonely bedroom.

"What would you like to know about him?" she asked cautiously before taking a sip of her wine.

"I guess first, what was his name?"

Smiling, she lowered her glass. "Jermaine."

"Jermaine," Daniel repeated with a healthy dose of respect. "How did you two meet? And more importantly, what did he do to make you fall in love with him?"

The tears continued to inch their way toward the rim of her eyes, yet, it felt incredibly wonderful to breathe life back into a man whose footprints walked beside hers for a brief time in her life.

"I don't remember how I met Jermaine," she stated honestly. "He was just always there and I can't remember a time when I didn't love him. Like I said, Talboton is a small place. Everyone knows everyone. Children you played with on your first birthday are the same ones you graduate with from high school. It was the same for Jermaine and I—except I'd dropped out of high school when I got pregnant and married Jermaine."

She caught the question in his expression before he had a chance to voice it. "I know I told you that I didn't have any children…but the truth is more complicated than that."

Daniel stretched his hand out to cover hers. "Look you don't have to discuss this if you don't want to," he assured her.

"I know," she whispered and gently flipped his hand over and caressed his palm.

Daniel sucked in a breath and pulled his hand away.

Surprised, Gia also pulled back and settled her hands into her lap. "Is something wrong?" she asked.

His eyes glossed, but no tears fell as he shook his head. "No." He stretched his hand across the table again and waited. "I have a feeling that everything is just how it's supposed to be."

Gia stared at his long fingers and then into his dark eyes. Without another thought, she placed her hand back into his. He's a keeper, a voice floated inside of her head.

But am I ready?

Their date floated like a dream and Gia never did get around to telling Daniel the truth about her daughter. Instead, the couple conversed about the trials and heartaches of being the spouse left behind. When dinner came to an end, Gia praised how much she enjoyed the evening.

"It's not over yet," he said, starting the car.

Gia glanced at her watch and noted it was nearing eleven. "I don't know. It's getting kind of late." The longer she was with him, the more in danger she was of losing her heart. "I really—"

"Come on. Trust me. You're going to love this next stop." Daniel winked, and then surprised Gia by taking her to Brooklyn to the Up and Over Jazz Café.

"You're a fan?" she inquired, gazing over at him.

"Fan is too mild a word," he confided as he led her to a small circular table near the front. "Wait until you get a load of the Eddie Allen Quartet," he whispered, pulling out her chair.

Gia didn't have the heart to tell him that she didn't know the first thing about jazz. Her music heroes were a weird mesh of Michael Jackson and Run DMC; however, when an older gentleman lifted his saxophone and played a soul-stirring melody, she was hooked. Throughout the song, she couldn't pull her gaze way from the musician. And though there were no words, she was certain that it was a song about loneliness and heartbreak.

When the haunting melody ended, she wiped her tears and applauded.

"I hope that means you like it?" Daniel asked.

"That was beautiful," she said, mopping her eyes again.

"Yeah. T. K. Blue can play a mean sax."

"Ladies and gentlemen, welcome to the lovely Up and Over Jazz Café," T. K. greeted the audience. "We hope you'll enjoy your evening with us tonight. If this is your first time, please make yourself right at home." He smiled and then squinted down into the front row. "Well, well. Look who we have here with us tonight."

Gia followed the man's gaze and was stunned that it landed on her date.

"Dr. Daniel Davis," their host laughed. "Mighty long time since we've seen you here."

Daniel gave him a tentative nod and a broad smile.

"Maybe if we ask nicely, we can get the good doctor to join us on a few numbers."

"No, no," Daniel chuckled.

However, the crowd applauded and tried their best to coax him up on the stage.

"You should play," Gia also encouraged. Dr. Davis was full of surprises.

He shook his head. "It's been *too* long."

"C'mon, man. Get your butt up here," T. K. commanded.

"I would love to hear you play," Gia said sweetly.

Daniel hesitated and stared into her eyes. "In that case, I'll do it…for you." He winked at her and stood from his chair.

She watched him as he made his way to the stage while the applause grew louder. The musicians huddled for a moment and then finally Daniel took his place behind the piano.

The band instantly launched into a snazzy number that had Gia tapping her feet and rocking in her chair. Daniel's talent left her utterly amazed. Pure unadulterated joy radiated from Daniel and, in turn, she enjoyed herself that much more.

After two head-rocking, toe-tapping songs, a beautiful

full-figured woman made her way from behind the drum-set to take the front microphone.

"I figured, we would do a little number to get everyone in the mood for the holidays," Daniel informed the audi-ence from his bench. "A few of you out there know that Christmas is my favorite time of the year." He glanced at Gia. "So we're going to do one of my favorite songs."

She smiled back and enjoyed the feeling of those flutter-ing butterflies.

He tickled the ivories for a brief while and Gia instantly recognized the song.

The female singer cooed seductively into the mike. "I really can't stay."

"But baby it's cold outside," Daniel's velvet voice joined in.

"I've got to go away."

Gia shook her head and laughed at the memory of their brief conversation before coming to the café. It was a great rendition and they received a thunderous ap-plause at the end.

By the end of the night, Daniel was right: She did enjoy their time at the jazz club. By the time he returned her to her door, it was well past three in the morning—but she didn't want the night to end.

"I guess this is good night." She smiled.

"Sorry I kept you up past your bedtime."

"I'll live."

He nodded and inched closer. "I really had a nice time."

"So did I," she managed to respond as the air thinned in her lungs.

"Does that mean we can do it again sometime?" He leaned in another inch.

"Sure. I'd like that."

"When?" His warm breath rushed against her cheek.

Her brain fogged and scrambled her thoughts. "Huh?"

Daniel smiled. "When would you like to go out again?"

"When?"

"Yes, when?"

It was on the tip of her tongue to ask him to come back in a few hours for breakfast, but she knew such a request would make her come off as too eager. "Whenever you're free," she finally settled on saying.

"Tomorrow night?" he asked.

His lips now were just inches away from her mouth. She was practically salivating for the taste of him. "Tomorrow will be great."

"Good. I'll pick you up at the same time tomorrow."

Gia opened her mouth to speak, but was caught off guard when Daniel's lips pressed gently against hers. A soft moan escaped her as her arms drifted up and around his neck. She drew him closer and marveled at how he tasted like heaven and sin at the same time.

He's the kind you keep. She moaned again though she knew the voice in her head spoke the truth.

He's the kind you keep. Gia could feel the tears rising behind her lashes.

He's the kind you keep. She sighed and finally ended their kiss. "Good night," she whispered and turned toward her door.

"Until tomorrow," he whispered back.

She closed her eyes and shivered at the feel of his warm breath against the shell of her ear. "Until tomorrow." She entered her apartment and closed the door without chancing a glance back. It wasn't until she secured the locks that she allowed herself to exhale.

She was on dangerous ground, she knew. After knowing Daniel for less than forty-eight hours, she already knew that she didn't want to go back to a life without him. She pondered that thought for a moment. She had completely lost her mind, but the revelation refused to change. "Oh, Jermaine. What should I do now?"

CHAPTER 7

The streets of Manhattan were a madhouse while Starr, Neve, and Daniel shivered and quaked for nearly five hours on Fifth Avenue, waiting for the lighting of the Christmas tree. As the time neared 9:00 p.m., the night was abuzz with excitement.

"Are you girls ready?" Daniel asked, draping his arms around each of the girl's shoulders.

Starr nodded. She would've answered, but she was more concerned about her inability to feel her toes.

"How cold do you think it is?" Neve asked as she tried to huddle closer.

"Like fifty below or something ridiculous like that," Starr answered and leaned against her dad.

"Hey, you're the one who wanted to come down here," Daniel reminded her with a chuckle. "We could've stayed in the comfort of our nice *warm* home and watched this whole thing on television."

"Yeah. How come we couldn't make our wish at home?" Neve asked.

"Because we had to be here in person for it to work," Starr reasoned with a flash of annoyance.

"Said who?" Neve challenged.

"It's common sense," Starr said. "Whoever heard of making a wish via a television set?"

"Girls, girls," her father interrupted. "Calm down. We're here, so let's make the best of it."

The friends' narrowed gazes softened and seconds later, they flashed each other smiles.

"We have less than five minutes," her dad announced after a glance at his watch.

"So how come you didn't invite your new lady friend to come here with us tonight?" Starr asked. "And when am I going to meet her?"

"Whoa. Whoa." Daniel held up his hands. "Please tell me that my daughter isn't butting her nose in grown people's business."

"C'mon. You know you like her." She elbowed him. "You've been out with her several nights in a row."

He shook his head. "I don't hear you."

"Yeah, you like her. I heard you singing in the shower this morning. It must have been some date last night. Where did you go?"

"Starr, I'm not going to discuss this with you," he reprimanded out of embarrassment more than anger.

In response, she twinkled a smile at him.

A minute later, he nodded. "Yeah, I like her."

"Ten, nine, eight…"

Starr turned expectant eyes toward the tree. "Don't forget to make your wishes exactly when the lights come on," Starr shouted.

"Four, three, two, one…"

The lights flashed on—and the Christmas tree was an instant glorious sight. Starr, Neve, and Daniel squeezed their eyes closed and made a wish…

Gia opened her eyes and sighed into the night.

"What did you wish for?" Bernie asked, leaning toward her. "Please tell me it was for the winning lottery."

Gia shook her head and exhaled a long stream of white frost. "Don't be silly. You know I don't believe in such nonsense."

"Oh, no?" Bernie's smile widened. "Then why were your eyes closed?"

"I'll tell you what I wished for." Tonya turned and popped into the conversation. "A car."

Bernie groaned at the major hint her sixteen year-old daughter tossed her way. "The only car you're getting after those pathetic grades you've been pulling is a Matchbox car."

"Amen." Bernie's husband, Vinny, tossed back his head with a hearty chuckle.

Tonya rolled her eyes and then gave Gia a wounded look.

She sympathized with a casual shrug. Of course, she knew Tonya's one *D* in a long list of *A*s was not going to deter her parents from buying the hard-working teenager a car. But her parents got a kick out of making the teenager squirm.

Gia returned her attention to the breathtaking seventy-nine foot Christmas tree and drew in a long cold breath. When Tonya told Gia to make a wish upon the star, she had at first thought to wish that her company would have a banner year, then she thought about Daniel, then Ma Belle—which surprised her.

The only time she thought about her grandmother was when she made out a monthly check to send back home—checks that were never cashed. Maybe this year she would call them on Christmas. When the crowd commenced the countdown, however, another thought bubbled to the top of her mind—actually it was a seed of hope that grew with each second of the countdown.

The moment the tree lit up, she squeezed her eyes closed and made her heart's true wish: *I want to be reunited with my daughter.*

Shivering in the cold with her eyes fixed upon New York's finest Christmas tree, she still felt a residue of hope bloom in her heart. But it was impossible, wasn't it?

Later that night, while lying in bed, Gia stared into the darkness surrounding her. Should she dare look for her daughter? What would she say if she found her?

The phone rang and startled her. It was the stroke of midnight and she knew precisely who was calling her.

"Good morning, Dr. Davis," she greeted, smiling.

"Good morning, Gia. I hope I didn't wake you," he said with a note of caution.

"No. Actually, I'm wide awake," she admitted honestly. "How did your evening go?"

"Great. Despite the fact that I froze my butt off," he chuckled.

"Ditto." Gia sat up and leaned back against the headboard. "Bernie and Tonya dragged me down there this afternoon as well."

"You're kidding me. You mean we all could've gone together?"

"Seems so."

Daniel's question implied he was ready for her to meet his daughter. Even though things were going well with them, she was pretty sure she wasn't ready for that gigantic leap.

Often, when Daniel spoke of his daughter it was with a glowing pride that left Gia envious. Her regret was an emotion that grew heavier each year. She was at a point now where she needed help shouldering the load, but asking for help was something she was unaccustomed to doing.

"I want to see you again," Daniel said.

She closed her eyes and allowed his words to stir her butterflies. "I'd like that." Mildly, she wondered if this *need* to be around him was such a good thing or was she just setting herself up for an eventual downfall. Too much too fast was a dangerous thing for a new relationship.

A new relationship—was that what they were in? She straightened, suddenly uncomfortable with everything having to do with this man.

"I do have to do some Christmas shopping tomorrow, but after that, I'm free. What about you?" he asked.

"I actually have some work I need to finish," she admitted. "I have three design boards I have to finish by the end of the week and—"

"Oh, yeah, yeah. You don't have to explain. I completely understand. We just met and here I am hogging up all your time."

"No. It's nothing like that," she rushed to explain, but her unease wouldn't go away. "I've enjoyed our time together."

Daniel heard a "but" in the hanging sentence and consequently felt like an ass. Had he been pushing too hard—going too fast? "I've had a good time, too." He drew a deep breath and exhaled it slowly. "Well, it's getting late. I should let you go."

"It's not...I mean, if you have to go—"

"Yeah. Just give me a call if you find some time tomorrow. I should be around here somewhere." He laughed awkwardly.

"Okay. I'll do that," she said softly.

They held the phone for a few long, awkward seconds, and then finally disconnected. Daniel stared at the portable hand held unit with a wave of dread crashing against his body. He pressed the instant replay button in his mind and was still unsure of what just happened and how it went wrong.

He didn't get much sleep that night and Starr accused him of being distracted during breakfast. So this was what it was like being back in the dating arena—a dizzying see-saw of emotions where you're constantly guessing and wondering what the other person is feeling.

Oh, joy.

The thing was, he really liked Gia. She was strong,

smart, and beautiful. My, was she beautiful. The way her eyes lit up when she smiled or laughed. She even had this way of making him want to drop everything to take care of her when at times she looked so sad about something.

It usually happened whenever he talked about Starr. He pondered that for a while.

"I know I told you I didn't have any children...but the truth is more complicated than that."

What exactly did she mean?

On the fourth day he hadn't heard from Gia, Daniel saw the writing on the wall: she wasn't interested. Though it was difficult to put the matter behind him, he was determined to the forge ahead, put a smile on his face, and prepared to enjoy the holidays with his daughter. Yet, in the back of his mind, he couldn't help but wonder at what could have been.

CHAPTER 8

"Twelve days before Christmas and you're not doing anything but staring at the phone," Bernie accused, plopping down a stack of accounts that needed review. "Why don't you do us both a favor and just call him?"

"I don't know what you're talking about." Gia shifted her gaze to the pile of swatches on her desk.

"Uh-huh." Bernie cocked her head and crossed her arms. "Then let me tell you what I'm talking about— Call Daniel. What's the point of pretending that you don't like him?"

"I never said I didn't like him," Gia said stiffly. "I've just been busy that's all."

Bernie stared.

"It wouldn't have worked out anyway," Gia added. "It never does."

"Sounds like you're scared."

"Don't be ridiculous," she huffed. However, her heart

quickened at just how close Bernie was to the truth. "I just dated the man for a week."

"Every night for a week and then ran away for another week. C'mon. Maybe this guy really is the one. Have you thought about that?"

In truth, she could think of little else. "It just can't be this simple," Gia mumbled.

"Believe it or not, sometimes love is simple."

"Love? Who said anything about love? I just said I liked the guy." She bolted to her feet and paced behind her desk. "Who wouldn't like him? He holds out chairs, opens car doors, and sings like…"

"He sings, too?"

"Oh, Bernie." She sank back into her chair. "He has the most incredible voice and the things that man can do on a piano."

Bernie's brow lifted.

"Get your mind out of the gutter," Gia reprimanded. "But all of that isn't why I…like him." She swallowed. "It's the way he talks about his daughter. The pride and love he has for her is so humbling…and in some ways it makes me feel so undeserving of a man like him."

"What? That's silly."

"Is it?" Gia challenged. "He's a man who's all about family and doing the *right* thing. I haven't even spoken to anyone in my family in years." She glanced down at her hands. She had never shared any of this with Bernie. Avoidance was Gia's specialty.

"What happened?" Bernie asked.

"I made one of the biggest mistakes of my life," she

whispered. "I sacrificed my child to save myself." When she glanced up again, tears streamed down her face. "How can a man who values family so much ever understand what I've done?"

Starr, Neve, and her dad meticulously combed through Goodman's Tree Farm. Hands down, this was one of Starr's favorite traditions: finding the perfect tree. She would always pick the ones that were too big to squeeze into the house and her dad would always pretend to fall in love with the puniest thing on the lot, and in the old days her mother would always stumble onto the one that was just right.

Starr smiled weakly at the memory.

"So what do you think happened between that lady and your dad?" Neve whispered.

Starr glanced at her father who was busily inspecting a three-foot tree. "I don't know. Like always, he's keeping things pretty close to his vest." She sighed. "I thought we were so close this time."

"Well, you know what I think," Neve hinted.

Instead of tossing up her usual protests or excuses, Starr felt herself wavering. Her father needed someone whether he wanted to admit it or not.

"Hey, Starr," her dad shouted. "What do you think?" he asked, gesturing toward a stick with three branches.

She played her role to the hilt by rolling her eyes and droning, "I don't think so, Dad."

"Is that supposed to be a tree?" Neve whispered.

"He's just playing," Starr assured, and then watched her father meander off to find another ghastly choice. In her mind, she cut back to the day her father had met the attractive interior designer and the way he lit up around her. What *did* go wrong?

Her thoughts danced around the question until the three of them stumbled upon the perfect eight-foot tree, two hours later—consequently, it gave Starr her next big idea.

Gia picked up the phone and dialed the first three digits to Daniel's home, but as her prepared speech jumbled in her head, she quickly hung up. She wanted to call mainly because she feared what Bernie had said was true: *maybe this guy really is the one.*

She sighed and tightened the belt on her robe. It was more like wishful thinking on her part. Her confession to her best friend today was dead on. She had no right wanting a man like Dr. Daniel Davis.

Standing at the window of her apartment, she gazed at the buildings across the street. Christmas lights, glowing Santas, and miniature nativity scenes could be seen in just about every window. In the street, she could make out a few teenagers engaged in a fierce snowball fight. It was just another sign of families enjoying the holidays.

She retreated to her bathroom to rummage through her medicine cabinet. How could she have allowed two weeks to pass without getting a refill of her antidepressants?

The doorbell rang and Gia frowned. All her friends knew her golden rule: Call before you come over. So who was at her door?

At the bell's second chime, she again tightened the belt

on her robe and headed toward the front door. After peering through the peephole, Gia couldn't make out what was on the other side. It sort of looked like something was blocking the door.

"Who is it?"

"Santa Claus."

Gia's heart leapt at Daniel's unmistakable voice. *What is he doing here?* Her hand flew to her wet hair and she glanced down at her attire.

"Hello," he called through the door when she hesitated too long.

"Yes, huh. Just a minute." She sweated a few more bullets while teetering in limbo on what to do.

"I know I should have called," Daniel explained through the door. "But while I was out shopping for a Christmas tree tonight, I was reminded of something you said to me."

"What was that?" she asked, leaning against the door and feeling a bubble of hope rise within her.

"I remember you wanted to turn over a new leaf this Christmas. So I'm here to help you out." Daniel waited. At the sound of the locks turning, he finally released a sigh of relief and allowed a broad smile to monopolize his face.

Gia opened the door and gasped in surprise at the sight of the large pine tree clogging the hallway. "You brought me a Christmas tree?"

Her gaze swung to him and he was warmed by its radiance. "You didn't have one the last time I was here, so I took the liberty to help you get into the spirit. I hope you don't mind."

She flashed him a smile that was more beautiful than he remembered before she stepped back and allowed him entrance into the apartment. It took a bit of work but Daniel finally squeezed the large tree through the door.

"Nothing says Christmas like a trail of pine needles," Gia joked.

"Ah. You might feel that way now, but wait until we get this baby up and decorated. I guarantee you'll be in the Christmas spirit by then."

"You also brought decorations?"

"Hey, I came prepared," Daniel winked, and then casually glanced over her attire. "I'm not complaining, but, uhm, you might want to put on something more appropriate for climbing trees."

Her cheeks darkened prettily. "In that case I'll go change."

Daniel nodded and watched her disappear toward the back. Starr's bright idea just earned her another gift under the tree. He was very aware of how badly things could have turned out—how things could *still* turn out.

A few minutes later, Gia returned to the living room dressed in a pair of formfitting jeans and a red sweater just tight enough to stir the blood in any man with a pulse.

"Can I get you anything—maybe something to drink?"

"Some coffee would great," he answered, jarring out of his trance. "I hope you're not angry with me for just dropping by?" he asked tentatively.

Gia retrieved a can of Folgers from the cabinet and smiled. "No. I'm not angry…just surprised."

He nodded, but still felt like he was treading on thin ice.

"Actually, I've been wanting to call you," she began.

He definitely didn't like the sound of that. "Oh?" he asked, drawing a deep breath and preparing for the worst.

"Yeah. Each time...I chickened out."

Daniel remained composed though his heart was trying to hammer its way out of his chest.

"But I'm glad you came over. You made my night." Her smiled brightened and she made the coffee.

Daniel relaxed, but then grew curious. "Why would you chicken out?"

Gia hit the brew button and crossed her arms. "It's complicated."

He studied her as he nodded. "Well, I'll let it go at that...but when you're ready to talk, I've been told I'm a pretty good listener."

"I'll remember that."

"Good." He clapped his hands. "Now let's go down to my car and get those decorations. Shall we?"

"Okay." Gia quickly bounded out of the kitchen and grabbed her coat by the door. "I can't believe that I'm actually doing this," she said, slipping on her gloves.

"Trust me. You're going to have fun." He winked.

The moment the couple stepped out of the apartment building, an errant snowball hit Daniel.

"Sorry, Mister!" a kid yelled.

Daniel held up his hands. "Not a problem."

Gia laughed and then clamped a hand over her mouth.

"What, you think that's funny?" Daniel asked, grinning.

"It's sort of—"

Bam! Gia was hit in the shoulder by another runaway snowball.

"Hey!" Gia turned toward the snow battling children.

"Sorry, Ma'am," the kids called.

"Now that was funny!" Daniel chuckled.

"Uh-huh." She knelt down and began gathering snow. "There are four of them, but I think we can take them."

"What?"

"Hey, I'm a woman who believes in revenge."

"We can't—"

Bam! Another snowball smacked him in the chest.

"Sorry, Mister!"

"You were saying?" Gia asked, smiling sweetly up at him.

Daniel knelt beside her. "You're right. We can take them."

Gia launched the first snowball. With an astounding aim, it hit one of the boys in the center of his back.

That was all it took to commence a war.

Daniel sent his own snowball flying and caught the shoulder blade of one of the teenage boys.

"Good hit!" Gia declared, but then was smacked soundly on the side of her head by return fire.

Squealing, she rocketed two balls in almost rapid succession. But nothing was as hilarious as watching Daniel take two in the face.

Temporarily flattened on his back, Gia struggled to help him up, but she took four hits and toppled over on top of him.

Laughing, the couple scrambled on hands and knees to find protection behind a parked car.

"We're surrounded," Daniel chuckled.

"We can't give up," Gia gathered more snow. The moment she stood up, however, she took a direct hit in the face and toppled right back into Daniel's lap.

"Yeah, that's showing them."

They laughed as she sat up in his lap, but it soon faded to small puffs of frosted air when their eyes and lips were just inches apart.

Daniel remembered the taste of her lips and, despite the cold, his body stirred to life. He didn't want to move too fast or scare her off again, but he wanted to kiss her, too.

To his surprise, she made the first move and closed the small gap between them. The petals of her lips were softer than he remembered and their taste was intoxicatingly sweet. For a brief moment he was lost to a roaring passion that threatened everything he'd ever known. Nothing that tasted this good or felt so right could ever be wrong, he reasoned.

However, their attackers had other ideas.

"Ah!" Gia screamed when another snowball hit the back of her neck.

The war was back on.

However, it wasn't long before Daniel and Gia had to reconsider their position. Sure they managed to get in a few good hits, but the kids had speed and agility on their side. Defeat loomed before them.

In the end, World War III lasted all of twenty minutes.

"We surrender, we surrender!"

Gia and Daniel waved their hands from behind a parked car and were relieved when there was a cease-fire.

By the time, they returned to Gia's apartment with bags of decorations, they were sopping wet and chilled to the bone.

"I definitely could go for that coffee now," Gia chuckled, lowering her bags onto the sofa.

"That makes two of us."

Gia slowly peeled out of her coat, amazed at the amount of snow that made it inside of her clothes. "I'm going to change again. You might want to get out of those clothes before you catch your death."

Daniel twisted his face in a fake frown. "Are you coming on to me?"

She smiled, feeling flirtatious. "What if I am?"

"In that case." He settled his jacket over the back of his chair and moved closer until he could feel the gentle radiation of her body heat. "I'd tell you that you don't have to work so hard."

He drew her close and sampled her lips once again. Problem was, he couldn't stop kissing her, nor could he stop peeling off her clothes.

CHAPTER 9

G ia was lost in a world of passion to a man she hardly knew. The array of candlelight had diminished somewhat, but it still provided enough light for her to watch as waves of ecstasy washed over his handsome features. She could recognize it because they were the same waves crashing through her.

Tears gathered and fell at the exquisite feel of him inside of her. In the back of Gia's mind, a voice reasoned that this coupling was nothing more than two adults seeking to satisfy a physical need.

But she wasn't buying it.

Something had clicked within her soul—something akin to two pieces of a puzzle finally snapping together. The completion of that puzzle was beautiful and divine.

Daniel produced a condom and then thought that he would die at how her body sheathed him. Like an addict, his lips returned to her mouth, and he was completely at peace to drown in their sweet taste.

She twisted breathlessly beneath him while her warm passage grew increasingly tight. Together their breathing and leisurely pace quickened until a spark ignited in the core of their souls.

He hiked her hips and dove deeper.

A cry of rapture tore from her lips and, soon after, an explosion erupted inside him and he clutched her body as his roar of release filled the apartment.

"Good Lord, you are incredible," he panted against her ear.

She chuckled lightly and brushed her breasts against his chest. "You weren't so bad yourself."

He stole a quick kiss. "Do we know what we're doing?"

"Haven't a clue," she answered honestly. "That's been the case since the moment I met you."

Daniel rolled onto his side, but still held her close. "I should tell you that I don't do one night stands." His heart sank a bit when her gaze lowered.

"You're not going to try and convince me that you're in love with me, are you?" she asked.

He wondered at the tremble in her voice. "You don't believe in love at first sight?"

"Things like that don't happen to me. I don't deserve it."

She pulled away, but Daniel held her firmly in place. "What do you mean by that?"

"Please, let me go." Her eyes glossed.

Daniel's heartstrings tightened but he refused to release his hold. "Talk to me." He kissed her. "Trust me."

Gia was tempted.

Daniel's lips slowly traveled the column of her neck and then languished lazily at the crook of her collarbone. "Talk to me. Tell me what you're afraid of."

Her lips trembled and struggled to hold on to her secrets, but as his lips continued their descent, her body grew warm and the truth about her past, her regrets, and her fears poured out of her.

"It's past midnight," Neve said, brushing on a final coat of nail polish on her toes. "That's a good sign, right?"

"I don't want to say that I'm a genius, but I *am* a genius."

"So when do you think we'll get the chance to meet her?"

"Soon I hope."

"What if she turns out to be like this awful stepmother and has children of her own? Next thing you know you'll be like this modern-day Cinderella."

"Oh quit it. That story had a happy ending, by the way."

"Yeah, but look at what she had to go through." Neve shrugged. "I'm not too sure it was all worth it."

"Look, my father would never fall for some evil, manipulative woman. Trust me on that. This Ms. Hunter has to be really someone special to snag my father. You saw how picky he was when we were trying to set him up."

"Yeah, I hope my mom will be easier." Neve brightened. "Maybe we can find her someone for Valentine's Day."

"Hey, what about Principal Hedley? He's single," Starr suggested.

"Our principal? Are you kidding me? How weird would that be?"

"Yeah, you're right." Starr waved her nails around in the air. "Don't worry. We'll think of something. First let's keep our fingers crossed about this Gia Hunter. I have a feeling that she really could be the one."

"So what about your plans to find your real mother?" Neve asked. "Are you still going to contact the adoption agency?"

Starr drew a deep breath and met her friend's direct gaze head on. "I already have."

Somewhere in between making love and confessions, Gia and Daniel finished decorating her first-ever Christmas tree. The beauty of what they created—both while making love and the tree—filled Gia with a warm glow. What truly surprised her was that there was no judgment in his expression—just complete understanding and support.

Yet, when she described the minefield between her and her family, it was the first time he looked at her with something akin to disappointment in his eyes.

"It's just complicated," she finally settled on saying.

Daniel said nothing, but continued to hold her.

"Besides, it's too late. Too much time has passed."

"As long as you're both alive," he said, kissing the top of her head. "It's never too late."

She shook her head and closed her eyes. She had plenty of time to figure this whole thing out. Right now, she just wanted Daniel to hold her forever.

Thoughts of Talboton and Ma Belle were put on the back burner. Gia's arms tightened around Daniel. After so many years, it was time for her to be happy.

* * *

Five days before Christmas, Glenda could barely pull herself together. She had cried so hard and for so long, her eyes remained puffy and bloodshot red 24/7.

Not only that, but the usually ornery Ma Belle had changed her tune and was now asking for Gia every hour on the hour.

"Call her," Byron growled through the phone and fixed his hard stare on her through the prison's Plexiglas. "How you goin' deny her dyin' wish?"

"You don't understand." Glenda raked her hands through her dry, unpermed hair. "Gia escaped this place once. I ain't gonna drag her back here and let this place dig its claws into her again. I won't do it."

"You talkin' nonsense. After all Ma Belle's done for us— takin' us in after Ma died, and then helped raised our chil'in, you gonna sit there and deny her dyin' wish? Hell, you still livin' up in her house, gurl."

Glenda wiped away another stream of tears. "You ain't got it in you to understand. I'm doin' this for Gia. If she wanted to see Ma Belle, she would've been here. I ain't tryin' hurt nobody. I'm just tryin' to do what's right."

Byron shook his head. "You wrong, Glenda. I can't do much about it while I'm locked up, but I'm going to be out of here in a couple of days. And you can bet your last dollar I'm callin' Gia as soon as I walk out."

A nervous Gia kept her eyes on the clock. Tonight, she was going to meet Daniel's beloved daughter Starr. Daniel had arranged for them to spend an evening at Radio City

Music Hall. One minute, Gia was excited and anxious, and in the next, she was nauseous and thinking of every excuse she could to back out.

"You're meeting the daughter?" Bernie plopped into the seat across from Gia's desk. "That's the equivalent of meeting the parents—if not more."

Gia reached into her desk and removed a packet of Alka-Seltzer. "Please, let's just change the subject."

"Are you kidding me? This is the longest relationship I've known you to be in and you want me to just drop it? Not on your life." She settled back in her chair and crossed her arms. "Do you know what I have to go through to get Vinny to get our tree every year? It's like pulling teeth."

"So if a man brings you a Christmas tree he's a keeper?"

"No. If a man brings you a Christmas tree, plays with you in the snow, and puts a smile of your face like the one you've been wearing for the last five days, *then* he's a keeper."

Gia knew she was right. It was hard enough not to melt every time she spoke his name or even thought about him. Daniel had a way of making her feel young and loved. And she was falling in love with him as well.

"Well, I, for one, am glad that this day has finally come. You deserve to be happy. Grab on to this man and don't you dare let him go."

Gia nodded, and then was startled when her phone rang.

"I'm going. I'm going." Bernice bounded out her chair. "It might be Dr. Davis again. You just remember what I said."

Shaking her head, Gia answered the phone.

"Hello. This is Wendy Robinson at the Independent Adoption Agency in Atlanta, Georgia. Is this Ms. Gia Hunter?"

Gia's heart leapt into her throat as she sat up in her chair. "Yes it is."

"Great. I'm calling because we received an inquiry from your daughter. She wants to meet you."

Daniel hadn't intended to read his daughter's personal mail, however, while he was straightening up the dining room, his eyes snagged on a company's letterhead: Independent Adoption Agency.

Starr was searching for her biological mother—and she hadn't said a word to him.

He lowered into one of the chairs at the dining room table. His hands trembled as his eyes scanned the letter. Yet, before he could finish, the front door opened and his daughter and her constant companion entered the house.

"Hey, Dad," Starr shouted. "Wait until you see the outfit I bought for tonight. You're just going to—"

Daniel's gaze clashed with Starr's when she finally strolled into the dining room.

"What are you doing?" she asked.

It was a simple question, but it was one he had trouble answering.

"That's mine." Her eyes narrowed. "Why are you reading my mail?"

"You left it out," he said simply, and then glanced to her frozen friend. "Neve, do you mind going home? I would like to talk to Starr in private."

Neve's sympathetic gaze shifted to Starr, but she wisely retreated backwards toward the door. "I'll call you later," she said, and then flashed a flat smile when she didn't receive a response.

The house became as silent as a tomb until the click of the front door announced Neve's final departure.

Starr slowly crossed her arms and lifted her chin. "Why are you reading my mail?"

"I didn't mean to," he answered softly and placed the offending letter down on the table. Though his brain was crammed packed with questions, he struggled to pull one out of the clutter.

Starr moved toward the table and picked it up.

"It says that they will be delivering your file within the week. Am I doing such a terrible job?" he finally asked.

His daughter's stern expression collapsed. "How could you possibly think that?" she asked with a tone of disbelief.

The tightening in his chest loosened a bit, but he still didn't know how to handle this latest information. Wasn't this the thing that Hilary always feared: the biological mother showing up and taking Starr away from the people who loved her. "If you wanted to meet your real mother I wish you would've told me." He held her gaze. "I would've helped."

"It's not what you think." Starr's shoulders deflated and she pulled up another chair. "In fact you probably wouldn't believe me if I told you what I had in mind."

Daniel patiently folded his hands in his lap. "Why don't you try me?"

"Well," she drew a deep breath. "I had hoped to pair you and my biological mother together—if she's still single."

Of all the things Daniel expected her to say that explanation was nowhere on the list. He took a few seconds to mull the confession again and then decided honesty should only be rewarded with honesty.

"Starr, that has to be the dumbest thing I have ever heard."

Gia paced inside her apartment with her nerves tied up in knots. She had several hours to digest the information from the adoption agency and she still couldn't believe the latest course of events. Her wish had come true.

She hadn't made a habit of believing in magic or anything else supernatural, but the call from the agency had her reconsidering. Now that the agency had gotten her okay, the next step was waiting for them to deliver her daughter her entire adoption file—complete with Gia's name and address.

A new waiting game.

There was the possibility that her daughter would receive the file and still never contact her, but she quickly pushed those thoughts aside. So far this season had brought her out of her depression, had given her Daniel, and now her daughter.

The doorbell rang and jarred her out of her stupor. She had forgotten to cancel her date. She glanced at her watch as she headed toward the door. It was an hour before show time and she wasn't even dressed.

She stopped at the front door with her hand on the knob when she suddenly remembered Daniel was coming with his daughter.

She glanced down just as the doorbell rang again.

"I'm off to a great start," she mumbled and pulled open the door. She greeted Daniel with a smile, but then Gia's gaze shifted. She froze unable to believe that she was staring into the eyes of her deceased husband.

CHAPTER 10

"Oh my God." Gia stepped back but her knees suddenly couldn't support her.

"Are you all right?" Daniel rushed forward and caught Gia before she hit the floor.

"Dad, what's wrong?"

Tears glossed Gia's eyes and then streamed down her face as her gaze took in the teenager's nose, cheeks, and lips. She knew those features all too well, but couldn't wrap her brain around how this was possible.

Daniel easily swooped her into his arms as though she weighed nothing. "Let's get you over to the sofa," he announced. "Starr, can you go into the kitchen and get her some water?"

Starr entered the apartment and meandered around until she found the kitchen.

Meanwhile, Gia dropped her face into her hands and

tried to get a grip on herself. It had to be stress that was doing this to her. She couldn't possibly be seeing what she thought she was.

"Are you all right, baby?" Daniel asked again as he gently brushed her hair back from her face. "C'mon talk to me."

"It's not possible," Gia mumbled, trying to convince herself that her eyes were playing tricks on her.

"Here, Daddy." Starr returned to the room.

Gia spread her fingers and peeked through them. She hadn't been dreaming. "How can this be?"

Starr nervously glanced at her father.

Gia lowered her hands and Daniel pressed a glass of water into it.

"Here, drink this."

She obeyed, but her gaze remained locked on his daughter. After draining the water in one long gulp, Gia quickly set the glass down on the coffee table and continued staring.

Starr fidgeted.

"Gia," Daniel said softly. "Do I need to call someone?"

Shaking her head, Gia pushed herself to stand up. However, when she took a step toward Starr, the teenager retreated. Suddenly, realizing how her behavior was probably frightening the young girl, Gia smiled to lighten the mood. It didn't help.

The room remained layered with tension and Gia quickly came up with a plan to relieve it. She rushed out of her living room and dashed to her bedroom. When she returned to her stunned guests, she handed Daniel a picture. "That's my late husband Jermaine."

Daniel stared at her as he accepted the picture.

"Look at him."

He glanced down, blinked, and then brought the picture closer to his face.

Now Gia fidgeted with her hand while sneaking more glances at Starr.

With disbelief etched into his features as well, Daniel glanced up at his daughter.

"What?" Starr asked. Finally tired of the adults' odd behavior, Starr moved toward her father and reached for the photograph in his hand. One glance at the handsome man posed in a military uniform and Starr also needed help standing.

The resemblance was too similar to be ignored. "Who is this?"

Gia swallowed. "My deceased husband."

Starr leaned more of her weight against her father. "Why—why does he look like me?"

Gia opened her mouth but couldn't speak. There was still a great possibility that all of this was just a coincidence.

"You gave up a child for adoption," Daniel said slowly. "And Hilary and I adopted a child."

Gia nodded.

Daniel looked as though he needed to sit down as well, but he continued to stand and support his daughter. "We received a letter today," he began.

Gia's heart leapt to her throat. "I received a call."

"F-from whom?" Starr asked.

"The Independent Adoption Agency out of Atlanta."

"Ohmigosh." Starr clamped a hand over her mouth. "You're my mother."

* * *

The next 24 hours passed in a blur as Gia, Starr, and Daniel got to know each other. The hardest part for Gia was explaining the circumstances surrounding Starr's adoption. But she took great pride in telling Starr about her real father. To be sure, Gia and Starr took a DNA test.

After nearly fifteen years, mother and daughter were finally reunited.

For Christmas Eve, Gia invited Daniel and her daughter over to her place for a small get together. Close friends and a few associates gathered for the opportunity to meet Gia's daughter.

Being that it was going to be her first Christmas with Starr, Gia had also gone on a mad shopping spree that amazed Bernie. She was driven by a need to give her daughter anything and everything her heart desired. So when Daniel and Starr showed up with their own armloads of gifts they were completely blown away by the amount of packages stuffed under Gia's tree.

"Ms. Hunter, you shouldn't have," Starr said with wide eyes.

"Please, call me Gia," she said, though in her heart she longed for her daughter to call her *Mom*. Maybe one day.

It became an exciting time for Gia and Starr; however, things grew a little awkward between Gia and Daniel.

"Hey, what are you doing hiding in here?" Gia asked, entering the kitchen.

"Oh, nothing. I just came in here for...for a few minutes." Daniel set his cup of eggnog down on the counter.

Gia drew a breath when she realized Daniel was going out of his way to avoid making eye contact.

"Have things changed between us?" she asked bluntly.

His gaze still refused to meet hers. "I don't know."

She nodded and braided her hands together. "I'm not trying to steal her away from you."

"Are you sure?"

Gia sucked in a breath, but waited until he finally looked at her. "I fell for you long before I knew about Starr."

"Now that you know?"

"I hope to always be a part of her life…even if it doesn't work out between us. Though I hope that it does."

"Why?"

She drew a breath but held his gaze. "Because you taught me how to love again. You pulled me out of a dark place, introduced me to jazz, and taught me how to love Christmas." Gia dried the corners of her eyes before the tears had a chance to fall. She couldn't tell if rejection was on the horizon and she felt stripped and vulnerable.

At last, Daniel smiled and closed the distance between them. "It has been a magical few weeks. I, too, didn't think that I would ever find love again."

"Love?" she asked in a shaky tremor.

"Am I going too fast for you?"

"Actually, this whole thing has felt more like a wild roller coaster—fast but exhilarating." She stared into the mirrors of his soul. "I love it and wouldn't have it any other way." A wide smile ballooned across her face.

Daniel leaned forward and savored a light kiss. "That makes two of us."

* * *

Starr and Neve stepped back from the kitchen and grinned at each other.

"Wow," Neve whispered. "Your wish came true. I wouldn't have ever believed this if I didn't see it with my own eyes."

Starr had a hard time believing it as well, but she couldn't deny that she was ecstatic about the whole situation. Gia Hunter was all that she had hoped for. After learning the circumstances of her adoption, she knew there was no way that she could hate her real mother. Not when such great parents had adopted her.

Yes, everything was just how it was supposed to be. "You know, Neve, this really is going to be the best Christmas ever."

Gia jumped away from Daniel when her phone rang and then laughed at herself. "Jeez, I'm being a lousy hostess," she said, heading toward the phone's wall unit. "Can you take those hors d'oeuvres out to the guests for me?"

"Certainly," Daniel answered with a chuckle. "Don't be too long. Your friends keep asking me when I'm going to propose."

"Oh yeah? When are you?" she asked, picking up the phone.

"Soon." Daniel replied. "Real soon." He exited the kitchen with a wink.

Shaking her head, Gia placed the phone against her ear and answered.

"Hello, Gia? I-it's me—Byron."

CHAPTER 11

Christmas, Talboton, GA

After the flight from hell, Gia rushed through the doors of Baptist Meriwether Hospital by noon with her heart lodged in her throat and tears streaming down her face.

"Can I help you, ma'am?" a woman inquired from behind the nurses station.

"Y-yes." She glanced around, and then swiped at her face with the back of her hand. "I'm here to see Maybelle Jackson. Can you tell me what room she's in?"

Daniel and Starr finally caught up with Gia while the nurse typed into the computer. "I'm showing she's in room three-twelve."

Gia turned and collided into Daniel. Before she had a chance to react, he gently kissed her forehead, and slid a supportive arm around her waist.

"C'mon. We'll help you find her."

Starr favored her mother with a nervous smile and it suddenly occurred to Gia that the young girl was within seconds of meeting more members of her biological family on, of all things, her birthday. How traumatic would it be for her to meet her maternal great-grandmother on the day that she…

Gia reached for her daughter's trembling hand and the small family walked down the hospital's empty hallways looking for room three-twelve. They rounded the corner and stopped when they saw a crowd spilling out of one of the rooms.

Family members—young and old all—stared at Gia slack jawed. Slowly, she inched toward them. Once the three of them maneuvered through the crowd to reach the door, Gia hesitated. What was she going to say?

"Baby," Daniel whispered. "You can do this."

Gia drew strength from him and lifted her head, but it took the squeeze from Starr's hand for her to push open the door.

The room was cold and dim.

The nerve-racking sounds of machines beeping and pulsing sent a shiver of fear racing down Gia's spine. Her attention locked on the outline on the bed and as she moved farther into the room, her gaze traveled its length.

A loud gasp came from someone sitting in a chair, but Gia blocked out the person as her eyes finally settled on the sleeping face of Ma Belle. It was a face both familiar and foreign to Gia, and she was suddenly overwhelmed by guilt.

"What are you doing here?"

Gia finally lifted her eyes to Glenda's hard gaze.

"I called her."

Gia jumped and turned around to see her brother Byron enter the room behind Daniel and Starr.

Glenda seethed. "I told you—"

"She's got every right to be here," Byron said with a dismissive tone, and then stared at Gia. "Ma Belle's been askin' for you."

Ma Belle drew a deep sigh and shifted in her bed, but her eyes remained closed. "Ya'll goin' keep all this racket up or are you goin' to let an ole woman get some rest?"

Gia smiled. Her grandma was going to be cantankerous to the end.

Byron maneuvered around the small crowd and moved toward the bed. "Ma," he said, taking her plump hand. "There's somebody here to see you."

"Honey chile, I'm too tired for more guests right now." She winced and shifted to get comfortable again. "Tell 'em to come back in the mornin'."

Gia immediately took a retreating step, but once again bumped against Daniel's chest.

Byron motioned Gia to the bed. "Ma, I think you want to see this person tonight. She came all the way from New York on account I told her you wanted to see her."

"New York?" Ma Belle questioned and finally pried open her eyes.

On trembling legs, Gia approached the bed. She was unprepared when Byron grabbed her hand and placed it atop of Ma Belle's. Her grandmother's hand felt more like a block of ice and it trembled as much as her own.

"G-Gia?" Ma Belle questioned. "Chile, is it really you?"

Gia opened her mouth but her warring emotions had choked off her vocal chords and she was unable to speak.

A smile slowly eased its way across Ma Belle's face. "My Lawd, I never thought I'd see your face again." She squeezed Gia's hand. "Glad to see I was wrong. 'Course, I realized I'm the reason you ran from town."

"No," Gia managed to whisper.

"Just 'cause I'm dyin' it's no reason for us to start lyin', chile. I pushed you to give up your baby and I had no right. It's just…"

"It's okay." Gia glanced over at Starr, who also had tears brimming in her eyes as she clutched her father. "Things worked out just fine, Ma."

"I tried my best with what little I had," Ma Belle went on. "I know you chil'en think I was always hard on you, but I treated you like my folks treated me. I always wanted the best for you and maybe I just didn't know how to go about gettin' it for you. I need you to forgive me because I had no right to—"

"*I* made the choice, Ma." Gia forced the truth out her mouth. "Me. I wanted to blame you, I tried to blame you. But it was *my* choice. You don't need to seek forgiveness from me because you did nothing wrong. I ran from Talboton trying to escape myself—but it didn't work." She sighed, thinking about the years she had spent depressed and then her thoughts turned to how things had changed. She didn't need pills to get through life anymore. Somehow, someway, a miracle had happened this Christmas. She had her daughter, the man of her dreams, and now the chance to mend the tattered bridge between her and her family.

"Ma, there are some people I'd like for you to meet."
Gia motioned for Daniel and Starr to come forward.

Ma Belle turned her head. "My Lawd, chile. Do you
know who you look like?"

"She looks like her father," Gia said.

Ma Belle's face pinched with confusion. "You mean to
tell me…but how?"

"I'm not sure how myself," Gia chuckled with fresh
tears.

"Gia, this is your daughter?" Glenda asked equally as-
tounded.

"Yes. Her name is Starr Davis. Isn't she beautiful?"

Starr blushed and fidgeted with her hands.

"My prayers have been answered," Ma Belle whispered
in awe as tears streamed down her face. "Praise be to
Jesus, chile. Come over here and give your great-grandma
a hug."

Starr blinked and glanced over at her father.

Daniel gave her an encouraging nod and then watched
as his daughter was enfolded in the elderly woman's arms.
His eyes stung with emotion watching his little girl with
her newfound family. His gaze swept toward Gia and he
was overwhelmed by the love he saw radiating there. The
fact that she was looking at him confirmed that there was
indeed a future for them—together.

"If I remember right, today is your birthday, chile." Ma
Belle said, gazing into Starr's eyes. "I'm 'fraid I ain't got
nothing for you."

"That's okay," Starr wiped her tears and then reached

for Gia's hand, and then motioned her father over. "I've already gotten the best birthday and Christmas gift ever."

Daniel's gaze again returned to Gia's. "That goes for me, too."

"And who are you?" Ma Belle asked, squinting up at him. "You a handsome devil. I'll give you that much. And you even look a little respectable, too."

"I'm Daniel Davis," he chuckled. "I'm Starr's adoptive dad."

"My dad," Starr corrected.

Daniel winked at her. "Starr's dad…I'm also the man in love with your granddaughter, Gia. And I'm hoping that she will have my hand in marriage."

Gia and Starr gasped.

"Well, well, now." Ma Belle's smile broadened. "The gifts just keeps on comin' this Christmas."

"Oh, Ma." Gia returned her attention to her ailing grandmother. "We should be letting you get your rest."

"Rest, hell. What is it you do for a livin', Mr. Davis?"

"I'm a doctor."

"Humph. I don't care too much for them." Ma Belle said bluntly and rolled her eyes. "The one I'm seeing is tryin' to tell everyone I'm dyin'. I'm fine I tell you. Women in my family live a long time. I just needed some time off my feet that's all…and maybe get some of these chil'in to quit worrin' me so much."

Starr slapped a hand across her mouth and snickered.

"Anyways, I hear that doctorin' makes a pretty good livin'. You think you can take care of my Gia?"

Gia glanced at Daniel again. Even in that cold and dim hospital room the intensity in his gaze stirred her butterflies.

"I think we'll do a good job taking care of each other," Daniel responded.

"We're going way too fast," Gia said, shaking her head.

"There's no such thing."

Joy burned the backs of her eyes while hope bloomed within her heart, but somehow words failed her.

"Gia," Glenda hissed under her breath and then a small smile curved her lips. "I think he's waiting for an answer."

"We all are," Ma Belle said, glancing from Daniel to Gia. "If you love him, marry him."

Gia blinked in surprise. She suddenly realized that the room was slowly filling with the Jackson clan.

"What can I say?" Ma Belle shrugged. "I ain't too old to change. Do you love him?"

All eyes turned toward Gia as tears leapt over her lashes. "I love him with all of my heart."

"Then that's a *yes*?" Starr asked, clutching Gia's hand.

Gia nodded. "That's a *yes*."

The Jackson clan applauded as Daniel pulled Gia into his arms and kissed her soundly.

"Well, chile," Ma Belle whispered to Starr. "Strange enough, it looks like your mom and dad is gettin' married."

"It's not strange. It's a wish come true."

EPILOGUE

One year later

"Four, three, two, one…" The lights flashed on and the Christmas tree at Rockefeller Center was once again a magnificent sight. Everyone with the Davis family squeezed their eyes shut and made a wish.

"What did you wish for?" Daniel whispered, cozying up to his beautiful wife.

"I wished for us to always be this happy for the rest of our lives."

"Sounds good to me." He kissed the tip of her nose.

"What about you?" she asked, gazing up at him. "What did you wish for?"

Daniel gently roamed his hands across the bulge of her belly. "I wished for a girl with your eyes and smile."

Gia glowed. "You're not disappointed that it's not a boy?"

"Heck, no. With boys you're a hero for a few years, but girls love you for a lifetime." He kissed her again. "Plus, there's always next time."

Gia laughed and tightened her arms around her husband.

Starr sighed as she watched her parents and then turned toward Neve. "Aren't they cute together?"

"Hardly," Neve moped.

Starr frowned, and then followed the direction of her best friend's gaze. "I wasn't referring to your mom and Principal Hedley."

"Yeah, well I was," Neve said. "Of all the men in New York, why in the world does she have to date *him?*"

"Hey, she looks happy. I thought that's what you wanted?"

Neve grunted. "Do you know how uncool it is for your mom to have a thing for the principal? It's humiliating."

"She looks happy," Starr sing-songed.

"Yeah, yeah, yeah."

"So what did you wish for?" Starr asked.

"For them to get married *after* I graduate."

Starr chuckled and turned toward her other guest. "What about you, Ma Belle?"

"I wished for ya'll to get me out of this damn cold. Good Lawd, it must be thirty below. How in the world do any of ya'll stand it? I get better and now ya'll tryin' to give me pneumonia."

Starr rocked her head back with a hearty laugh. Ever since Ma Belle and her aunt Glenda moved to the city, Starr delighted herself in her great-grandmother's off-the-cuff remarks. Though most of the family marveled over Ma Belle's miraculous recovery, others like her uncle

Byron believed Ma Belle was simply suffering from a broken heart and had practically willed herself to death.

Aunt Glenda was fun, too, because she treated New York like it was some fantasy land, and she was amazed by almost everything she saw. This Christmas Uncle Byron's family promised to come up and everyone was to meet the members of the Davis family. In other words, it was going to be one *large* Christmas dinner—just like Starr wanted.

"So what did you wish for?" Daniel slid his arm around Starr's shoulders.

"You mean since my *dumb* plan worked?"

"All right, all right. I deserved that one. So what did you wish for?"

"Nothing," Starr said smiling. "Everything is just perfect, Dad."

"I'm about to be mushy in public," he warned.

"Me, too," she said, and leaned up on her toes to kiss him softly on the cheek.

Daniel returned the favor by planting one against her forehead.

"You know, there is *one* thing, Dad. With the family exploding like it has, I'm going to need an increase in my allowance."

"Sounds reasonable to me," Gia cut in.

Daniel chuckled and rolled his eyes. "What am I going to do when there's three of you?"

"The only thing you can do," Gia said, leaning against him.

"Yeah," Starr said, flanking his other side. "Just keep loving us."

Daniel nodded. "I think I can handle that."

BLIND FAITH

KAYLA PERRIN

PROLOGUE

Andrea Dawson knew she was going to die.

As much as she wanted to deny that truth, as much as she wanted to hang on to hope, she knew she had to face reality. If she hadn't been found already, it was unlikely she ever would be.

The accident had happened in the blink of an eye. One minute she had been driving, the next she had been flying off an overpass somewhere on the outskirts of Buffalo. It had all happened so fast. So fast, in fact, that she hadn't had time to be scared. Her car had crashed through layers of branches of numerous trees before finally coming to a stop.

She wasn't exactly sure where she was, nor how long she had been out here. She only knew that after screaming until her throat was raw, it had become painfully obvious that no one had witnessed her accident. And if no one had witnessed the accident…

God help her, she didn't want to believe that she would never be found—not before it was too late.

It was dark—again. How many nights had come and gone, she wondered. She had been in and out of consciousness since the accident, so she couldn't be sure. Two nights? Three?

More?

Uttering a soft moan, Andrea tried to swallow. Her mouth was so dry, she didn't know how much longer she could last without something to drink. Yesterday—at least she thought it was yesterday—she had been able to stretch her fingers out the window and scoop up the light frosting of snow. Now, she just didn't have the energy.

Something was broken. A rib probably, and maybe her left wrist. She hadn't been able to move her left arm immediately after the accident.

She angled her head toward the back seat, as if by just looking in that direction, she could will her purse into her hands. With the force of the collision, her purse had somehow ended up in the back seat.

"Why is this happening?" she asked aloud, trying not to despair. Her cell phone was in that purse—and out of reach. She had tried desperately to move her body, to see if she could somehow squeeze herself out from behind the steering wheel, but the front end of the car had smashed on impact, trapping her in the driver's seat.

Terrence… She closed her eyes and thought of her four-year-old son. Thought of him and tried with all her might to fight the tears.

"Think of his smile," she told herself. "Think of how much he needs you."

Sighing softly, she thought of the picture she loved most of Terrence—the one where he had his arms wrapped tightly around her, and his face pressed against hers as if he wanted to bond their bodies together. Both were wearing grins as wide as the moon. It had been taken just a few months earlier.

Suddenly, Andrea felt a burst of determination and strength, even as a tear slid down her cheek.

I can't die out here, she told herself. *I can't.* She had to fight to stay alive. She couldn't die here, cold and alone in the middle of nowhere. Not when she had a son to get back to. A son who was young and needed her desperately.

With all her might, Andrea stretched her body, ignoring the pain that ripped through her ribs. She reached her right hand toward the left-side window. Slipping her fingers through the crack, she felt for drops of moisture.

The window was dry.

Andrea softly cried. She wanted to stay strong, but with each passing moment, it was getting harder and harder.

"Dear God," she silently prayed, "please let someone find me. I don't want to die here like this."

Her stomach grumbled, reminding her just how hungry she was. And she was so cold, she could no longer feel her toes. How could she survive being out here much longer?

"Give me strength, God. Please…"

Andrea's eyes fluttered shut, and she forced them open.

The energy she'd expended trying to move had exhausted her. But God help her, she had to stay awake. If she went to sleep, she didn't know if she would ever wake up.

Maybe if she kept her mind active, that would help her stay up.

For the past however many days she had been trapped in her car, Andrea had tried to keep her thoughts on Terrence, her reason for getting out of here.

But now, she finally allowed herself to think about what she had tried so hard to block from her mind. The very reason she had ended up careening over an overpass and into this bushy abyss in the first place.

CHAPTER 1

Fifty hours earlier…

Andrea rounded the corner in the restaurant and stopped dead in her tracks. Then she jumped backward, taking cover behind a potted plant.

Good Lord, it couldn't be him.

Not here. Not now.

No way.

When Andrea Dawson glimpsed that handsome brown face, her first instinct was to flee—into the kitchen, into the bathroom, into a hole in the ground. Heck, even an alien abduction would be nice right now. Anything to get her out of this potentially embarrassing situation.

There was no way she could go over to that table and serve the people there if one of the men dressed in the expensive Italian suits was Mark Potter.

Mark Potter. Oh God, could it really be him? Wiping her now sweaty hands on her burgundy apron, she peered through the plant leaves for a better look. The man she thought might be Mark had his back to her—a broad, well-sculpted back if she ever saw one—and she'd originally only seen the side of his face. But that face… How could she forget the face of the first man who'd claimed her heart?

"What are you doing?" Andrea nearly jumped out of her skin when she heard Trevor's angry voice. "You have three tables waiting for lunch, there's a line at the door, and you're standing behind this bush? You better have a damn good reason for this."

Andrea swallowed as she turned to face Trevor Churchmuch. His narrow face was red as a beet and she felt two inches tall beneath his intimidating gaze. She could tell her manager that she wasn't feeling well, which, as of right now, was quite true. Or, she could muster up the courage to go to her table and face the men there, even if Mark Potter was one of them.

Her manager chose for her. "Table three wants their bill. And table six is *still* waiting for a greeting. You've got food in the kitchen waiting to go out. Unless you want to be standing in the unemployment line tomorrow, I suggest you get moving."

Inhaling a deep, steadying breath, Andrea took a step forward. Despite her mind's protest, one foot followed the other until she was at table three, handing the Crawfords their bill. The elderly couple came in weekly for lunch.

"Take care," she said to them, forcing a smile.

But that was the easy part. The hard part was going to

table six—the table where she thought she'd seen Mark Potter. With dread flowing through her veins, she turned and faced the table in question. She could do this. She had to—since she could still feel Trevor's eyes boring into her back. Praying that Mark wasn't really sitting at the table, she slowly walked toward it.

Her heart sped up as she neared the table. Oh God, the man was looking more and more like Mark! She sucked in air, forcing herself to breathe—and nearly choked. Who was she kidding? She couldn't do this. If the man indeed was Mark Potter, she wasn't about to stick around and find out. Barely pausing at the table, she blurted, "I'll be with you in a minute," then, before any of the men could respond, ran into the kitchen. If Trevor fired her, so be it, but right now she needed to collect her wits. Ignoring the waiting food, she flew to the bathroom, cursing her bad luck every step of the way.

Inside she found Pamela, her co-worker, on yet another smoke break. "Pam," she said, immediately relieved. "Thank God you're here." Maybe her luck was turning. "I need you to take table six for me."

Pamela took a long drag of her cigarette, then ground it out in the sink. "Sorry, hon. I can't. I'm in the weeds."

If she was in the weeds, meaning totally swamped, then what was she doing here having a cigarette, Andrea wondered, but didn't ask. Instead, she pleaded, "I'll take one of your tables. Two if you want. I just really need you to take table six for me."

"I can't." She flashed an apologetic look. "I'm already behind. I only took a quick smoke break because I was

going to die if I didn't have a cigarette." Shrugging rue-
fully, Pamela opened the bathroom door and sauntered
out.

"No, Pam, wait—" But Pamela was gone. Groaning,
Andrea turned and gripped the edges of the sink, then
stared at her reflection in the mirror. Her normally bright
brown eyes were now bulging with terror. Lines of concern
were etched on her forehead. Oh God, she couldn't go
back out there. She couldn't face Mark Potter.

Stop acting like a fool! she told herself, then drew in a slow,
steady breath. She was being ridiculous, acting like a
spoiled child having a conniption fit. She was a mature
adult with a job to do. She would go back out and do it. If
the man at the table really was her old flame—and she
prayed he wasn't—he probably wouldn't recognize her
anyway. After all, ten years had passed since she'd dumped
him and gone on with her life.

Gathering all her courage, she left the bathroom and went
back to work. She brought out the lunch entrees for table
four, then, curling her lips in a grin, approached table six.

"Afternoon gentlemen." She couldn't sound more
cheerful if she was doing some cheesy commercial. "How's
everyone doing?"

"Starving," a dark-haired man replied, glancing at the
Rolex watch on his thick wrist. "I think we're all ready to
order."

"Okay, what would you like?" Normally, she would have
suggested the lunch special, but right now she wanted to get
away from this table as quickly as possible. Thankfully, the
men knew what they wanted. Writing down the orders of the

first three men on her order pad, Andrea carefully avoided eye contact with the possible Mark Potter. And when it was his turn to place his order, she focused all her attention on her pad and pen, not daring to look him in the eye.

"Great," she announced when he was finished, her tone deceptively calm despite the realization that it was truly Mark at her table. The voice was unmistakable. "It shouldn't be too long."

As she turned on her heel to leave, grateful that he hadn't recognized her, his familiar velvety-smooth voice stopped her dead in her tracks. "Andrea?"

A shiver of dread skittered up her spine. *No!* her mind screamed. *Please, no...*

"Andrea Dawson?"

Swallowing down her panic, Andrea turned around slowly. Mark's face lit up with recognition, and his lips formed a wide, sexy grin. "I can't believe it."

"Mark?" Andrea asked, pretending to be just as shocked as he.

His eyes crinkling as he beamed at her, he nodded. "It's me, Andrea. Mark Potter. Wow, what a surprise."

He wasn't kidding. This kind of surprise could give someone heart failure. "Yes, it certainly is," she said, feigning delight at seeing him again. "Um, uh, I've got to uh, run...back into the kitchen. You know, um, for food. So, I'll, uh, talk to you in a minute."

"Okay. I'll be here."

Turning, she whimpered. *Armani!* That was an Armani suit Mark was wearing! As she scooted to a computer terminal to punch in their order, she realized that this was the most humiliating day of her life. Mark was clearly some kind of businessman, and if his expensive suit was any indication, he was doing very well. While she, Andrea Dawson, was waitressing in a greasy spoon!

She could just imagine Mark's feeling of victory, of sweet revenge, after the way she had dumped him ten years ago. The irony of the situation did not elude her. Years ago, she was the one who'd had everything going for her—social status and wealth. Mark, on the other hand, had come from an average, working class family. Eventually, despite their love for one another, they hadn't been able to get past their differences. Now, it seemed their situations were totally reversed. How would she ever live this one down?

When she delivered the lunch orders to table six, Mark was smiling widely at her. Was it an arrogant, look-how-times-have-changed smile, or a genuine one? *Of course not,* she told herself, acknowledging that she was being paranoid right now. Mark had never been the petty type, and she couldn't imagine him being that way now.

Still, she wondered if he wasn't secretly getting a kick out of having the woman who had once dumped him serve him spaghetti with Mama's special meat sauce.

"There you go, gentlemen," she said in a sing-song voice. She certainly wasn't going to let Mark know that seeing him again had phased her in any way. "If you need anything else, just give a holler."

Before she could escape, Andrea felt a warm, callused hand on her arm. The hand of a man who used to help his father fix cars. Tiny currents of electricity ran up and down

BLIND FAITH 267

her arm, startling her with their intensity. Finally she turned, facing the man she had once loved so fiercely.

"I know you're busy, but can I have a moment of your time?"

"Um…"

"Let me at least introduce you to my associates." Gesturing to the men at the table, Mark said, "Andrea, this is Michael Di Carlo, Robert Tremont, and Greg Yates. Gentlemen, this is Andrea Dawson. An old friend."

She was more than an old friend, but was glad that Mark hadn't mentioned that. His associates merely nodded at her, but seemed more interested in their lunches than in an old friend of Mark's.

Which was fine with her.

Mark turned his attention back to her. "So tell me, Andrea, what are you doing here?"

It was the question she had dreaded. How could she tell Mark the truth? That she wasn't as well off as she once was and now worked in this restaurant to support herself?

She couldn't. "You know, Mark, I'd love to stay and chat, but as you can see the restaurant is quite busy and I *do* have other customers."

His smile fading, he released her arm. "Of course. Well, whenever you get a minute, I'd love to chat with you."

Nodding, Andrea said, "Sure."

What was she going to do? she wondered as she flew into the kitchen to retrieve more food orders. Avoid Mark's table and just have another waitress bring them their bill? That was an option, but what if they wanted dessert? Lord, this was truly the worst day of her twenty-six years. Why did Mark have to show up in *her* restaurant today, after ten years of not being in her life?

She avoided him as much as possible as she served other customers, but while at a table with a young mother and her daughter, Andrea noticed Mark waving at her. Damn him for still being so incredibly handsome. He was even more attractive than when she had first fallen for him years ago, and he'd been pretty fine then. His slender face was the complexion of milk chocolate, and except for the small scar on his chin that gave him character, his skin was smooth and flawless. But his two deep, sexy dimples had always been her weakness.

She excused herself from the mother and daughter, then coolly sauntered over to Mark's table. As his smile widened, those two incredible dimples made an appearance.

And suddenly Andrea remembered another time, another place. She remembered being sixteen and in love. She remembered stroking that smooth, dark face, kissing those full, sexy lips. She remembered the way just one of Mark's looks made her feel warm all over.

"Andrea?"

Startled from the reverie, Andrea found her voice. "You all finished?" she asked, then began clearing their plates. She hoped they hadn't noticed her space out. "Can I get you any dessert, any coffee?"

The men agreed on coffee. Within a few minutes, she returned with four steaming cups, along with milk and cream. Thankfully, Mark was absorbed in what looked to be a serious conversation, over something in a file folder. Andrea pivoted on her heel and said, "I'll just get your bill."

"Wait a second."

Andrea swallowed painfully before turning around. "Uh-huh?"

"You didn't answer my question. About what you're doing here."

Andrea's back stiffened at Mark's words. She'd have to think of something to tell him; she couldn't avoid him forever.

Turning to meet his gaze, she shrugged. "Oh, you know how it is. One can never have too much extra cash."

"So that's why you're waitressing here?" Mark asked. "For the extra cash?"

Andrea fiddled with her ponytail. "Yeah."

Mark pinned her with a dubious gaze. "Are you sure you're the real Andrea Dawson?"

He may as well have added, "The Andrea Dawson I knew wouldn't be caught dead working as a waitress." And that would have been true. But her life had changed substantially over the past ten years, something she didn't feel like sharing with him.

So she said simply, "People change."

Mark shrugged, seeming to accept her explanation. But if he expected her to ask him what his profession was, he had another thing coming. It was humiliating enough to know that he had obviously succeeded in life, whereas she had not.

Yet. She'd make her dreams come true one day.

She was thankful that Mark and his associates didn't want a coffee refill. She'd seen the anxious looks on their faces and knew that they were ready to leave. When she handed them the bill, Mark gave her his Platinum Visa card.

Not even Gold, but Platinum. Could this day get any worse?

So what? a voice asked her. *So what if he has a Platinum credit card, a top of the line Mercedes, or even a lakefront mansion?*

So what indeed? She went to the computer terminal and entered his payment.

Mark was the only one still at the table when she returned with his credit card and the Visa slip to sign. Just looking at him as he sat, Andrea's heart went wild. It was bad enough dealing with him when he was with the other men, but to have to deal with him alone... Something strange was tingling in her belly. Something like...attraction.

But how could that be? Their relationship had ended years ago, and she had moved on with her life.

Pushing the thought from her mind, Andrea hoped Mark would sign the Visa slip, leave her a decent tip, then head out the door and out of her life.

When he finished settling the bill, Mark rose to his full six-foot-one-inch height. Absolutely gorgeous, he was a picture of cool confidence and success. And Andrea suddenly felt like a complete failure.

God, she was so pathetic, even her hands were shaking. "It was, uh, nice seeing you again," she announced. "Take care."

"That's it?"

"Should there be anything else?"

"Andrea, I know we haven't seen each other in years, but at one time we meant something to each other. Surely you've got to be curious about what I've been up to."

"It's obvious that you're doing very well."

"All right then, let me just say what's on my mind. I'm

only in town until tomorrow night, but maybe we could get together some time and talk. Have coffee."

Andrea's fake smile disappeared. No! She couldn't see him again. She wouldn't. Not after the way things had ended between them. And it wasn't like there was a chance of a future with them now.

Still, she knew that there was something about Mark Potter that was dangerous to her heart and her sanity. She might start daydreaming about what once was and could never be again if she actually got together with him.

"Mark, I wish I could, but I'm just so busy with Dawson Enterprises and this job…I…" She was lying about Dawson Enterprises, and felt bad for it, but she couldn't bring herself to admit that her family's clothing business had gone belly-up. "I couldn't possibly fit in any time to see you. But it was nice running into you again." The fake smile returned. "All the best."

Mark withdrew a business card from his shirt pocket and passed it to Andrea. Taking the card, she looked down at it. Embossed gold letters showcased the company's name: Creative Image Advertising. Beneath that was Mark's name, and his title—Founder & CEO.

Wow. If she weren't so embarrassed, she would have been impressed.

"If you get some free time, call me," Mark said. "Even if it's just to talk for a few minutes."

Andrea stuffed the card into her apron. "*If*," she agreed. "But I don't think I will. You take care now."

And then, before Mark could say anything else to weaken her resolve, she practically sprinted to the kitchen.

She held her breath as she peered through the small window in the kitchen door, only releasing it when she finally saw him walking toward the front exit.

Walking out of her life.

Again.

CHAPTER 2

Ten years.

Had it really been that long?

Swiveling the black leather chair toward the floor-to-ceiling windows in his hotel room, Mark locked his hands behind his head and gazed out at the gray-blue sky. It looked like it would snow.

"Andrea," he said softly. He had never expected to see her again, and he'd expected that if he ever *did* cross her path it would be at some ritzy ball for the most important people in the state of Illinois. He certainly hadn't expected to run into her in an airport restaurant in Buffalo—working as a waitress, no less. The Andrea he'd known and loved for a short time would never have been waiting tables.

Unless she had to. Several years back he'd heard that Just My Size, the once successful chain of children's clothing stores started by Andrea's father, Stewart, had been bought out. But considering the size and wealth of the company, he figured the Dawsons were still worth millions. What he learned today had him wondering if the rumors he'd heard were even remotely true.

First of all, he knew Andrea was lying to him when she said she was busy working for Dawson Enterprises. That company didn't exist anymore. She obviously didn't know that he knew that. But what intrigued him more was *why* Andrea had lied. Just because the company didn't exist anymore didn't mean her family didn't have money. And if they did have the small fortune Mark expected they'd have, why was Andrea waitressing in a greasy spoon that could hardly bring in decent money?

His nagging curiosity had prompted him to call John Kreuger, one of his contacts in the clothing industry, and have him do a little digging into the Dawson's background.

His cell phone rang. Spinning back around to face the hotel desk, Mark grabbed his phone off the table. "Potter here."

"Mark, it's John Kreuger."

Great. The call he'd been waiting for. "John, hi. What did you find out?"

"I did a little digging, and it seems Dawson Enterprises went out of business six years ago. Actually, they went belly-up."

"Bankrupt?" Mark asked, surprised. "I thought they were bought out."

"You know spin doctors. You can't believe everything you read in the papers."

"Bankrupt," Mark repeated.

"Mmm hmm. Seems they were in way over their heads, owed a lot of money to suppliers…and the bank."

"You're kidding." This was very surprising, and very interesting. "So what next? They liquidated their assets, opened another store?"

"What assets? Apparently, after all the bills were paid, they couldn't even keep the mansion. My source says they moved clear down state, to Bridgeport. As far away from Chicago as they could get, apparently."

"Wow. That's unbelievable. I thought that was a solid company."

"Bad management, I guess. Who knows?"

If her parents were in Bridgeport, then what was Andrea doing working in Buffalo? He hadn't seen a ring, so he didn't think she was married. "So no word on what they've been doing these past six years?"

"Nothing I've been able to find out. But it's clear they're not living the glamorous life they were once used to."

Very interesting indeed. "Thanks, John. I appreciate the info."

"No problem."

"I'll be in touch. Maybe we can get together for a game of tennis this weekend when I'm back in town," Mark suggested. He and John routinely played tennis at a club in downtown Chicago.

"Sure," John replied. "Just let me know."

"Will do."

Mark hung up, his mind reeling with the information

he'd just learned. In fact, he was wondering if he should head back to Mama's Place and see Andrea again.

He was curious about why she'd lied to him, but it was more than that. Call him crazy, but he still had questions about the way she'd dumped him. About why. She had told him that she simply didn't love him anymore, and he'd never believed that.

However, he'd never had the chance to talk to her again, to tie up the loose ends between them.

Had fate just handed him the chance?

When Andrea finished the final count of her cash, she heaved a sigh of relief. Thank God the day was over. She had worked a double, both lunch and dinner, which was always stressful. But at least she had earned a little more than a hundred bucks in tips.

In the restaurant changing room, she stripped out of her now filthy white shirt and black pants, then changed into a pair of jeans and a burgundy turtleneck sweater. She didn't normally like turtlenecks, but this had been a gift from her best friend and classmate, and it was both warm and comfortable.

She was pleasantly surprised when she stepped outside and felt the mild night air. The day had looked so glum, she was certain it would be freezing. But there was a fresh dusting of snow, and it was never as cold outside when it was snowing.

As she made her way to her car, she let out the frustrated growl she'd held inside all day. Mark Potter! She still couldn't believe that he'd shown up in her restaurant, and of all places, at her table! What kind of a cruel joke was fate playing on her? After ten years and a disastrous turn of events in her life, he was the last person she wanted to see.

Andrea slipped into her blue Pontiac Sunfire, jammed the key into the ignition, and tossed her purse onto the passenger seat. Life wasn't fair. She remembered only too well when she had once had it all, when she had enjoyed the perks her parents' money had given her. Mark always used to tell her she was clueless about the way normal people lived. Then, she hadn't known what he meant. In reality, she hadn't cared. She hadn't known any better because her parents had spoiled her.

So this was the punishment for her arrogance—seeing Mark on top of the world, while she was now on the bottom. Mark's suit alone could pay her rent and more. Once, she had been able to spend hundreds on a new outfit, and the truth was, she'd taken that life for granted. She hadn't expected it to end. But it had ended, and she'd learned the hard way what it was like to suffer. Now, making ends meet was such a struggle that she sometimes didn't know if she'd make it from one pay day to the next.

"Don't start feeling sorry for yourself," she said, then started the ignition to begin warming her car. She still had plenty to be thankful for, like the fact that she was still breathing.

And she was especially thankful for Terrence, even if he had changed the course of her plans. Who ever thought a little boy could bring so much joy to one's life?

"Why am I even thinking like this?" she asked herself. She hadn't wallowed in self-pity when she got pregnant and had to drop out of college. She had accepted the challenges thrown at her and she was still going strong. She had a lot to be thankful for—something she had never questioned before.

It was just that seeing Mark again had thrown her for a loop. The last time she'd spoken to him, he had been heading to Kent State in Ohio on a football scholarship. Was that where he had gotten his money? From professional football?

No, she decided. If Mark Potter had made it to the pros she would have heard about it.

He was a bit slimmer than he had been in high school, but still muscular and just as gorgeous as ever. Even Pamela, after seeing him at table six, had regretted her refusal to take that table. "Man, he's hot," Pamela had later whispered in Andrea's ear. "If he wants to come to my place I'll serve him anything he wants." Andrea had merely shrugged.

Mark, former high school football star, was no doubt a hit with the women. He had the killer good looks, and from what she remembered of him, he was a charmer. But he'd also been a total gentleman, and serious about his feelings for her. No, Andrea decided. Mark wasn't a player. He was probably happily married and enjoying family life.

A pang of jealousy hit her hard as she considered that thought. At one time in her life, she'd thought they would end up married. In fact, she had been convinced of it.

Though their relationship ended a decade ago, she felt a modicum of regret that things hadn't worked out for them. And a part of her couldn't help but wonder what their life together might have been like if she hadn't allowed her parents to interfere with her happiness. Would they have been happy together?

As she drove her car out of the parking lot and away from Mama's Place she tried to force the memories of Mark Alexander Potter to the back of her mind. As the saying went, there was no point crying over spilled milk.

Then why couldn't she stop thinking about him?

Why now? she asked herself. *Why did he have to show up in my life now?* She had never forgotten him. She had told him that she wasn't in love with him anymore, but that had been a bald-faced lie. A lie to make sure he stayed away from her, as her parents had ordered. The look in his eyes had broken her heart, but she couldn't let him know that.

From time to time she wondered how he was doing. From time to time, she felt regret about what could have been.

What could have been but never would be.

"Why does this matter to me?" she asked herself. "Stop this pathetic trip down memory lane."

The car was sufficiently warm, and Andrea started to drive. For some reason, she didn't feel like going home yet. It was late, and Rhonda, her babysitter, was sleeping over, so she didn't have to worry about Terrence. With the roads so quiet, it was the perfect time to take a long drive to clear her head and gain some perspective.

And she definitely needed perspective right now.

It was shocking that Mark's reappearance in her life had rocked her to her core, but it had. She couldn't deny that.

She headed to the 33 Expressway, but instead of heading home, she found herself merging onto the interstate.

Before long, she was taking the I-190 North exit, heading toward Grand Island. It was as good a spot as any.

The snow was lightly falling, but the roads had been pretty much cleared from the previous night's downfall. It was a picturesque time of year, with the snow and Christmas lights that many people had just put up after the Thanksgiving holiday.

Andrea would drive around and view Christmas lights and think of Terrence and the upcoming Christmas holiday. Last year, when he was three, he had finally understood what all the fuss was about. The look of excitement in his eyes had made her heart fill with a joy she hadn't known existed before becoming a mother. Terrence's excitement had been contagious, and she had fully enjoyed the holiday for the first time in years.

Andrea made a series of turns. Somehow, she was on a stretch of road in an industrial area, nowhere near the Christmas lights she was hoping to see. She didn't know this part of town.

She drove over a set of train tracks, then continued over a short bridge before she slowed and turned her car around to retrace her steps. "Go back over the bridge," she said aloud, "turn left..." She gazed out the right window at the wintery landscape. Even in the night, the snow covering the tree branches looked entirely enchanting.

As Andrea looked ahead again, she saw something dart before her car.

Startled, she swerved to miss it. Her car started to skid, spinning out of control. She yanked on the steering wheel, trying desperately to correct its direction.

The car kept skidding, like there was a patch of ice under the snow, and Andrea had no control of the car. She was heading straight for the side of the road, and the overpass.

She hit the brakes, but the car didn't stop. The next thing she knew, the car was crashing through the guardrail and flying in the air.

"God help me," she cried out.

Then everything went black.

CHAPTER 3

Mark was finding it hard to concentrate on the presentation about using the Internet effectively to enhance a company's sales. His brain was preoccupied with thoughts of Andrea, though he wasn't sure why.

After she had rejected him ten years ago—then had refused to take any of his calls—he had vowed to move on with his life and forget her. But seeing her yesterday brought everything back. How he had been smitten with her instantly. His foolish dreams of happily ever after with her. Oh, how young and naïve he had been. In his heart, he truly believed that his love for Andrea would overcome all odds—even her parents' staunch disapproval of their dating. He had met them, tried his hardest to impress them, but all in vain. They hadn't thought him good enough to date their daughter, and Andrea had eventually caved under their pressure.

Frowning, Mark looked up as the conference room lights dimmed. A colorful graph appeared on a screen. *Pay attention,* he told himself. Yet still he couldn't.

It had taken him years to forgive Andrea for her rejection, yet seeing her again, the pain was suddenly fresh. She didn't know it, but her dumping him—because of her family's disapproval—was the catalyst for his drive to become a huge success. He wanted to prove to the world that he wasn't inferior to anyone. And a part of him had always hoped the day would come when he could show Andrea just how far he'd come.

That day had come, of course. But Mark was a man now, one who knew he didn't have to prove his worth to anybody. The truth was, he simply wanted to talk to Andrea. Even after all this time, there were questions he wanted answered.

He wondered what she was doing right now.

Mark's cell phone vibrated on his waist, giving him the perfect excuse to leave the conference room. He quietly walked out and pulled his phone from his waistband. "Potter here."

"Mark?"

Mark's stomach sank at the sound of Cynthia Nichol's voice on the other end of the line. Her tone was high-pitched, vulnerable. She was good at playing the victim.

"Cynthia, make it quick. I'm very busy."

Her exaggerated sigh reverberated through the phone line. "Why do you always talk to me like you can't stand hearing from me?" she asked. "Didn't I mean *anything* to you?"

Mark didn't have time for this. But he had to be careful how he dealt with Cynthia. She was the type to call back over and over until she felt she'd been heard.

"I'm sorry if I was abrupt," Mark said. "But I'm out-of-town right now, at a conference."

"Oh, I should have known. I didn't mean to snap at you. It's just that…I miss you. We haven't seen each other in God knows how long, and I just want to spend some time with you. What are you doing this weekend? Say, Sunday?"

Mark rolled his eyes toward the ceiling. What planet was she from, anyway? He hadn't seen her in months, not since he'd found her rifling through his wallet. But she conveniently seemed to have forgotten that fact. "I'm busy this weekend."

"Oh, come on. You must be able to spare *some* time on Sunday evening. I was planning a romantic, candlelight dinner. And we can drink champagne in the hot tub, just like we used to…"

Cynthia's gall never failed to amaze him. Did she figure he was so hard up for a woman's affections that he'd forget she was after only one thing? He may have been blind before, but he knew her now. She didn't want him. She wanted his money. How had he ever thought he was attracted to her?

"Cynthia," he said gently. "I can't make it. And you know why."

"Please, Mark. Don't start that again."

"I think I've been more than patient with you. In fact, probably too patient. But don't misread my intentions. Our relationship is over. You need to accept that."

"Why are you so mad at me? I told you that you misunderstood what you saw. Why can't you give me the benefit of the doubt?"

Easy for her to say. She wasn't the one who'd been deceived. "I know what I saw."

Tension-filled silence hung in the air. "Fine," Cynthia finally said. "There's no pleasing you. Call me when you're ready to see things from someone else's perspective."

"Thank God," Mark said aloud when she hung up the phone. He hoped that this time Cynthia had finally gotten the message. But he wouldn't hold his breath. Somehow, she always found a reason to call him.

She was a prime example of the kind of women he met these days: a golddigger. A woman who wanted the finer things in life but didn't want to work for them. Well, after busting his butt to build Creative Image Advertising from the ground up, he wasn't about to be any woman's meal ticket.

In fact, since his seven-month relationship with Andrea ended bitterly ten years earlier, Mark had not had another serious relationship. The women he'd met in college didn't seem to know what they wanted from life, and the women he'd met since he started his business seemed only to want a sugar daddy.

Before his mother died, she used to say that he was too picky. Mark frowned. Maybe she was right. He didn't know why, but he managed to find fault with even the most attractive women he dated.

Maybe, he acknowledged, he just didn't want another woman to stomp all over his heart—like Andrea had.

Man, what was wrong with him? Just thinking of Andrea now had his pulse racing. He could dismiss it as a case of nerves, but deep down he knew it was more than that. The moment he saw her, his body came alive with a purely macho reaction to her delicate femininity.

She was the only woman who had ever gotten to him in quite that way. He had to get in touch with her. He had a late flight back to Chicago, and wanted to talk to her before he left, perhaps even spend some time with her this evening.

Ever since he had run into her again, she had dominated his thoughts. He didn't like the way she had dismissed his suggestion that they get together. But he was a man now, not a teenager who would take *no* for an answer. He shouldn't have let her walk out of his life without a fight then, and he sure wouldn't walk away without the chance to talk to her now.

Mark dialed information on his phone.

Less than a minute later, he had the number for Mama's Place. He punched in the number to the restaurant.

"Good afternoon. Thank you for calling Mama's Place."

"Um, hi," Mark began cautiously. "I'm trying to reach one of your waitresses. Andrea Dawson."

"Andrea's not due in until five o'clock."

"Oh. Okay. I guess I'll call back."

"Can I take a message for her?"

"No, that's all right. No message. I'll just…call back."

Mark ended the call and headed back to the conference room. He took a seat at the back and listened as the speaker talked about how his company had grown substantially once he'd really invested in Internet advertising.

This was Mark's second time attending the Young Entrepeneurs Conference in Buffalo. He believed in supporting black entrepreneurs and sharing knowledge, as well as making contacts while he was here.

That's what he *should* have been thinking about. That, or the Campelli ad campaign on which he was currently working. The Campellis ran a mom and pop chain of grocery stores in Illinois, and were trying to grow their customer base with a hip new ad campaign.

Instead of thinking about business, however, Mark was thinking of how he would head to Mama's Place later and surprise Andrea with a visit.

Maybe I'm an idiot, Mark thought. What else would explain the fact that instead of thinking of the Campelli ad campaign—which is what he should have been doing in his spare time—he was driving to Mama's Place, hoping to see Andrea.

Worse still, he was hoping to see Andrea even though her reaction to seeing him yesterday had definitely been wary. There had been no doubt in his mind that she'd been uncomfortable seeing him again, something that went beyond surprise, as far as he was concerned.

He had a flight later tonight. He had his own life to which to get back. Maybe he should just get on the plane and walk away from Andrea again, the way she had done ten years ago.

Mark glanced out the window of his rented Grand Am. A thick layer of snow had blanketed the area overnight, making the drive slow. It was hampered even more by the fact that it was still snowing. It was certainly a beautiful view, one that made him think of Christmas. Christmas was a nostalgic time of year for Mark—both happy and sad. Happy because of the memories of his parents, but sad because he'd lost them both within a year. His father to a heart attack, and then his mother in a tragic car accident.

This was a time of year for family. He had always wanted one of his own, more so now that he didn't have his parents anymore. Seeing Andrea again reminded him of the dreams he'd had about the two of them. One more reason why he knew he couldn't head back to Chicago without the chance to sit down and talk to her.

He drove past the airport, past the gas station at the corner, and then, his heart hammering in his chest, turned left into the parking lot of Mama's Place.

Mark felt unexpected butterflies as he stepped inside the restaurant. His eyes did a quick sweep of the place. It was packed, and filled with chatter. There were workers whizzing around, but he didn't see Andrea.

A woman with a harried expression rushed toward the front. "Hi," she said, offering him a half smile. "Table for one?"

"Yeah," Mark replied. "But I'd like to sit in Andrea Dawson's section."

"Andrea? Oh, she's not in tonight."

Mark frowned. "I called earlier. I was told she started at five."

"She was supposed to, but she didn't show up."

"She didn't? Is she sick?"

"How should I know?" the woman replied somewhat testily. "She didn't even call, and we're busier than usual tonight. Even I've had to help the waitstaff to pick up the slack." The hostess made no attempt to hide her annoyance.

"I see," Mark said, disappointment swirling inside. "I was really hoping to see Andrea."

The hostess glanced behind Mark's shoulder, and he quickly whipped his head around. A man and woman, arms linked, stood behind him.

"I'm sorry," he said, quickly stepping aside. "You go ahead."

As he watched the hostess lead the couple to a table, Mark debated what to do. He was hungry, but the reason he had come was to see Andrea.

Before the hostess could return, Mark slipped out of the restaurant. He would order room service back at the hotel.

Andrea's eyes opened instantly. Panicked, she glanced around in the darkness, and saw immediately that she was in her car. The memory of how and why suddenly came back to her.

She wasn't sure how many days it was now that she'd been stuck here. She only knew that she had far less energy now, and she was thankful to have slept as much as she did. Sleep gave her relief from the pain, the hunger, and her thirst.

Through it all, though, she kept saying silent prayers. She would not let despair get to her. Despair would not help her get through this ordeal.

"Mark," she whispered. He was back home now, and Andrea felt a pang of regret. Would it have hurt to have sat down and chatted with him, to act like an adult who had her life together? Now, she would probably never see him again. No matter how hopeful she was trying to be, she had to accept that she might not make it out alive.

The saying that you shouldn't put off for tomorrow what you can do today was so true.

"If only I'd taken the time to talk to him…"

She thought back to a happier time in her life—a time when she had been hopelessly in love with Mark Potter. She had been a sophomore and he'd been a senior at their respective high schools. Like it was yesterday, she could remember the first time she'd met him. She had gone to one of his high school football games with her girlfriend, Maggie, because Maggie had wanted to see Tom Stoddard, the new love of her life. Once there, Maggie had disappeared with Tom, leaving Andrea to fend for herself. Bored out of her mind and with nothing better to do, she watched the game with the hundreds of other spectators. But she hadn't really been interested, not until she'd noticed a certain football player on the field.

Magic was the only way to describe what had happened. As she'd looked down on the field, he'd looked up at her, and their eyes met. Instantly, there was a spark between them, something that made her stop and stare. He had stopped and stared, too—so much so that he'd missed a ball he should have easily caught. Knowing he had missed the ball because of her, Andrea giggled. She'd never distracted a guy like that before, and it was a nice feeling. Even as Mark had retreated to the sidelines, he'd held her gaze and flashed the sexiest smile she had ever seen. From that moment on, Andrea had been hooked.

They met after the game, and it was clear they both liked each other. It didn't take long for Andrea to realize that he was a special kind of guy. Most other guys at her preppy private school had wanted to date her for one thing only: her body. But Mark had been different. Sweet and gentle and totally sincere. She had been so happy with him.

Perhaps too happy. She had been caught up in her first love and could think of nothing else. She knew nothing of the conflicts and pressures of being from two different worlds. Foolishly, she believed that they would get married when she turned eighteen and live happily ever after.

"Mark." His name fell from her lips on a sigh. To this day, she regretted what had happened between them. Her parents had opposed their dating, and Andrea had eventually given in to their pressure. She ended her and Mark's seven-month relationship with cruel words about how she just didn't love him, and she knew she had hurt him beyond repair.

Andrea's head throbbed from thinking about Mark. She wished she could turn back the clock. She wished she hadn't caved to her parents' pressure. They had acted like they were better than the Potters just because they had more money, and now her parents were the ones living a modest life.

They still had some small savings, and on more than one occasion they'd offered to help her out financially so that she didn't have to work so hard to pay her tuition and rent. If she accepted a loan from them, she could devote all her energy to making her dream of owning a business a reality.

But if she did that, she would also be admitting that she couldn't make it on her own, something her mother had angrily told her after she'd gotten pregnant with Terrence. Even though her parents had grown to love Terrence dearly, they had never forgiven her for getting pregnant, especially before she finished her degree. Despite the heartache she had experienced after getting pregnant and dropping out of Princeton, however, she was certainly happier than she had ever been. And that happiness was because of what that small boy, who needed her so much, brought to her life every time she looked at his innocent face.

No, Andrea knew she would never take money from her parents.

She would make it on her own. She was a fighter.

That's right. You're a fighter. You'll get out of this, too. You need to get out of this for Terrence.

She would tell herself that as many times as she needed, to sustain her will to survive alive.

She would cling to the hope that she would see her precious son again, sooner rather than later.

CHAPTER 4

Mark stood at the back of the car, the trunk open, his luggage still on the parking lot floor.

Something was preventing him from loading his luggage into the trunk. The overwhelming feeling that something was wrong.

He couldn't pinpoint the feeling exactly, except that it was a mix of fear and anxiety deep in his gut, much like he'd felt the day his mother had died.

He knew it had to do with Andrea.

He still hadn't been able to reach her, and he was worried about her.

"She was sick," he told himself. "She didn't show for work. No big deal."

And he had a plane to catch. He certainly couldn't stick around just because he hadn't been able to spend more time with the woman who had broken his heart.

Still, as he lifted his suitcase into the trunk, something was nagging at him. The feeling that he shouldn't get in the car and drive away.

But he had a schedule. He had to get to the airport now if he was going to catch his plane on time. Tomorrow, he had an early meeting in the office regarding the Campelli campaign.

He had to get going.

He glanced around as he put on his coat, as if the empty underground parking garage could give him any answers.

Mark slipped into the driver's seat and started the car.

At the airport, Mark called the restaurant again. He had a sinking feeling again when the manager told him that Andrea still hadn't shown up.

"Has she ever done this before—not shown up?" Mark had to know.

"Never," the manager replied. "And she won't do it again, I can tell you that much."

Mark ended the call, then leaned against one of the airport's floor-to-ceiling glass windows. Why did he feel so strongly that something was wrong?

He didn't know, but he suddenly knew that he couldn't get on a plane. Not yet. That meant he would miss tomorrow's meeting, but Michael, Greg, and Robert could handle it without him.

They would have to.

He simply couldn't go back to Chicago until he located Andrea and knew that she was okay.

He rolled his luggage to United's business class line and went straight up to the counter. The woman there greeted him with a big smile.

"Good evening," Mark said. "I'm supposed to fly out tonight, but I'd like to change my plans."

"I can certainly help you with that. What's the name on the reservation?"

"Potter. Mark Potter."

The woman typed on her keyboard. "Ah, I see it. We have a flight at eight tomorrow morning to O'Hare, and one at nine-fifty-five. I can check later in the day as well."

"Actually," Mark began, "I'm not sure when I'll be leaving. Let's keep it open."

"Mark…"

It was the faintest of sounds, a whisper in the room.

"Mark…"

He opened his eyes. There was Andrea, at the foot of his bed, her arms outstretched to him.

Mark scrambled to a sitting position. "Andrea. H-how, w-what?"

"I need you, Mark."

Mark felt a moment of confusion. "I'm right here. What is it?"

"I'm in trouble, Mark. Help me."

He leaned forward and reached for her, but couldn't quite touch her fingers no matter how hard he tried.

And then Andrea disappeared, literally evaporated into thin air.

"Andrea!" Mark yelled. "Andrea!"

His eyes popped open. Mark was stunned to find himself lying on the hotel bed, his heart racing.

He'd been dreaming.

He sat up as a breath oozed out of him. A dream? That was almost hard to accept, it had seemed so real.

Guided by the moonlight coming into the room, Mark climbed out of bed and walked to the bathroom. There, once he turned on the light, he splashed cold water on his face, then looked at his reflection in the mirror.

His heart lurched when he saw Andrea in the mirror.

He whirled around. Found himself alone.

Damn it, something was wrong. Either that or he was losing his mind. But he had a strange feeling, a feeling that told him the dream hadn't been just a dream. That somehow, some way, Andrea had been reaching out to him to let him know that she was in trouble.

"How crazy is that?" Mark asked his reflection.

Entirely.

Mark went back to bed, determined to get some sleep.

By the next morning, instead of feeling like he was paranoid, Mark was more certain than ever that Andrea was in trouble.

Once he'd fallen asleep, he dreamed the same dream again—only this time, much more vividly. He pictured a blue car spinning out of control and flying off a bridge in an industrial area. The scenery was so real to him, like he had seen it in the light of day rather than just dreamed it. He knew the bridge was over a ravine with lots of trees. He also knew this bridge was near a railroad track, one he had the feeling wasn't in use anymore.

With every fiber of his being, Mark believed that the place he had dreamed of was indeed real.

He wasn't exactly sure what to do, so after calling his office and having a light breakfast, he called Mama's Place.

"Good morning. Thank you for calling Mama's Place," a woman said in a pleasant voice.

"Hello," Mark began. "I'm looking for Andrea Dawson. Is she in?"

"I'm sorry, sir. No." The woman paused briefly. "Are you a friend of Andrea's?"

Mark leaned forward in the room's leather chair. "Yes, I am. Has something happened to her?"

The woman sighed. "That's what the police think."

"The police?" Mark asked, unable to mask the alarm in his voice.

"Uh-huh. We thought she just didn't show up yesterday, but she's missing. Anyone who knows Andrea knows she'd never abandon her son."

"Her son?" Mark swallowed hard. If she had a son, then she must have a husband. A husband who would no doubt be looking for her.

"It's so awful. She's just vanished."

Mark wanted to ask more about her son and husband, but knew that didn't matter right now. What mattered was finding Andrea. Because now more than ever, he knew that his instincts had been dead-on. No one would believe him, but somehow, some way, Andrea had reached out to him for his help.

Why not her husband's?

Pushing that thought out of his mind, Mark scrambled out of the chair and hurriedly dressed. Andrea was trapped somewhere in her car. It didn't matter who found her.

He was debating whether or not he should stop to call the police, but decided that he could do that on the road.

Right now, he needed to get to Andrea. And the sooner the better.

The trouble was, Mark had no clue where to start.

He drove to Mama's Place, and circled that area extensively, hoping for some sign of something he recognized from his dream. More than an hour later, he felt somewhat defeated when he saw nothing suspicious.

He pulled the car into a building parking lot and reached for his cell phone. He dialed information to get the local number for the Buffalo police.

Minutes later, he was calling them.

"Hi," he said when a man answered the phone. "I'm wondering who I should speak to about a missing person."

"Hold a moment, please."

Mark held, listening to elevator music through his phone, until finally someone else came on the line. "This is Detective Shaw."

"Hello, Detective Shaw. My name is Mark Potter, and I'm calling about an Andrea Dawson. I understand she's missing."

"Yes, that's right. She was reported missing last night."

Mark hesitated, not sure how to phrase what he had to say. "I think I have...I may have information."

"What kind of information?"

"This is going to sound weird, but I had a dream. I got this vision of where she might be."

"You did?"

"Yeah. And I'm pretty sure she's over an overpass somewhere. Trapped in her car."

"Ahh, I see," the cop said, in a cynical voice. "So you're some kind of psychic?"

"No, I wouldn't say that. I just had this dream, like Andrea was calling to me for help. It was very real."

"Thanks for your call," the detective said dismissively. "The department will take your information into consideration."

"Wait," Mark said. "You-you're not going to do anything?"

"First—I can't begin to tell you how many overpasses there are in the city and surrounding area. And second, we get all kinds of calls from psychics and nothing ever pans out."

"But I'm not—"

Mark stopped talking when he heard the dial tone in his ear.

Great. The cop thought he was a raving lunatic.

His story *did* sound crazy. He understood that. But as offbeat as it seemed, he knew his dream had revealed the truth to him.

Mark groaned in frustration as he started the car. If the cops weren't going to help him, he'd just have to keep searching for her. Buffalo wasn't that big of a city. How long could it take him to find her?

Four and a half hours later, Mark was tired and frustrated. He'd surely covered every inch of Buffalo by now, and he still hadn't found Andrea.

"I'm doing something wrong," he said as he drove back toward Mama's Place. "What am I missing?"

He had taken the interstate and driven for a while without getting any strong sense that he was going in the right direction. When he'd circled the Walden-Galleria Mall, he had seen a couple of areas of interest where a car *could* be hidden, but ultimately hadn't seen a blue car stuck anywhere.

"I know you want me to find her, God," Mark said. "Show me which way to go."

Mark was in the left hand lane and slowed down to turn right into the airport. He was going to stop and think of another plan of action, but something told him he should keep going. He drove until he reached the main road again and headed in the direction of the 33 Expressway. He had gone that way already, but he hadn't veered off onto the interstate that would take him north, out of Buffalo.

"Let this be the way," he whispered silently. "God, let this be it."

Mark felt butterflies in his stomach when he saw the sign leading to Grand Island. "Grand Island," he said aloud. "Grand Island. This could be it."

Was he really feeling strongly about this area, or was he simply desperate to find Andrea? He couldn't be sure. He only knew that he was running out of time. The sky was starting to darken, and he would lose the light very soon.

He continued to drive, hoping against hope, and decided to get off at the second exit on Grand Island. At the light, he looked both left and right—and instantly realized that there was an industrial area to his far right.

Okay, he thought. *I know I'm onto something.*

He turned right. Mark's skin began prickling with each inch the car moved.

He recognized the scenery, he realized, as if he had seen it before.

He had—in his dream.

A sense of nervous excitement started to fill him, making his hands sweat as they held the steering wheel. *This is it,* he told himself. *I know it is.*

There was the large, gray building. And the gas station that looked abandoned.

Mark jerked his car to the right. He was the only person driving on this road, so he slowed to a crawl. His eyes searched right and left for some sort of spot that a car could disappear from without anyone noticing.

And then he saw it. An overpass.

Not any overpass—the one he'd seen in his dream. Shrouded by many trees, a car could easily get lost in the brush if it fell over.

Now he sped up, hurrying toward it. Lord have mercy, there were the train tracks, just beyond the bridge. Mark pulled his car to the side of the bridge and quickly shut it off.

He scrambled out of his car and looked over the bridge. Beneath the trees, he could see train tracks—just like in his dream.

"Andrea!" he yelled. He craned his body as far as he could over the railing and didn't see anything.

Standing upright, he quickly whipped his head around and looked at the other side of the bridge. Instantly, he saw the telltale sign of an accident. Even though the guardrail was covered with snow, it was obvious something had collided with it.

"Oh my God." Mark ran to that side of the overpass and stretched his body over the guardrail. The trees were thicker on this side, making it hard for him to see through the snow-covered branches.

But this was it. He knew it.

He ran back to his car to get his phone, and realized he had no clue where he was. So despite the fact that he wanted to stay here and search for Andrea in the ravine below the overpass, he knew he had to drive back to the main road so he could find out exactly where he was.

He was already dialing 9–1–1 as he started his car.

"9–1–1," an operator said. "What's your emergency?"

"That missing woman, Andrea Dawson. You have to send help right away. I just found her car!"

CHAPTER 5

The fire truck was the first emergency vehicle to arrive. Mark drew in a relieved breath. He hadn't wanted to venture down into the ravine before anyone arrived, for fear they wouldn't find the right spot. But now that they were here…

"Sir," a firefighter said as he approached Mark. "There's a car down there?"

"Yes," Mark replied, even though he hadn't seen it. "You can see the impact with the guardrail right here."

The firefighter looked down into the ravine. "I don't see anything."

"I know she's down there," Mark said. "I'm heading down."

"Sir…"

But Mark was already hopping over the guardrail. "We

don't have time to waste. Within minutes, it will be too dark to see anything."

"Let us outfit you with a harness—"

Mark started down the steep hill, ignoring the firefighters above. His heart deflated when he didn't see the car. Could he be wrong?

He pushed through the trees, straining his eyes to see shapes beneath the snow. And then his stomach dropped when he saw the unmistakable tail end of a car.

"Down here!" he yelled. "It's down here!"

Mark began scrambling, sliding down the snowy slope because he couldn't get his footing. "Andrea! Can you hear me?"

If she was in that car…

God, let her be alive, he prayed. *Don't let me be too late.*

"Andrea…"

The sound creeped into Andrea's subconscious. Was someone calling her name?

She tried to move. Tried to open her eyes.

Were there people around her? She thought she heard voices. But why couldn't she open her eyes?

She tried to speak. The truth was, her brain was so clouded, she didn't even know what she wanted to say.

Lord, she was tired. So very tired.

Her brain tried to make sense of what was going on. Was something happening? Or was she hallucinating?

She still couldn't open her eyes, and suddenly she felt drained of energy. There was no point fighting sleep any longer. It was easier to drift away.

* * *

Feeling entirely helpless, Mark stood back and watched as the rescue team secured Andrea in a stretcher. There had been a flurry of activity and excitement, complete with police, ambulance, and media crews. Mark stood to the side, keeping his eyes on the stretcher. He knew she was alive, but he didn't know how she was doing. He had no clue if she'd even make it. He had asked one paramedic, and he'd been instructed to simply wait.

Mark inhaled a frazzled breath. He wished there was something he could do.

There was something, he realized. He could continue to have faith. He'd been led to Andrea by divine intervention. She was alive, and by God's grace she would stay that way.

Mark hadn't expected the media attention.

A couple hours after Andrea had been rushed to the hospital, he was giving a press conference at the hospital's front entrance. There was a slew of media standing in front of him. Some had cameras and microphones, while some held notepads and pens. It had already been a very long day, with no signs of ending any time soon.

"Mr. Potter—how did you know where Ms. Dawson was?"

It was the same question the police and paramedics had asked him. There was only one answer he could give.

"It's a miracle," he answered simply.

"Mr. Potter," someone practically shouted. "Can you elaborate?"

Mark surveyed the crowd of curious reporters. He was tempted to tell them that he really didn't want to be down here—he wanted to be upstairs with Andrea.

But this was the holiday season, a season for miracles, and this was indeed a miracle. Any way you slice it, this would be a positive, uplifting news story, and perhaps a reason for those who had lost faith to believe again.

"I had a dream," he answered. "I had a dream that Andrea was trapped in a car somewhere and needed my help."

"Amazing," he heard someone mutter.

"Exactly how did you know where she was?" a male reporter asked.

"I wasn't sure. But I had a very vivid picture of a certain landscape, which turned out to be exactly where her car was."

"But how did you—"

"How did I find this place I dreamed of?" Mark interjected. He shrugged. "It wasn't easy, let me tell you. It took nearly all day of searching the neighborhoods in Buffalo. Finally, when I started toward Grand Island, I had a very strong sense that I was heading in the right direction, and when I did, I got the most overpowering feeling when I came to this overpass. It looked exactly like what I had dreamed about."

Reporters scribbled. Cameramen fought for the best angle.

"So you believe this was a miracle?" a woman asked.

"It *was* a miracle," Mark replied. "Now, if you'll excuse me…"

"Mr. Potter," people called.

"That's the whole story," he replied.

"Who is Ms. Dawson to you?" someone yelled as he turned on his heel.

The question stopped him cold. A bittersweet feeling washed over him. He remembered ten years ago, how much Andrea had meant to him then. And he remembered how she had broken his heart.

There was a part of him that believed their meeting again was fate. But then, she had a son. So he was sure there had to be a man in the picture somewhere, whether or not she was married to him.

"She's a friend," he replied softly, then turned to head into the hospital.

Andrea had the distinct feeling that something was different. She abruptly opened her eyes.

Where am I? she wondered as her eyes focused on the pale blue room. She turned her head to the right, feeling pain shoot through her neck as she did. There was a large window, letting in sunlight. Her gaze darted to the left, and she saw a door.

This was a hospital, she suddenly realized.

And then snippets of memory started to come back to her. The car. Driving. Careening off the overpass.

Her heart started to race.

Her car. *Terrence!* Good, Lord. Who was looking after Terrence?

She reached for the nurse call button on her bed and began to press it in rapid succession.

The door turned. As she whipped her gaze in its direction, all her anxiety ebbed away. Her heart melted at the sight of her son—in her mother's arms.

"Terrence." She was surprised to hear that her voice was hoarse.

Andrea's mother, Gretta Dawson, broke out in a smile. "Oh, Andrea."

"Mummy, Mummy!" Terrence yelled. He wriggled his way out of his grandmother's arms and bounded toward Andrea.

"Terrence, be careful," Gretta cautioned. "Your mother's hurt."

"Mom, it's okay," Andrea said when Terrence stopped and looked at her with caution. She reached her right arm out in invitation. Her left arm was tightly bandaged and she could hardly move it. "Come here, baby." She wanted to take Terrence in her arms and squeeze the heck out of him.

Terrence's cute little laugh was music to her ears. He skipped across the room and leapt onto the chair beside her bed. Then he crawled onto the bed with her, planting kisses on her face.

"Mummy, Mummy, Mummy!"

"Oh, my sweet baby." Andrea squeezed Terrence as hard as she could with her good arm.

The door turned again. This time a nurse entered, a wide smile on her plump face. "So, you're awake."

"Yes." Andrea's eyes flitted between her mother and the nurse. "I hate to ask this, but how long have I been here?"

"You came in last night," the nurse answered. "But you were trapped in your car for two days. You're one lucky lady."

"The last few days are a blur to me."

"You were barely conscious when the paramedics got to

you. And let me tell you, things could have been a lot worse. With the snow, the weather was actually fairly mild. You were dehydrated and your body temperature was low, but you escaped without even frost bite."

More memories came back to her. She remembered voices, and the feeling that she was being taken out of her car. It had seemed like a dream to her, but obviously it hadn't been.

Andrea watched as the nurse took her blood pressure and then her temperature. "Who...who found me?"

"Sweetheart," the nurse said, "it's a miracle. The guy who found you said he dreamt that he knew where you were. Every news station has been covering this. They can't wait to talk to you."

"You're kidding."

The nurse shook her head. "Where this guy found you...it's nothing short of a miracle. I hate to say it, but you could have been there until the spring thaw."

Andrea shivered. If she hadn't been found until the spring, there was no way she would have survived.

Thank you, God, she said silently, remembering now all the prayers she had uttered while in the car. She squeezed Terrence tighter.

"You seem pretty healthy," the nurse announced. "Your blood pressure's a little low, but nothing to worry about." She paused. "I'm sure you're hungry. I'll make sure a plate of food is sent up right away."

"That would be great, thanks," Andrea said. Though she hadn't eaten for so long, she'd passed the stage of hunger pangs.

The nurse left the room.

Her mother, Gretta, squeezed Andrea's hand. "You gave us quite a scare, young lady."

"At least I probably lost ten pounds."

"Oh, don't say that," her mother scolded. "We were out of our minds with worry."

"I can't believe you're here."

"We're all here."

"What do you mean, all?"

"Your father. And your brother and his wife. Your nephew and niece."

"Wow." The family hadn't gotten together for Thanksgiving this year because everyone lived far apart and had been busy doing their own thing. It was sad that it took a near tragedy to bring everyone together.

"We got word that you were missing about thirty-six hours ago when your babysitter called. We knew something had to have happened because there was no way you would have ever left Terrence. We got on a plane first thing the next morning."

And if she hadn't been found, her family could have been mourning now instead of rejoicing. Tears filled Andrea's eyes.

"Everyone's in the cafeteria. Terrence and I came to check on you. But now that you're awake… Will you be okay while I go and get them?"

"Of course." Andrea stroked her son's cheek. "Just leave Terrence with me."

Gretta was at the door when it occurred to Andrea that she hadn't asked the most important question.

"Mom," she called.

"Yes, honey?" Gretta replied, turning.

"I didn't ask this, but who found me?"

"Oh," her mother said, her face changing to an expression Andrea couldn't quite read. "Mark Potter."

"M-M-Mark?"

"Yes, honey. The same Mark Potter you used to know years ago."

CHAPTER 6

Andrea's mind was reeling as her mother left the room. Mark Potter. Everything came back to her now. Seeing him at the restaurant. Feeling distraught about his sudden reappearance in her life. Being distracted as she was driving and then skidding out of control.

"Oh my God," she said softly. *Mark* had found her?

But how? How could he have found her where she was? Had he been following her?

Sitting there and wondering wasn't going to give her answers, so she concentrated on the here and now and gave Terrence a kiss on the temple. "Am I ever glad to see you, sweetheart."

"I'm glad to see you too, Mummy. I was so scared."

"Oh, sweetheart. You know your mommy would never leave you, right?" Though the awful reality was, many parents died and left children in need of care. Bad things happened in the world all the time. She was Terrence's only parent, and the thought that she almost hadn't come home to him had her throat swelling with emotion. He needed her more than anything, and she needed to be here more than anything.

"I can't believe I was so stupid."

"You're not stupid, Mummy."

Andrea didn't realize she had spoken out loud. She kissed Terrence again. He had his little arms wrapped around her waist like he didn't want to ever let go.

"I know I'm not stupid. I'm not sure why I said that. I guess I'm just upset with myself for being away from you for more than two days."

"But you're here now, Mummy."

"You're so smart," Andrea said, smiling down at her son. Terrence was right. She was here now, and that was all that mattered.

Holding a bouquet of white carnations, Mark entered the hospital and headed to Andrea's room on the third floor. After last night's press conference, he had checked on Andrea and found that she was still unconscious. Given that he wasn't family, he wasn't allowed to stay with her, so he'd decided to leave and head to his hotel for the night.

He had briefly run into her parents and brother, all of whom had thanked him for saving Andrea's life. He knew he shouldn't judge them by their past actions, but that didn't make him feel any more comfortable around them, not after knowing how much they had disliked him ten years ago. He had been friendly, but hadn't hung around long. He did need rest after his very long day, and there was a part of him that didn't want to be around when Andrea's significant other showed up.

As the elevator climbed, Mark's stomach clenched with anxiety. Here he was, now a successful businessman, yet he was still uncertain about seeing people who had once considered him not good enough for their daughter. It was amazing that no matter how successful you became, you still had battle scars and insecurities.

The truth was, Andrea's family had opened their arms to him. After all, he had saved their daughter's life.

As the elevator doors opened, Mark wondered what Andrea's boyfriend or husband looked like. He supposed it shouldn't matter after all this time—they'd both gone on with their lives—but it did.

Mark headed toward Andrea's room. Mrs. Dawson was standing in the hallway, as well as Andrea's sister-in-law, Melissa, whom he'd met last night. Melissa's young daughter and son hung close to her side.

Mark picked up his pace. As he neared them, he asked, "Is there a change?"

Gretta's smile was ear-to-ear. "Oh, Mark. She's awake, and she's doing so well." She wrapped him in a warm hug. "God bless you for bringing our daughter back to us."

"Can I see her?" Mark asked as he pulled back.

"Her father and brother are in there right now. And Terrence, of course. They only want two people in at a time, but Terrence won't leave her side."

"I'll bet," Mark said, smiling. He had met the little boy last night.

"I'll just knock on the door," Gretta said.

Mark waited while Gretta went to the door. Moments later, Andrea's father, Stewart, exited the room, followed by her brother, Albert, who was carrying Terrence.

Stewart Dawson was a much thinner version of the man he had once been, but he still had a smile that lit up a room. "Mark," he said, "she's all yours."

"Hi, Mr. Potter!" Terrence exclaimed happily.

"Hey, little man." Mark rubbed his head, then started for Andrea's room.

Gently pushing the door open, Mark peered inside. Andrea lay quietly on her side, facing the window. He suddenly had doubts about disturbing her.

Stop making excuses, he told himself.

"Mmm mmm." He cleared his throat as he walked into the small room, and Andrea instantly turned her head in his direction.

"Hey," Mark said softly.

"Hey," Andrea echoed, her eyes lighting up as she looked at him.

Mark hesitated, then said, "These are for you."

"From what I hear, I should be the one giving *you* flowers."

"You certainly have a lot of them," Mark commented, looking at the many gorgeous bouquets along the windowsill.

"Let me tell you, it's like a florist shop up in here. I've been getting flowers from people I don't even know."

Mark frowned, confused, but then it hit him. "The news story."

"Uh-huh. I had no clue people would care so much."

"There's a lot of bad in the world, but there's also a lot of good."

Mark lowered himself onto the chair beside Andrea's bed and handed her the carnations. She grinned as she took them, instantly bringing the bouquet to her nose for a good whiff.

"So," Mark began. "It's been a long time."

Andrea couldn't help but chuckle, it was such an odd thing to say under the circumstances, even if it was true.

"Yeah, it has been," she agreed. "With a lot more drama than I'd bargained for."

Mark offered Andrea a small smile. "What happened—"

"How did you find me—"

They both spoke at the same time.

After a pause, Mark asked, "Have you seen the news?"

"I did, yes. And it's been crazy up in here, with all the reporters and cameras. They left about an hour ago."

"You heard what I said, right? That I had a dream that you were in trouble." Andrea nodded. "Incredible, I know, but it's true. It was like an angel spoke to me, told me you were in trouble. And showed me where to find you. I can't really describe it any other way."

Andrea shook her head in amazement. "I could ask you a million more questions, but there's only one answer to what happened. It was a miracle. The Lord works in mysterious ways. I've always known that, and this is just proof."

"Amen to that."

Andrea's expression saddened a little as she looked at Mark. "I'm sorry," she said. "Sorry I said *no* to meeting with you."

"Shh. That doesn't matter. I'm here now, whether you like it or not."

Mark's smile was contagious. "I do want you here. I hope you know that."

"Hey. We're friends, right? Even if we haven't been in touch over the years."

Friends. The word stung a little, because it made Andrea think of all the hopes she'd had for her relationship with Mark.

"I guess we haven't been great friends over the years, have we?" Andrea asked.

"That's not important. Not right now. What matters is where we go from here."

Andrea reached for Mark's hand. "You're right."

Mark lowered his gaze to their linked hands. It was shocking how good Andrea's hand felt in his, after all this time.

"I met your son," Mark said after a moment. "He's a cutie."

"Thank you. Oh, Mark. The thought that I might not make it back to him…"

"But you did."

"Thanks to you."

A moment of silence passed between them, then Mark asked, "I've seen your parents and your brother, but what about…your husband, boyfriend…?"

"Are you fishing?" Andrea teased.

"I'm curious."

"I have neither. It's just me and Terrence."

"Oh," Mark said, hoping he didn't sound too eager about her admission.

"What can you do? That's the way life goes sometimes. Terrence has been my biggest blessing, my greatest joy."

The door opened, and both Mark and Andrea looked in that direction. The nurse entered the room.

"Time for me to do my thing," she announced.

Mark got to his feet. "I'm gonna get going."

"Will I see you later?" Andrea quickly asked.

"Sure. Of course."

Mark started for the door, and the nurse began taking Andrea's blood pressure.

"Mark," Andrea called just as he reached the door.

Slowly, he turned to face her. "Yeah?"

"How long are you staying in town?"

He shrugged. "I figured I'd at least stick around for the weekend, make sure you're okay."

"Well, my family and I figured that when I get out of here, we'll have a post-Thanksgiving dinner since we didn't get together then. Why don't you stay in town and have dinner with me and my family? I mean, it's only fitting. You should be there. Unless you have to get back home. Oh my God. I didn't even think that you might have a wife, or children…" Andrea stopped talking when she realized she was rambling. In fact, when the nurse asked her to open wide to stick a thermometer in her mouth, she was grateful for the excuse to shut up.

"I'd love to be there," Mark said. "Dinner certainly beats my offer of coffee," he added with a wink.

Andrea watched him leave the room, a feeling of warmth growing deep in her soul.

CHAPTER 7

"Why don't you let me do that?" Gretta asked, taking the oven mitt from Andrea's hand.

Andrea plucked the oven mitt from her mother's fingers. "I've got it."

"You're sure?"

"Yes, I'm sure."

"You really should take it easy. Melissa can help me in the kitchen."

"I'm not an invalid, Mom."

"I know that," Gretta said softly. "But you only have one good arm. Let us help."

Two days after Andrea had been released from the hospital, she, her mother, and Melissa were getting their family dinner ready. She was still a bit tired, and her left arm was pretty much useless because it had been fractured, but

Andrea was surprisingly upbeat. She had a lot for which to be grateful, and she wasn't taking a moment for granted.

"Okay, Mom," she said to her mother. "You take care of the turkey. I'll make sure the table's in order."

As Andrea made her way to the small dining room area in her apartment, she glanced at the wall clock. It was twenty after four, and she'd told Mark four-thirty. She was anxious for him to get here.

She was recounting the silverware when there was a knock on her door. Her heart pounded hard in her chest.

"I'll get it," Melissa said.

"No," Andrea said, quickly heading in the direction of the door. "Let me."

It had to be Mark. She couldn't help smiling from ear-to-ear.

Then she felt a moment of self-doubt, wondering if she looked good enough. Should she quickly reapply her lipstick?

"Open the door," she told herself.

Inhaling a deep breath, Andrea did just that.

There stood Mark, his hands pushed in the pockets of his slacks, his long leather jacket making him look like he'd just stepped off the cover of *GQ* magazine.

"Hi," she said softly. *You look fine!*, she added silently.

"Hello, Andrea."

"Come in," Andrea said, stepping backward and opening the door wide.

Mark stepped into the foyer, his masculine presence seeming to fill the area entirely. It made Andrea think of how much she had missed a man in her life.

It made her think of how much she had missed Mark.

Oh, she had pushed away every memory of him over the years, but that didn't mean he didn't still have a special place in her heart.

"I'm glad you came," she told him.

"It sure smells good in here," Mark commented.

"There's turkey, candied yams, collard greens, sweet potato pie." Andrea paused to grin up at Mark. "I hope you brought your appetite."

"I did."

Mark shrugged out of his coat.

"Oh, let me take that." She took the coat from him and placed it on the coat tree. Then she linked her arm through his. "Come on in and say hi to everybody."

She's still so beautiful, Mark thought as he walked with Andrea. Her light brown skin looked good enough to eat. Her body had rounded to give her soft feminine curves that she didn't have in high school. Her shoulder-length straight hair had a delicate floral scent, the kind that made him want to bury his nose deep in her raven tresses and inhale the essence of her.

As they reached the living room, Mark's heart started to race. He did a quick sweep of the room and adjoining kitchen, noting that the place was small, but cozy. Andrea's brother and father were sitting on one sofa, while Terrence and his two cousins were on a second sofa, laughing.

Andrea's father instantly got to his feet, a warm smile lighting up his face. Stewart started toward him at the same time that Gretta floated toward him from the kitchen.

"Mark," Gretta said warmly, wrapping him in a strong hug. "It is so good to see you."

Then Stewart was hugging him, and then Andrea's brother and her sister-in-law. And when the adults finally let go of him, Terrence practically threw himself into Mark's arms.

"Hey, little man," Mark said. He ignored the slight pang in his heart. More than anything, Mark wanted a wife and some children.

"I helped Mummy cook the turkey," Terrence announced proudly.

"You did?" Mark asked with encouragement in his voice.

"Uh-huh."

"Then I bet it tastes real good."

"It's gonna be yummy," Terrence assured him.

"Make yourself comfortable," Gretta told Mark when he put Terrence down.

Stewart patted Mark's back. "Come on into the living room, Mark. Let's have a beer."

The irony wasn't lost on him that had this been ten years ago, Andrea's parents and her brother wouldn't have been so welcoming. He was the same person now that he was then, except that he had more money now.

And of course, he'd saved Andrea's life.

"Mark?" Stewart said.

"Hmm?"

"I asked if you wanted a light beer or regular."

"Light, please."

"One light beer coming up," Melissa said cheerfully.

Mark watched her scramble toward the kitchen. Beyond Melissa, his eyes met Andrea's. And held. Her lips pulled in the slightest of smiles, a smile that tugged at his heart.

Much later, warm laughter and good cheer filled Andrea's apartment. It pleased her immensely.

"Mark, how about another piece of pumpkin pie?" Gretta asked as she got up from the sofa.

"Oh, no." He patted his belly. "I'm stuffed."

"Another glass of wine, then?"

"No, thank you. In fact, I really must be going."

"So soon?" Stewart asked.

"Stay, please," Melissa urged. "We have *got* to play another round of monopoly."

"Yeah," Albert agreed. "And this time, I won't be such a pushover."

"Ha." Mark laughed. "I wish I could, but I can't. Though I did have a great time." And he did. His anxiety regarding the Dawsons had dissipated as they'd spent time together. He'd once figured them snobby and uncaring, but they were good people who obviously loved their daughter immensely.

Mark got to his feet, and Andrea immediately followed suit. "You really have to leave already?" she asked.

"Yeah. I have a conference call in the morning. In fact…" His voice trailed off as he looked at Andrea, then her family. "I might have to head back to Chicago by the afternoon."

"Oh, no." Andrea frowned.

Mark simply shrugged. "I'll see. I wouldn't mind sticking around for another day or two."

He let his statement hang between them, and Andrea knew what he was getting at. He wanted to spend more time with her. She wanted to spend more time with him, too.

Mark looked around the room. The children had gone to bed an hour before. "Mr. and Mrs. Dawson, Melissa and Albert—good night to you all."

"Good night," they said in unison. Gretta gave him a warm hug.

"Well, let me walk you out," Andrea said.

She walked Mark to the doorway, aware that her family's eyes were boring holes into her back. They were all wondering what was happening between her and Mark.

So was she.

"Mark," she began in a low voice, "I'm really glad you came. I had a nice time. We all did."

"I had a nice time, too."

Andrea took a moment to search for his coat. Handing it to him, she said, "So, you might be heading back to Chicago?"

Mark nodded. "I have to present an ad campaign to the company I told you about."

"Oh. Well."

"But…I do have to head back to Buffalo soon. I made some new contacts and we've already been in touch about setting up some meetings."

Andrea perked up. "Oh. Then that means I can see you again. Soon."

"Looks that way."

"I'm proud of you, by the way. You certainly have made a success of yourself."

Mark slipped into his coat. "I'm blessed."

But was he dating anyone? He hadn't specifically told her, so she didn't think he was, but she wanted to be sure. "Will someone be happy when you return to Chicago?"

Mark shrugged. "Yeah, sure."

Andrea's stomach lurched. "Really?"

"Uh-huh. My partners, for one. Those guys can't seem to run things smoothly with me gone. Do you know how many calls I got with crisis after crisis while I've been here?"

"Oh, you!" Andrea's shoulders drooped with relief as she laughed.

"What—oh, you were trying to find out if I have a girl-friend?" Mark asked innocently.

"The thought crossed my mind. You haven't said one way or the other."

"No. There's no one special." He paused. "Is that okay?"

"Fine by me."

"All right, Miss Dawson." Mark looped his arms around her waist and pulled her close. "I have to be going."

The low timbre of his voice made a shiver of delight dance down Andrea's spine. As he hugged her, she squeezed him as best she could with her good arm.

All too soon, he pulled away from her. "Wait," Andrea suddenly said.

Mark looked at her with concern. "What?"

Andrea subtly flicked her eyes upward. Mark followed her line of sight.

"We *are* standing under the mistletoe," Andrea said.

"Ah." Mark chuckled warmly. "We are. In that case."

He reached for her face, trailing a finger along her cheek. A jolt of electricity zapped through her body. Andrea gazed up at him with expectation, savoring the feel of his hand clutching her back and her breasts pressing against his chest.

And then his lips came down on hers, soft and feathery and completely exhilarating.

"And now," Mark whispered in her ear, "I have to go."

Andrea practically melted like butter. She watched Mark leave her apartment, her heart full of more happiness than she had felt in a long, long time.

CHAPTER 8

"I am higher than a kite, that's how amazing I feel," Andrea said the next day, aware that she was smiling like a fool as she chatted with her friend. Allison, a fellow student in her business class, had brought her class notes, but Andrea was too distracted to go over them. All she wanted to do was talk about Mark, and how the feelings she'd had for him years ago had come rushing back.

"I was sad when he called me this morning to say he had to head back to Chicago, but then he told me he hadn't stopped thinking about me." Andrea sighed with glee. "Honestly, I can't remember feeling this…this good about a guy since…"

"Since the first time you were involved with him?"

Andrea drew in a deep breath. "Maybe. Yeah."

"*I've* certainly never seen you this excited about any guy before. You know I was starting to get concerned."

"Shut up," Andrea said, chuckling.

"Hey, I'm happy for you."

"I know it probably seems sudden, but it's like the accident knocked me over the head. It made me realize how much I want him in my life."

"Are you sure this isn't a savior-worship complex thing?"

Andrea shook her head as she reached for her coffee mug. "If I hadn't known him before, I might think that. But with Mark, it's more about me realizing that life is short, and too precious to waste a moment of it not going for what you want." She paused to sip her coffee. "I want Mark."

Allison's lips twisted in a lopsided grin. "And how does he feel about you?"

"The kiss last night—it was the most sweet and gentle and exciting kiss I've ever experienced. It was like my whole body came alive."

"Oooh," Allison crooned. "So, when do you see him again?"

Andrea sighed wistfully. "Some time this week, I think. He's back here for business. Or maybe just to see me. He said he was going to miss me every second he was gone."

"He sounds romantic. You know I love a romantic man."

"Maybe you'll get to meet him soon. Christmas is less than three weeks away. I plan to invite him to spend that day with me and Terrence. Something small and intimate."

"I'm so happy for you," Allison said. "Really, I am. You deserve it, especially after what you've been through."

"Thanks," Andrea replied, already wondering when her phone would ring and she could talk to Mark again.

* * *

That night, as Andrea looked over the notes from her business class, the phone rang. She instantly dropped the notes and grabbed the receiver. "Hello?"

"Hey."

Andrea bit down on her bottom lip to suppress a happy giggle. "Hey, yourself."

"What are you doing?"

"Nothing much. I put Terrence to bed not too long ago and was doing some studying."

"Trying to get caught up on your studies. Should I let you go?"

"Not a chance. I've been thinking about you all day."

Mark chuckled softly. The sound always made her feel woozy inside.

"I've been thinking about you, too," he said. "How's your arm?"

"A lot better. I might even go back to work by the end of the week."

"What?" Mark asked, surprised.

"If I do, I'll only do hostessing duties. I wish I didn't have to, but unfortunately, I need the money."

"Can't your parents help you out?"

"They'll be here for the week, helping me with Terrence."

"I meant financially."

Andrea paused. "I know we didn't really talk about it in detail, but things aren't the same for my family as they used to be. My parents lost their business."

"Your father mentioned that," Mark said. "But surely they have some money.

"They do, yeah, but I'm trying make my own way in the world."

"Which is admirable, but if you need help—"

"My parents would never let me live it down. Well, maybe not in an I-told-you-so way. But in a way that would make me feel like I couldn't make it on my own. And I would hate that."

"Are you sure?" Mark asked. "They seemed nothing but warm and accepting of you when I saw them."

"I don't know. Maybe things have changed. Guess I'm too proud to ask them for any help, or to accept any if they offered." She paused. "When I was a child, I had no clue what it took to make money. And then we lost everything." She had listened while her father talked frankly about this with Mark yesterday, humbled by the change in him. It was sad to say, but without millions in the bank, her father was much more down to earth, much easier to relate to on a real level.

"I know how much it means to earn something for yourself," Andrea went on. "Like you did. No one can ever take that away from you."

"You're right about that."

"It might be hard, but anything worth having isn't easy."

"The way it wasn't easy for us?" Mark asked.

"I…" Andrea began, stumped by his candid question. "I guess, yeah. What are you saying?"

"I don't know. I suppose I'm trying to figure out what's happening between us. *If* there is something happening."

"I…I think there is," Andrea answered softly. "I think

we've been given a second chance to explore what might have been."

Mark was silent, and Andrea was wondering what he was thinking, but afraid to ask. Instead she said, "So, when are you coming back to see me?"

"Is two days too soon?"

"Two days!" Andrea practically shouted.

"Is that excitement...or panic?"

"You know the answer to that. I'm thrilled. I just didn't expect you back so soon."

"One of my new contacts in Buffalo wanted to set up a meeting right away. So, off I go."

"Mark, I can't wait to see you."

"Just keep the mistletoe out. Because I'd like to pick up where we left off."

On Wednesday, Andrea practically lived by the phone while her parents were at the mall with Terrence. Her nerves were fried, she was so anxious to hear from Mark.

When it rang, she jumped. Then she snatched up the receiver. "Hello?"

"Andrea, it's Mark."

"Mark," Andrea said, relieved. "How are you? How did your meeting go?"

"I'm fine, and the meeting went really well. Looks like I might have myself a new account."

"Congratulations."

"Thanks." Mark paused. "Are you busy right now?"

She wasn't, but she said, "Not particularly, why?"

"I thought...I was wondering if we could get together soon. Maybe get some dinner, see a movie."

"You have time for that? You don't have more meetings?"

"I'm free."

"Well, it just so happens that I'm free, too. My parents have taken Terrence to the mall."

"Can you be ready in half an hour?"

She had been ready all day. "Sure, half an hour is fine."

Andrea was waiting in the lobby of her building when her parents and Terrence suddenly started up the walkway. Seeing her immediately, Terrence tore his hand from his grandmother's and raced toward the building's glass doors.

Andrea swung open the door and bent to accept her son. "Ooh," she said as his body collided with her left arm. "Terrence, sweetheart."

"Mummy!"

Andrea glanced in her parents' direction. They were carrying several bags, which meant they had probably splurged on Terrence.

"Did you have a good time, sweetheart?" Andrea asked him.

"Uh-huh," he replied, nodding vigorously. "Mummy, where are you going?"

"Oh. Well, I'm going out for dinner with Mark."

"Can I come?"

The door opened and Gretta and Stewart stepped into the lobby. "Hello, Andrea," Gretta said. "Were you heading out?"

"I was just telling Terrence that I'm going out for dinner with Mark."

"I want to go," Terrence proclaimed.

"I won't be gone long, Terrence," Andrea assured him.

"Why won't you take me, Mummy?"

Andrea looked into Terrence's eyes, not sure what to say. "It's not that I don't want to take you, it's just that… Don't you remember that Mrs. Shields is taking you swimming tonight? You and Bobby."

"That's tonight?"

"Mmm hmm."

"Oh." Terrence pouted a little.

"By the time you get back from swimming, I'll be here, ready to tuck you in. Okay?"

"But what if sumthin' happens to you again?"

Andrea hugged her son. "Oh, sweetheart. Nothing's going to happen to me."

Worry tugged at Terrence's lips. "You promise?"

"Cross my heart, I promise." She made the sign of a cross over her heart.

Her answer seemed to satisfy Terrence, because he gave her a big smile. "Okay."

"Come, Terrence," Gretta said. "Time for us to go upstairs."

"Buh bye, Mummy." Terrence waved a little hand at her.

"Bye, sweetheart. I love you."

A horn beeped, and Andrea whipped her head around. A red Pontiac Grand Am was parked at the curb.

Mark.

"We'll see you later," Gretta said.

"Yes, later," Andrea replied, looking at her mother. Gretta was giving her a pointed look, though a grin played on her lips. "Call me if you need me."

Andrea gave her family one final wave, then was out the door.

Before she made it to the car, the driver's side door opened and Mark stepped out. Once again, the sight of him took her breath away. His long leather coat was open, revealing a black turtleneck. It fit his body to perfection.

"Hello, Andrea." Mark walked toward her and wrapped her in an embrace.

"Hello, Mark." Andrea wished she could stay in his arms all day.

"I checked out movie options. Do you want to see funny, or scary or—"

"Actually," Andrea said as she pulled away from Mark, "I think it will just have to be dinner tonight. I promised Terrence I would tuck him in. I'll have to take a rain check, okay?"

A rain check would be easier if he lived in Buffalo, but Mark didn't say that. "I bet the little guy's worried about you, right?"

"He gets scared every time I leave. I hope that passes soon. I keep assuring him that nothing's gonna happen to me."

"You're a good mother. It's obvious Terrence adores you."

A soft smile touched Andrea's lips. "Thank you. I adore him, too."

"Let's get out of this cold," Mark suggested. He walked to the car and opened the door for Andrea. When she was securely in the car, he closed it.

"So, where are we going?" Andrea asked.

"I was thinking we could head to Mama's Place."

Andrea threw a sideways glance at him. "You're kidding, right?"

Mark chuckled. "No, we're not going to Mama's Place. I called around, and there's a restaurant downtown I'd like to check out."

"Sure." Andrea paused. "Not that the food at Mama's Place isn't good, mind you. I just don't—"

"You don't have to explain yourself," Mark told her as he started to drive. "I understand. In fact, I'd think it was strange if you *did* want to eat there."

"Oh." Andrea's laugh said she was relieved. "I forgot all about your sense of humor."

"I forgive you."

Andrea laughed again.

Mark drove to the intersection, then turned right onto the main road.

"Did you have a nice time at the dinner?" Andrea asked him. "Because you seemed a bit quiet. I wasn't sure."

"I had a great time. It was nice, especially since I didn't do anything for Thanksgiving."

"I didn't ask, and you didn't say, but how are your parents?"

A pang stabbed Mark in his heart. "They've passed, Andrea."

"Oh my God. I'm so sorry."

"Two years ago, within six months of each other. My father had a heart attack, and my mother was killed in a car accident."

Andrea reached for Mark's hand. "Oh, Mark. How awful for you."

"Yeah." Mark drew in a deep breath. "But they're with me. All the time." He tapped on his chest with a finger. "In my heart."

Andrea's eyes filled with tears. She remembered Mark's parents well. They had loved her just as much as she had loved them.

"I…I really liked your parents. I…"

Mark squeezed her hand, offering *her* comfort. "It's okay."

Andrea wiped at a tear.

"Let's talk about Terrence," Mark suggested.

Instantly, Andrea smiled.

"There. That's what I want to see. Your smile."

If Andrea had ever doubted it before, she didn't now. Mark was an incredible man. He had a warm and giving heart and knew just what to say to make a person feel better.

And even though he could have let go of her hand, he didn't. Andrea didn't want him to.

She settled back against the seat and looked out the window. She didn't talk, and neither did Mark. They drove in comfortable silence, as if they had done this a million times before.

Their connected hands seemed to say all that was in their hearts.

CHAPTER 9

Andrea was in awe the moment she stepped inside Amoré, a five-star Italian restaurant in downtown Buffalo. The walls were covered in dark red velvet. The place was filled with dim lighting and lots of candles, creating a romantic atmosphere.

"Mark," Andrea whispered, clutching his arm, "I don't think I'm appropriately dressed."

"Andrea, you look beautiful."

His tender compliment relaxed her instantly—and filled her heart with happiness.

Mark walked up to the hostess. "I have a reservation for two. Potter."

"Come this way, Mr. Potter."

She led them to a table in a corner. It was more private than the rest. There was a bucket on the table, chilling a bottle of champagne.

"Mark?" Andrea looked up at him.

"Thank you," he said to the hostess.

Ever the gentleman, Mark held her chair for her. As Andrea sat, she said, "You arranged this for us?"

"I figured we had a lot to celebrate. Your recovery, for one thing."

And perhaps something more?

"You are just the sweetest—" Andrea stopped short. If she continued, she just might blurt out that she loved him. Did she? Could she, after all this time?

In a way, it seemed impossible. But that's what she was feeling in her heart, like things had picked up where they left off with Mark ten years ago.

Their waiter arrived and poured the champagne. When he was gone, Mark lifted his glass in a toast. "To life's surprises," he said.

"To miracles."

They clinked their glasses.

They spent some minutes going over the menu and ordering their food.

With that out of the way, Andrea spoke. "I have to tell you, Terrence had such a great time at dinner on Sunday. He was raving about you the next morning, saying how much fun he had decorating the tree with you. It was nice, Mark, to see him so happy."

Mark nodded as he looked at her, but a question popped into his mind. He wondered if she meant that Terrence had been happy to have a man around, a man who could be a father figure.

"Tell me about Terrence's father," he said.

Andrea rolled her eyes as she sipped her champagne. "There's nothing to tell. He was a guy I met at Princeton, I was wildly in love with him, and I thought he felt the same way about me. He said he did. And then I got pregnant." Andrea shrugged as if to say the rest of the story was obvious.

"Does he ever see Terrence?"

Andrea shook her head vehemently. "It drives me crazy when I think about it. But if he's the kind of man who doesn't care about his child, then we're both better off without him."

"Did you love him as much as you loved me?" Mark was horrified to realize he'd asked that question aloud. He quickly said, "You know, forget I asked that. I'm not sure where that came from."

Andrea reached across the table and covered his hand with hers. "No, you're right to ask. I mean, I think it's something we've both wanted to talk about, but neither of us really has brought it up. That's why we're here, isn't it? That's why we're spending time together. We're trying to reconnect…aren't we?"

Mark nodded. "I know I still have feelings for you."

"But?" Andrea asked. Because she sensed there was one.

Mark shrugged. He fiddled with the stem of his champagne flute. "I know it's been ten years, but I *do* have some questions."

"I'm sure you do." Andrea sighed. "But first, let me apologize to you. You know the truth now, that my family lost their business. I didn't mean to lie to you that day at the restaurant. It was just that seeing you caught me off guard, and I was self-conscious about not being at the place in my life I had planned to be…"

Mark waved a hand dismissively. "That's neither here nor there."

"You sure? Because it just slipped out. I don't want you to think that I'm the type of person who would lie to you."

"Why'd you end things, Andrea?" At her confused look, he said, "I know what you told me, that you didn't love me anymore. That you realized your parents were right and we were from two different worlds. But I never believed that."

A lump suddenly lodged in Andrea's throat, a lump caused by the bittersweet memories of yesteryear. How had she ever said those words to Mark?

It was seeing him with Marsha Whitfield that had gotten her so riled, so completely insecure. She'd never given him a chance to explain. She'd simply dumped him before he could dump her. Given everything that had happened, she wondered why Mark even wanted to be within five hundred feet of her. At least he didn't hate her for what she'd done.

"You want the truth?" she asked.

"The truth."

"I loved you deeply. You knew that. But my parents forced me to break up with you. Even still, I wasn't sure I would. Then, when I showed up at your football game and I saw you with that cheerleader, Marsha Whitfield—I guess I kinda lost my mind."

"Marsha?" Mark looked confused.

"She was flirting with you, and I freaked out. I waited until she walked away from you and then I went to you and told you what I did."

"I was never interested in Marsha."

"I was young and insecure and jealous. And torn. My parents were forcing me to end my relationship with you. So when I saw you with her, that became a convenient excuse to do what they'd demanded." Andrea paused. "I'm sorry."

The memories came rushing back. As if it were yesterday, Mark remembered how, after he had graduated from Belfield High, he had asked Andrea to come see him at the school's football field. He and a bunch of guys had gotten together to hang out and throw the football. Mark had wanted to spend every free moment with Andrea before leaving for Kent State, where he had been awarded a scholarship. Instead of being her normal cheery self, she had pouted and shrugged away from his touches. At first, he'd thought she was angry because he was going off to Kent State, even though he promised he would visit her as often as he could.

It was when he told her that he was going to miss her that she shattered his world, leaving him wondering what on earth had happened. "I don't love you anymore," she'd told him. She had gone on to make things worse by saying, "It was fun while it lasted."

The words had hurt, more than he'd ever thought possible. Over the next few weeks, he had tried to reach her, but she had not taken any of his calls.

"Mark…"

The sound of Andrea's voice brought Mark back to the present.

"I'm sorry," she said again. "I can see it in your eyes, the same thing I saw the day I ended things. It's a look that's haunted me so much…"

Mark finished the champagne in his glass and poured himself another one. "I just…I never…" He shook his head, not completing his statement.

"Mark, please believe me. What I said to you was a lie. I was young and stupid. There's nothing more I can say."

Andrea shoulders slumped as she stared across the table at Mark. He wasn't meeting her eyes.

He finally lifted his gaze to hers. "I can't believe it still hurts."

"It still hurts me, too. But I hope we can move on. To a new place."

"I hope so, too."

They were interrupted by the food arriving, and spent the rest of the evening talking about more pleasant things. His career, her aspirations of opening her own business.

"You'd think that after my parents lost their business, it's the last thing I'd want to do. I want to open a children's clothing store as well."

"That doesn't surprise me," Mark said.

"Really? It surprised my parents. They keep telling me how hard it will be, especially with me being a single mother. But I can't let that stop me."

"People succeed despite the odds all the time."

"Exactly. I'm not planning on a chain of stores like my parents owned, but a small, personal boutique. If I can make a name for myself with one store, then I'll consider expanding."

Andrea's eyes suddenly lit up. "You know, I already know

that one of my assignments next semester will be to interview an entrepreneur. Maybe I can interview you."

"Sure."

Andrea and Mark fell silent when the waiter came to clear
their plates. He proceeded to tell them about dessert options.

Andrea opted for the flan, while Mark settled on a specialty coffee.

"You know," Andrea began, "I don't think I answered
your question."

"What question?"

"If I loved Terrence's father, Richard, as much as I loved
you." There was a flash of something in Mark's eyes, something Andrea couldn't read. She reached across the table
and covered his hand with hers. "The answer is, *no*, Mark. I
never loved Richard the way I loved you. I've never loved
anyone the way I loved you."

Mark didn't say anything, just linked his fingers with
hers and ran the pad of his thumb over her skin.

All too soon, the evening ended. Now, Mark was parked
outside Andrea's building. She didn't want to get out.

"I had a nice time," she told him. "I'm glad we…talked."

"I'm glad, too. It doesn't matter how old the pain is, if
there's no closure…"

Closure! Andrea's brain screamed. Was that what this was
about? Getting closure on their ten-year-old relationship?

The thought made Andrea's stomach clench.

She had to let him know that this was about more than
that for her. That despite everything that had happened

between them, she still cared for him deeply and hoped this could be a new beginning for them.

"Mark?" she began tentatively.

"Hmm?"

I love you, she almost said, surprising herself. *Did* she love him? And if she did, would it seem too sudden to tell him that—too contrived?

Instead she asked, "When do you leave town?"

"Some time tomorrow. I have to get back to the office."

Andrea groaned.

"I know," Mark said, sensing her frustration. "But Chicago's not that far. I can always catch a flight here to visit you. I know I'll have some time near the end of next week."

Andrea had lived without him for ten years, and now being apart for a week seemed too long. Since her accident, however, she didn't want to waste another moment. Her heart told her she should be with Mark, and she wanted to do everything in her power to make that happen.

"Christmas is just around the corner," she said. "Do you have plans?"

Mark shook his head. "No. Not really."

"Then maybe you could…spend it with me and Terrence?"

"We can certainly talk about that."

Andrea tried to read in Mark's eyes what he was thinking, but she couldn't. "Will you come by tomorrow before you leave for Chicago?"

"Definitely," Mark said. "I'll call you in the morning."

Andrea couldn't deny the sadness she felt at the thought of Mark leaving again, especially with so much unresolved between them. On Sunday, she'd had so much hope, but today she felt uncertain about where their relationship was headed. It wasn't anything specific Mark said.

Perhaps it was what he *hadn't* said.

"I wish we lived in the same city," Andrea told him. "It would be so much easier."

"You said yourself, nothing worth having ever comes easy."

Andrea wrinkled her nose. "I did, didn't I?"

"I'm sure Terrence is waiting for you." Mark opened his door. "Let me help you out."

Mark bristled against the cold as he stepped outside. Andrea watched as he hustled to her side of the car, wondering why some woman hadn't already snagged him. She almost asked him that as he walked her to her apartment's entrance, but thought better of it.

Inside the lobby, she gazed up at him. "Tomorrow?"

"Not so fast."

"Hmm—"

Before Andrea could finish her question, Mark drew her to him and planted his lips on hers. She gasped in surprise, then relaxed against him, slipping her good arm around his waist. His lips played over hers skillfully, gently nipping and suckling and leaving her breathless. When he finally pulled away from her, she collapsed against him with a satisfied sigh.

"Wow," she said.

"I hope that'll hold us until the next time we see each other."

"I'm kinda doubting that."

Mark's lips curled in a smile. "You're still something, you know that?" He gave her a soft peck on the cheek, which, surprisingly, had her heart racing as much as the previous kiss. "Tomorrow, okay?"

"Okay."

"Give Terrence a kiss for me," Mark told her.

"Sure. He'll like that."

Mark pulled the lobby door open and headed out of the building. Andrea didn't take her eyes off him as he sauntered to his car, occasionally glancing over his shoulder to see if she was still looking at him.

And she knew, without a doubt, that she *did* love him.

CHAPTER 10

"Mummy."

Andrea spun around at the sound of her son's voice. Terrence was standing behind her chair where she sat at her desk, clutching his favorite stuffed giraffe. He was barefoot on the cold tiled floor, and she immediately reached for him, pulling him onto her lap.

"Hi, sweetie," she cooed softly in his ear. "Did you sleep well?"

Resting his head against her bosom, Terrence nodded. "But I'm thirsty now. I want some juice."

"What kind of juice? Orange or apple?"

"Orange!" he announced proudly.

Giggling, Andrea planted a soft, wet kiss on Terrence's temple. "Orange it is. Go put some socks on, sweetie, and I'll get you something to eat."

Andrea's parents were still sleeping. With them around, and with seeing Mark, her life had been slightly more hectic than normal, so she had gotten up early this morning to work on her school assignment. It was due in a week, just before the Christmas break began. Thanks to Allison, she had been able to stay on top of her studies.

A short while later, Terrence entered the kitchen and climbed onto a chair. His little feet dangled in the air. Some days, he seemed like he had grown so much, and others, she was reminded of just how small he was. He would always be her baby, no matter how old he got.

Andrea passed him a plate of whole-wheat toast, a boiled egg, and orange juice in his favorite Goofy cup. She had already cooked the eggs, but had waited for him to get up before eating. Putting her plate of breakfast down beside him, she slipped into her seat.

With a wave of emotion washing over her, she paused for a moment to watch her son eat. Where had the years gone? Once he had been a small, innocent baby in her arms. Now he was old enough to question things he didn't understand—like why he didn't have a father. Most of his friends in the neighborhood had two parents, and he'd recently realized that he didn't. Now, he had so many questions, but Andrea was uncomfortable giving him answers. How did you tell a four-year-old boy that his father wanted nothing to do with him?

Richard's outright rejection of her after she'd told him she was pregnant had been the hardest pill to swallow. Richard proved to be an utter and complete jerk, and had denied the fact that the baby was his. He'd accused her of sleeping with other men, which had been far from the truth. Making love with Richard had been her first sexual experience, and to this day she wished she hadn't let herself be pressured to have sex before she was ready. It had cost her her last year of college, because she had to drop out once she got pregnant. Richard was long gone from Princeton and from her life by the time Terrence was born.

So far, Andrea had answered Terrence's questions carefully, telling him that his father was away for a long time and that she didn't know when he would come back. Although he seemed to accept her explanation, she could tell that he still didn't understand. A boy needed his father.

When he got old enough to understand why his father really wasn't around, he might be devastated. She could only hope that by showering him with all her love, he wouldn't be scarred for life.

Maybe Mark can fill that void, she thought.

"Bobby went to the zoo yeserday, Mummy. He saw monkeys and giraffes. Can we go to the zoo today?"

Reaching out, Andrea tenderly stroked Terrence's adorable face. "You know how cold it is outside?"

"Yeah."

"And you still want to go to the zoo?"

"Uh-huh. I wanna see a giraffe!"

"Of course you do." Giraffes were Terrence's favorite animal, and his room was decorated with all sorts of giraffe paraphernalia. "Well, I guess we can. We'll have to make sure we're bundled up nice and warm. But if the animals survive in the cold, I suppose we can, too." She hadn't planned to go to the zoo this weekend, considering that she had to finish her paper, which was due next week. But how could she say *no* to Terrence?

Just seeing him smile made her life seem complete.

Terrence threw his hands up in the air. "Yay!"

Andrea regarded him with affection. He was such a good child, he deserved the best.

He deserved two parents.

Andrea glanced at the clock on the kitchen wall. It was almost nine-thirty. She wondered when Mark would call.

"Mummy," Terrence began.

"Yes, sweetheart?"

"Can Mark come with us to the zoo?"

"Oh." Andrea frowned. "I don't know if he can, but I can ask him."

"Yay!" Terrence exclaimed.

"I didn't say he could, Terrence. He's very busy. But I'll find out if he can."

"Tell him I reeeeeaaaaalllly want him to go, okay?"

From the first time Terrence met Mark, it had been obvious that he was smitten with him. "Okay, I'll tell him," Andrea assured her son.

"Is he gonna be my daddy?"

Andrea nearly choked on a piece of toast. She quickly drank some juice. "Sweetheart, why would you ask me that?"

"Because I want him to be my daddy. I like him."

Oh my God, what do I say now? Andrea struggled to find the right response. She finally settled on, "He's our friend. He can visit us as often as we like. And maybe we can visit him."

"But I want him to be my daddy."

Andrea was saved by the sound of footsteps. She looked up to see both her parents heading into the kitchen. "Mom, Dad. Good morning."

"Good morning." Her father kissed the top of her head. "How's your arm today?"

"It's my neck that's bothering me, because it's hard for me to find a good position to sleep in."

"Andrea," her mother said. "Can you come here for a minute?"

Andrea got out of her seat. "I'm sorry. I already boiled the eggs, so they're a little cold. You just have to heat them up—"

"That's not why I called you over," her mother said in a hushed voice.

Andrea looked at her in confusion. "I don't understand."

"How long have you and Mark been seeing each other again?" Gretta asked in a sing-song voice.

"Oh, Mom," Andrea said dismissively.

"You had to know I'd have questions. We show up and there he is at the hospital, the one who found you. Imagine our surprise."

"You think because he's the one who found me that means we've been secretly involved?"

"Have you?"

"No," Andrea said in a tone that she hoped her mother would take to mean the conversation was over.

Gretta shot Andrea a curious look. "But he was in Buffalo. He found you and saved your life."

"You know the whole story, Mom. It was a miracle."

Andrea opened the microwave door and put the boiled eggs inside.

Gretta frowned playfully at her. "You won't tell me anything?"

"The truth, Mom, is that there's nothing to tell. You know everything." Andrea shrugged. "Maybe it was fate. I did see him before the accident. He came into the restaurant and was seated at my table. Imagine *my* shock."

"And…?"

"And nothing. The next thing I know, I'm hearing he saved my life."

Gretta placed her hand on Andrea's. "You still love him, don't you?"

Andrea knew she did, but how did her mother know? "We're getting to know each other again."

"I saw the way he looked at you at the hospital. And then at the dinner. I also saw how *you* looked at him."

Andrea couldn't help smiling as she took the eggs from the microwave. "I can't keep much from you, can I?"

"Do you think it bothers me now, the fact that you still care for each other?"

"Does it?" Andrea reached for the bread. "When we saw each other again, he asked if we could meet for coffee or something. I told him, *no.* I had no plans of pursuing anything with him again. But now, after the accident…"

"You realize that life is short."

"Yeah, pretty much."

"I'm sorry I kept you both apart. Mark is a fine young man."

"He's the same person he was ten years ago. Is he good enough now because he has his own business?"

"No, that's not it at all. Despite what you think, I want

you to be happy. If Mark makes you happy, then you should be with him."

"We'll see," Andrea said.

She buttered the toast and put it on a plate, thinking that was the end of it. But then her mother said, "I heard what Terrence was asking you, about Mark being his daddy."

Andrea threw a glance in Terrence's direction. He was engrossed in conversation with his grandfather, a smile on his face. "I know, Mom. I'm not sure what to tell him. He just likes Mark so much…"

"It's natural. The boy *does* need a father."

What was her mother saying? "And you think Mark can fit the bill?"

"Well…it's something you need to consider. If you don't think Mark would be a good father to him—"

"Actually, if things worked out between us, I *do* think he would be a good father."

Gretta smiled. "So do I."

"What exactly are you saying, Mom?"

"We leave tomorrow, but I didn't want to go before I had this talk with you. It's obvious you and Mark still care for each other. And I say go for it. Now that you've found him again, don't ever let him go."

Don't ever let him go.

Gretta's words sounded in Andrea's mind as she walked with Terrence and Mark at the Buffalo zoo. He had graciously agreed to accompany them because he didn't have to be on a plane until late afternoon.

"Wow, look at those zebras," Mark said with excitement.

"I like all their stripes," Terrence said.

"They're beautiful creatures, aren't they?"

"Uh-huh," Terrence agreed, nodding his head vigorously.

The three of them headed past the zebras and strolled toward the elephants.

"Now that's an animal I love," Mark said. "The elephant. It's so big, no one can mess with it. Yet, it's a gentle creature."

Terrence looked up at Mark, and Andrea could see a question in his eyes. He asked, "Are you gonna be my daddy? Is that why you saved my mummy?"

Mark's eyes widened in shock. He looked at Andrea, who shrugged helplessly at him.

"Terrence," Andrea said. "Remember we talked about this."

"I know…"

Lowering himself to Terrence's level, Mark looked him dead in the eye. "Is that what you want?"

"I think so." He pouted. "I have a daddy, but he never comes to see me. So I wanna new one, and you're really nice."

Mark didn't quite know what to say. He rubbed his hand over the top of Terrence's head. "I know I couldn't ask for a better son than you."

Terrence's grin melted Mark's heart. He meant what he said. Terrence was a special little boy, the kind any man would be proud to call his son. Mark wrapped him in a hug.

"Oh, look," Mark suddenly said. "There are the giraffes."

Terrence whipped his head in the direction where Mark pointed. His eyes lit up with excitement, he sprinted off in that direction.

"Terrence," Andrea called. "Don't go too far ahead of us." As Terrence slowed to a walk, Andrea looked at Mark and said, "I'm so sorry. I didn't know he would ask you that."

"It's all right."

"I hope you don't feel too awkward. He's at the age now when he's realizing that he doesn't have a father. I...I'm sorry."

"There's no need to apologize, really."

"Come on!" Terrence called.

"Okay, okay. We're coming." Mark took Andrea's hand.

"Wait," Andrea said.

Mark looked at her. "Hmm?"

"I...I love you." There, she said it. And the world didn't end. "You don't have to say it back. I just want you to know how I feel, that I'm glad we found each other again, and I hope we make things work this time."

"Mummy!" Terrence called.

"All right, sweetheart. We're coming."

Before Mark could say anything, Andrea, still holding his hand, hustled toward Terrence. Terrence immediately pushed himself between them and reached for their joined hands. With Mark and Andrea's hands secured in his, Terrence looked up at them both and smiled.

It was the kind of smile Andrea had seen before—on other kids. Kids with two parents, walking together in the mall or the park.

Or the zoo.

Lord, Andrea hoped Terrence would get his wish. That things worked out with Mark, and he became her son's new father.

CHAPTER 11

A week later, Andrea could hardly concentrate on her paper for thinking about Mark and the fact that he was arriving later that day. Somehow, she got her assignment done and she could only pray that it was decent.

"Earth to Andrea." Allison snapped her fingers in front of Andrea's face.

"Oh, sorry. What did you say?"

"Girl, never mind. You're way up in the clouds."

Allison was at Andrea's place to pick up her assignment and take it to class for her. "I appreciate this," Andrea told her. "Make sure it gets there in one piece," she added with a smile.

"Have I ever let you down?" Allison asked.

"No." Andrea hugged her. "Never. That's why I love you, girl."

As they pulled apart, a smile danced on Allison's lips. "What time is Mark getting in?"

Andrea glanced at the clock in her foyer. "His flight arrives a little after four." A week ago, it seemed this day would never come. Yet here it was. "I can't believe I get him for the whole weekend."

Allison's eyes lit up. "Woo hoo. It's about time you got lucky!"

"Allison!" Andrea bopped her on the arm. "He's staying at a *hotel*."

"Hey, if you need me to watch Terrence for the night—"

"Okay, enough. Don't you have to turn our papers in?"

"All right, I'm gonna head out. But make sure you give me *every* detail on Monday."

Andrea chuckled. "You know I will."

"And I was serious about watching Terrence—"

Andrea started to push her friend out the door.

"All right, all right," Allison protested. "Enjoy yourself, whatever you do."

"Thank you," Andrea said in a sing-song voice.

When Allison left, Andrea walked into her living room, looking around for any loose ends she'd missed. The place was neat and tidy, and vanilla-scented candles gave the room an enticing smell. Everything was in order—so why did she still feel on edge?

Andrea knew why. She had told Mark that she loved him, and since that time, he hadn't said a word about it.

Yes, she'd made sure to tell him that he didn't have to say the same thing to her. But now she couldn't help feeling doubt about what he felt for her. Their talks had been nice, and Mark obviously still wanted to see her. But Andrea couldn't help feeling like she had put herself out there and didn't know if she was going to get her heart broken.

The way you broke Mark's heart…

The thought made Andrea uneasy. Mark wouldn't string her along, just to hurt her the way she had hurt him.

Would he?

"Good grief, you're being paranoid," she said as she marched into her kitchen for some juice.

She had waited ten years to be reunited with her soul mate. She could certainly wait a bit longer.

Much later, Andrea didn't feel much better.

Terrence was with his sitter, and she and Mark were once again at Amoré.

They'd had another wonderful dinner, and to look at them, one would think they were a happy couple. Even their waitress had gushed over them, treating them like they were newlyweds or a young couple in love. Mark had been nothing but pleasant to her, and polite as always, but something seemed off to Andrea.

"So, it's been a crazy few weeks," Mark was saying. "But I'll get a bit of a break, which I'm definitely looking forward to."

When he finished speaking, Andrea lowered her cup of coffee and looked him dead in the eye. "Mark, is something wrong?"

"At work?" he asked.

"I don't know. Maybe it's work. Maybe it's something else. But I get the feeling something is up."

He glanced down at the dessert menu. "Like I said, it's been a crazy few weeks. But other than that, everything's fine."

Why wouldn't he look at her when he answered the question? Andrea's stomach knotted with worry. "Are you sure?" she asked again.

"Mmm hmm. Yeah, I'm sure." After a beat, he asked, "Do you know what you're going to have?"

Andrea glanced at her menu. "I was thinking of the pineapple sorbet. There's a place in Chicago where they serve it, and it's to die for."

"Maybe I'll try that, too."

When Mark put his menu to the side of the table, Andrea reached for his hand. "Christmas is six days away, Mark. Do you know yet if you'll spend it with us?"

He sighed, a weary sound, and still wouldn't look directly at her. "I don't know."

Pain wrapped its fingers around Andrea's heart and squeezed hard. "Mark, please. If something is wrong, tell me. If I did something, said something—"

"All right." He finally met her gaze head-on. "I have had a lot on my mind."

"About?"

"About…about us."

Andrea swallowed. "What about us?"

Mark shook his head. "I don't know. I'm not sure if this is…right."

Exactly what was he saying? "Don't know if what is right?"

"Andrea…"

"No, tell me," she insisted. "What isn't right?"

"Fine." He looked away uncomfortably before meeting her gaze again. "You and me."

Andrea's stomach lurched painfully as she stared at Mark in shock. She didn't quite know what to say.

"Maybe our time has passed," he continued. "Maybe we're not supposed to be doing this again."

He couldn't mean what he was saying. She had seen how he looked at her. Her mother had seen it, too. There was still something between them.

She couldn't be so wrong.

"Mark, where is this coming from?"

"Am I really the only one who's questioning anything?" he asked her. "Doesn't this feel forced to you?"

"No," she told him, fighting sudden tears. "It doesn't."

"We met again by chance. You didn't even want to get together with me for coffee, and suddenly…" Mark's voice trailed off.

Andrea leaned across the table. "And suddenly I got knocked over the head, right? Well, yeah, I did. And maybe that's what I needed because I finally see the light."

Mark's expression said he wasn't convinced. "This is all so fast."

"Wait," Andrea said, a horrible thought coming to her. "Is this because I told you I loved you? My God, please don't tell me you're like every other guy out there who freaks out at the mention of commitment."

"You've got a son. He's growing attached to me. He wants a father. He deserves one. But I don't want to hurt him by continuing things if this is just…"

"Just what?"

Mark hesitated. "Just two people who used to be in love, trying to recapture something they once had."

His words left Andrea cold. "How can you say that?"

"What if we hadn't met again? Would you be feeling anything for me?"

"Don't you think we met again for a reason?" Andrea asked him pointedly. "Call it fate, call it destiny—"

"Did you ever think of me?" Mark asked, cutting her off. "Think of me and wish that we had been together? Did you ever consider me the love of your life?"

"And if I didn't think of you every day, that changes how I feel now?"

"I guess that answers my question."

"No, it doesn't." Andrea stared at him, wondering exactly what he was afraid of. "Because I *did* think of you. A lot. Maybe not every day, but I certainly never forgot you. You think I never wondered what could have been if I hadn't been swayed by my parents?"

"What about Terrence's father? You wanted to marry him."

Andrea drew in a deep breath and released it slowly. "Life goes on, even if we don't want it to. When I was involved with him, I never thought I'd see you again."

"Or maybe you never thought I'd have enough money for you."

Andrea gaped at him. "You know I never cared about your family background, how much money you did or didn't have."

"No, but your family did. It just feels wrong, them accepting me all of a sudden. Like it's not real. I'm the same person I was ten years ago."

"My parents have learned some hard lessons in life. They've been humbled. They like you for you. How can you not know that after the dinner?"

Mark didn't answer.

"Fine—question them all you want. I guess I can't blame you. But there's no need to question me. You were the first man I ever loved."

"You were the only woman I ever loved."

His statement hung in the air between them. Andrea wasn't sure what she was supposed to say. He seemed to be saying that because she had loved someone else, that had ruined what could be between them. Whatever she said now, she knew it would be wrong.

Mark looked around impatiently. "I'm not in the mood for dessert anymore."

"We don't have to have dessert. We can call it a night and talk tomorrow. I think a good night's sleep will do us both some good."

"Actually…I think I should head home in the morning."

Panic filled Andrea. "You're leaving?"

Mark didn't answer.

"Are you going to come back?"

Mark didn't look at her. "Maybe I shouldn't."

"You can't be serious."

"I've got all kinds of thoughts going through my head. I don't know. I just need some time," Mark told her.

Their waitress arrived and asked if they wanted dessert. Mark told her he wanted the check.

Andrea felt helpless as the woman walked away. But she had to get through to Mark. She just had to.

"You're right, Mark, things *have* been moving fast. But when it's right, what's the point in waiting? Life is short. I've learned that first hand. We're together now, right here, because this was meant to be. Please, Mark. Look at me." She stared at him until he met her eyes. "You heard what Terrence asked at the zoo. He wanted to know if you had saved me because you're supposed to be his daddy."

"That's exactly why I say things are moving—"

Andrea held up both hands. "Hear me out. I'm not saying we have to rush down the aisle, or that we'll ever make it down the aisle. But I am saying that things happen in life for a reason. There was a reason you sat at my table that day, a reason you had the dream about where to find me. A reason we've been trying to reconnect. I know you believe in God. And I know you know He works in mysterious ways. What if this is all part of God's plan? What if we were meant to be together from the start? We messed up when we were younger, but what if this is our second chance?"

The waitress arrived with the check, sparing Mark from answering Andrea's question.

But it was on his mind, even as he drove Andrea home and said goodbye to her. It was still on his mind the next morning when he got on a plane and headed back to Chicago.

CHAPTER 12

Mark spent the entire weekend in a foul mood, even if he did feel that his leaving Andrea was for the best. He meant what he said about things moving too fast, so fast that he wasn't sure if he was really feeling what he thought he felt, or if he was just caught up in emotions of the past.

That and the drama of having saved her.

It was a romantic notion to believe that fate had brought them together. Andrea believed it, and he wanted to believe it, too. Indeed, since the story of Andrea's rescue had become national news, it seemed that everywhere he went people recognized him and asked him about her. The flight attendant on his flight to Buffalo asked if he was going to see her, and when he'd said *yes*, she joked that the two of them were bound to get married.

That's when Mark had realized that he was caught up in

the middle of a story, the story of a man who had saved the life of a woman he'd once loved. It made for good press, and everyone wanted a happy ending, especially at Christmas. But Mark's life wasn't simply a story, and happy endings weren't guaranteed in real life.

He had tried to work off some stress by playing tennis with his colleague, John, at the club, but that hadn't helped much.

Monday morning came, and he was glad to be back at work. Work could always help him forget his personal life. Or so he thought, because so far this morning Andrea still occupied his thoughts.

His last conversation with her continued to play out in his mind. *What if this is our second chance?*

Could it be?

The only thing Mark knew for sure was that he needed some space. Space to figure out if what he was feeling was real. And Andrea needed to figure out the same thing, whether she accepted that or not.

"Mr. Potter?"

Startled at the sound of his name, Mark looked up from the papers on his desk and stared into the emerald green eyes of his secretary, Shirley McNamara.

"Yes?"

"Mr. Feinstein has arrived. He's waiting in the lounge."

Damn. Mark had completely forgotten about his ten o'clock meeting with George Feinstein, local owner of Feinstein Art, a gallery that imported and sold fine art. Fishing for his client file among the ton of papers on his desk, Mark groaned when he couldn't find it.

"If you're looking for his file," Shirley announced, "you won't find it on your desk. It's in your filing cabinet." She smiled.

Once again, Shirley had cleaned up after him when he'd left in a hurry Friday afternoon to head to the airport. In her late fifties, his administrative assistant had proven to be a godsend. She always knew where everything was and she knew his schedule like the back of her hand. She was with the company when he'd first started Creative Image Advertising six years ago, and Mark couldn't imagine what he'd do without her.

"Thank you, Shirley," Mark said, returning her smile. "Just give me five minutes, then send him in."

The meeting with Mr. Feinstein went well. He liked all the suggestions Mark made regarding an advertising campaign, and even agreed to a series of commercials. Mark prided himself on living up to the name of his firm, always offering his clients innovative ad campaigns.

His business was going well, but he still longed for a woman to complete his life.

Rising from his soft leather chair, he strolled to the windows. The sky was gray, and he wondered when the sun would make another appearance.

You left the sun in Buffalo, a voice in his mind said.

The thought disturbed him, even as an image of Andrea's smile suddenly warmed him all over.

Damn, he missed her. But was he really missing her, or missing the dreams he'd once had for them?

His desk phone rang, and Mark snatched up the receiver. "Mark Potter."

"Mr. Potter," Shirley said, "Cynthia Nichol is on the line. I told her you were busy but she's demanding to speak to you," Shirley added in a weary tone. "Says it's urgent."

Not Cynthia again, he thought. But he said, "Put her through."

"Mark, hi," Cynthia began in her best bedroom voice. "I thought I would have heard from you by now."

"Cynthia, you really have to stop calling me. I am tired of telling you that our relationship is over."

"Mark, please. Christmas is on Thursday. I want you to spend it with me. Let's put all the bad stuff behind us and start over."

Mark couldn't quite believe his ears. Perhaps Cynthia was delusional. "There *is* nothing to start over."

"When will you stop being angry with me?"

"Is that what you think is going on—that I'm angry with you?" When Cynthia didn't say anything, Mark continued. "Let me make this clear. I'm not angry. I'm not hung up on what happened between us. It's not about me needing to trust you. Cynthia, it's simply over. I don't feel anything for you anymore."

Cynthia started to sob. "How can you say that? I thought you loved me."

Now he knew she had to be delusional. "I'm sorry you're hurt. That's not what I want. I just want you to accept that it's over. You have to move on with your life."

And suddenly, Mark realized why it was so easy to walk away from Cynthia, while walking away from Andrea hurt like hell. Cynthia had never had his heart, not for a minute. In fact, on the occasions when she expressed her love for him, his stomach always twisted because he didn't feel the same way about her.

Yet, when Andrea had told him those words not too long ago, something inside of him had come alive. Something inside him had also started to ache. For the first time in ten years, he realized just how close he was to bringing down the wall around his heart. And that was a scary prospect.

He had *wanted* to tell Andrea he loved her, too, but fear had held him back.

Fear, because Andrea was the one woman with the power to hurt him. The one woman who *had* hurt him so badly he had barely recovered from it.

It was obvious now why he was pushing her away. He didn't want to give her that power again, but who was he kidding? He had given her his heart ten years ago, and she still had it now.

Mark tuned in to hear Cynthia saying something about how they could make it work. He cut her off. "Cynthia, you can't make something work if it isn't there to begin with. But I thank you so much for your call. You have helped me in a way you'll never know."

"What are you talking about?"

"You've helped me realize that I'm in love with someone else. I've just been too afraid to face that."

For a moment, Cynthia was silent. Then she said, "You're a jerk. Go to hell."

She hung up on him, and Mark felt relieved. Because for the first time since he'd ended things with Cynthia, he truly believed that he would *not* be hearing from her again.

* * *

Things were definitely back to normal at Mama's Place.

"Andrea," Trevor began when she emerged from the staff bathroom, "I know you're doing hostessing duties, but you've seen how busy this place is. You can't be taking breaks like this."

"Sorry, Trevor." What was she supposed to do, never take a bathroom break?

"Everyone's in the weeds. I need you to go around and refill coffee for the waitstaff, okay?"

"But what about the hostess stand? Like you said, the place is extremely busy."

"Forget hostessing. I can cover it. Just get to the coffee ASAP."

Ooooookaaay, Andrea thought. Sheesh, you'd think the guy could cut her some slack, considering she was even back at work. But no, Trevor didn't spare anyone his sharp tongue.

For goodness sake, Christmas was two days away. Couldn't Trevor *try* to fake some holiday cheer?

It was times like this that Andrea wished she didn't need the money so badly because she'd definitely quit this job. The past weeks she'd spent at home had been a luxury. It had been wonderful to spend more time with Terrence.

With a coffee pot in her right hand, Andrea made her rounds on the restaurant floor. She was tired of "Mama's Special Tuesdays." Everyone and their dog seemed to come out for the half-price specials. Even though she normally made great tips, she definitely ran herself ragged.

She was about to turn the corner toward the second half

of the restaurant when Rosalie, one of the waitresses, blocked her path. "Andrea, I need a favor."

"What?" Andrea asked warily.

"I'm so busy. Do you mind running this bill over to table fifteen?"

"I only have one good hand," Andrea pointed out.

"Here." Rosalie took the coffee pot from her and slipped the bill into her hand. "Thanks so much!"

"Sure, don't mention it," Andrea said with sarcasm as she watched Rosalie sprint in the direction of the kitchen.

Andrea headed toward table fifteen. The person there had the *Buffalo News* open covering his or her face. "Excuse me," she said. "Your waitress asked me to bring you your bill."

The newspaper lowered, and Andrea gasped.

Mark!

His dimples came to life as he smiled up at her. Damn, he was still so gorgeous, still so irresistible. She knew she wanted to spend the rest of her life with this man.

But he didn't want the same thing as her.

Or did he?

"Mark." To her own ears she sounded breathless. "What are you doing here?"

"Would you believe it if I said fate?"

Butterflies began dancing in Andrea's stomach. "Mark…"

"I'm sorry," he told her. "Sorry about what happened the other night. Sorry I walked away from you the way I did."

His dazzling smile unnerved her, much the same way it had on the day they'd first met.

"So you're here to apologize…?"

"Is that why you think I'm here?"

More butterflies. "I don't know. Maybe you're here to tell me that you feel bad about what happened, but you still want us to be friends."

"Fate didn't bring us back together just to be friends."

There was movement to Andrea's right, and she looked over her shoulder. Rosalie, Trevor, and other staff members stood not more than twenty feet away from her, grinning as they watched the interaction between her and Mark.

She whipped her head back around to face Mark. "Were they in on this?" she asked him.

"They did what they had to to get you over here. Now it's my job to do the rest." Mark reached for her hand and took it in his. "When you told me that you loved me—"

"Oh, Mark. We don't have to—"

"Yes. We do." He paused. "When you told me that you loved me, something inside of me came alive for the first time in many, many years. And it also frightened me because you had hurt me so badly."

Andrea's knees started to wobble. "Can I sit down?"

"Of course." Mark got to his feet and pulled out a chair for her. As he sat back down, he continued. "You still have my heart, Andrea. That's why I was so afraid of what was happening between us, because I didn't want to give you the power to hurt me again. Now, I realize that if I walk away from you, I'm only hurting myself."

Andrea drew in a long, shaky breath. "So you want to continue seeing me?"

Mark shook his head.

"No?" Andrea asked, confused.

"I want it all," he told her, the truth in his voice touching the deepest place in her heart. "I want you in my life today, tomorrow, always. I want Terrence in my life. Because I love you, Andrea. I always have and I always will."

"Oh, Mark." Andrea started weeping softly. And when he drew her into his arms, the entire restaurant erupted in cheers.

Andrea smiled through her tears.

Mark framed her face. "I do believe in fate. I believe God brought us together to give us a second chance. How can I walk away from that?"

Tears streamed down Andrea's face. "I'm so happy. And I'm so sorry about the years we've been apart."

Mark shook his head as he wiped at her tears. "No, don't be sorry. If things had worked out differently, you wouldn't have Terrence."

She knew right then that Mark was the most special man in the world. As long as she lived, he would have her heart.

"You're right, Mark. You're so right." And she wouldn't change Terrence for the world.

"We weren't ready to make it work before. We were too young and we both needed to grow up. But now…there's nothing to keep us apart."

"Mark, I love you so much."

"I love you, too, Andrea. And I want you to be my wife."

Andrea's heart filled with more love than she thought possible. "You don't have to say that. We can take things slowly."

"You're my destiny," he told her. "We both know that. So why wait any longer than we already have?"

Andrea gazed lovingly into Mark's eyes. "You're right. You're absolutely right."

"I know I am. Now kiss me. Right here, in front of all these people."

Andrea looked around self-consciously, but saw only a room full of smiling faces. She giggled as she faced Mark once again. "Right here, right now?"

"Right here, right now."

She sighed happily, knowing that finally her dream had come true. She had a man who loved her, a man who also loved her son.

Leaning forward, she framed his face. "How can I refuse the man I love?"

She couldn't.

So she kissed him in front of a hundred witnesses, a kiss that healed the hurts of the past and promised a wonderful future.

A CHRISTMAS SERENADE

JANICE SIMS

Dear St. Nick, here is my suggestion…umm, plea
for what to leave me under the Christmas tree.

One straight male specimen, healthy and tall,
who actually follows through when he says he'll call.

He doesn't have to be rich, and he doesn't have to be pretty.
But he must be kind, and faithful and witty.

Make him intelligent and sympathetic to others.
And as a gift to my sisters, let him have brothers.

So, St. Nick, I'm whispering this plea into your ear
in hope that you'll grant my wish this year.

—*The Book of Counted Joys*

CHAPTER 1

"You don't remember me, do you?" asked a sweet, southern-accented voice. Jack Cain was surrounded by at least six curvaceous beauties, but Joyce Hart elbowed her way into the inner circle. The women let her pass either out of respect because she was an older woman, or out of fear that they'd get more than a sharp elbow in the side if they didn't. Jack inclined his head in Joyce's direction, his light brown eyes squinting. He was near-sighted. He had to wear either glasses or contacts on stage.

She was attractive—from his mother's generation—petite, and plump. Her café au lait skin was practically unlined, and the crinkles around her eyes were few.

He had missed the beauty of African-American women, especially those from South Carolina. His father, John Sr., used to say that South Carolina had more beautiful black women than anyplace else on earth. Jack suspected that was his father's opinion because his wife, and Jack's mother, Dahlia, came from South Carolina.

Joyce laughed and cocked her head, her brown eyes twinkling.

"Darlin', you were only seven years old the last time I saw you." She placed a soft hand atop his. "You and your parents attended my wedding and then, the following week, you were off to Germany."

Jack smiled down at her. The wedding was a big clue to her identity. She had to be none other than Joyce Hart. How could he forget a wedding during which the bride had fallen into a pond? Over the years his mother had regaled him with the story on many occasions. "Mrs. Hart?" Jack said, with a note of incredulity in his deep voice. Joyce beamed her pleasure. "It's gone from Hart, and then to Campbell after my Clarence died, and I married again. Big mistake! Husband number two took me on a fast ride to nowhere! I was so glad to get rid of him, I'm not looking for anybody else!"

Jack laughed with her. "Well, you look as lovely as the last time I saw you."

"You're a charming liar," Joyce said, taking him by the arm and leading him away from the other women who were clamoring for his attention. "But at my age, a lie is better than no compliment at all." Joyce was on a mission. Those other women, all of whom were young and glamorous, were trying to make time with a world-famous concert pianist who was the guest of honor at this shindig. She would let them at him as soon as she'd had her say.

"I will always regret losing touch with your mother," she said as they walked toward French doors that led to a private balcony. "Dahlia and I were best friends from first grade, when my family moved here from Augusta, Georgia. And I was so sad when I heard about the plane crash, and how you'd lost both of your parents. You were only nineteen. Lord, that must have been hard on you. So young, and no relatives to lean on. I wrote several letters to the U.S. Army asking about your welfare. The last letter I received from Dahlia came from somewhere in France. I tried the address she'd given me first, but I never heard anything. Then out of desperation I wrote to the army. They told me that you were a student at the Sorbonne, and that you were well. I didn't try anymore after that. You were well, and that was good enough for me."

Jack didn't know what to say. Here was a link to his past, the very reason he'd returned to Charleston, South Carolina: to find his roots. All his life, he'd gone from one country to another, never really feeling at home anywhere. Both of his parents had been born here. *He* had been born here. There were no relatives left to speak of. A distant cousin, perhaps, but no one he had had contact with in years.

He couldn't resist asking, "What was she like as a child?"

They were outside now, standing on the balcony. The October night was cool and the sky, pitch black with a smattering of stars. Joyce wrapped her arms around herself. Jack removed his suit jacket. "Here, put this on."

She did, and thanked him for his kindness. She gazed wistfully at the sky. "Dahlia was such a little lady. She was quiet and soft spoken. She wore dresses to school every day, with Buster Browns and ankle socks with lace around the edges." She smiled up at him. "You inherited her talent for the piano. Oh, she played *beautifully*. By ear, mostly. She never had lessons. Mrs. Gaylord, her foster mother, would not pay for lessons. But Dahlia didn't let that stop her. She could hear a song once, and play it on the piano. My daughter, Callista, was born with that ability, too. You've got to meet her. Every time Callista would be practicing her lessons, I'd think of Dahlia." She sighed heavily. "When your mother was sixteen she won the statewide talent competition for high school students. Did she ever tell you about that?"

"Yes, ma'am."

"She was the first black student to ever win. Oh, we were so *proud* of her! She got to play for the governor. She was awarded a trophy and her picture was in the papers." She laughed suddenly. "Funny thing is, if she hadn't won, she might never have met your father. During her performance at the governor's mansion, she was accompanied by the army band, and your father played the trumpet in the band. I guess you inherited your musical talent from *both* your parents. Anyway, she and John wrote letters to each other for five years before they finally got married. By that time, he was already an officer. Your father worked hard to achieve rank in the army, especially since he didn't come from a privileged background like some of those other officers. He was an orphan, like your mother. I suppose that was one of the things that attracted them to each other. They both knew the loneliness of not having relatives." She looked up at him with such compassion then that Jack knew she was thinking he was in the same boat. He was also an orphan, of sorts.

But she brightened and said, "You must come to my house and let me make you a meal while you're here, John."

"Oh, my friends call me Jack," he told her. "John Cain feels more like a stage name than anything else."

Joyce gave him a stern look. "John Cain was your father's name, and it's a mighty fine name, too! I'm going to call you, John. You're the spitting image of John. He was a handsome devil!"

Jack couldn't help smiling at this tiny woman whom he'd only met fifteen minutes ago and who already felt comfortable enough to chastise him. "John, it is, Mrs. Hart."

"Then, that's settled," Joyce said, sounding satisfied. "Now, look, John, I didn't come out here among all these *fancy-dressed* folks tonight just to make your reacquaintance. No, I came because I wanted to recruit you for a special project." Jack listened intently.

"I was a social worker for thirty years," Joyce told him. "I'm retired now. My mission these days is to make the community a better place to live, and to keep the young folks who're about something, those who know the value of hard work, on the right track. The youth center where I volunteer my time puts on a Christmas festival every year. It serves to showcase the talents of our young people, and to raise money for scholarships for those who're getting ready to graduate from high school. I thought it would be nice if you would come and give us a concert. Nothing taxing. I read in the paper about your being here over the holidays, and how you're resting up until you have to do a series of concerts over in Europe after New Year's. So, two or three songs with a holiday theme would be sufficient. Plus, Callista will perform as well. She performs every year. The kids love her because she plays their kind of music—hiphop, rhythm and blues, jazz… You name it, that child can play it. But I thought it would be wonderful if they could be exposed to a little classical music. There is one child, Randall, who I believe could one day become a classical pianist. The other kids call him a wimp because he likes that kind of music. But you, John, are living proof that a man can play classical music and still be masculine. I don't know where these kids get their ideas. Anything they don't understand, they make fun of!"

She took a deep breath after that long monologue. "So, think about it. You don't have to give me your answer this minute. I'll give you my phone number and you can call me after you've decided."

Jack didn't have to think about it. "It would be my pleasure to perform for the kids, Mrs. Hart," he said.

Joyce threw her arms around his waist and hugged him tightly. Jack's chin came to the top of her head. She smelled like orange blossoms. "Thank you, darlin'," she said happily. She peered up at him. "Well, I've monopolized you enough for one evening. I'm going so those young ladies can have a crack at you. I'm sure they'll be *thrilled* to see me go!"

They stepped back inside the grand ballroom of one of Charleston's finest hotels.

Jack glanced up at the banner that read, WELCOME HOME, JOHN CAIN, OUR NATIVE SON.

Joyce removed his jacket and handed it to him. Afterward, they took the time to exchange business cards. "Don't be shy about phoning me if you want to talk, John. I was serious about that meal, too. Cooking is my best talent. I don't dance, and I don't sing. But put me in the kitchen, and watch me work my magic!"

"I'll be calling about that meal," Jack promised.

Joyce looked him straight in the eyes. "No jive?"

Jack smiled. He hadn't heard that expression in a long time. "None whatsoever."

Joyce smiled up at him. "All right, then. I'll be expecting it."

She turned and walked swiftly toward the exit. Jack had never seen such a tiny woman move so fast. She must really feel uncomfortable among all of these "fancy-dressed" people, as she'd referred to them. She'd only come around them to talk to him. Truth was, she was the most interesting person he'd met since his arrival two weeks ago.

Sandra Gerrard, lead news anchor for the local ABC affiliate, saw her chance when Joyce Hart walked past her. She knew Joyce from a story she'd done on children and families, the governmental agency for whom Joyce used to work. Joyce had been an unflinching children's advocate. The agency had come under fire for "losing" children in the system, and Joyce had given Sandra an interview in which she had not minced words about the many weaknesses in the system, and how the agency could go about improving them. The problem was, she said, the caseworkers were given too many children to supervise. And there weren't enough checks and balances in the system to ensure that the welfare and safety of each child was effectively maintained. Sandra had learned later that Joyce had nearly gotten fired for her outspokenness.

"Mrs. Hart! Hello!" Sandra said.

Joyce turned and regarded her with warmth. "Sandra! Honey, you're a sight for sore eyes. Are you covering John's big return?" She grasped Sandra's hand.

Sandra laughed. "Well, I'm hoping to, if I get the chance to talk to him."

Joyce glanced back at the spot where she'd left Jack. He was once again surrounded by predatory women. "Then, you'd better get over there before there's none of him left!"

Sandra followed Joyce's line of sight. "I'd sure better!"

Joyce fondly squeezed her hand. "Good to see you again, honey. Good night."

"Good night, Mrs. Hart."

They parted, and Joyce continued toward the exit. "Lord, I hope my feet hold up until I make it to the car," she said under her breath. Her new shoes were pinching her toes. Sure enough, once she reached her Ford Taurus and got behind the wheel, she removed the offending shoes and drove home barefoot.

Inside, the party was a long way from winding down.

Jack fielded questions on every subject from his training, to his opinion of European women versus American women. He told them he thought all women were wonderful, which earned him appreciative looks rife with speculation, and several phone numbers were slipped covertly into his coat pocket.

When Sandra joined them, some of the other women voluntarily gave up their positions out of respect. Most of them had come here tonight to celebrity-watch, and Sandra Gerrard was one of Charleston's most beloved news anchors. Everyone knew her.

"Good evening, ladies," she said sweetly. "Don't you all look lovely tonight."

A flash of white teeth, expertly applied lipstick, and a smile that could melt the coldest of hearts. They were all her trademarks. She used them as weapons tonight. The other women didn't know what hit them. Sandra had cleared the field in less than five minutes with a compliment here, a keen observation there, and sharp repartee. When she saw that her efforts needed that something extra, she cooed, "Isn't that Donnell 'Quicksilver' Robinson over there by the entrance?"

Donnell Robinson was the quarterback for the Carolina Panthers—North Carolina's professional football team. He'd been born and raised in Charleston, South Carolina, though.

The remaining hangers-on gave Jack a once-over. He was rich, handsome, and talented. But Donnell had just negotiated a multimillion-dollar contract! They made their apologies and abandoned poor Jack without so much as a backward glance.

"You're good!" Jack complimented Sandra when they were alone.

Sandra gave him a bright smile. Her dark brown eyes

swept over him. "You have no idea!" She laughed because she didn't know *where* that comment had come from.

The surprised look on Jack's face was priceless. Brows knitted in a frown, he took a step backward as if he didn't know what to make of her.

Sandra laughed harder. Then, she held her wedding rings under his nose. "My name is Sandra Gerrard, Mr. Cain, and all I'm after is an exclusive interview. I saw all the other media types bombarding you tonight. I simply wanted to make my pitch to you in private. We're the ABC affiliate. We can get you on *Good Morning, America*, if that's what you want, or we can keep it intimate and for our local viewers only. It's your choice."

"Yes, but wouldn't it be more advantageous for you if we went national?" Jack asked with skepticism. Journalists had burned him in the past.

Sandra smiled. "Yes, it would be. But, you see I'm not interested in going to New York. I've already done that. I moved back to Charleston because I wanted to get married and have kids. I've done both, and I'm happy here. So, I'm not out to ride your coattails to fame and fortune. All I want is to sit down with you and let you tell the people of Charleston what brings you back here after a thirty-year absence. That, to me, Mr. Cain, is a good human-interest story."

"Give her the interview, Jack. It's good publicity," said a male voice from behind them. Jack turned and found his former agent, Morris Findlay, standing there. Jack had not been expecting Morris, especially not after their last phone conversation during which Jack had fired him.

Jack narrowed his eyes at the shorter, older man.

Morris strolled up to them as if his welcome was assured. He smiled at Sandra.

"I saw you on the six-o'clock news tonight. You're quite good. I could have you back in New York in no time."

Sandra cocked a knowing eye at Jack. "I take it he's your agent?"

"Not anymore," Jack said pointedly.

Sandra gave Jack her card. "Please phone me, Mr. Cain. I'll do right by you."

Jack smiled down into her upturned face. He liked her. "I'll give it some serious thought, Ms. Gerrard."

Sandra left them.

Jack grimaced, and said, "What did you do, bribe somebody who works for Doris?"

Doris Gamble was his new agent, a sister from the Bronx who was sharp, aggressive, and tenacious on behalf of her clients, but who genuinely cared about their welfare.

"Yes," Morris freely admitted, not ashamed of the lengths to which he'd go to get what he wanted. "And I'd do it again."

Jack might have told him to go to hell, but when he looked up and saw the women, who'd abandoned him in favor of a jock a few minutes ago, heading back his way after learning they'd been hoodwinked, he beat a hasty retreat with a fast-talking Morris dogging his steps.

"You were unfair to me, Jack. After ten years of making you the most sought-after concert pianist in the world, you dropped me when all I wanted to do was secure your future."

"You mean, secure *your* future," Jack said through

clenched teeth. "You wanted to book me well into 2007. You wanted to work me like a slave—fifty weeks out of fifty-two. I'm tired, Morris. I have been living out of a suitcase for nearly all my life. I'm getting too old for that crap! From now on, I play when I want to play. And when I don't want to, I don't."

"Lucky for you, you have the luxury of being able to do that, and I'm happy for you," Morris said. "But that's not why I'm here. I'm here because I've been approached by a publisher about you writing your memoirs."

Jack paused in his steps, and scowled at his former agent. "Are you on something?"

"I kicked that habit eight years ago, and you know it!"

Jack narrowed his eyes further.

"I swear I'm not using," said Morris hastily. "This is a legitimate offer."

Jack stood there looking into Morris's watery brown eyes for a full minute, wondering why he'd ever hired him in the first place. Of course, they'd both been a decade younger when Morris had approached him about representing him. And, to be honest, in the beginning, Morris's take-no-prisoners attitude had been just what he'd needed in the cutthroat world of classical music. It was such an exclusive world, and in many ways those who were not born to money and privilege were barred from it.

Over the years, as his star had risen, so had Morris's greed. Jack's main focus had always been his music. He'd hired an agent in order to free him up so that he no longer had to worry about the business end of his career.

This proved to be a mistake because he found himself playing more venues every year, and enjoying it less.

Morris had asked for a higher percentage of his earnings, to which Jack had agreed. He had his lawyer go over the agreement and found it was fair. Unbeknownst to him, however, Morris was negotiating one amount for his appearances, telling him another amount, and pocketing the difference. That went on, to Jack's estimation, for approximately five years out of the ten Morris had represented him. When Jack found out about it, quite by accident when he changed accounting firms, he fired Morris.

"You cheated me, Morris. You're lucky I didn't have you prosecuted and thrown into prison for what you did."

"I know that," Morris said regretfully. "I'm trying to make it up to you. They want to offer you an amount in the high six-figures, Jack."

"Don't use agent-speak with me," Jack said. "Tell me the amount in round numbers."

They had gone out of a side door and were now standing in a small garden. Jack thrust a hand in his coat pocket, looking for an imaginary pack of cigarettes. He'd quit more than a year ago but sometimes, when he got upset, he still reached for them.

"Nine-hundred-thousand," Morris said. "But I think I can get them up to 1.2 million if you take me back."

Jack laughed shortly. "As I understand it, to keep an advance legally, the writer actually has to deliver a publishable product by a certain date."

Morris looked puzzled. "Yes, that's how it works."

"You've forgotten one salient point, Morris."

"What's that?" Morris asked, his eyes wide with confusion.

"I can't write worth a damn!" Jack shouted.

"Oh, that," Morris said, dismissing Jack's concerns. "We can get you a ghostwriter. Pamela Anderson used one, and her book made the *New York Times* bestsellers list."

Jack sighed. "I have no desire to write my life's story, Morris. I'm not finished living it yet. I'm only thirty-six, for God's sake! Maybe I'll dictate it to a ghostwriter when I've got one foot in the grave. But not now."

"The cardinal rule that entertainers live by is, *strike while the iron is hot*," Morris told him. "You've just come off a tour that anyone who's anybody is still talking about! You've got how many more good years left? Perhaps ten or twenty if you take good care of yourself. Even your idol, André Watts, has accepted a position at a university. Age catches up to all of us." He was almost poignant in his delivery.

Luckily, Jack was fully aware of his former agent's persuasive powers. "No dice, Morris."

"But I've changed!" Morris said, pleading. "I'll work for you for five percent less than the last fee we negotiated."

"No," Jack said, implacably.

"I'll suspend my fee for a year!" Morris offered.

"No!"

"I'll prove to you that I've changed!" Morris said, suddenly full of indignation.

Jack simply shook his head sadly as he turned away. "You do that," he said softly, without anger.

"I know you're disappointed in me," Morris said to Jack's retreating back. "But I'll find a way to make up for what I've done!"

Jack kept walking. If he hurried, he could arrive home in time to catch three back-to-back reruns of *The X-Files* on TNT. Besides, if he left Winslow at home by himself for too long, the dog tended to get destructive, and "home" for them nowadays was a rented house on the outskirts of Charleston. Jack could imagine the fat deposit he'd had to pay going down the drain because of damage done by an overly energetic one-year-old golden retriever.

CHAPTER 2

"One more sad song, and I'm gonna slit my wrists," Reid Harris, owner of The Blue Bird, one of the few remaining blues clubs in Atlanta, whispered into Callie Hart's ear.

Callie was in the middle of "How Long Has This Been Going On?" and from the rapt expressions on the faces in the audience, she had them enthralled. Her deep, sensual voice was in fine form tonight, undoubtedly because her emotions were in turmoil.

Reid, tall and dark, dressed completely in black, stepped off the small stage and let her complete the song without further interference. He went and stood in the back, watching Callie's face as she sang. She sounded like her heart was breaking. But when was the last time he'd seen Callie with a man? Not since that pompous ass,

Raymond Warner. Ray could almost make a tenor saxophone speak. But he couldn't keep his pants zipped, and Callie wasn't the type of woman to put up with that kind of behavior.

Reid had told Ray he had to find himself another Saturday night gig. He wasn't going to have him coming around upsetting Callie, who was the reason The Blue Bird was packed every Friday and Saturday night.

Callie smoothly transitioned into an old Dinah Washington tune, "Is You Is or Is You Ain't My Baby?" The subject matter was betrayal, but it was a bouncy ditty that put smiles on the listeners' faces. Her fingers flew over the piano keys during the solo, and when she wrapped it up she was rewarded with thunderous applause.

Grinning broadly, Callie rose from the piano bench and blew kisses to the audience before scurrying offstage and into the dressing room. She hadn't been sitting in front of the makeup mirror for five minutes before there was a knock at the door.

"Come in!" she called.

Reid strode in. "Haven't I told you to keep the door locked?" he said. "Atlanta ain't the same as it used to be. Or have you forgotten that crazy who stalked you last year?"

"How can I forget him?" Callie said with a laugh. "He writes me from prison every week."

Reid leaned against the long counter. There was space for three performers in front of the lighted mirror. Three tall red swivel chairs stood before the counter. Callie was sitting in the one farthest from the door. She drank half of the contents from a Dasani water bottle.

"You wanna tell me where that set came from?" Reid asked.

"My soul?"

"Don't be a smart ass, little lady." Reid pursed his considerable lips. "What's going on?"

"Nothing," Callie said, looking away from his intense gaze. "I got fired, that's all. Well, actually, all of us got fired, so I shouldn't be taking it personally. The parent company decided they could do without another lifestyle magazine. I called Oprah, but she doesn't need any more editors on her staff."

Reid gave her a firm hug. "Poor baby," he commiserated.

Callie glanced at the two of them in the mirror and had to smile. Reid Harris was one gorgeous brother. Dark brown skin, eyes the color of honey, blue-black dreadlocks that hung to his waist, an utterly masculine body that any woman would love to have wrapped around hers. Probably for the millionth time, she wished he weren't gay.

Sometimes God played tricks on her.

"Don't worry about me," Callie said. "I've been saving up to buy a house. That money is gonna tide me over until I can find another job, so I won't starve."

"I wouldn't let you starve, honey," Reid assured her. He bent and kissed her forehead. "I'll pay you your normal salary. And, if you need to, you can put a tip jar on the piano. Then, more than just dirty old men can slip you rolled-up bills."

Callie smiled up at him. "You're too sweet to me." But she shook her head. "No, I'm going to find another job. Joyce Hart didn't raise no quitter. I'll find something before Thanksgiving."

Reid gave her a squeeze. He glanced in the mirror at the two of them. Callie's skin reminded him of coffee with cream in it, but not too much. Her auburn curls were naturally that color, and they fell nearly halfway down her back. She was a breath of fresh air, a beauty with dangerous curves. Whenever she walked across that stage every straight man in the club watched the ebb and flow of those hips, those thighs, those long, shapely legs. He'd told her she should never wear pants. Even *he* liked looking at her legs. Tonight, she was wearing a spicy little number in red.

"What you need to do is get married and give me some godchildren," he joked.

Reid had always known he was gay. He'd never been with a woman. Since his heart was broken a few years back by someone he'd lived with for more than twenty years, his subsequent relationships tended to be of brief duration. This was due largely to the fact that he didn't want to get his heart broken again. Besides, celibacy was something he'd learned to embrace. He filled his time with the club, volunteering at a home for AIDS patients in transition, and with his many friends—one of whom was in his arms right now.

He'd told Callie years ago that he planned to adopt her children as his own. Callie, of course, had heartily agreed. "With one stipulation," she'd said at the time, "that you have to become my surrogate father and walk me down the aisle at my wedding."

"Done!" Reid had said.

He released her and gazed into her dark brown eyes now. "So, are you going home for Thanksgiving?"

"Yeah, my mom's counting on my being there. She says she sees Cal and Derrick all the time. She'll be really disappointed if I don't come."

"You don't sound like you're looking forward to it," Reid observed.

"Well," Callie said, hedging. "It's not that I don't want to see my family, it's just that both of my brothers and my cousins are doing so well. They've got such stable lives. They're all married with children. They own beautiful homes, and drive nice cars. I'm the only one who's kind of…"

"Free-spirited, doing what she wants to do with her life, instead of going to a nine-to-five that pays the bills, but doesn't excite her?"

Callie impulsively kissed him on the mouth. "Thanks for not letting me hold a pity party up in here!"

Reid laughed. "If you kiss me like that again, I just might have to rethink my sexual orientation."

"If only!" Callie said with an exaggerated sigh.

"If only I were straight, I'd be the perfect guy for you, huh?"

"Exactly. You're kind, thoughtful, and faithful. You're a talented musician. You have a successful business, so you're not a bum. And on top of all of that, you're *hot*, Reid Harris!"

"It's my curse," Reid said. "To be so devastatingly handsome that women fall in love with me and I can't do a damn thing for them." He gave her one last hug. "I've got to get back out there. Clive should be finished bombing by now."

Clive Edmonds was the house comic, but not a very good comic. Reid liked to give young people a chance. He'd given a twenty-one-year-old singer/pianist a chance seven years ago when she'd walked into his club. Today, she was the headliner.

He grinned at his headliner in parting. "You'll find your prince one day, Callie. Just don't tell him your first name is Callista. God knows where your mama got that name from!"

"For your information," Callie said with mock indignation. "Callista happens to be my father's mother's name, and I'm proud to carry it."

"Liar," Reid said as he walked out. "If you were, you wouldn't go by Callie! Get ready for your second set. And ease up on the sad songs."

"Just for that, I'm gonna sing 'In My Life,'" she warned.

Reid turned back around, a frown marring his handsome face. "Your rendition of that song always makes me cry!"

"I know!" Callie chortled.

A little over a week after Jack's encounter with Morris, his new agent, Doris Gamble, phoned to say, "You're not going to believe who called me not twenty minutes ago!"

Jack was sitting at the Steinway in the living room of the rented house, a large, modern, glass and wood structure built on the side of a hill. There were floor-to-ceiling windows along the walls of the living room, and throughout the house, which meant lots of direct light during the day. And drawing the blinds at night was quite an undertaking.

It was around noon, and Jack had been playing Beethoven's Sonata no. 23, "Appassionata" when Doris had phoned.

He spoke into the cordless handset. "I was practicing, Doris. Give me a hint."

"Eleanor Arenz!" Doris said, excited. She named the publishing company where Eleanor Arenz worked and suddenly Jack was excited too. "Wow!" he couldn't help saying.

"They want you to write your life's story, Jack," Doris went on to tell him. "And don't die of a heart attack or anything, but it was your former agent who approached them about it, and then told them to contact me with their offer because he was no longer representing you." Doris sounded astonished. "I didn't know he had it in him."

Jack was silent a moment. So, that was Morris's grand gesture—his way of proving that he wanted to make up for stabbing him in the back. Jack told Doris about Morris's visit to Charleston.

"Well, it's the least he could do," was Doris's opinion when he'd finished. "You were very generous in not pressing charges."

Jack knew all of that, but he was still touched by the selfless act. Not touched enough to rehire Morris, but touched nonetheless. "Listen, Doris, what do you think I ought to do? I'm no writer. I write music, and that's all. I don't want to sign a contract unless I know I can deliver the goods, you know?"

Doris sighed. "I think you have an interesting story to tell. I mean the contradiction of how you look and how you play would sell a million copies!" She laughed. "That's not to say that folks only come to hear you play because you're a sex god. But you have to admit that women come to your concerts in droves, and they don't just throw roses at you, but photos of themselves with their phone numbers written on them. On a serious note, the story of your childhood and how devoted your parents were to making sure you got the training you needed makes for a wonderfully inspiring tale. I say, go for it, Jack!"

The thought of paying tribute to his parents appealed to Jack. They had sacrificed a lot to support his ambitions over the years. Indeed, they had been *his* ambitions. John and Dahlia Cain had not been stage parents, seeking to realize their deep-seated dreams through their son. His father would have been deliriously happy if he'd gone into the military like he'd done. His mother would have been pleased to see him become a doctor, or a lawyer. But music had been Jack's compulsion. From the age of three when his mother bought an old upright piano from an estate sale in Charleston he had known no greater love. His mother had been his first teacher. When she realized he'd surpassed her knowledge of the piano, she found him another teacher. When they moved to Germany, she searched high and low until she tracked down maestro Karl Salzinger who had been Jack's instructor until he left Germany for France, when his father was transferred, yet again. In France, he was given special dispensation to attend the Sorbonne at age fifteen. A year later, he debuted with the New York Philharmonic orchestra. He was still studying at the Sorbonne when his parents were killed in a private plane crash while vacationing in the Bahamas. He had been too busy with school to go with them.

"Okay," he said to Doris now. "I'm coming around. But there's still the matter of finding a writer I can work with. I refuse to put an inferior book on the market."

"Yes, I know what a perfectionist you are," Doris said with a short laugh. "Don't worry, sweetie. I'll find you a good writer. Any preferences?"

"Like what?"

"Male, or female?"

Jack thought for a moment. He had a lot of practicing to do in preparation for his European tour in January, plus there was the fact that he hadn't been with a woman in nearly six months. Not since he and Nadia had called it quits over breakfast in Berlin. Nadia was the last in a string of beauties he'd casually dated over the past two years. Before that, he'd been a one-woman man. Cecylia Canady was an Afro-British artist he'd met in London. She was the only woman he'd ever loved, but she could not live with his schedule. She left him, tearing him up inside. Three months later, he heard that she'd married a lawyer and was living in a suburb of London. He supposed she preferred having a husband whom she could count on to come home every night.

His heart still felt pain at the thought of her.

"I'd prefer a male," he answered.

"You don't need any distractions, am I right?" Doris said, being astute as usual.

"Right."

"Okay, sweetie. Leave it to me. So, I can tell Eleanor that you're interested, but you need at least…what? Six months to work on the book? I don't want to get you a deadline that's going to have you all stressed out."

"Doris, having never written a book, I don't know how long it's going to take."

"What you need is a writer who'd be willing to move in with you for several months."

"Move in with me?" Jack said, startled by the notion. He hadn't lived with anyone since he'd left home for the Sorbonne, not even with Cecylia.

"Put the brakes on, Doris," he said. "I can't do this if it means someone is going to invade my privacy."

Doris laughed. "Okay, what if I can get someone to move to Charleston and he can come in every day?" She paused, thinking. "But then you have the tour, and after that, more engagements in about a zillion cities over the next five months. Sweetie, what you need is a *wife* who writes."

"Really, Doris, if I wanted an agent who does stand-up comedy I would have hired a struggling comic for much less than what you're getting!"

Doris laughed even harder. "The thought of marriage scares you that much?"

"Doris, where am I going to find a woman who understands the music world, likes to travel, and will put up with a moody artist?"

"If you're the moody artist, I can give you about ten names right now."

"Keep the names, and find me a writer who can be here in about a week. If we work diligently maybe we can get through the first draft by New Year's Eve."

"Chicken!" Doris said of his reluctance to talk seriously about her fixing him up with a nice woman.

"You bet I am," Jack said. "Bye, Doris, and thank you!"

"It was my pleasure," Doris said before hanging up.

Jack felt so optimistic after their conversation that he decided to give Sandra Gerrard her interview. Little did he know, that phone call would set in motion a chain of events that would change his life forever.

Sandra and the Channel 9 News crew showed up bright and early the next morning. Sandra, who anchored the evening news wasn't taping the interview for a segment on that program, but for a weekend local entertainment show that aired every Saturday morning at ten.

It had rained last night, and Jack was suddenly apprehensive about the amount of mud the crew was tracking into the house. Three weeks in Charleston, and he still hadn't hired a housekeeper, something he'd been promising himself he'd get around to doing. Sandra had asked if they could tape at the house because they wanted shots of him seated at the Steinway. The interview would last about an hour. With commercial interruptions when the showed aired, it would run for thirty minutes.

Jack was casually dressed in a well-worn, but neatly pressed, sky-blue denim shirt, a pair of Levi's, and brown leather Italian loafers, without socks. While the men set up in the living room, he and Sandra toured the house, with Winslow trailing behind them.

"What a beautiful house," she said, her face a mass of smiles. "A lake, and I noticed on the way here that your closest neighbor is about half a mile down the road. Were you surprised by how remote it is?"

"No, the realtor told me it was isolated."

They were standing on the side deck. The house had three decks: one that was accessed from the kitchen, one from the master bedroom, and this one from the living room. Jack could see Sandra's crew setting up and positioning lights a few feet away.

Sandra wore a smart navy blue pantsuit with low heels. Her black shoulder-length hair was upswept, and her makeup was at a minimum. There was no makeup artist assigned to this shoot. Sandra liked the Saturday morning show to be as laid-back as possible. She smiled up at Jack. The camera probably loved him. He had the kind of lean good looks for which she knew Hollywood stars would pay a fortune. A large square head with wide-spaced light brown eyes, straight black brows, and thick lashes, a rather long, but well-shaped nose above a generous mouth, and a masculine, square chin. His short, curly hair was dark brown and, she noted, the morning sunlight gave it reddish highlights. What's more, his golden-brown skin was so healthy-looking, and the muscles of his body were so noticeably well-toned beneath his clothing that she knew he worked out. Nobody looked that delectable without some effort.

She chided herself. This was the second time she'd had improper thoughts in his presence. While she was married, she was not immune to every sexy man she encountered.

She knew that her heart belonged to Bruce, her husband of five years.

"You don't want neighbors nearby, or you simply like being able to play the piano at all hours?"

"A little of both," Jack said. "I do like the freedom of being able to get up in the middle of the night and play without disturbing anyone else."

Sandra laughed. "What am I doing! I should save these questions for the interview, and I *will* ask you that again."

She saw Bill, the lead cameraman, beckoning them. "They're finished," she said. "Let's get started, shall we?"

Jack lowered his six-foot-one body onto the large piano bench, and Sandra sat down beside him. She turned to smile at him. "Just relax and pretend I'm a friend who dropped by for a chat, okay?"

"All right," Jack said.

Winslow went and sat by the bench on Jack's left. Sandra was on his right.

Jack glanced down at Winslow. "Be a good boy, and I'll take you to the park this afternoon."

"That's how I bribe my son, Matthew," Sandra joked. "Does he obey?"

"Not usually."

"Mattie, either," Sandra said.

Shortly after that, they were cued, and Sandra looked into the camera. "Good morning, Charleston! I hope you're all up and you've had breakfast, and now you're getting ready to attend the twelfth annual Multicultural Arts Festival downtown. But, before you go to have fun at the arts festival, please join me at the home of renowned concert pianist, John Cain, for a little chat and, hopefully, a musical interlude before we're done."

Regarding Jack warmly, she continued. "Good morning, John!"

"Good morning, Sandra, and, please, call me Jack."

"Okay, Jack." Sandra turned toward him a bit more, getting comfortable. "You were born here in Charleston, weren't you, Jack?"

Jack nodded. "Yes, that's right. So were my parents. All native to Charleston."

"But sadly you lost both parents about seventeen years ago. I'm sure our viewers would like to know what brings you back to Charleston after a nearly thirty-year absence? You were seven years old the last time you were here, am I correct?"

"Yes, you are."

"Then you don't remember much about the city."

"Not very much, no," Jack confirmed. "In fact, my decision to come here was probably fueled by my parents' memories of Charleston, not my own. They often spoke fondly of the people they left behind."

"According to local sources, your parents were both orphans."

"Yes," Jack said cautiously.

"And you have no relatives in the area."

"None that I know of."

Sandra gave him a concerned look. An almost pitying

expression spread across her pretty face. "Not that we're
not delighted to have you, Jack. But why would you choose
to spend your downtime in a city where you don't know
anyone? You're a world traveler. You could have gone to
any major city in the world. Why Charleston?"

"Probably for that very reason, Sandra. I *am* a seasoned
traveler. I've lived out of a suitcase for more years than I
care to admit. Like anybody else, I want to live in a place I
can call home. Charleston is where I was born. I was hoping to discover that special 'something' that made it home
for my parents. No matter where we lived in the world,
they would always tell people, 'I'm from Charleston, South
Carolina.' I have no city I can say that about."

Now, Sandra was definitely looking at him with profound pity mirrored in her big, brown eyes. She missed a
beat, a no-no in the world of TV journalism, and there was
dead air for nearly fifteen seconds. Then, she came to herself. "Well, we'll do our best to make you feel at home,
Jack!" she said enthusiastically. She looked into the camera
again. "Won't we, Charleston?"

Back to Jack. "Jack, you've played before royalty in
Europe and heads-of-state all over the world. I was wondering if I could get you to play a little something for your new
friends and neighbors?"

"I'd love to," Jack said, glad for something to do. Talking
about his feelings was making him very uncomfortable.
Next, Sandra would have him boo-hooing and he would
wish he'd given Barbara Walters that interview for *20/20*
last year, instead.

He began playing Beethoven's Piano Sonata no. 14 in

C-sharp minor, op. 27, no. 2 "Moonlight," better known as *Moonlight Sonata*.

On Saturday, when the show aired all over Charleston, viewers turned the volume up on their TVs. If they were standing, they sat down. Parents shushed their loud, rambunctious children and threatened to withhold some treat if they didn't obey.

Women, especially, sat and watched intently, wondering how music that beautiful could come out of a man with such broad shoulders. They were entranced by the intense concentration in his hooded eyes, and the manner in which his big hands seemed to caress the piano keys. Some closed their eyes and sank into their chairs with longing-filled sighs.

Others had a more aggressive response to Jack's playing, and phoned the station, demanding a number where they could get in touch with him. By the next day, the station had received more than two hundred e-mails, all wanting to know more about Jack.

Joyce Hart was watching in the kitchen of her home with her grandkids, LaShaunda and Brett, whom she'd babysat last night so that her son, Calvin, and his wife, Rhonda, could have some time alone. She'd popped a tape into the VCR and pressed *record* as soon as Sandra and Jack had appeared on the screen. She didn't know why she was taping the program. She rarely taped anything except her soap operas so that she wouldn't miss them when she was out.

The kids' mouths were filled with her homemade pancakes, so she didn't have to tell them to be quiet. She watched Jack, marveling, once again, at how much he looked like his father. And when he spoke about wanting someplace to call home, tears formed in her eyes and moistened her cheeks.

After the program ended, Joyce rose from her chair at the table. "Y'all finish eating, Grandma has to go make a phone call."

A minute later, a groggy-voiced Callie answered her phone. "Hullo?"

"Sorry, honey, I know you sleep late on Saturday mornings. Was the club hopping last night?"

"Mmm, huh, the place was packed. Reid even gave me a bonus." *Uh, huh*

"Good, old Reid. Listen, honey, do you remember my talking about my childhood friend, Dahlia Cain?"

"Of course, Ma. You said I reminded you of her."

"Yes, well, her son's back in town."

"Oh, that's great. How long is he staying? Maybe I'll get to meet him at Thanksgiving or Christmas."

"There's no doubt about that. He's going to be sharing the spotlight with you at the Christmas festival," her mother calmly informed her.

"He's a musician?" Callie asked, calmly, as well.

"He plays a little piano. His name is John Cain."

Callie was momentarily speechless. "The concert pianist?!"

"Don't scream in my ear, Callista."

"Sorry," Callie said, lowering her voice. "You never mentioned that Dahlia Cain's son is John Cain. I'd be too nervous to perform in front of him."

"He's just a man, honey."

"No, he isn't. He's a genius. Ma, I'm not coming anywhere near Charleston if you're going to force me to play on the same stage as John Cain. How did you get him to agree to do the show, anyway? He must charge thousands for a performance. Doesn't he live in Europe somewhere? I think the liner notes from his last CD said he lived in London. What is he doing in Charleston?"

"Will you be quiet, and listen?" Joyce asked with an exasperated sigh. "The package I told you I'm sending is a tape of an interview John gave Sandra Gerrard. He played this beautiful song." She started humming it.

"Beethoven's *Moonlight Sonata*," Callie told her.

"Anyway, the first thing I thought after watching it was that you had to see his performance. So, watch it, Callista, and then decide if you're brave enough to share a stage with this genius who's really just a man. Bye, honey. Try to go back to sleep if I haven't gotten you too excited."

"Bye, Ma. And don't forget to put that tape in the mail!"

Joyce laughed. "I won't. Love you."

"Love you more."

CHAPTER 3

Two days after the interview, Jack was in the kitchen preparing a ham sandwich for lunch when the doorbell rang. Winslow was shamelessly cadging bits of ham off his master, even though he'd already eaten.

Jack gave one more sliver of ham to Winslow, then trotted through the house in bare feet wearing jeans and a T-shirt, to see who was at the door.

A neatly dressed young black man stood on the front porch, a large box in his arms.

"Mr. Cain?" He held his driver's license up for Jack to see. His name was Charles Levi.

"Yes?" Jack said, his gaze lowering to the box now that the man's identity was known.

"I'm Chaz Levi, Sandra Gerrard's assistant. She asked me to deliver this package to you. She asks that you open it at your earliest convenience."

Jack accepted the box. "All right, thank you."

"No problem," Chaz said with a grin. "Have a great day!"

"Yeah, you, too."

Jack turned away and went back into the house, closing the door behind him. He took the box back to the kitchen with him and set it on the counter. He'd open it after he finished lunch, and before he went back to practicing "Appassionata." He was having a problem with the second movement. But before he could take a bite from his sandwich, the telephone rang. He glanced at the caller ID. Coincidentally, it was Sandra.

"Sandra, hello, your assistant just delivered your package. Thank you, but I haven't had the chance to open it yet."

"Jack! Hello, yourself. I asked Chaz to let me know via his cell phone after he'd given you the letters," Sandra said, cheerfully.

"Letters?"

"From your admirers."

Jack laughed. "Sandra, what are you talking about?"

"Jack, in the past two days we've received more than five hundred phone calls, around two hundred e-mails, and more than two hundred letters from people who want to know more about you. My assistant tells me that the majority of them are from women. No surprise there! I asked Chaz to bring you the letters. We didn't open them. But, don't worry, all of our mail gets scanned for bombs and other harmful things. They're safe."

"You never mentioned I could be inundated with mail before I did the interview," Jack said, almost accusingly.

"This has never happened before! I'm as surprised as you are. My boss is after me to do a follow-up interview with you to satisfy the hungry hordes!" Sandra said, laughing.

Jack wasn't amused. "Haven't you done enough harm already?"

"I understand your concerns, Jack. You were probably left pretty much alone by the fans in Europe. They went to your concerts, tossed roses at your feet, and let you have your privacy. But this is South Carolina, and folks are excited to have you among them. Give them time, things will die down soon. Believe me, most of them mean well. Until then you'll have to put up with the adulation, and a few nuts who will propose marriage, or something a little less permanent like a one-night stand. Ignore them, and they'll eventually go away."

Jack sighed. "You're right, this sort of thing happens to pop singers and actors in England, but they usually leave me alone."

"Like I said, the mail will trickle off, and you'll be old news in a few weeks. But for now I'm afraid you're the talk of the town. Did you look at the tape I gave you? Jack, it was wildly romantic! My husband, Bruce, accused me of nearly swooning while you were playing and, you know what, he was right! So, don't blame those women for wanting to know more about you. Hey, maybe some good will come from this, and you'll meet someone special. Or at least find that missing 'something' that you said you were looking for."

Jack suddenly felt sick to his stomach. How had he come off during the interview, anyway? He hadn't watched the tape yet. He'd filed it away, never to watch it. He didn't like watching himself perform. A perfectionist, watching himself play brought his obsessive–compulsive tendencies to the surface. He would watch it over and over again, analyzing it, and finding fault with every aspect of his performance.

"No, I haven't seen it," he told Sandra. "I guess I'd better take a look."

"Yes, you do that," Sandra gently said. "Jack, I'm sorry this didn't turn out the way that you imagined it would."

"It's not your fault, Sandra. Besides, as long as they don't have my address or phone number, I'm okay."

"It's against station policy to reveal any personal information about interview subjects," Sandra assured him.

"Good."

Sandra laughed. "I guess I'm not going to get that second interview, then?"

"Let's leave well enough alone, shall we?" Jack said with a short laugh.

" 'Nuff said." There was a note of regret in her voice. "However, if you should actually *accept* one of those marriage proposals, I want an exclusive!"

Jack laughed. "You'll be the first person I'll call. Bye, Sandra."

"Bye, Jack."

Once he'd hung up, Jack succumbed to curiosity and ripped the box open. As Sandra had said, it was full of letters. He reached in and picked up one of them.

Tearing it open, he read,

Dear Jack, After I saw you on TV, I went to the library to look you up. I'm sorry, I'm not a fan of classical music, but you can bet I went to the mall and bought all of your CDs after hearing you play! If I'd known Beethoven could be this cool, I would have paid closer attention in my music appreciation class! And as for sex appeal, Harry Connick, Jr. has got nothing on you!

He put that letter down, picked up another one, and carefully opened it. He was both curious and cautious, as he always was when reading fan mail. Sometimes people could be uncommonly cruel in their assessment of your performance. His agent's people usually handled his fan mail.

Jack, the second letter began, *I'm lonely too. Maybe we could get together for drinks sometime soon. Here is a recent photo of me. My number's on the back.*

She was very attractive, and scantily clad. He dropped the letter and photo back into the box. Is that how he'd appeared? Like some lonely piano geek, looking for love?

He went to the sink and washed his hands as if the letters had been tainted, and he could wash away the doubt they'd left on his psyche. Was that how the majority of viewers had perceived him? Did they feel sympathy for him because he craved a place to call home? That's not what he'd meant at all! Granted, he did want Charleston to embrace him, but not *embrace* him! He didn't want strange women writing him, giving him their phone numbers, and enclosing photos of themselves in provocative poses!

He tried his best to ignore the box with the letters in it as he went back to his sandwich. But as he sat at the counter eating, and using the remote to channel surf on the TV, his mind was split. Try as he might, he could not stop thinking that he had made a complete and utter fool of himself during the interview.

What he needed was an unbiased opinion of the program. But he didn't know anybody in Charleston except a few members of the arts group that had sponsored the welcome home gala and Mrs. Joyce Hart. Out of those few people, he felt most comfortable with Mrs. Hart. So, when he was done with lunch, he went into his office and got Mrs. Hart's card out of the desk drawer, sat on the corner of the desk, and dialed her home number.

He glanced at his watch. It was nearly 12:30 on Monday. Would she be at home? The phone rang three times before someone picked up. "Hello, Hart residence."

"Mrs. Hart?"

"Yes, this is she." There was a sharp intake of breath. "John, is that you?"

"You have a good ear for voices."

"Process of elimination. I don't give my number to just anybody, and the only men who phone me are my sons, Cal and Derrick, and my brother, Calvin. You don't sound like any of them."

Jack laughed. "I could have been a salesman."

"Honey, not if they know what's good for them. Now, I hope you're phoning because you're ready to take me up on my offer of a meal! I've got some young collard greens in my fall garden that are ready to eat. And I've been waiting for an excuse to make a sweet potato pie."

After that, Jack didn't have the heart to say he was only phoning to see if she'd seen that disastrous interview from a couple of days ago and, if she had, what she thought of it.

"I haven't had collard greens in years," he said. If he remembered correctly, they could be quite tasty if prepared by a competent chef. "And sweet potato pie is one of my favorites."

"We're on, then," Joyce said, happily. "By the way, John, I saw your interview with Sandra, and it made me cry."

Oh, no, Jack thought, *even Mrs. Hart pities me.*

"You played so beautifully, I got to thinking of Dahlia and how proud she must have been of you!"

Jack could barely contain a sigh of relief. She didn't pity him; memories of his mother had made her cry. "I miss them every day," he said of his parents.

"I'm sure you do," Joyce said softly. Then, she revived, and cheerfully gave him directions to her house.

"Will there be other guests?" Jack asked.

"Not tonight," Joyce told him. "I'll have you all to myself."

Jack had no trouble finding the house, a small well-kept ranch house in an older neighborhood where trees lined the streets, and people kept their yards manicured.

It was dark when he arrived, and lights were on in the windows of the houses. Savory aromas were in the air, and music danced all around him. Rhythm-and-blues over here, gospel over there, hip hop, everywhere.

Joyce answered the door and hugged him hello. "Look at you, all dressed up for my collard greens and ham hocks! And, flowers too?"

"Ham hocks?" Jack asked as he walked inside and handed her the bouquet of red roses.

"Just kidding, I use smoked turkey nowadays. But back

in the day I used ham hocks. They come from the pig's leg," Joyce told him as she closed the door and took his coat, which she hung in the hall closet. "It's cured, or slowly smoked in a smokehouse, where it get a real thick, kind of tough skin on it. All it really is is a piece of thick skin around a bone, a lot of fat, and a little bit of ham. You have to cook it to death to get it tender! When I was a girl we ate every part of the pig. Even the part that goes over the fence last," Joyce said, laughing. "Now, we know that all that fatty pork isn't good for you."

"I had no idea," said Jack, feeling as though he was getting a history lesson and a cooking lesson, simultaneously.

Joyce took a moment to inhale the heady fragrance of the roses. "Thank you, John. They're beautiful."

"Truly, they don't do you justice," Jack said sincerely.

Joyce found herself giggling like a schoolgirl. She didn't know where he'd learned how to be so charming, but she knew men who needed to go there and take lessons.

"Stop that," she told him. "You're going to get me so flustered I'll burn dinner or some nonsense. Come on in, and let me show you around."

Jack followed her to the living room. Because, he supposed, the house was small, Joyce had furnished it sparingly, and in neutral colors. The furniture was a deep shade of beige, and well made. The rugs on the hardwood floors had short naps. The artwork, consisting of paintings and wood carvings, was influenced by Asian and African cultures.

"You have a lovely home," he complimented her.

"It's taken me years to get it exactly the way I want it," Joyce said as she led him to a wall in the back near the dining room. She gestured to the first framed photo on the wall. "These are my children, Calvin, we call him Cal, Derrick, and Callista. That was taken last Christmas."

Jack peered closely at the photographs. Her daughter Callista was a knockout. He had to school his expression before Joyce, perceptive woman that she was, noted it and found some way to use it to her advantage. He'd come up against quite a few match making mothers in his time. He didn't want to give her any ideas.

"You have a good looking family," he commented.

"They're okay," Joyce said modestly. He noticed that she rocked back on her heels a little when she said it though. She was proud of them.

"What do they do?"

Joyce hummed as though she had to think about it. "Uh, mm, Calvin, who's the first, is a dentist. Derrick, who is in the middle, is a teacher, and, finally, Callista, is an editor at a lifestyle magazine. As the baby of the family, I think I might have spoiled her when she was a child. I let her indulge her interests anytime she had a whim. Now, she's kind of a jack-of-all-trades. She's an editor, she's working on a novel, and she is the main act at a blues club in Atlanta. To say that she likes keeping busy would be an understatement."

A woman who willingly took on all of that interested Jack. Especially the part about being the main act at a blues club. "So, she doesn't just appear in the Christmas Festival once a year, she works steadily."

"Oh, yes," said Joyce. "She's been working professionally for the past seven years. She's no amateur. I have tapes of her performing in the club. I'll show you one after dinner.

Don't worry, I'm not going to drag out all ten tapes. But, she's quite good. She could easily get a recording contract if that's what she wanted, but she's not interested. She says she likes the intimacy of The Blue Bird, that's the name of the club where she works." Joyce laughed suddenly. "I know this kind of talk coming from a mother means nothing. But you can judge for yourself later."

She went on to show him a few more photographs and then said, "Come on back to the kitchen. We don't stand on ceremony around here. Besides, it's hard to be proper when you're eating collard greens and cornbread."

She glanced at his cream-colored shirt with some concern. "You're going to need an apron to protect that nice shirt."

An apron! Jack thought, slightly panicked.

In her scrupulously clean kitchen, Joyce directed him to the counter where she'd left two plump, ripe, freshly-washed beefsteak tomatoes. "You can wash up at the sink, and then cut those tomatoes into nice, thick slices. They'll be delicious with a little salt, pepper, and vinegar on them. I've got some fresh red pepper too if you like your tomatoes spicy."

Jack was busy appreciating the mouthwatering aromas all around him. "Yes, ma'am."

While he washed his hands, Joyce went to the pantry in the rear of the kitchen, got a vase and went to the other side of the sink to run water into it. She smiled up at him. "Do you cook much, John?"

"No ma'am. I eat out a lot."

"Well, if you hang around me long enough, you'll learn.

All of my children can cook. They had to learn. I was a single mother for a lot of years after Clarence passed on."

Jack realized he'd missed out on a lot of interesting experiences when he was a kid because he'd been practicing the piano. Of course, if he hadn't made sacrifices, he wouldn't be where he was today.

"I can make a good tomato sauce for pasta," he said. "I learned from an Italian chef when I was in Tuscany for a few months. And I can make my Mom's pancakes. She taught me how to make them when I was eight."

"Well, that's breakfast, lunch, and dinner," Joyce joked. "You're doing okay."

Jack smiled as he cut the tomatoes into quarter-inch thick slices with a serrated knife.

After Joyce had put the roses in the vase, she walked out of the kitchen to the dining room where she placed them in the center of the table she'd already set for her and Jack.

When she returned to the kitchen, she went to a drawer and got a large red apron for Jack to put on. Standing behind him, she said, "My sons use this when they're here."

Jack turned around and bent down so she could slip the bib-apron over his head, then he turned back around so that she could tie it around him.

Satisfied that he wouldn't ruin his shirt, Joyce went to the gas stove to check the pots she had left simmering on the stove top. Lifting the lid on a large Dutch oven, she inhaled deeply.

Her eyes watered a little. She thought she might have used too much cayenne pepper. All her people loved spicy foods. She'd turned the heat down a little for John Junior.

"Does Merlot go with beef stew, John? I'm not a wine drinker myself, but I thought you might be, having lived in Europe all those years. Mercy Jones, she's a good friend of mine, told me Merlot was a good choice. Though, Lord knows what the vintage is like. I bought it from the local liquor store."

"Merlot is perfect," Jack told her, touched that she would go to all that trouble for him. He imagined that she had never set foot in a liquor store.

"Personally, if I'm going to drink an alcoholic beverage, I prefer Scotch, straight up," Joyce said matter-of-factly.

Jack tried his best to suppress the guffaw, but somehow it escaped and soon they were both laughing uproariously. Joyce never could forego a good belly laugh.

She looked at him with tears in her eyes. "What did I say?"

"I was thinking that you had probably never gone into a liquor store before, and then you said you prefer Scotch, straight up. I'm sorry, it just didn't fit with my image of you."

"Well, you can't judge a book by its cover," Joyce said, still smiling. "Come on, let's eat. Wrestling comes on in an hour, and I don't want to miss it."

They talked throughout the meal. Jack wanted to know about African-Americans in Charleston's history. "Oh, honey, we have a long history in this town," Joyce told him. "Lots of slave ships docked here, and many African-Americans can trace their family trees back here. My favorite historical figure is Robert Smalls, who hijacked a Confederate steamship and sailed it to the Union side during the Civil War. He disguised himself as a white man in order to do it. I would've loved to have seen that!"

Jack was enjoying the food and the company. Mrs. Hart hadn't been boasting when she'd said she was a good cook. Jack had to remind himself that if he ate too much of the food in front of him, he wouldn't have room for the sweet potato pie, and he'd been dreaming of it all day long.

After dinner, Joyce suggested they have dessert and coffee in the living room in front of the TV. As it turned out, she'd been joking about watching wrestling. She put a video tape into the VCR and went to join Jack on the sofa.

Jack sampled the sweet potato pie as the tape began. It was delectable. Not too sweet, creamy in texture, delightfully spiced, and with a crust that was crisp and flaky.

Then, he heard a man's voice say, "Hello, Momma Joyce, this is Reid coming at you from Hotlanta. I've got a special treat for you tonight. Yes, it's the one, the only, your baby girl, Miss Callie Hart, singing, 'Fine and Mellow.' Happy birthday!"

"That's Reid Harris talking," Joyce explained. "He owns The Blue Bird. Callista sends me a tape every year for my birthday."

Callie had Jack's attention from the opening bars on the piano, and then she began to sing: "My man don't love me, he treats me so mean…"

Reid, or whoever was shooting the video, zoomed in closer to her and Jack could see the sheer joy she felt mirrored in her dark eyes. Her voice, a deep contralto, wasn't like any other singer's that Jack had ever heard. If he were to try to compare her with someone, it would be Anita

Baker, but Callie Hart had a more playful quality to her voice. It was extremely sensual. He felt flush. He hoped that reaction was due to Mrs. Hart's spicy food, and not to her daughter. But he knew that hope was in vain.

He was embarrassed by his response, especially with her mother sitting less than four feet away from him. Joyce wasn't watching him, though. She was smiling at the image of her daughter on the TV screen. "That's my favorite Billie Holiday song," she told Jack. "It's one of mine, too," Jack said, his voice cracking a bit.

After that, they fell silent and simply watched the tape. Callie sang four more songs, "Stormy Monday," "Blue Skies," "Embraceable You," and a bluesy version of "Wade in the Water." "She throws in a gospel tune to let me know she hasn't forgotten where she came from," Joyce said of that selection. "She grew up singing in the church. Her grandma, Eva Jean, played the piano at St. John A.M.E. for nearly thirty years. Callista played there, too, until she went away to college."

The tape ended, and Joyce went to remove it from the VCR. She put it back in its box. "I don't want to be a pushy parent or anything," Joyce said as she was putting the tape back on the shelf next to the others that Callie had sent her over the years. "But there are six others, and if you'd like to borrow them, you're more than welcome to them."

Jack dearly wanted to take those tapes home and watch every last one of them, but he politely refused because he didn't want it to appear as if he had more than a passing professional interest in her daughter.

"She's very talented," he said sincerely as he rose and stretched, preparing to thank his charming hostess and call it a night. "But I wouldn't have the time to watch them. I'm practicing for an upcoming series of concerts. And, besides that, I've been talked into writing an autobiography I'm ill-equipped to write since I'm not a writer!" He laughed. "I should have my head examined for agreeing to do it."

Joyce didn't miss a beat when she suggested, "Honey, you ought to give Callista a call! I'm sure she could help you with that."

Jack tried to ignore her comment as he bent to pick up his empty dessert plate, fork, and coffee cup from the coffee table. "Let me help you with the dishes."

"I have a dishwasher for that," Joyce said. She was busy choosing one of the tapes of Callie's performances from the shelf. "Just take one, John. You can return it anytime. That way, I can be sure you'll come for another visit. I know you're busy, but you can watch it before drifting off to sleep one night, or something. No biggie."

Jack put everything back on the coffee table and accepted the tape Joyce held out to him. "All right," he said. "But, I assure you, after such a wonderful evening, this won't be the last time I come to bum a meal off you."

Joyce laughed. Her face was aglow with pleasure. "Thanksgiving's coming up. I'll put you to work in the kitchen just like I do my children."

As Thanksgiving approached, however, Jack was determined to take the tape back to Joyce, and give her a very good reason why he would not be anywhere in the vicinity of her house come Thanksgiving Day.

The tape never left his VCR. He played it so often that even Winslow got attached to the sound of Callie's voice. Jack would turn the tape on, and Winslow would come running from whichever room of the house he was in to sit in front of the TV and watch it. Jack didn't know what it was that attracted Winslow to Callie Hart. But as for him, he found *everything* about her attractive. Her skin, her hair, her teeth, her nose, her eyes, and *especially* her mouth, which was so undeniably sexy, his gaze stayed glued to it as she sang. He adored her voice, and could listen to it for hours on end. He *had* listened to it for hours on end!

By the fifth day of this, he couldn't look at himself in the mirror without thinking, "You're getting weird. Take the damn tape back to Mrs. Hart and get it over with!"

He could not bring himself to do it, though. He kept the tape until well into November. He played it every day, realizing he was becoming obsessed with a woman he didn't know anything about except what her mother had told him. She could be a married woman for all he knew. No, he distinctly remembered Reid, the club owner, referring to her as *Miss* Callie Hart. So, chances were that she was single. Or she *had* been when that particular tape had been recorded!

The day before Thanksgiving, Jack and Winslow got into his SUV to drive to Joyce Hart's house in order to return the tape before he ruined it by overuse.

Hours earlier, Callie had begun her drive from Atlanta in her old, reliable Toyota Corolla. She had a thermos of black coffee, bottles of water, tapes of her favorite artists, most of whom were piano players like Nina Simone, Ray Charles, Stevie Wonder, Alicia Keys, Elton John, and the offending John Cain tape, which she was going to return to her mother—and never may it darken her door again!—on the seat beside her.

She glanced into her eyes in the rearview mirror. Those were the eyes of an insane woman! She'd watched that darn tape every day for nearly six weeks. She was happy to get it out of her apartment. Well, it might not be her apartment for long because she still hadn't found a job, but she was digressing. The point was, the more she watched John Cain perform *Moonlight Sonata*, the more she dreamed of kissing him in the moonlight. God help her, the man was beautiful with those dark, hooded eyes, large nose—it flared when he became emotional. This was something an obsessed woman would notice after watching his performance forty-odd times. He also had a strong chin, sensual mouth, and wonderful hands. Strong hands that played the piano as lovingly as he might caress a woman's body.

She returned her attention to the road and her driving. Of course, the harm was done by the time she did this because the right rear tire had picked up a nail somewhere between her musings about John Cain's nose, and his hands.

Because she was listening to Elton John singing, "Your Song," she didn't at first hear the high-pitched whine that was her tire rapidly deflating. She did, however, feel the sudden jerk of the steering wheel. It had been a long time since she'd had a flat tire. But some deep-seated memory told her to hold on to the steering wheel firmly and slowly ease up on the accelerator.

She coasted to the soft shoulder of the highway, put the car in park, set the parking brake, and turned off the engine. She let out a long breath and, hands still clamped to the steering wheel, lay her head on it for a minute. That had been a little nerve-racking.

The first thing she did after gathering her wits about her was to dig in her shoulder bag and get her cell phone. Peering closely at it, she was disappointed to find that she had forgotten to recharge it. So, she would not be able to phone her auto club or, better yet, one of her brothers who would get there faster than the auto club's tow truck.

There was only one thing left to do. She would have to change the tire herself. For that, she would have to focus. Did she even remember how to change a tire? She'd done it once before, perhaps fifteen years ago when she was in high school, and then she'd had three other girls with her. They'd been returning from cheerleader camp in her battered Chevy. Between the four of them, they'd gotten the job done.

Well, she thought with a resigned sigh, *it's not going to change itself.* But first, she reached in her purse and got a Ferrara Pan Atomic Fireball, opened the wrapper, and put it in her mouth. She was addicted to the extremely spicy jawbreakers. Like chocolate soothed some people when they were upset, Atomic Fireballs steadied her nerves. Plus, they cleared her sinuses. She got out of the car, and went to unlock the trunk.

CHAPTER 4

Jack slowed the SUV when he saw the disabled car on the side of the road. Its trunk was open, and someone—even with his contacts in he couldn't tell from this distance whether it was a male or a female—was bent over trying to remove the lug nuts from the damaged tire. He knew it was the damaged tire the person was working on because he could see the spare leaning against the back bumper.

The person straightened to her full height, and that's when he saw mounds of curly auburn hair, and the tall, unmistakable shape of a woman. He slowed further.

Winslow began barking enthusiastically. He stood up on the seat and turned around to look at the woman after Jack had passed the car.

"Will you calm down?" Jack asked as he pulled the SUV off the road a few yards in front of the Toyota Corolla. "I'm going back to see if I can help. But I'm blaming you if she's a carjacker and I wind up with a blow to the head, and you end up dognapped."

Winslow barked again and wagged his tail happily. When Jack got out and began walking toward the Corolla, his pooch leaped across the front seat, onto the back seat, and stuck his head out of the open back window to watch.

Callie had managed to get all but one of the lug nuts off the wheel. She was using the hubcap as a receptacle for the huge bolts. Using it would remind her to put it back on once she'd changed the tires.

It was all coming back to her. You didn't have to be a genius to change a tire, after all. You just needed common sense. The evening breezes were blowing pretty fiercely though. Charleston must be in for an unusually cold winter. She was glad she'd worn a sweater, jeans, and her good leather ankle boots. She couldn't recall the last time they'd had snow in South Carolina for Christmas. She'd been really young. But it would be nice if it snowed a little the night of the Christmas festival.

Even though she wanted to get out of doing the concert, she knew she wouldn't be able to tell her mother, *no*. No, she wouldn't do her part to help underprivileged kids go to college? The guilt would be unbearable.

She could hold her stupid crush on John Cain in check for one evening, couldn't she? It wasn't as if she'd see him much before or after the concert. He certainly wouldn't want actually to get together and collaborate on a couple of songs, now, would he? She'd never known him to perform with other pianists. He'd performed with symphony orchestras the world over, but he was always the sole pianist.

She smiled when she got the last lug nut off and dropped it into the bowl the hubcap made. Then, she took the opportunity to turn the wheel on its axis in order to examine the ruined tire. There it was, the reason she was here on her knees on the side of the road only about ten miles from her mom's house: A large, rusty nail was embedded in the tire.

"There will be no saving you, buddy," she said sarcastically. Something else to subtract from her ever-decreasing savings that were supposed to tide her over until she could find another job.

"Do you talk to all tires, or just the ones you're changing?" asked a deep male voice from behind her.

Callie started, jerked her head around, and looked up into the face of John Cain. There was no way she would not recognize him in the flesh. And it was such nice flesh, too!

She abruptly rose and stood staring at him with her mouth slightly open.

Jack's heart was beating in double-time. *Callista Hart.* He felt off-kilter, as if someone might jump from behind a bush any minute now, and yell, "Smile! You're on *Candid Camera!*"

The possibility of this being a ruse ran through his head. What were the odds that Callista Hart would be on this road the very evening he was heading to her mother's house? Probably pretty good seeing as how it was the day before Thanksgiving, and she was on the way to her mother's house for the holiday. Clearly, she had as much of a reason to be traveling this road as he did.

In the end, his attraction to her won over intellect. His greatest fear had been realized. He was even more turned on by her *now* than he'd been while watching her image on tape. She took his breath away, plain and simple.

Callie swallowed hard. Why was he staring at her like that? Was she looking bug-eyed at him or something? Did she have axle grease on her face? She self-consciously reached up to smooth a strand of wind-blown hair out of her face. Now, she probably *did* have grease on her face.

Jack found his voice, and said, "Let me finish that for you."

Callie's eyes stretched in horror. She stood in front of the car, arms out, effectively preventing him from getting any closer to it. "No!"

Jack smiled. "Don't worry," he said gently. "I'm harmless. I just want to help."

Jack tried to get around her. She blocked him. "Listen, I recognize you, okay?" Callie finally said, exasperated. "And I'm not letting you risk your career by changing a tire!"

Jack laughed heartily. "I should have known Joyce Hart's daughter would inherit her perception. So, you know who I am. Well, I know who you are, too, and I'm not going to let you risk *your* hands by changing a tire!"

They stood, at an impasse, eyeing one another. Jack loved the obstinate curve of her bee-stung lips. How her chin jutted out defiantly as if she were certain she would get her way in the matter.

"Surely we can compromise, Callista?"

"Callie."

"Callie," he said, trying out her name on his tongue.

"I don't see how we can compromise on this, John."

"Jack."

"Jack," Callie said, her voice husky.

Jack felt the pleasure of hearing his name on her lips spread from the pit of his stomach to the rest of him, until it settled in an area that had never before been stimulated only by the sound of a woman's voice.

"What if we do it this way?" Jack asked reasonably. "I'll do it, and you can watch over my shoulder and make sure I'm extra careful."

Callie made him wait a few seconds before agreeing. "Okay, but if I see you about to do something daring, I'm taking over," she warned.

Jack laughed as he took his jacket off and placed it on the car's roof. "What could I do that could possibly be construed as daring while changing a tire? And you shouldn't be so bossy. It ruins my image of you as Joyce Hart's daughter. She hasn't got a bossy bone in her body." He bent to take the flat tire off the axle.

Callie humphed. "Goes to show how well you know my mother!"

Jack lifted the damaged tire, and walked around to the back of the car to retrieve the spare. He tested it for inflation, pressing firmly down on it. It appeared to be properly inflated. "When was the last time you had your spare checked?" he asked as he put the tire on and Callie handed him the first lug nut.

"I always get it checked before a trip," Callie said. "I know I should probably get it checked more often."

"Most people wait until they're preparing for a trip," Jack said. "You're average."

"Well, thanks," Callie said, sounding none too pleased to be described as average.

Jack laughed softly. "You don't like being average, do you?"

He'd tightened the bolt and held his hand out for another one. Callie placed it in his palm. "Who does? We all have dreams of standing out in the crowd. Of being special."

"You are special, Callie. I don't know when I've enjoyed a performance more."

Callie gazed down at him. His burnt caramel-colored eyes held an amused glint in them. "Where did you see me perform?" she asked.

"Your mother had me over for dinner a while back, and showed me one of her birthday tapes that you sent her."

Callie's face grew hot with embarrassment. She touched her cheek, probably putting more grease on her face. "Oh, no, she didn't!"

"Yes," Jack said. "And when I was about to leave, she gave me one to take with me."

"I don't believe she did that!" Callie cried, thoroughly discomfitted. "What was she *thinking*?"

"She is understandably proud of you, and she wanted me to see you play," Jack said. They continued with the work at hand. "I think it was sweet. When she first told me she had a daughter who played piano and sang in a blues club, I assumed she was one of those parents who can't see that their child has no talent. But I was wrong. You're very talented, Callie Hart."

Callie smiled her pleasure. "Thank you, Jack."

Jack returned her smile. "You're welcome." They worked in silence for a couple of minutes, then Jack said, "So, how did you recognize me? Please tell me you didn't see that awful interview of several weeks ago."

"My mom sent me a copy of it," Callie confirmed.

It was Jack's turn to groan in protest. "She's a busy woman, your mother."

"Very," Callie agreed. She handed him the final lug nut. "Why did you think it was a bad interview? I thought you did a great job."

"You didn't think I appeared too needy, telling folks I wanted a place I could call home?" He paused before tightening the last bolt to look into her eyes.

"Jack, that's a normal human desire, wanting to belong somewhere. I thought you were being extremely candid, and I liked that about you."

"So, you appreciate honesty in a person?" Jack asked, going back to work on the bolt. "How much honesty?"

"You can never be too honest."

"That sounds like something I would expect from Joyce Hart's daughter. She doesn't believe in pretense or putting on airs, either." He checked again to make sure all of the bolts were tightened sufficiently, then he replaced the hubcap. Rising, he brushed his hands together to get rid of the grit.

He used the jack to slowly lower the car. This done, he

bent and disconnected the jack and picked up the flat tire. Callie bent and retrieved the tire iron. Once everything was in the trunk, Jack closed it and turned to face her.

"I watched your tape more than once. I watched it several times, wondering what you were like. You intrigued me."

The wind lifted Callie's hair off her shoulders as she stood there with her hands on her hips, watching Jack. A thrill of excitement shot through her body at his confession.

This couldn't be happening. John Cain couldn't be telling her he had a romantic interest in her! She didn't know if she could handle that. Dreaming of kissing him was one thing, but the thought that there was a possibility that her dreams might come true was incomprehensible. A girl had to take a chance once in a while, though, didn't she?

"I think I must have watched your tape at least forty-seven times," she admitted. "Is that bordering on obsessive?"

"If it is, then we're both borderline obsessive," Jack said with a laugh.

"How many times?" Callie wanted to know. Her dark eyes bore into his.

Jack paused as if he were mentally counting the days he'd watched her tape. "Actually, I don't know. But I watched it once, sometimes twice, a day for a solid month."

Callie laughed delightedly. "You could have watched it more than I watched yours!"

"Does that make you feel any less crazy?" Jack asked with a grin.

"A little," Callie told him, still laughing.

Jack grabbed his jacket from atop the car and started putting it back on. Callie stepped forward and helped him with it. When she got close to him, he immediately felt the warmth of her skin and smelled the fresh, flowery scent of her cologne. He wanted to bend his head and inhale her fragrance, but resisted.

Callie let her hands fall to her sides after helping him with his jacket. "Thanks for stopping. I hope I haven't kept you from something important."

"I was on my way to return your tape to your mother," he told her, a smile curving his lips. "And to give her an excuse as to why I can't come to Thanksgiving dinner."

Callie frowned. "Not come? Why ever not?"

Jack thrilled to the soft, southern-toned sexiness of her voice.

He looked her straight in the eyes. "Because I didn't know if I'd be able to resist staring at her beautiful daughter the entire time, that's why."

"Well, it's settled then," Callie told him with a soft laugh. "You'll sit next to me at dinner, and if I catch you staring I'll pinch you. Problem solved. You'll be there?"

"All right," Jack agreed, marveling at how bossy she was. He kind of liked it. He tore his gaze away from her face. "If you don't mind, there's someone I'd like you to meet. He's kind of a fan of yours."

Callie glanced at the large SUV a few yards in front of her car. She hadn't noticed anyone else in it. But she walked with Jack to his car anyway, and as they got closer she saw a golden-brown head sticking out of the back window.

Winslow barked a greeting, and danced on the back seat

in anticipation of Jack opening the door. When Jack let him out, he bounded down and headed straight for Callie. Callie let him sniff her hand. Then, when he licked it, she bent and gave him a hug.

"He's friendly," she said, peering up at Jack. "What's his name?"

"Winslow."

"Hello, Winslow, aren't you a handsome boy?"

Winslow shivered with happiness and licked Callie's cheek.

Laughing, Callie said, "He acts like he knows me."

"Well," Jack said, "he watched your tape as often as I did."

Callie gave Winslow one more hug, and rose. Looking into Jack's eyes, she said, "You two are good for a girl's self-esteem. I'd better be going." She slowly backed away. "Come early tomorrow if you can, and wear athletic clothes. My brother, Calvin, likes to get up a game of touch football in the backyard before dinner. The neighbors join in. It's a yearly tradition."

"Around what time?" Jack was fairly devouring her with his eyes.

"Two," she answered a bit breathlessly. She felt naked. It wasn't an unpleasant feeling, having Jack Cain look at her with such intensity. It was wildly stimulating, in fact. "See you, Jack!" She abruptly turned and swiftly walked back to her car.

Jack had to hold onto Winslow's collar to prevent him from following Callie. "Down, boy, I saw her first," he joked as he led Winslow to the car, and opened the passenger-side door for him.

When he got in, he saw the videotape on the seat. He'd intended to give it to Callie, but tomorrow would be soon enough to return it.

Callie blew her horn and waved at him as she got on the highway and drove off. He smiled and waved, turned the SUV around, and headed back to his house.

"Put me down, you big lug head!" Callie shouted, laughing so hard tears were in her eyes. Donnell Robinson, quarterback for the Carolina Panthers, ran across the yard with her thrown over his shoulder. "Why aren't you somewhere playing ball today, anyway?"

He put her down only after they'd made it past the imaginary goal line. "Touchdown!" he yelled triumphantly. "Not every pro team can have a game on Thanksgiving Day!"

"You're supposed to take the *football* across the goal line, not me!" Callie said with consternation, looking up at him from her seat on the ground.

She got up and brushed grass and sand from her shorts.

Her brother, Calvin, came over, shaking his head in mock disgust. "How are we gonna get a real game going if you two keep cuttin' the fool?"

"Oh, loosen up, Cal," Donnell said. "I haven't seen Callie in months, I guess I got carried away."

Callie gazed up at Donnell with her love for him shining in her eyes. Donnell's family had lived next door to them since she was five years old. She and Donnell had started kindergarten together. In grade school, she'd had a huge crush on him and, finally, in high school he'd noticed her and asked her out. They'd gone steady their senior year in high school. But after they graduated, they drifted apart. They would always be each other's first love. Although, now, their feelings were purely platonic. That is, until another *rooster* stepped foot in the yard.

Donnell looked up. "Who's that?"

"That must be Callie's new boyfriend," Calvin joked.

Callie punched her brother hard on the upper arm.

"Ouch!"

"Then, be good," Callie said as she jogged over to greet Jack who was looking mighty fine in a pair of navy athletic slacks, white Reeboks, and a white T-shirt. The day was bright and clear, the temperature in the low sixties. Perfect football weather.

In Callie's absence, Donnell asked, "Were you serious? That's Callie's new guy?"

Calvin shook his big head. "Naw, man, as far as I know they've just met. He's the son of one of Ma's old friends. He's visiting from England."

"England?" Donnell crossed his powerful arms over his broad chest, frowning.

"He's one of those concert pianists." Calvin said it as though being a concert pianist was an odd occupation.

"I don't like the way he's leaning down to her," Donnell said, proprietary all of a sudden. The two of them looked over at Callie and Jack who were standing close and laughing about something.

"Why do you care?" Calvin asked. "You've got women coming out of your ears."

"It ain't like that," Donnell denied. "I just don't want to

see her get hurt again after how Ray Warner treated her. I wish she would've let me pound him!"

"Get in line," Calvin said.

A few feet away, Callie was in the throes of that wonderful magnetic pull one felt for the opposite sex when the relationship was only a bud of the flower it would become. She found it impossible not to thrust her chest out, hold her stomach in, stand up straight, and grin like a pure idiot at everything Jack said.

After they'd spoken, she had asked, "How is my handsome boy today?"

"Oh, I'm fine, how are you?" Jack returned deadpan.

"I meant *Winslow*."

"He's fine, too. He'll probably be miffed because I didn't bring him with me when I return home with your scent on me." That's when he leaned close to her and gently touched his clean shaven cheek to hers. "There, let him be angry."

Callie smiled up at him when he straightened, and reached for his hand. "Come on, let me introduce you to everybody."

Jack took her hand, and let her lead him over to two large men, one of whom he recognized from the photograph Joyce had shown him.

At six feet, Calvin was the shorter of the two men. Donnell was six-three and in top condition, while Calvin's daily workout consisted of walking for twenty minutes before going to his dental office.

"Jack, this is my brother, Calvin."

The two of them shook hands. "Good to meet you," Jack said.

"Same here," Calvin told him, taking the measure of him with a glance. Calvin was always wary of anyone his sister showed a romantic interest in, and there was no doubt that Callie liked Jack.

"And this is Donnell Robinson. We all grew up together."

"We were high school sweethearts," Donnell shamelessly corrected her.

He turned narrowed eyes on Jack. "I crush heads for a living now."

Callie laughed. "He's the quarterback for the Carolina Panthers, the pansy!"

"Ah," Jack said. "So, *you're* Donnell Robinson." He went on to tell them about the incident at the gala. How the women who'd been hanging on his every word abandoned him in a flash after Sandra Gerrard had mentioned Donnell was in the room.

The three men wound up laughing companionably, while Callie shook her head at the fact that stroking a man's ego always got the desired effect. A minute ago, Donnell had been belligerent toward Jack, and now he was Jack's best friend!

The other six men in the yard came over and joined the conversation. Calvin took over the introductions, and Callie whispered in Jack's ear, "I'm going inside to help with the cooking. See you in a few. Have fun!"

Jack reached out and grabbed her hand, squeezing it gently. "Don't stay away too long," he said softly.

Callie's ears burned, and her grin grew wider. Lord, but this man was ultrasexy! She wished she could have him all to herself today. But Thanksgiving was for family.

"I won't," she promised, and left.

In her absence, one of the men spoke up. "Hey, I know you!" he said to Jack. "You're the man responsible for my wife wanting to get 'romantic' all of a sudden! I had to take that woman to dinner three weekends in a row after she saw you on TV. And I can't even watch a little tube when I get home from work. All she wants to do is play your CDs and cuddle on the couch!" He sighed with exasperation. "You've made my life miserable, dude!"

The other men laughed at him. Jack too. "You can't tell me there are no fringe benefits for you when you treat your wife well," he asked hopefully.

The man, a tall, stout fellow in his mid-thirties grinned sheepishly. "Well, okay, I admit that things have been more interesting in the bedroom."

"Mm, huh," said Jack. "A little give and take."

Soon, the conversation turned into an advice session with the men asking Jack for pointers on how best to romance their wives and girlfriends. Suddenly Jack, by virtue of the fact that he was a concert pianist, was an expert on the subject.

He laughed as hard as the rest of them, enjoying the easy camaraderie and down-home Southern manners they were inadvertently teaching him. "If you want a woman to do anything you want in bed, you have to rub her belly real soft-like," one of the men said. "Of course, if you've gotten as far as her belly it ain't far to the Promised Land!"

"Amen!" the rest of them wholeheartedly agreed.

After that, they played a little football until they started complaining about pulled hamstrings and cramps all over their bodies. Calvin herded them all to the picnic table under the big oak tree in the backyard where he'd left a cooler filled with ice and Coronas. They spent the next few minutes lying about how well they'd played the game, knocking back a few tall ones.

At around four o'clock, Callie went outside and announced that dinner was ready. The men who were neighbors left to go have Thanksgiving dinner with their families. Callie hugged Donnell goodbye and told him to give his mother a kiss for her. He dropped a quick buss on her cheek, cocked an eye at Jack, and said, "He's all right."

"I'm glad you think so," Callie replied. *As if I need your approval*, her tone said.

Donnell laughed and jogged off.

She and Jack let Calvin get ahead of them. "It seems we're not fooling anybody," Jack said of Donnell's comment. "Maybe you ought to stop looking at me with big, soulful eyes."

Callie pursed her lips. "Maybe you ought to stop touching me every chance you get."

In fact, he was holding her hand right now. Jack looked down at their entwined hands. It had been a subconscious act. Their eyes met and held. They stopped in their tracks. Calvin continued walking. They were alone next to the gazebo. Callie pulled Jack behind the small structure, and pressed his back against it. She was in his embrace in an instant and Jack lowered his head just to breathe in her essence. He wasn't going to kiss her unless she instigated it. It was enough to simply hold her this close and smell her skin, her hair, her breath, which smelled like cinnamon.

But Callie wasn't satisfied with an embrace alone. She moistened her lips and tilted her head back. Jack kissed her softly. She sighed a little, and the kiss deepened. Opened her mouth, and their tongues touched, dipped, and danced. They parted and looked into each other's eyes.

"I could get used to you, Jack."

"It would be kind of nice to have you around, too," Jack told her, his voice slightly hoarse.

Callie smiled up at him, hugged herself, and turned to continue the walk to the house.

Joyce met them at the back door. "What kept you two?" She didn't expect a reply. "Callie, come help me in the kitchen. John, you can go in the den with the rest of the family."

Callie looked over her shoulder at Jack. "Not bossy, huh?"

Jack laughed softly and said, "I'm not going to touch that."

Out in the shaded backyard, Callie hadn't noticed her lipstick on his mouth. Inside, in better lighting, she clearly saw it. Joyce had walked over to the stove to peer into the oven. Callie hurried over to the sink and grabbed a paper towel from the holder above it.

Returning to Jack, she whispered, "You've got lipstick all over your mouth."

He bent and she gently wiped it off. He smiled at her. "Now, you know your mom saw that, don't you?"

Callie glanced worriedly at her mother. "Probably."

"If she asks, tell her my intentions are honorable."

Callie looked at him. He wasn't joking. She was touched. Fact was, she wanted to kiss him again as soon as possible. "If she asks, I'll be sure to tell her," she said, ushering him out of the kitchen.

When she turned back around, her mother was watching her with a knowing expression on her pretty face. "Tread carefully, Callista. I sense that he's been hurt, and you're not entirely over Ray. Two tender people can find it hard to figure out how to get around the past hurts, and get on with living."

Callie smiled. "Ma, it was just a kiss." She hadn't told her mother about her conversation with Jack concerning the number of times they'd watched each other's tapes. She felt that it should stay between her and Jack. She'd told her about their meeting on the side of the road, and that they'd been attracted to each other, but that's all. She believed that if she told her mother how close she felt to Jack already, after watching him perform *Moonlight Sonata* over and over again, her mother might laugh and say that she was putting too much store in emotions. For now, their connection felt magical to her, as if they were somehow destined to meet. She'd never experienced anything like it before. Why shouldn't she simply go with the flow, sit back, relax, and see what happened between her and Jack?

She sighed, and there was a dreamy look in her dark eyes. "Ray, who, Ma?"

Joyce shook her head. "Help me get the food on the dining room table. Maybe some work will help clear your mind."

"I doubt it."

"Well, try, Callista, *try*," her mother implored. "I don't want something disastrous to happen between you and

Dahlia's son. I see how you two look at each other. I know a love affair waiting to happen when I see one! And I've been young, you know. I can see the appeal of going to bed with a man like Jack. But if it turns out to be only sexual attraction and one, or both, of you end up getting hurt, it'll spoil the friendship he's developing with this family. I was out of touch with Dahlia for a lot of years, I'd like to keep in touch with Jack when he goes back to England. So, for my sake, take things slowly. Don't simply act on your impulses!" All of this was said very intensely, and very quietly. The quietness of her mother's voice had more of an impact on Callie. She immediately recognized the truthfulness of her mother's words. She had to resist succumbing to Jack's charms too soon.

Over a meal that consisted of an appetizer of Carolina crab cakes with dill lemon dressing, a main course of Creole braised chicken with golden rice, various garden vegetables, and a dessert of praline bread pudding, all recipes from Joyce's favorite Low Country chef, Marvin Woods, the family caught up on their lives, making sure to include Jack, who was the only nonfamily guest at the table, in the conversation.

Unlike some families, the Harts did not insist on the children sitting at a separate table. Calvin and Rhonda's two children were near their parents so they could keep an eye on them, and Derrick and Iris's six-year-old son sat between them. Callie sat beside Jack, and Joyce sat at one end of the table, and Calvin, as the eldest son, sat at the other end.

The children were also encouraged to join in the conversation, so it was not a surprise when Calvin and Rhonda's daughter, LaShaunda, who was eight, turned to Jack and asked, "Was it fun playing the piano for the Queen of England?"

"We saw your performance at Buckingham Palace when it aired on PBS," Rhonda explained. "LaShaunda is following in her auntie's footsteps and is taking piano lessons. We're trying to introduce her to the classics, and show her that black people can excel at any kind of music, not just hip-hop."

Jack smiled at LaShaunda. "I was honored to have been asked to play, LaShaunda, but I was nervous the entire time."

"Nervous?" LaShaunda asked, her eyes even bigger looking with her astonishment. "Why were you nervous?"

"Because if the Queen didn't like the way I played, she could have said, 'Off with his head, off with his head!' And then, dear LaShaunda, I would have been headless."

LaShaunda giggled. "You're silly! That's in *Alice in Wonderland*. The Queen won't really have your head cut off!"

"But I didn't know that!" Jack cried.

The other kids were cracking up, too. The adults chuckled softly, liking Jack even more for his easy manner and apparent love for children.

Callie admired his macabre sense of humor.

A little later, Iris, who faithfully read the lifestyle magazine Callie worked for, asked how things were going at the job. Callie smiled at Iris, who was tall, had meat on her bones, and had the prettiest dark chocolate skin, and said,

"I wish I could report that everything was great, but *Atlanta Lifestyles* is no more."

Everyone expressed sympathy.

"What happened?" Joyce asked. "And why am I hearing this for the first time?"

"They called a staff meeting in early October and told us that the parent company no longer felt *Atlanta Lifestyles* was cost effective, so they folded the magazine. But, don't worry. I'm still working for Reid, I've filled out applications all over Atlanta, and I have savings. I'll be all right until something else comes along."

"What you need to do is move back here," Joyce said emphatically.

Everyone at the table, except Jack, knew that Joyce had been trying to talk Callie into moving back to Charleston for years. She had both sons near her. Was it selfish of her to want her daughter close by?

Jack suddenly felt as if he and Joyce were on the same wavelength because he would have liked nothing better than to have Callie in Charleston, too. He wanted to offer her the job as his ghostwriter; however he felt it wasn't his place to speak up during a family discussion, so he didn't say anything at the dinner table.

Later that night, as Callie was walking him to his car, a plate of food for him wrapped securely in a leak-proof bag in one of her hands, he turned to her and said, "You can come work for me, Callie."

Her mother hadn't told her that Jack had mentioned he was writing his autobiography, so Callie had no idea what sort of job to which he was referring. She calmly handed him the plate of food and waited until he placed it on the seat of the passenger side.

They faced one another. The street was quiet. The neighborhood was winding down for the evening, and even the children had gone inside for the night. "As what?" Callie asked softly. "I'm gonna tell you now, I can't cook as well as my mom. My food is edible, but nothing close to being as wonderful as hers. I love to clean, though. Don't tell anybody. It's sort of a fetish, cleanliness. But you wouldn't want me yelling at you for tracking mud into your own house, now, would you?"

"I like things kept clean, too," Jack said. "But if you'll be quiet for a moment, I'll tell you about the job."

And, so, he did. When he was finished, Callie laughed. "You don't even know if I can write!"

"That is what you did at the magazine, wasn't it?"

"Sometimes, if I was desperate for an article and couldn't hire a freelancer in time."

"And your mother told me you're writing a novel."

"That I've been working on for three years!"

"How far along are you?"

"Five-hundred and forty-six pages. And I'm not finished *yet*."

"You need an editor."

"Don't I *know* it!"

"I don't plan on doing that many pages, three-hundred and fifty at the most. Do you think we could get started tomorrow?"

Callie stared at him. "You're serious?"

Jack sighed. "I haven't been talking for the past ten minutes for nothing." He went into the car and retrieved a pad and pen he kept in the glove compartment. After which he wrote his home number and address on a slip of paper, and handed it to her. "Call me if you need directions. Shall we start at say, nine o'clock in the morning?"

Callie shrugged. "I guess."

Jack offered her his hand to shake.

When Callie took it, he drew her close, bent his head and planted a kiss on her mouth. "Don't be late."

He left her standing there on the sidewalk, slightly stunned, more than a little turned on by his kiss, and scared to death that she'd made a bad decision. She'd done exactly what her mother had warned her against, let her impulses rule.

If she had been thinking straight, she would have known that she could not possibly concentrate on work when Jack Cain was in the room!

CHAPTER 5

When Callie arrived fifteen minutes early the next morning, she spotted Jack walking Winslow down by the lake. The air was brisk, and Jack wore a thick, wheat-colored crewneck sweater, khaki's, and brown leather hiking boots. Callie thought he and Winslow looked like an ad from a J. Crew catalog.

Winslow barked happily and loped across the lawn to greet her. Callie got out of the car and bent to fondly rub his head, then underneath his chin. "I missed you yesterday, handsome!" Winslow responded by enthusiastically wagging his bushy tail.

She looked up to find Jack silently watching her with a smile on his face. "Good morning," he said. "You look very secretarial."

Callie was wearing a gray silk blouse that was buttoned

all the way up to her neck, a darker gray skirt whose hem fell about an inch, if that, above her knees, pantyhose, and black pumps with two-inch heels. A dark gray cardigan was on the car seat next to her laptop. Her shoulder-length hair was twisted into a French roll.

Still, in spite of the extremely safe clothes she had on, Jack couldn't help noticing what a shapely form she had underneath it all. Long, gorgeous legs, slim ankles, a plump behind—he liked it when women had curves—full breasts, and a long neck.

His light brown eyes, rendered golden by the morning sunlight, settled on her graceful neck. It was long and lovely, the skin delicate-looking, and that dip at the base of her throat begged to be kissed.

"Good morning, Jack. After a good night's rest, have you come to your senses and realized offering me the job as your ghostwriter was a huge mistake?" Her expression was alternately wary, then expectant.

"No." Jack was adamant. "You're the one that I want."

Callie smiled. "Good, because I think I can do a good job for you." She tried to get around Winslow but found he wasn't going anywhere, so she carefully opened the car door and got her laptop, shoulder bag, tape recorder, and cardigan off the front seat. Winslow was right behind her, sniffing her ankles.

"Winslow, come here," Jack ordered.

Winslow looked at his master, whined, and went back to sniffing Callie's ankles.

With her arms full, Callie straightened, and grinned at Jack. "Okay, I'm ready to get started."

Jack went and took the laptop from her. "I thought we'd have coffee first and talk about the hours we want to work. And my agent faxed the terms to me this morning. You'll want to know how you'll be compensated, I'm sure."

"I can work Monday through Thursday. I'll need Friday, Saturday, and Sunday off. I have an obligation to Reid Friday and Saturday nights. I have a contract with him up until January first when we usually renegotiate. I hope that's okay with you, Jack."

"I understand," Jack said. "Four days a week is all right with me. I have to practice, anyway." They walked up the steps to the porch. "Maybe I'll come see you play."

Callie followed him into the house.

"I'd like that," Callie told him, looking around. Hardwood floors, high ceilings, and windows everywhere that let in a lot of the morning light. "Great house."

"Thanks. I'm renting. If I like it here, I'll look for something more permanent. It came furnished, so I had nothing to do with the decorating." He glanced up at a rather bad painting of a bullfighter above the fireplace in the living room, where the piano was. Callie wrinkled her nose. "I see what you mean." But then she caught sight of the Steinway, and something akin to desire flashed in her dark eyes. She dropped her purse, cardigan, and the tape recorder onto a nearby chair.

As if he sensed that was where she was headed, Winslow darted past her and settled down next to the piano. He was already sitting beside the piano bench when she finally made it across the room to the gleaming instrument.

Jack placed her laptop on the big coffee table in front of

the long tan sofa, and slowly followed her to the piano, a contented smile on his face. He recognized when someone was under the spell of a fine instrument. That's how he'd felt when he'd walked into the piano showroom in London about ten years ago and first laid eyes on the Steinway that was in his London home right now. It was love at first sight. Some piano virtuosos have sworn that a certain instrument "called" them, and that they were unable to resist buying it. Jack had never regretted his purchase. It was as if his piano was made especially for him. He didn't have that connection with this rented Steinway. Perhaps that was why he was having trouble with the second movement of Beethoven's "Appassionata."

Callie stood beside the piano. She hadn't even reached out to touch it yet. "May I?"

"Please," Jack said. "Take her for a ride."

Callie eagerly sat down. As soon as she sat, she was transformed. Her posture became perfect. Her left leg remained perpendicular to her body; however, her right leg slid slightly forward. Then she lowered her hands and began to play Patsy Cline's "Crazy." The song was written for the piano, and it was hauntingly lovely. Jack closed his eyes as the notes drifted throughout the huge house.

A few minutes into the song, Jack, who was familiar with the original, knew that this was Callie's arrangement. She imbued it with a bluesy quality that in turn made it somehow more emotional. It was mellow, sexy, and mournful all at once. As he stood there listening he hoped she would sing, but she was content to simply play and enjoy the sound of a superior instrument.

She finished, and almost reverently lifted her hands from the keyboard. "That was very satisfying. Thank you, Jack."

She rose.

Jack wasn't ready for her to quit playing. "Please, play another."

Callie smiled at him as she walked over and picked up her shoulder bag, cardigan, and tape recorder. "I'd love to, but we've got work to do. Remember the autobiography?" She laughed when she saw the disappointed look on his face. "Jack, I don't think you realize how much work we're going to have to do in order to do justice to your life's story. We don't have time to waste!"

Jack laughed as he went to retrieve her laptop. "You Hart women are awfully bossy."

"True, but men tend to love us anyway."

"Just tell me one thing," he said as they walked down the hall to his office. "Do you do all of the arrangements?"

"Who else?" Callie asked.

"Then, you can read and write music?"

"Of course I can."

"Your mother said you played by ear."

"She's right. That's how I learned. I used to watch my grandma, Eva Jean, play in church. I must have been around three or four when I climbed up on the piano bench and started picking out notes. The first piano I played belonged to St. John AME Church. After Grandma Eva Jean noticed I was drawn to the piano, she started letting me sit next to her on the bench. She played by ear. Never learned to read music. So, she couldn't teach me. But when I went to college, I was a member of the band,

and I had to learn how to read music. I found out I had a talent for composition. Over the years I've written nearly a hundred songs."

Jack remembered that he hadn't been familiar with at least two of the songs that she'd performed on the tape he'd borrowed. "You put me to shame," he said quietly. "I used to write, too, but I let my performance schedule keep me from it. I haven't written anything in more than seven years now."

"You put all of your creativity back into your playing. That's why you're so good at what you do, you feel it intensely. When it's time for you to write again, you will."

She sounded so confident that Jack felt it, too. Maybe he would be inspired to write again. Writing music, after all, had been his initial dream when he began studying the piano. He'd wanted to compose beautiful sonatas like Beethoven, his first musical influence.

They weren't in the office thirty seconds before Winslow entered the room and went to Callie, who was sitting behind the desk, opening her laptop. Winslow went and lay on the floor next to her.

Jack, who was sitting in a chair opposite Callie, looked at his constant companion with amusement. "He doesn't follow *me* around *this* much!"

"Maybe he misses having a female around?" Callie asked hopefully.

Appearing to read her thoughts, Jack said, "Is that your way of asking if I'm seeing anyone special?"

"Could be," Callie said, unwilling to give him an affirmative reply. "Although, as your employee, I can't see where it's any of my business. But feel free to answer the question, anyway."

Their gazes were locked. Both were smiling, but both of them felt the seriousness behind Callie's light-hearted way of putting the question.

"No," Jack replied. "I'm not seeing anyone, special or otherwise. And you?"

He was not afraid to ask the question pointblank.

"No, not for about a year. He cheated on me, and I broke up with him even though he swore he'd never do it again. Can we speak candidly with one another?"

"I insist on it."

"I'm just glad I always made sure we used a condom. Life's complicated nowadays. Infidelity can kill."

"Me, too," Jack said. "Always used a condom, I mean. Although my last relationship didn't end because of infidelity. It ended because she couldn't live with my career. She wanted someone who would always come home at the end of the day. So, she left me for a lawyer."

"It was a trust issue, then," Callie said.

"What do you mean?"

"She wanted a man whom she could keep an eye on. You travel a great deal. She probably would not have been able to go on all of those trips with you. She didn't trust you to be faithful to her when you were away."

Jack's brows knitted in a frown. "You could be right. Do you still have trust issues?"

"More than likely," Callie said truthfully. "I want to believe that, should I fall in love again, I'd be able to trust him. But I think that's something we'd have to work through."

"But you do believe yourself capable of loving again?"

"Oh, definitely. I'm only twenty-eight. I do plan to marry someday."

"Twenty-eight! I'm eight years older than you."

"We met at the right time."

"Why do you say that?"

"When you were eight, I wasn't born yet. When you were sixteen, I was eight. When you were twenty-four, I was sixteen, and jail-bait. When you were thirty-two, I was twenty-four. That might have worked. But now you're thirty-six and I'm twenty-eight, we're better suited for one another. That is, if we want to take this past friendship."

"I think after those kisses yesterday, we've already taken it past friendship."

"Yes, but that was before you asked me to come work for you. If we're going to work together *and* play together, I think we should set forth a few rules to live by."

"Such as?" Jack reluctantly asked. He was up to a little playing during the work day. In fact, he wanted to kiss her right now.

"Such as, no kissing, touching, or anything remotely along those lines during work hours. We need to be strictly professional. I intend to do a good job on this book, Jack, and I won't have you distracting me from it!"

"Well, how about during lunch? And breaks? Can we play a little then? We'll be off the clock."

Callie shook her head in the negative. "No, that won't do. We'd risk getting carried away if we allowed that. And if we get carried away, there goes a perfectly good work day.

No, we have to behave ourselves from...what, nine 'til five? Or nine 'til six? It's up to you."

"Nine 'til five," Jack said. "I don't want you traveling at night if you can help it, and I intend to kiss you from five 'til six."

Callie reached across the desk so that they could shake on it. Jack pulled her toward him as he rose, bent low, and kissed her. Callie stood and they held each other close, their mouths hungrily giving and receiving the pent-up pleasure that they'd held in check since they'd laid eyes on each other this morning. When they finally drew apart a couple of minutes later, Jack raised his gaze to the clock on the wall. It was 8:59 a.m. "It's not nine yet," he said.

Winslow, who'd been watching them kiss, barked as if he agreed with his master's reasoning.

Callie smiled down at Winslow. "Don't encourage him!"

After that, they got down to work.

Callie sat poised at her laptop. She'd opened a file, and was ready for the words to begin flowing from Jack; however, Jack wasn't sure of where to start.

"My life," he said. "My life." He shook his head. "Who in the hell is going to want to read about my life?!"

"All of the people who faithfully go to your concerts," Callie replied. "All of the people who buy your CDs. A black teenager in Harlem who is a piano virtuoso, but doesn't know of any other blacks who have made it playing classical piano. Women who just want to dream of being a part of your life if only for the few minutes they spend reading your book, that's who! *I* want to read it, Jack."

"But where do I begin?"

"Let's try two tactics," Callie suggested. "First, let's start at the beginning of your life, and see how that feels. Then, if you think it's too stale, we can begin at the end."

"The end? I'm still breathing, Callie."

Callie laughed. "What I mean is, you can begin the story with what you believe is your greatest accomplishment, and then tell them how you got to that point in your life. You're in control here. Do what makes you feel good."

Smiling faintly, Jack said, "I do like the idea of talking about performing at the Kennedy Center in honor of Joseph Mbeki. He was a great inspiration to me. And he gave me the best advice anyone has ever given me on how to handle my career."

"Never let them see you sweat!"

Callie laughed. "I like that! That could be the title of the book. Joseph Mbeki, now his is an inspirational story. A child prodigy, but because he was born in South Africa under apartheid, he was denied the right to study. Then he escaped to America and became a legend in his own time."

"He told me," Jack began, his voice low and awe-filled, "that no matter who I played for, I should never let my composure slip because in this business appearance is everything, especially for a black man. There are still those who would prefer it if you were not there to remind them that their world isn't as exclusive as they thought it was. Then, he joked that since perfection is impossible to maintain, it was okay to be 'just a man' in your everyday life."

"It was so sad when he passed away last year," Callie said. "Did you go to the funeral?"

"Yes, I went. There wasn't a dry eye in the church.

Bishop Desmond Tutu gave the invocation. And Nelson Mandela did a wonderful job on the eulogy. Then, Denyce Graves sang one of his compositions, *Requiem*, which he wrote for his mother. When I sat down to play *Resurgence*, his most famous composition, I remembered what he said about not letting them see you sweat, but I was weeping. Not only did they see me sweat, they saw me weep."

Touched, Callie smiled at him. "I bet you still played beautifully."

"The old man's spirit wouldn't let me miss a note," Jack confirmed with a wan smile.

"That's the beginning of your story," Callie said, eyes sparkling with excitement.

"You can begin with the anecdote about Joseph Mbeki telling you never to let them see you sweat, and then you could recount the emotions you felt while playing at his funeral. From there you can tell the readers about your journey to that moment in time."

"Begin at the high point in my career," Jack said, considering it.

"The high point as defined by you. Others may think the high point was your playing for the Queen of England. However, the important thing is, you're telling the story. It's your life that will be revealed. So, tell it the way you want to tell it."

"But above all, be honest," Jack said, understanding where she was coming from.

"Yes, because raw honesty touches people, and the last thing anyone wants to read is a watered-down version of someone's life. They want the bitter with the sweet."

Jack pondered the idea of telling everything. "I don't want this to be one of those autobiographies that people buy only to find out who a celebrity has slept with."

Callie smiled at him. "Jack, you don't have to reveal anything you don't want to."

Jack got up and walked over to the window closest to the desk. Peering out, he said, "It's just that I don't want to embarrass anybody. Some of them are married with children now. They may not want anyone to know they had a sex life before marriage. Plus, I think it's tacky to name names just to sell books." He turned back around. "I will just say we dated, and that's it."

Callie inwardly breathed a sigh of relief. The last thing she wanted to hear was the entire list of Jack's lovers. She had no doubt there had been plenty of them. A man with Jack's attributes would never lack for female companionship.

"Did you say something about coffee when I arrived?" she asked, hoping to get off the subject. Jack laughed softly. So, talking about his past lovers didn't sit well with her. For some reason that was comforting news to him. At least she was thinking about sleeping with him in the future. A woman didn't care about past lovers unless she was considering sleeping with a man.

"I'll go make a fresh pot," he volunteered.

Their eyes raked over one another before he strolled from the room. His held an amused look in them. Callie's were once again wary, as if she were still wondering if she was doing the right thing by agreeing to work with him.

Winslow had made himself comfortable on the floor

next to Callie's chair. He did not move an inch when his master left the room.

Callie visibly relaxed after Jack left the room. She slumped in her chair, and let out a long breath. Her heart would definitely get a workout for the next few weeks. She wondered if she'd ever become blasé about Jack's presence. It wasn't as if the man was huge, like Donnell, who actually filled a room when he was in it. No, Jack had the kind of electric energy that charged the air, and melted your resolve to be unaffected by his charm.

"I don't know if this is going to work," she said to Winslow.

She got up and went to the window to look out. She wanted to satisfy her curiosity about what Jack had been looking at. Below was a lovely view of the deep backyard. As little as ten years ago this area had been undeveloped woodland. The owners of this property had allowed some of the palmetto trees to remain on the edge of it. Otherwise, the lawn was manicured, and the flowers were not indigenous varieties like the Carolina jessamine, but imported. Callie's mother's backyard was full of the delicate, fragrant vine with its yellow trumpet-shaped flowers.

The phone rang and when it stopped Callie assumed Jack had answered it in the kitchen. She went and sat down at the desk. *It won't hurt to get started*, she decided, and began to type.

In the kitchen, Jack had the receiver to his ear, listening to Doris as she told him everything she'd found out about Callie since he'd phoned her with the news that he wanted her to ghostwrite his autobiography.

"She's never published a book. But she's had plenty of

articles published in both popular magazines and literary magazines. She's a good writer. So, we don't have to worry about that. However, I think the best thing about her is that she's a musician, and she'll understand that part of your life, Jack. Also, since she has no publishing credits, we can get her services for a song, so to speak," Doris said, laughing softly.

"I want her to be paid well, Doris. Make sure she gets a good deal."

"But, Jack, the deal is, she gets an advance and royalties, part of *your* advance and *your* royalties. The lower her percentage, the higher yours will be."

"I'm serious about this, Doris. Make sure she gets a fair percentage of both the advance and the royalties. I don't need the money but, as I told you, she lost her job last month and she may be in need. I don't know, I haven't asked. But I want her to be well compensated. See to it. Please."

"You like this girl," Doris said. There was a short pause. "Okay, Jack. I'll look out for her. But you know, as her agent, too…"

Jack laughed. "I know, Doris. I'll explain that to her. Who knows, she might want to get her own agent to negotiate for her. Then you'd lose her fifteen percent."

"God forbid," Doris said. "I'm on the case!"

"Good. See you," Jack said, still laughing.

"Bye, Jack," Doris said.

Jack put the receiver back in its cradle and went to pour coffee into two mugs. By the time he returned to the office, Callie had written two pages of copy. He stood and read them over her shoulder. When he was done, he smiled. "You made what I said sound like poetry."

Callie looked up at him. "It *was* poetry."

For lunch, they made turkey sandwiches and ate them on the deck that overlooked the lake. Winslow ran down the steps and into the yard where he burned off pent-up energy by leaping into the air and snapping at late-season monarch butterflies. Then, when they flew out of his range, he was reduced to trying to pounce on unsuspecting grasshoppers.

It was a cool, clear day, and Callie was enjoying watching him play while the sun warmed her face. Callie was watching Winslow, Jack was watching Callie. Never before had he realized how sexy a woman could be while all covered up. There was a definite advantage to leaving something to the imagination. He imagined removing that staid blouse and skirt and then peeling off her underwear. He imagined how silky her skin would feel against his. The smell of her skin, the taste of it on his tongue. Her kisses were the sweetest he'd ever had. *Why*? He never would have thought that a man as well-traveled as he would have to come back to his birthplace to find a woman who interested him this much.

Callie didn't take her gaze off of Winslow's antics, but she knew Jack was looking at her. She felt his stare. From now on she knew she'd be able to sense when he was watching her. That's how acutely aware of him she was. His desire for her relentlessly made its presence felt, too. It was heavy in the air between them, like a nearly tangible spirit, magnetic in its force. He was sitting on her right, only about five inches away from her. His body heat enhanced the scent of his citrus-scented aftershave lotion. Perhaps it was a combination of his aftershave and the pheromones he gave off that was wreaking havoc with her senses. Her nostrils flared in an effort to breathe him in.

She turned to look into his eyes. They said nothing, just looked into each other's eyes for a few moments. Then, as if by tacit agreement, they turned their heads to look at Winslow who had tired and had stretched out on his back on the lawn for the sun to warm his belly.

By five o'clock, Callie's nerves were on edge from trying to resist Jack all day. She was in the office transcribing the final page of Jack's narration. Winslow was asleep underneath the desk. He had been thoughtful enough not to lie on her feet, but he was very close to them.

When Callie finished the page, she looked down at the page number on the bottom left-hand side of the screen. They had done thirteen pages. She closed the file, shut down the laptop and closed it firmly. Tonight, before going to sleep, she would reread what she had written, editing it as she went.

About thirty minutes ago Jack had left her to go practice, saying, "I never knew that talking about myself could be so tedious." He'd grinned at her before leaving the room, and she'd known that in spite of his self-deprecating remark, he was enjoying himself.

She rose and walked down the hall to the bathroom to freshen up before saying goodbye to Jack. She used the toilet, then washed her face and hands, brushed her teeth, and reapplied what little makeup she wore on a daily basis: no foundation, just a bit of moisturizer, and lipstick.

As a final touch, she took her hair down and finger combed the curls. It fell down her back, to her shoulders, full and dark and in slight disarray. Its state didn't bother her, she wanted to feel the wind in it on her drive home. She gave no thought to whether or not Jack would like her hair like that. She liked it, and that's what counted. The worst thing she could do was to pretend to be something she wasn't. After work, she generally let everything hang out. The sooner he realized that, the better.

She undid the first three buttons of her blouse, and removed her shoes. This done, she went and put her belongings in a chair near the front door, then she followed the sound of Jack's playing to the living room, where she stood in the doorway until he looked up and saw her.

Jack immediately stopped playing and rose. She saw at once that he'd taken the time to freshen up, too. He'd even changed into a pair of jeans and a sky blue denim shirt. She glanced at his feet, which were bare. So, they had that in common—the desire to loosen up in the evening, shed clothing, shoes, and, perhaps, inhibitions?

"Don't let me interrupt," Callie said, stopping at the entrance. "I just wanted to let you know that I've finished today's pages, and I'm leaving now."

Jack's golden-brown eyes narrowed as he walked toward her. Was that a hint of cleavage he spotted? He smiled. All day long she'd remained off-limits to him. Did she really think she was leaving without his at least holding her in his arms?

"What did I tell you I intended to do to you from five 'til

six?" he softly asked when he was within three feet of her. His brows arched arrogantly as he awaited her reply. He felt like Don Juan, about to seduce a virgin.

Callie pushed away from the doorjamb she'd been leaning on and languidly sighed. She lowered her gaze, her long, curly black lashes nearly touching her cheeks. It was a coy maneuver if he'd ever seen one, and when she raised her eyes to his again, he saw a saucy challenge in their depths.

"I thought you said something about kiss…" She was unable to complete the sentence because in the time it took her to get the words out, Jack had pulled her into his arms and covered her mouth with his.

He kissed her slowly and with intense pleasure. There was no desperate thrusting of the tongue, as if enthusiasm made up for skill. Callie had been kissed by men who thought kissing was only a means to an end. The sooner they got the kissing part over with, the sooner they'd get to the real deal, sex itself. But Jack kissed her as if he really *could* kiss her for an hour, and enjoy every minute of it! His lips, warm, firm yet supple, didn't smother her, but teased and tempted. When she opened her mouth and invited him in, he did not rush in as if the invitation might be withdrawn. He gently enticed and parried as if they were accomplished fencers and he was waiting for her to join in the play, which she did, with abandon.

Jack was such a sensory delight for her, she felt like a hungry woman at an all-you-can-eat banquet. A firm, sweet mouth, here. A delicious tongue there. A great big portion of hard male anatomy from one end of the table to the other. And nary a calorie anywhere. He would become her exercise routine: *Climb Jack every day for at least an hour!*

Every pleasure point in her body was at red-alert when they parted.

Jack nuzzled her neck. "Callie, I don't think it comes as a surprise to you that I want you in my bed." He peered into her eyes. "But, that would complicate things, wouldn't it?" He looked almost hopeful that she would say no.

Remembering what she and her mother had discussed about Jack's staying a friend of the family, Callie replied, "I'm afraid so."

Jack looked sober. "I don't normally behave this way. I usually prefer to wait a while before intimacy. But, I suppose, because of that blasted tape of you I feel as though I already know you." He closed his eyes momentarily, and when he looked at her again, Callie saw a new resolve in them. "But I'll be patient."

Callie kissed his chin. "Thank you, Jack."

Jack lowered his head for another brief, but deep kiss. "But not too patient." He took her hand. "Come, I'll walk you to your car."

That's how it went for more than two weeks, from the end of November to the middle of December. Jack and Callie worked diligently on the book. They lunched together, sometimes taking Winslow for walks during their break, and at the end of the day they would kiss each other goodbye. Consequently, during the course of everyday events, as it has often happened to unsuspecting lovers, they fell quietly in love, although neither of them could give a name to the emotion just yet.

Callie drove to Atlanta on weekends, a six-hour drive from Charleston, and entertained the loyal crowd at The Blue Bird. She was grateful she hadn't given up her apartment.

When she told Reid about her arrangement with Jack, during the intercession between sets her second weekend back in town, Reid had been unable to hide his concern. He sat in one of the ruby red chairs, and clasped both her hands in his. "John Cain definitely ain't nobody to play with," he said in awe, something Callie had rarely seen the self-assured Reid express. He had hobnobbed with numerous celebrities and had said on more than one occasion, "Their breath stinks in the mornin', too!," to convey that celebrities were as human as he was, and shouldn't be put on pedestals.

"Are you in love with him?" he asked, peering into her eyes. Callie's eyes never lied. She might tell a lie with her lips, but never with those smoky orbs that held more wisdom in their depths than he'd seen in people twice her age. She had an old soul.

Callie crossed and uncrossed her long legs. The hem of the bronze dress rode up her thighs. She pulled it down, lowering her eyes as she did so.

"*Callie?*" Reid said more urgently. "Please, look at me."

Meeting his gaze again, she blew air between her lips and slumped in her chair. "Oh, God, Reid, what am I going to do?"

"Honey, I don't know what you're going to do. But you'd better call me if you go into crisis while you're away." Every year, Reid closed The Blue Bird the last two weeks of December in order to spend time with his mother. Mrs.

Harris, a widow from St. Paul, Minnesota, looked forward to spending two weeks in the relative warmth of Atlanta, and in the bosom of her loving only son.

That meant this was the final weekend Callie would perform at The Blue Bird in 2005. Outside, the club was packed. Reid had had to turn some folks away in order not to be in violation of the fire code.

Reid stood up and planted a fatherly kiss on Callie's forehead. "My Callie's in love. I'm so happy for you, even if you *are* miserable right now. Don't worry, I'm sure he loves you, too. *I love you*, and I'm very discriminating."

Callie smiled lopsidedly. "I love you, too."

She watched him stroll to the door, his long dreadlocks swinging behind him, and that tall, powerful body looking delectable in black leather pants and a long-sleeved white silk shirt. He exuded no effeminate mannerisms. No wonder women kept hitting on him.

He turned and looked back at her. "Do me a favor? Sing "Your Song" tonight? There's someone in the audience I want to hear it."

Callie stood, excited all of a sudden. "You're dating someone special?"

"Now, don't go getting all up in my business. Do I pry in your private life?"

"Yes!" Callie looked at him in jaw-drop astonishment.

Reid laughed as he left. "I'll introduce you after the set," he promised.

Callie sat back down, finished her Dasani water, went to the bathroom to use the facilities and freshen her makeup, and then she was on again.

CHAPTER 6

The Blue Bird's patrons cheered when Callie returned to the stage for her second set. There was something in the air that night. Callie could not put her finger on it, but she felt expectant, restless, excited, and pensive all at once. Maybe it was the collective vibe the audience was giving off, or maybe it stemmed from the fact that she was not certain of where her relationship with Jack was going.

At any rate, as she looked out over the smiling faces of people she knew, and some she didn't, she pushed aside the angst and said, "For those of you who are regulars, I don't have to tell you how much I love the music of Elton John. He's been a mentor to me, whether he knows it or not. So, I'm going to do one of my favorite Elton John songs for you, with my own flavor, of course." Then, she began playing. With the first few notes the audience recognized "Your Song," and applauded.

When she started singing, however, a hush came over them. Some of them leaned forward in their seats a little. Others closed their eyes and smiled, remembering someone they'd loved as much as the protagonist in the song must have to say such heartfelt things about his lover. "It's a little bit funny, this feeling inside." Callie's deep, sultry voice dipped and glided over the notes. Her fingers skillfully coaxed gospel, rock, and soul from the strings of the piano.

At a table in the back, three men sat quietly watching her, their drinks and conversation forgotten. One of them was particularly mesmerized by her. Not just her voice, but her stage presence. It was impossible not to want to stare at her the entire time she was up there. Her auburn hair caught the lights and sparkled, deep and red. Her skin fairly glowed, and those lips, those parted lips from whence the song came, were so plump, so enticing that he had to close his eyes against their beauty to keep from going up on stage and kissing them right now. He frowned deeply.

"Jack, are you all right?" asked one of his companions, a middle-aged British gentleman with intelligent brown eyes and an impish smile. "Are you in pain?"

Jack opened his eyes and smiled at Elton John. "Yes, I am."

Reid picked up his bourbon and took a good long swallow. "So is she."

Jack turned to regard Reid, his frown back. "What? Has something happened to Callie that I should know about?"

Reid cocked an eyebrow at him. "She's in pain because she doesn't know how you feel about her," he said almost angrily. Straight men were so dense when it came to the matters of the heart. "I swear to God, if that child up there gets hurt because of you, I'll personally wring your neck. And don't think I can't do it."

Jack laughed, and returned his gaze to Callie's face. "She's in love with me?"

Elton sighed. "And you're in love with her. Why else would you phone me and tell me I had to see her? You love her, and you want to help kick-start her career. But from what I'm told about Miss Callie Hart, being rich and famous is not on the top of her list. With talent like that, and the way she looks, she doesn't need my help. Now, will you two be quiet? This girl is going to *church* with my song!"

"How do you know she's in love with me?" Jack whispered harshly to Reid.

"Because she told me, that's how," Reid whispered back, just as harshly.

They were two men who loved the same woman, but in different ways. Reid wanted to protect her, whereas Jack wanted to protect her and love her forever.

Seeing that he wasn't going to get any peace and quiet at their table, Elton rose and began walking toward the stage. When Callie finished the song with a highly charged piano solo, liberally spiced with gospel, he applauded enthusiastically.

Some of the patrons, seeing this short, stocky, rather average-looking white dude, peered more closely at him. When they recognized him, they got out of their seats, clapping and shouting, "Elton, Elton!"

Callie squinted at the man, then her breath caught in her throat and she was off the stage in what felt like an instant, hugging one of her idols. Elton laughed and hugged her back. "You made that song your own, darling," he told her.

Callie was crying. She took a step back, apologizing for grabbing him the way that she had. Elton only laughed. "Don't be silly. I'm cuddly that way." He firmly took her by the shoulders and pointed her in the direction of the stage. "Now, darling, the show must go on. Pull yourself together and go thrill me some more."

The audience went wild with applause. What a treat it was to come out tonight to see Callie Hart's final performance of the year, and be surprised by a legend like Elton John. It just goes to show, the bigger they are, the *nicer* they are.

Callie somehow gathered the strength to return to the stage. She sat trembling for a few seconds before leaning toward the microphone and saying, "I don't know how I can go on after that lovely surprise. But if Sir Elton says sing, I *sing!*"

She turned to give Elton a stunning grin, and then launched into Fats Waller's "Honeysuckle Rose." "Every honeybee fills with jealousy, when they see you out with me…" Her voice didn't quaver, but was clear and lovely.

She's a pro, Elton thought fondly as he turned and went back to his table, shaking several thrust out hands as he did so.

Jack and Reid were in the middle of an argument when Elton sat down. "I'm telling you that's a bad idea," Reid was saying. "Callie's old fashioned in a lot of ways. She won't traipse around Europe with you without a wedding ring on her finger. She's never lived with any man, and she isn't going to start with you. She won't do it!"

"Then what do you suppose I should do? I have to go back to England right after Christmas. I don't want to be without her."

Elton laughed. Looking at Jack, he shook his head sadly. "Jack, just marry the girl! You love her. She loves you. So what if you haven't known each other very long? You knew Cecylia for years, and she betrayed you."

"She didn't betray me, she decided that she couldn't live with my traveling."

Elton rolled his eyes. "She got married three months after she dumped you. She was already seeing the other bloke. Face it, Jack. If she had loved you the way you loved her, she would not have looked at that other guy, let alone married him." He looked up at Callie and smiled. "You're cautious because you're afraid you're going to get dumped again. If I were so inclined, I'd definitely take a chance on Ms. Hart. Take a chance, Jack!"

Callie began singing, "Why Can't You Behave?"

The three men grew quiet: Jack was pondering what Elton had said. Reid was nursing his bourbon, his forehead wrinkled in a frown. He took his job as Callie's surrogate father seriously. If Jack offered Callie anything less than marriage, he would have *him* to deal with! And Elton, who was enjoying Callie's performance, was happy the other two were in pensive moods. He got to listen in peace.

Several couples got up to dance to the slow, mellow standard. Jack rose. "Excuse me," he said to his companions. He walked to the back of the club and stood in the shadows. He wanted to be alone with his thoughts. Elton had been right when he'd accused him of not being willing to take a chance on love. Love could break your heart.

Elton had also been right when he'd said he was in love with Callie. What was there *not* to love about her? She would be the last person to suggest she was perfect. In fact, she would probably laugh in his face if he tried to put that label on her. He was aware of her shortcomings. She'd admitted it would take her a while to trust any man for whom she fell. She was also too damned impulsive. What was more, she nearly overdosed on those devilishly hot jaw-breakers she liked. They did, however, add an interesting flavor to her kisses, which were already spicy enough.

Also, on the plus side, he was in love with her because of her infectious laugh, the way she moved, completely unconscious of how sexy she was, the love she had for her friends and family, and the affection she showed Winslow, who adored her.

The truth was, he would marry her tomorrow if he were certain she'd say *yes* to his proposal. But he wasn't certain, and that was the problem. Did he have it in him to bite the bullet and ask her, without the reassurance of a positive outcome?

He might be a man of the world, but somewhere deep inside of him beat the heart of a little boy who was deathly afraid of rejection.

He focused on Callie. She loved to perform. He could see it in her eyes, in her body language, and hear it in the inflection in her voice. It would never occur to him to ask her to give it up in order to support his career. But logistics would be a problem if she accepted his marriage proposal. No more than a fourth of his concerts were booked in the United States, most of the time even less than that. He worked all over Europe. For many Europeans, classical music was as important as eating and sleeping. They routinely bought season tickets to concerts. They brought their children so that the appreciation for classical music would be inculcated in them at a young age. Also, classical music wasn't seen so much as the province of the rich in Europe as it was in the United States. Everyone had access to it.

Callie finished "Why Can't You Behave?" A man in the audience yelled, "Hey, Callie, it's our twentieth anniversary. Would you sing 'Our Love Is Here to Stay' for my baby and me?"

Callie peered into the audience. The guy, a sharp-dressed, average-sized black man in his forties was standing and trying to pull his wife, a tall, pretty woman with a short layered hairstyle to her feet. She blushed, and finally rose.

"Congratulations!" Callie said into the microphone. "What are your names?"

"Sid and Sharon Monteille," Sid told her, grinning.

"Sid and Sharon Monteille," Callie repeated for the benefit of the audience. "Twenty years is quite an accomplishment. May you have many more happy years."

The audience clapped to congratulate the happy couple. The Monteilles sat down again, Callie played the intro with a flourish and began to sing, "It's very clear, our love is here to stay…" It was during the chorus that Callie's emotions got the best of her. Tears pricked the backs of her eyes. Although her voice didn't crack, she got full, and feared that she might burst into a full-fledged bout of sobbing at any moment.

If only she could get Jack off her mind. Unlike the Monteilles, she and Jack probably had no future together. Who was she fooling, except herself? She was not the type of woman a man like Jack required in a wife. He needed someone worldly and poised. Someone totally at home in polite society, not a blues singing, unemployed magazine editor who had never set foot outside of the United States.

Her mother had been right. She should have held her emotions in check. But, no, stupid woman that she was, she'd gone right ahead and fallen in love with him.

She sang with such angst-filled emotion that some women in the audience burst into tears, and men cleared their throats nervously and fought back unmanly tearing in their eyes by blinking rapidly.

Callie laughed softly when she finished. "That one almost got me," she said, as she often did when a song had touched her. "Let's liven things up a bit, shall we?"

She made the bass notes rumble like thunder as she played the intro to "Jesus Gave Me Water," an uplifting gospel tune made famous by Sam Cooke and the Soul Stirrers.

Closing her eyes, she let the words and the music transport her to the past when she played piano in St. John AME Church, and Miss Delphine would get happy, dance down the aisle, her dress riding up her abundant hips. This was considered unseemly behavior by others in the church but when the spirit hit her, Miss Delphine danced until she fainted dead away, her legs wide open, and you could see her white bloomers, the kind that looked like men's jockey shorts. Miss Delphine was a trip!

Callie finished to explosive applause, and rose, tossing kisses to the audience. "Thank you for coming," she said. "Have a safe, and happy holiday season!"

She hurried off the stage, but did not get far because she was waylaid by eager patrons who wanted to personally thank her for a delightful evening. Although she was tired, and wanted nothing more than to get home and take a shower, then phone Jack, she was sincerely thankful for their support and stopped to exchange pleasantries.

Reid stepped up and rescued her by getting between her and the fans. He thanked them profusely for patronizing The Blue Bird, giving Callie the opportunity to slip away.

Out of the public eye, she let the tears flow. Her vision blurred by tears, she didn't see Jack waiting by her dressing room door. He saw the state she was in, and stepped in her path, his hands reaching out for her. "Callie, baby, what's the matter?"

Callie froze in her tracks and stared at him. The man was breathtaking dressed entirely in black: A leather jacket, a long-sleeved shirt, pleated slacks, and oxfords.

"Jack, what are you doing here?" she asked calmly, even though what she wanted to do was run and jump into his arms. "When did you get here?"

Jack had walked up to her and taken her by the shoulders. He looked her in the eyes. "We got here just before the second set," he told her. "Reid put us at a table in the back so we could watch you, but you couldn't see us. We didn't want to unnerve you."

"Ah," Callie said. "You and Elton came together."

"Yeah," Jack replied. "I called him and invited him to come tonight. He loved you, Callie, really loved you."

Callie smiled wanly. "I love *him*. I have ever since I was ten years old."

Jack laughed. "I hope you didn't tell him that. It would have made him feel old."

"No, of course not. When we hugged out there I was too busy gushing over him to say anything remotely coherent."

Smiling, Jack put his arm around her shoulders. "Come on, I'm sure you want to relax a bit." He opened the dressing room door and waited for Callie to precede him.

After closing the door behind them he immediately took her into his arms. They hugged tightly, both of them sighing with pleasure. "God, I missed you," he said against her neck. He gently pressed his lips to her warm flesh.

Callie breathed in and expelled a sob. Jack straightened and tilted her head back so that he could look into her eyes. "Those tears aren't because of me, are they?"

Callie lowered her gaze. Her lashes, wet with tears, glistened. She was not the type of woman to avoid the truth, no matter how much it hurt. So she told herself to get a grip and show Jack Cain that she was someone to be reckoned with, and fully capable of dealing with the fact that she loved him and he didn't love her. One-sided love affairs happened all the time. It was probably not the first time a woman had fallen in love with with him and he'd had only a passing interest in her. The thought had an unsettling effect on her. She had been about to confess her love for him. Instead, she got angry and said, "I suppose this happens to *you* all the time!"

Sensing her pique, Jack reacted to it with sarcasm. "Standing in the dressing room of a singer? Yes, I've been in lots of dressing rooms in my time."

Eyes flashing, Callie walked out of his reach and tossed over her shoulder, "Yeah, I bet you have!"

Jack didn't like her tone. He went and grasped her by the arm. "What's all this about? Why are you behaving this way when all I wanted to do was surprise you with Elton's presence here tonight and show you how much I care about you?"

Some of the fight went out of Callie. Why was she turning her anger on him? It wasn't his fault that she'd fallen in love with him. She was the one who took him up on his offer to write his autobiography. She had known, deep in her gut, that she was asking for trouble, and had done it anyway.

Sighing, she reached up, removed his hand from her arm, and smiled at him. "It was a fabulous thing that you did, Jack, and I'm appreciative. Truly, I am. I'm just in a foul mood tonight and it has nothing to do with you."

"Are you sure?" he asked, looking concerned. He was remembering Reid's comment earlier tonight. Reid had said Callie was in pain because she loved him, but she didn't know how he felt about her. Armed with that kind of information, Jack wasn't about to let it go uncorroborated. He wanted proof that what Reid had told him was the truth. If it was, he would be the happiest man alive.

Callie laughed half-heartedly as she walked over to the

counter and sat down in one of the red stools. "Jack, I should know why I'm upset." She met his eyes in the mirror. "Believe me, you have nothing to do with it." She reached for the container with her makeup removal pads, got one of the pads out, and started taking the foundation off her face. She wore it only because if she didn't, when she started perspiring during her performance her face would get shiny. She never wore it when she wasn't performing. "You don't mind if I remove my makeup while we talk, do you?"

"Of course not," Jack said casually. He sat in one of the high-backed stools.

Callie didn't speak as she quickly removed the makeup. When she was finished, she rose and said, "Excuse me."

She went into the adjacent bathroom, and Jack could hear water running. He assumed she was washing her face. Actually, Callie had turned on the faucet because she needed to use the toilet. While she was in the bathroom, she also brushed her teeth—her mouth always felt cottony after a performance—and washed her face.

She came out of the bathroom patting her face dry with a clean washcloth.

To Jack, she looked even more beautiful without the makeup. Her skin was healthy and unblemished. What did she need with makeup?

He got to his feet. "Okay, you're refreshed. Can we talk now?"

In the space of the time she'd been in the bathroom, Callie had decided that it didn't matter whether or not Jack loved her. She loved *him*, and she would be a fool to waste time worrying about the future. She should enjoy the time they had together.

"Jack, how did you get here tonight?" she asked as she began gathering her belongings. She put the washcloth in her tote bag, went to the counter and shoved all of her makeup into it as well.

"With Elton. He picked me up at the airport, and we came straight here. He has a house here now, you know."

Callie nodded. "He's been here a few years now. Atlanta's home to several recording artists." She'd finished packing. Meeting his eyes, she said, "Then you came here tonight to seduce me?"

Jack started to deny it, but thought better of it. "Yes, I did."

Callie laughed delightedly. "And I didn't appear pleased to see you. Poor, Jack!"

She went to him and lightly kissed his mouth. Her eyes raked over his face. "As much as I'd like to make love to you, I can't do it. I promised my mother I wouldn't. Well, I didn't implicitly say I was not going to sleep with you. What I agreed to was not to rush into anything with you. You see she's afraid that if you and I become lovers too soon something might happen to break us up, and then you wouldn't feel comfortable remaining a friend of the family. It bothers her that she didn't stay in touch with your mother and now that she is back in touch with *you*, she doesn't want to lose that. And neither do I, Jack. So, I've been trying my best to resist you."

Jack gave her a naughty look. "How is that working out for you?"

"Not too well," she admitted, tossing the tote bag onto the counter and going into his arms. His mouth descended on hers, and Callie simply let go of any residual anger that had stubbornly kept her from him. She felt his relief as he also let go and allowed the pleasure of being in each other's arms carry them past petty differences.

"Baby, how could you deny me those sweet lips?" he groaned. He bent his head again to kiss the side of her neck, her throat, and to bury his nose in her cleavage and breathe her in. Callie kissed his forehead, jaw, ear, and chin.

"Jack, just kiss me, don't talk."

Jack was more than happy to oblige. He picked her up and sat her on the counter. Callie opened her legs and welcomed him between them, then wrapped them around him. They kissed like that, Callie sitting, and Jack standing between her legs for a long time, enjoying the taste and feel of each other's mouths. Jack suckled on her bottom lip. Callie moaned with pleasure and threw her head back so that he could lick her neck.

"Make love to me, Jack," Callie breathed.

"But what about your promise?" Jack teased.

"We'll share custody of my mother if we break up," Callie told him.

Jack laughed, grabbed her bottom with both hands and pressed her closer to his erection. "This counter, though sturdy, doesn't look very comfortable to me. My plan was to feed you, then take you back to my hotel room and have my way with you."

Callie's eyes were smoky with pent-up desire. "What kind of a girl do you think I am? I don't go to hotels with men, Jack. You're sleeping in *my* bed tonight!"

There was a knock at the door, and the two of them

quickly parted and straightened their clothes. "Come in!" Callie cried.

Reid walked in and immediately knew he'd interrupted them in a passionate clench.

Callie's hair was sticking all over her head. Her nipples were hardened and quite noticeable beneath the fabric of her gold dress, and Jack, well, Jack's evidence was the hardest to hide.

"Sorry, kids," Reid sincerely apologized. "I just wanted to say goodbye to you before you left, Callie. You know I'm going to be here awhile making sure the clean-up crew does a good job, and then shutting up the place for my two-week vacation."

Callie went to him and kissed his cheek. "I would have found you and said goodbye before I left."

"You're a little distracted," Reid told her, looking pointedly at Jack.

Callie smiled at him. "I'm going to miss you."

Reid hugged her. "Did he tell you?" he whispered.

"Not yet," Callie whispered back. "But I really don't care anymore. Just so we're together *now*."

Reid gazed into her upturned face. "You're a big girl," he said, but she could tell by his tone that he didn't think that was good enough. She deserved to be loved in return.

Reid hugged her again, then let her go.

He went and shook Jack's hand, squeezing it much too tightly. "Tell her!" he said for Jack's ears only. "Well, Jack, it was nice meeting you," he said for Callie's benefit.

"A pleasure," Jack said.

He had to work the kinks out of his hand after Reid let go of him and left the dressing room.

Callie was picking up her belongings and putting on her jacket. "Shall we go?"

She and Jack left the club hand in hand.

A few minutes later she was unlocking the door of her apartment. "Come in. It's about the size of your living room in Charleston, but it's charming if I do say so myself."

"Very nice," Jack agreed. The floors were hardwood and gleaming. The walls in eggshell white. The furnishings were in neutral shades, but the accent pillows were in bold colors. Like her mother, she didn't believe in clutter. Everything looked picture perfect, even the miniature Christmas tree, replete with flashing lights, on the hall table.

After Callie had closed and locked the door, she and Jack helped each other off with their coats and she hung them in the hall closet.

That was the end of propriety for the night.

Callie turned her back to him. "Unzip me, Jack."

Jack wasted no time doing so.

That little gold dress hit the floor so fast, it made his head spin. It brought a lascivious grin to his face too. Callie had a beautifully proportioned body. A little on the voluptuous side, which he liked, what with those full breasts, shapely hips, and thighs. Her legs seemed to go on forever.

He reached for the closure at the front of her lacy bra, but Callie laughed and turned to hurry down the hall. "I want you wet and slippery, Jack."

Jaws clenched in frustration, Jack grimaced and followed her.

By the time he got to the bathroom, Callie was already nude and turning on the water in the big, sunken tub. She looked like a brown-skinned water nymph. Jack stood transfixed in the doorway, his heart doing double-time. Callie saw him standing there and smiled invitingly. She had been turned to the side as she poured bath oil underneath the running tap but now she turned and faced him and he saw the full frontal view of her. Her skin was a lovely shade of red-brown all over. Except for the areolas, which were dark brown. Her nipples were distended. His eyes were on the triangle of dark, curly hair that formed the V where her thighs met.

Callie went to him and began unbuttoning his shirt. "Do you like what you see?"

Jack pulled her into his arms. Her skin was silkily soft and warm. He lowered his hands to her backside and squeezed, delighted. "More than that, I like what I *feel*."

She was unbuttoning his shirt too slowly for him. "Let me," he said, and quickly removed his shirt, slacks, shoes and socks. Callie stood back, watching and enjoying the play of muscles as he undressed. His skin was golden brown all over as if he got some sun from time to time. Strong, muscular arms and legs, and a washboard stomach. She had already seen his feet, which were big. His nails were clean and neatly clipped. She had a thing about nails on men's hands and feet. They had to be clean and neatly manicured. Jack took care of himself.

She held her breath when he removed his boxer-briefs.

At this unveiling, the key was to not show any sign of disappointment because men were especially sensitive about that part of their anatomy. She was not into huge genitalia, but she'd never been with a man who didn't wish he was better endowed. What she cared about was that he knew how to use it, not whether it was gargantuan or not.

Jack nonchalantly took off his underwear and tossed them onto the pile of clothes in the chair in the corner. Callie glanced down. He was well endowed. No wonder he'd been so unconcerned about it. She breathed a sigh of relief. Finally, a man who was satisfied with what God had given him!

"Like what you see?" Jack asked with self-confidence.

Callie went to him and wrapped her right hand around his erect penis. Jack trembled with pleasure. She gave him a saucy smile. "Honey, I like the way you look and I like the way you feel to my touch. Now let's see how you feel inside of me."

She released him and bent to turn off the bathtub's faucet. She glanced down at the filled tub, then back at Jack.

Jack's eyes held a mischievous glint in them and the next thing she knew, he'd picked her up and was carrying her to the outer room and to the bed. "Where are the condoms?" he asked breathlessly.

"Nightstand," Callie answered.

He dropped her onto the bed and went to get a condom. He tore it open almost violently. Callie took it from him and rolled it onto his disgorged penis. She kissed his thigh next to it, and it jumped. She smiled.

Watching her, Jack knew two things. This woman was

not ashamed of her body. She'd proved that by getting naked without his having to undress her, and not being coy about it, either. Second, she enjoyed a man's body. He was looking forward to turning her out and exploring every inch of her.

That would have to wait until later, though, because, for now, he simply had to have her, and with an urgency he'd never experienced before. All he could think about was plunging deeply into her and hearing her moans and sighs in his ears.

He pushed her onto the bed and straddled her. Callie brought his head down to her breasts. He suckled them each in turn, enjoying the taste of her hot skin. He found himself slowing down in order to relish the sensations. Callie writhed beneath him, her sex warm and moist against his manhood. All he had to do was position himself at the entrance and he would be inside of her. Instead, he left a trail of kisses between her fragrant breasts, down her belly, to her mound, and stuck his tongue inside of her. Callie cried out. He felt her body quiver. Smiling, he plunged in and out of her, massaged her clitoris until she pushed herself up on her elbows with a gasp and fell back down onto the bed, spent and sweetly ravished.

Her breasts heaved. She was breathing erratically, and her body was covered with a light sheen of perspiration. Jack took his time and kissed the insides of her thighs while his hands were gently massaging her breasts, her belly, her sex. Callie closed her eyes and sighed contentedly.

Momentarily, he got up, pulled her legs apart and

quenched the savage desires he'd held in check in favor of satisfying his woman first. He was so hard, his erection was painful. She was tight. He took his time pushing. Callie opened her eyes and smiled at him. Jack looked down into her sweet face, and pushed harder. He was inside of her then, and Callie began returning thrust for thrust. Jack wanted to suspend this moment in time, make it last forever, it felt so wonderful, so right. But Callie was a vision. An erotic dream beneath him. And unfortunately for him, he was ruled by his eyesight, like most males, and the sight of her sent him over the top. He yelled in release. Callie laughed. He laughed. And collapsed on top of her.

They went and sat in the bath shortly afterward and as soon as they toweled dry they made love again, and again. It was 5:00 a.m. before they left the bedroom, exhausted, and went to the kitchen to scramble eggs for some much needed sustenance.

CHAPTER 7

Callie and Jack spent the next two weeks in a fog of love. During the week, they worked on the book together and tried their best to maintain a business relationship, but once they'd made love the thought of not touching each other during the day was unbearable. Consequently, they didn't get much work done on the book, and poor Winslow spent quite a bit of time whining to be let in at the bedroom door.

"Let him in," Callie cried sympathetically.

"I am not going to let him watch me make love to my woman," Jack told her as he pulled her back down onto the bed. "That would creep me out."

Of course, when the bedroom door opened, Winslow got spoiled outrageously. Their guilt made them easy marks for extra bits of beef, and longer romps on the lawn. So, everybody was happy.

Everybody, that is, except Joyce.

The date of the Christmas festival was nearing, and Joyce had not been able to pin down either her daughter or Jack for a rehearsal time. One evening, when Callie came home from work, Joyce cornered her in the kitchen.

Callie's whole persona had changed recently, and Joyce hadn't missed the happiness that shone in her daughter's eyes. She waited until Callie went into the kitchen to get something to drink, as was her habit, and came in as she was drinking a glass of water.

"How was work today?" she casually asked as she sat down at the breakfast nook and picked up the newspaper that had lain there all day. She went to the entertainment section and waited for Callie's reply.

"Mm, it was good," Callie said. She was wearing jeans and a sweater. Her skin glowed with health and vitality, and there was also a kind of sinuous rhythm to the way she moved nowadays. Joyce noticed all of that. It was, also, hard to miss that love bite on the side of her neck.

Callie sat down across from her mother and smiled at her. "Jack's story is so fascinating. I'm sure the book's going to be a bestseller."

Joyce looked at her over the top of the paper. "Is it Jack's story you find fascinating, or Jack himself?"

"Both," Callie said dreamily.

That was it. Joyce became livid at the sound of pure sex in her daughter's voice. She slammed the paper down on the counter and rose. "Callista Joan Hart, I will not have you prostituting yourself with that man, I don't care if I have come to love him like a son!"

Aghast, Callie rose too and stared at her mother, incredulous. "*Prostitute* myself?"

"What else do you call it when a woman takes money from a man, and sleeps with him?" her mother asked, hands on her hips.

"I love him. I'm not selling myself to him," Callie tried to explain.

"Well, has he said he loves you?"

"No, but I know he does. He shows it in so many ways…"

"Yes, I'm sure he does, but the thought of Jack using you without some reassurance that he wants more from you than your body really burns me up, Callista. You were not raised that way."

Callie had tears in her eyes. She was torn between her love for Jack and her desire to hold onto some modicum of pride. What her mother was saying resonated with her, but she stubbornly felt in her heart that Jack did love her. He just didn't know how to tell her. He was still stinging after being rejected by the last woman he'd loved.

Callie met her mother's eyes. "Ma, I'm going to give Jack a little more time to state his intentions. In my gut, I know that this isn't just a love affair."

Joyce went around the breakfast nook and hugged her tightly. "I've had my say. You know I'll stick by you, whatever you decide."

That's how it was with Joyce and her children. She would let them have it with both barrels, but always, *always*, had their backs.

The night of the Christmas festival, Callie was excited to be there. This was a yearly event that brought out everyone from the community in support of their sons and daughters. The civic center was packed with more than 3,000 people. Joyce and the other event organizers had managed to borrow two Steinways and arranged them on the stage facing each other. Jack would play one of them, and Callie would play the other.

The program began with the students' talent show. The ages of the contestants ranged from five to eighteen. They sang, played musical instruments, danced, and enacted scenes from well-known plays or from skits they'd written themselves.

Jack and Callie stood backstage, watching the kids' performances and waiting for their cues to go on. Callie was beautiful in a sleeveless, black velvet dress that revealed just enough cleavage, and a lovely glimpse of her long legs. Jack kept stealing glances at her, and it was difficult not to touch her, but they had to maintain a sense of decorum around the other talent backstage.

Jack looked handsome in a formal black tuxedo with a white bow tie and vest over a crisp, pleated white silk shirt. He was nervous tonight, but not because he was about to perform. There was another reason his stomach was in knots.

He gazed at Callie. She turned at that moment, looked him in the eyes and smiled.

"Thank you, Jack."

His brows rose in a questioning gesture. "For what?"

"Just for being you."

Jack was about to tell her he should be thanking her for bringing him back to life, but Joyce rounded the corner and yelled, "Callista, you're on, honey! Get out there!"

Callie grinned at Jack. "Well, see you on stage."

And she was gone, hurrying around the heavy burgundy curtains, her heels clicking on the hardwood floor. Jack could hear the announcer say, "Ladies and gentlemen, please welcome Charleston's own, Miss Callie Hart!"

Callie walked on stage to thunderous applause, sat down at one of the gleaming Steinways and leaned toward the microphone that had been set up for her. "Good evening, Charleston. I'm delighted to be here tonight to help you celebrate the holiday season. I'm going to start with an old favorite that my grandmother used to play every Christmas. Grandma liked Mahalia Jackson's version of it."

"Go Tell It on the Mountain" was a gospel lover's dream, and Callie played it with passion and sang it with deep-throated conviction. The notes came up from her soul, spilled from her mouth and by the time they reached the listeners' ears they were rich with promise, and made their spirits glad. People were rocking in the aisles.

After that, she toned it down a bit with "Silent Night." Then raised their spirits again with a rousing rendition of "Didn't It Rain?"

Jack went on half an hour later and played "Adeste Fideles…O Come All Ye Faithful," "Angels We Have Heard on High," and "What Child Is This." After that he spoke into the microphone and said, "I ask your indulgence as I play the next song because it's not a Christmas song, it's a serenade. A love song."

Callie was standing backstage with her mother, watching him. Her heart was in her throat when he mentioned he was about to play a love song. But she didn't let herself hope the sentiments in the song were meant for her.

Jack put her mind at rest with his next words. "It's called 'Callie's Song'."

Joyce reached for her hand and squeezed it so hard Callie was afraid her bones would crack under the pressure. She patted her mother's hand. "Calm down, Ma. It's gonna be all right." Joyce eased up a bit.

Jack began to play, and the audience immediately sat up straighter in their seats and strained to hear the lilting notes as they filled the auditorium. If music was indeed a gift from God, then there was no better proof than the heavenly sounds that issued from Jack's heart that night. It played havoc with one's emotions, running the gamut: sadness, exultation, bitter remorse, and unmitigated joy. There wasn't a dry eye in the house when he finished nor a posterior in a seat because everyone was on his or her feet giving Jack a standing ovation.

Jack had tears in his eyes as he leaned forward and spoke into the microphone.

"Callie Hart," he said softly. "Will you marry me?"

"Yes!" cried a lone female voice from backstage. But it wasn't the voice of his heart. It was his love's mother's voice crying out.

Jack looked up and saw Callie walking toward him. The audience members started hooting and hollering, shouting, "Callie, Callie!"

Jack stood and Callie went into his arms. "Yes, Jack," she said in a tremulous voice. "A million times, yes!"

They kissed to the sound of applause in their ears.

* * *

Jack and Callie were married in St. John AME Church at 2:00 p.m. on Sunday, January 2. Reid gave her away. Jack's best man, long-time friend, musician Shane Arioli, flew in from London. Among the guests was a well-known singer who tried to appear incognito, but everybody recognized him anyway.

Jack and Callie did manage to meet the deadline for the book, and when it was published a year later it debuted at Number 5 on the *New York Times* bestseller list.

* * * * *

Dear Reader:

Thank you for picking up one of my books. I hope Callie and Jack's story provided you with a few hours of reading enjoyment. I had a ball writing it!

If you'd like to drop me a line to tell me what you thought of it, you can leave me a message on my Web site at *http://www.janicesims.com*, or e-mail me at *Jani569432@aol.com*. I love getting mail the old-fashioned way too. My mailing address is Post Office Box 811, Mascotte, FL 34753-0811.

Warm regards,
Janice Sims

As the author of more than 25 nationally acclaimed novels, *Rochelle Alers* is hailed by many readers as inspiring positive change in their lives. A native New Yorker, she holds a bachelor of arts degree, with a double major in sociology and psychology. Alers is the winner of Gold Pen, EMMA and Vivian Stephens Career Achievement for Excellence in Romance Writing. Now a full-time author, Alers lives in Freeport, New York.

National bestselling author *Adrianne Byrd* has penned twelve Arabesque novels, using her imagination to craft heroes that are gorgeous and women who are worth whatever trouble they manage to get into. Her books have consistently garnered critical praise, and her novel *Comfort Of A Man* went on to win eight prestigious awards. An army brat,

Byrd traveled throughout Europe and learned to appreciate and value different cultures. Now she calls Georgia home.

Kayla Perrin, a *USA TODAY* bestselling author, has legions of fans for her eight Arabesque romance novels. Praise for Perrin includes *New York Times* bestselling author Eric Jerome Dickey, and *Romantic Times*, which awarded her a Lifetime Career Achievement Award. Raised in Canada, she earned a sociology degree from the University of Toronto, and an education degree from New York University. She also works in the film industry as an actress. Perrin makes her home both in Toronto and Miami. An incurable romantic at heart, she plans to be writing stories of love and adventure for a very long time.

A native Floridian, *Janice Sims* is a full-time writer who strongly believes in family, fidelity and true love, and has turned her passion for writing into ten expertly crafted Arabesque novels. Sims's characters can often be found in settings and occupations that are nontraditional for African-Americans, as she finds this empowering for herself and her many fans. Sims has perfected romantic suspense and consistently garners literary praise from *Romantic Times*. Sims currently lives in Central Florida with her husband and children.